thus making MacGregor's stellar debut a must-read for any fan of Regency historicals." —*Booklist* (starred review)

"An impressive debut . . . plenty of sizzle."

—*Kirkus Reviews*

"This charming tale features a refreshing array of happy families, solid relationships . . . The book's promise of a delicious story is well realized, building anticipation for future installments." —*Publishers Weekly*

"Well-paced, powerfully plotted debut where love and revenge vie for center stage. Here is a romance that reminds readers that love is complicated, healing, and captivating. MacGregor's characters are carefully drawn, their emotions realistic, and their passions palpable. Watch for MacGregor to make her mark on the genre." —*RT Book Reviews*

"Delightful! Janna MacGregor bewitched me with her captivating characters and a romance that sizzles off the page. I'm already a huge fan!"

—*New York Times* bestselling author Eloisa James

Also by
Janna MacGregor

WILD, WILD RAKE
ROGUE MOST WANTED
THE GOOD, THE BAD, AND THE DUKE
THE LUCK OF THE BRIDE
THE BRIDE WHO GOT LUCKY
THE BAD LUCK BRIDE

Praise for

WILD, WILD RAKE

"Passionate, tumultuous." —*Publishers Weekly*

"Incandescent." —*Booklist*

"Will delight those looking to warm their hearts with a tender read." —*Library Journal*

ROGUE MOST WANTED

"A decadently delightful love story that refuses to conform." —*Publishers Weekly*

"An unforgettable love story." —*Booklist* (starred review)

"Deliciously romantic and poetic." —*Fresh Fiction*

THE GOOD, THE BAD, AND THE DUKE

"Sparkling . . . a richly engaging romance with a heroine we should all resolve to be more like." —*Entertainment Weekly*

"Utterly delightful in every possible way." —*Bookriot*

"Effervesces with lighthearted romance . . . sweet and sultry in equal measures." —*Publishers Weekly*

"[An] emotionally rich, exquisitely wrought tale that superbly celebrates the redemptive power of love." —*Booklist*

THE LUCK OF THE BRIDE

"Sparkling dialogue, a dash of deliciously tart humor, and just enough soul-searing sensuality to keep romance fans sighing happily in satisfaction." —*Booklist*

"Brimming with family, hope, and tender sensuality, this shrewdly plotted, gently paced romance is especially satisfying." —*Library Journal*

"A lovely, sweet, and touching love story."
—*RT Book Reviews*

THE BRIDE WHO GOT LUCKY

"Rising star MacGregor once again demonstrates her remarkable gift for effortlessly elegant writing, richly nuanced characterization, and lushly sensual love scenes."
—*Booklist* (starred review)

"A heady mix of action, wit, and sexual tension. Readers will eagerly turn the pages to see how this intense story concludes." —*Publishers Weekly*

"Deliciously provocative in historical detail . . . there is everything in this novel and more. *The Bride Who Got Lucky* is absolutely brilliant!" —*Romance Junkies* (5 stars)

THE BAD LUCK BRIDE

"With its beautifully defined, exceptionally appealing protagonists, intriguing secondary characters, and graceful writing deftly leavened with wry wit, this classic romantic story line becomes something marvelously fresh and new,

A Duke in Time

Janna MacGregor

St. Martin's Paperbacks

For Rossella

First published in the United States by St. Martin's Paperbacks, an imprint of St. Martin's Publishing Group

A DUKE IN TIME

For information, address St. Martin's Publishing Group, 120 Broadway, New York, NY 10271.

www.stmartins.com

ISBN: 978-1-250-76159-0

Printed in the United States of America

St. Martin's Paperbacks edition 2021

10 9 8 7 6 5 4 3 2 1

Chapter One

London, 1815
The Office of Malcom Hanes, Esquire

He was a good man." Katherine patted the family solicitor's arm while the poor man hung his head in grief. She didn't belabor the point that her husband's horse certainly didn't share the same opinion. Not when the beast had thrown Meriwether into a mud puddle, where he'd drowned. Seems his steady steed didn't care to participate in a midnight steeplechase during a deafening thunderstorm with a foxed Meriwether handling the reins.

That act meant she was now the *widowed* wife of Lord Meriwether Vareck, the second son of the previous Duke of Randford. Her chest tightened, making it difficult to draw a deep breath. Indeed, she was sad her husband had died, and equally regretful that most of her grief was for the end of her too-brief marriage.

"Thank you for your kindness, Lady Meriwether." The distinguished solicitor, Malcom Hanes, bowed over Katherine's hand as they stood at the threshold of his office. With a heavy, soulful sigh, Mr. Hanes murmured, "Please accept my deepest condolences. Such a shame you were only married for a year. I'm sure you're at a loss."

She nodded briefly. That was putting it mildly. *Lost* would have been a more accurate description. She *had* lost him. Katherine had last seen Meriwether on their wedding day. She'd always hoped he'd come home. Yet as the days between his infrequent correspondence had multiplied, the reality that he might never return had grown stronger.

Now it was a certainty.

"There are a few complications"—the solicitor pinched the bridge of his nose—"before we start the reading of the will."

"Is anything amiss?"

"No," he objected a little too quickly. "Absolutely not." His lips pursed in an expression that reminded Katherine of a tightly fastened reticule. "We'll begin shortly. I'm simply waiting for the Duke of Randford to deliver Lord Meriwether's will. It seems His Grace had it in his possession the entire time he was in France."

This time Katherine's lips were the ones to press together. She would not utter a peep against the Duke of Randford, her brother-in-law. Newly arrived in London after three years fighting the French, the duke was Meriwether's only family. Having the same father but different mothers, the duke and Meriwether were half brothers. Truthfully, a person couldn't tell by the duke's actions. Randford had treated Meriwether like a stranger.

Worse than a stranger really.

The duke acted as if Meriwether were a disease, one to be avoided at all costs. The fact that Randford didn't even write to Katherine when he received word of Meriwether's tragic passing, let alone call on her when he reached London, showed the selfish man's true colors. Whether he was a decorated war hero or not made little difference. A man of integrity and good manners should have shown some respect for his brother and his widow.

One of Mr. Hanes's clerks came to the door. With a flushed face reminiscent of a volcano ready to erupt, the young man frantically waved for Mr. Hanes to follow him.

"If you'll excuse me, Lady Meriwether?" Mr. Hanes nodded before taking his leave.

Katherine walked to the window and gazed at the gray London morning. How fitting the heavens looked gloomy today. Though she didn't love Meri, her husband's preferred name, his larger than life personality had shimmered with a brightness and light that had drawn people near. When he turned his brilliant blue eyes your way, a whirlwind erupted and you were swept into his carefree world.

Certainly, she had been.

She fisted her kidskin gloves. No good would come from feeling morbid about her husband's death. Meri certainly wouldn't want anyone to feel that way, particularly when his end came doing what he loved best—riding in a horserace and gambling on the outcome. Though they'd only spent six hours together as a married couple, Meri's infrequent letters informed her of his travels. First, he'd made his way to Portsmouth, then Cumberland, all in the pursuit of investments—or so he claimed. Katherine had a suspicion the "investments" were nothing more than racehorses.

If he would have stayed by her side, they could have started their marriage.

Nor would he have been dead.

"If you'll follow me, ma'am." Another of Mr. Hanes's numerous clerks, a young man with bright red hair, escorted a woman heavy with child into the room.

The woman caught Katherine's gaze and smiled slightly.

"May I offer you something before we begin?" the clerk asked.

The woman nodded. "If it wouldn't be too much bother, a glass of water would be lovely."

Katherine's eyes widened when the young man glanced her way then darted out of the room like it was on fire. But what caused her the most amazement was that the woman stood in Mr. Hanes's office at all.

Dressed in a dark mauve muslin gown, she was elegantly attired. Whoever she was, she looked uncomfortable with the weight she carried in her middle since she was rubbing her lower back. Though Katherine was no expert, the stranger before her had to be in the last couple months of confinement. What would cause her to venture forth on such a dismal day?

Surely, the woman was in the wrong office. She couldn't be there for the reading of the will. It was only for the immediate family, Katherine and the Duke of Randford.

Nevertheless, the petite woman stood before Katherine. With an ethereal beauty enhanced by bright blue eyes and wisps of escaped hair, she exhibited a calmness in direct contrast to Katherine's stomach, which swooped endlessly like a bat hunting in the wee hours of the morning.

"Would you mind if I sit?" the young woman asked as she waved a hand to one of the chairs in front of Mr. Hanes's desk. Mountains of paper were stacked on top with more mounds on the floor, a troubling sign that today's proceedings could last well into the evening.

"Of course not," Katherine answered. She quickly scooted one of the chairs toward the woman. "Please, let me help you."

"Thank you." The woman lowered herself into the chair.

"Are you somehow related to the deceased?" Katherine asked gently.

The young woman nodded. "Allow me to introduce myself. I'm Lady Meriwether Vareck."

Katherine's heart skipped mid-beat. Struggling to keep her bearings, she reminded herself she wasn't the type of woman to faint. "Pardon me? I must have heard you incorrectly."

Another Lady Meriwether Vareck?

Before the woman could answer, a different clerk escorted another beautiful woman into the office. Tall, thin, and elegantly attired, the lady tilted her head in a manner that was the embodiment of pure grace. It was difficult to see her since her hat hid most of her face.

With his mouth gaping, the clerk stood motionless while his gaze darted between Katherine and the other two women.

The red-haired clerk who had left to fetch the first woman a drink appeared with a full glass of water. When he saw the scene before him, his face paled. "You weren't supposed to bring *the third one* here. Not until Mr. Hanes had a chance to talk to the duke."

The clerk who had brought in the last women huffed in revolt. "And you weren't to bring *the second one* here"—he waved his hands in the direction of the pregnant woman—"until Mr. Hanes had a chance to talk to the duke. Who escorted the *first* one"—he nodded in Katherine's direction—"in here?"

Seeking purchase to keep from falling to her knees, Katherine reached for the closest chair and dug her fingers into the supple leather, clinging to it like a safety line in rough seas.

It was inconceivable. Meri had another wife. She shook her head, hoping it was all a bad dream.

No. Not another, *but two.*

The bad dream twisted violently into a nightmare that hit her with the force of a sledgehammer. She couldn't breathe, but the dull pounding of her heart continued.

The *bloody* bastard had three wives, and one of them with whom he'd obviously found the time to consummate the marriage.

Her burning lungs protested the lack of air. She gasped for breath, but thankfully, the clerks' verbal attacks muffled the ungodly sound. The other women's gazes flew back and forth between the two young men. They'd completely forgotten about Katherine.

Outside the room, the crisp click of boot heels against the wooden flooring grew louder.

"Three? As in wives? Why should I be surprised?" The deep baritone voice echoed from somewhere in the building. "Here's the miscreant's will. That's what I pay you for. Handle it, Hanes."

"But, Your Grace," Mr. Hanes pleaded. "We can't find the money."

Abruptly, the footsteps stopped. "What?"

Katherine slipped from the room, softly closing the door behind her. She leaned against the mahogany panel, hoping the cool wood would calm the overwhelming sense of dizziness. How could Meri have done this to her? One word came to mind. Bigamist. Yet, if he had three wives, then trigamist correctly identified him. She closed her eyes for a moment. For the love of heaven, if he had more than three, that made him a polygamist. The thought sent her reeling. Plus, he'd never sent a word or a peep about meeting someone else, only humorous observations about his travels.

She forced herself away from the door. Not more than twenty feet in front of her, Mr. Hanes stood wringing his hands before a giant of a man.

The stranger still wore his beaver top hat on his head. The multiple capes of his black greatcoat fell about his shoulders, giving him the appearance of Hades emerging from the underworld to conquer all. His thick black hair brushed his shoulders. Though the long length was out of fashion, it suited him perfectly.

Slowly, he turned his attention to her. Katherine straightened to her full height, ready to battle the beast before her. His brown-eyed gaze swept from the top of her head to her feet, then came to rest on her face.

As he stared at her, she stared right back. She pursed her lips and narrowed her eyes for effect. After watching her mother on the stage for years, she'd learned how to deliver a formidable look that could scare a mortal man senseless.

For that one moment, all sound and thought ceased except for the man before her. He wasn't conventionally handsome. His patrician nose was a tad on the large side, and his huge eyes reminded her of a hawk hunting for prey. His full lips were presently turned into a scowl, and his strong square jaw accentuated his confident demeanor.

Such sureness was rare and to be admired. At least, Kat had always admired it.

Unquestionably, he would get to the bottom of this travesty.

He nodded ever so slightly in acknowledgment.

Her breath accelerated as he continued to stare at her. His gaze dropped to her hands for a moment before his attention returned to Mr. Hanes.

Bloody hell. She'd been twisting her fingers together, a nervous habit she'd acquired in childhood. It completely destroyed her effort to appear disapproving. But after learning her fickle husband had three wives, it was a miracle she could stand at all.

Though the duke didn't continue examining her, she took the opportunity to further study him. For weeks, the newspapers posted weekly accolades of his success on the battlefield. The accompanying drawings bore a remarkable likeness. He didn't share Meri's looks. Meri had light hair and blue eyes like an angel.

With his dark hair and strong features, the duke strongly favored an archangel. Standing in the hallway, he appeared invincible, like an otherworldly being.

The duke turned one shoulder to keep his conversation private. "Is she one of them?"

Even with his lowered voice, Katherine heard the words clearly.

"She's your brother's wife," Mr. Hanes mumbled.

"Will you make the introductions?"

Goose bumps broke out across her arms at the roughness in his quiet voice.

By then, Katherine's companion, Willa Ferguson, had joined her. "Sitting in the waiting room, I couldn't help but notice the solicitor's office looks like an ant colony. Everyone is running back and forth as if they've lost their heads. Is there trouble?"

Willa's Scottish lilt normally soothed Katherine whenever she was tired or irritated. But this was more than irritation.

This was anarchy.

"The worst type of trouble," Katherine whispered. "I'm not the only wife Meri had. There are two others in Mr. Hanes's office."

"Nae! For all that's holy." Willa practically spit her displeasure as her eyes widened. "I knew there was something wrong with that lad." Slowly, her gaze narrowed on the duke. "Who's he?"

"Meri's brother, the Duke of Randford."

"He looks like a Highland barbarian. Stay away from that one," Willa warned.

"I can't." Katherine blew an errant curl from her face. "I heard the solicitor say the money is missing. I'm assuming that's my dowry."

Willa's gaze whipped to hers. "What?" she asked incredulously.

"Shush, Willa. My money is missing," Katherine whispered.

"*Pfft. Bloody English*," Willa murmured. "They never stop stealing what's not theirs. Especially the rich ones."

The duke returned his attention to Katherine and narrowed his eyes.

Katherine turned her back on the duke so she and Willa could speak softly without the two men overhearing. "He wants to meet me."

Willa's eyes widened.

Katherine nodded. "Hopefully, the duke and Mr. Hanes have devised a plan on how to right this wrong quietly and quickly. I'll speak to the duke, then see what I can glean from the solicitor. Once I know my money is safe, I'll ask that it be deposited in the bank. Then we can leave."

She hated to worry about money, but there was no helping it, not after what she'd just heard.

"I'll get your dowry for ye. I've brought some protection," Willa answered as if sharing state secrets while she padded her cloak pocket.

Her darling Willa's Scottish accent always thickened when she was excited.

"You brought your knife?" Katherine asked softly.

"My dirk." Willa shrugged. "Kat, I thought there might be a wee bit of trouble. An' I was correct."

Katherine shook her head.

"At least I dinnae bring my claymore," Willa added defensively.

"Thank God for small miracles," Katherine murmured. "We'd both be thrown out of the office if you drew your sword."

Yet, she couldn't be angry. Tall, spry, and in her forties, Willa had been with Katherine since she was a small girl, first as a nursemaid, now as her companion. Even when

Katherine's mother was alive, it was Willa who tucked her into bed and tended to her when she was sick. More than a companion, Willa was Katherine's only family—well, besides Meri the "trigamist" and perhaps the duke.

"Don't let anyone see it," Katherine scolded softly. "Will you fetch my cloak from Mr. Hanes's office while I speak with them about my money?"

Willa nodded, upsetting several curls of her graying red hair. "What about the will?"

"I doubt if Meri left me anything." Katherine tried to smile but failed. She wanted to summon nice thoughts of her dead husband, but it was uniquely difficult after he'd left her to fend on her own. Now, it was inconceivable after learning he had two other wives. She exhaled. "We were only together a day."

"Six hours," Willa corrected as her green eyes flashed. "Not even enough time to consummate the marriage. Yet the bastard ate the bridal breakfast afore he left."

"Hush, please," Katherine begged. "I don't need to be reminded, and I don't want them to know."

"What about 'im?" Willa threw her head in the duke's general direction.

"I'll take care of it." Katherine patted Willa's hand.

"*It*," Willa grunted while eyeing the duke. "That's a good description of 'im." She nodded reluctantly, then left.

Katherine took a deep breath and turned to face Meri's brother and Mr. Hanes once more. The duke stared at her while continuing his discussion with his solicitor.

She smoothed her hands down her skirt, then started forward. The duke nodded briefly in her direction then turned his focus to the solicitor.

"I don't care what you have to do. Take care of this mess," the duke commanded in a voice that demanded results.

Once Katherine stood beside them, a flustered Mr. Hanes

turned in her direction before his gaze whipped back to the duke's daunting visage. "Your . . . Your Grace, may I introduce your late brother's wife?"

Miraculously, the duke smiled and, for a moment, Katherine could have sworn the sun had burst through the clouds in welcome. The room practically swam in light. Two perfect dimples appeared on his angular cheeks.

Immediately, she changed her opinion. He was handsome. Too handsome, if truth be told.

Another clerk motioned Mr. Hanes forward, leaving Katherine alone with the duke.

The imposing man tucked his hat under the arm adorned with a simple black armband to show he mourned his brother. He clasped her fingers in his. In a show of respect, he slowly bent over her hand.

"I'm so sorry we meet under these circumstances," he murmured. "Randford at your service, Lady Meriwether."

"Thank you, Your Grace." Though he acted the perfect gentleman, the heat of his long fingers clasping hers sent a slow meandering chill down her spine. Ignoring the response, Katherine dipped a curtsey. When she rose, she smiled demurely.

"How are you faring under this trying situation?" he asked with a deep, smooth voice that could charm harpies from the ocean.

Completely captivated, Katherine leaned forward. His sandalwood scent surrounded her, and she inhaled deeply. "Well, Your Grace. Thank you for asking."

His eyes softened. "I'm glad to hear that."

The rumbling sound resonated within her chest, warming her insides, and she smiled in return. This man was the definition of dangerous, a celebrated war hero who led his men into battles that others ran from. He always won, no matter the odds. If he had asked her to follow him into one of his heroic war campaigns, Katherine didn't know if she could have refused. Thankfully, this wasn't war.

Or at least, she didn't think so. But heaven knew this was a disaster beyond epic.

"If you'll excuse me? It was lovely to meet you," he said.

The vision of a warrior who conquered all dissolved before her eyes. "Wait, you can't leave."

"Indeed, I can," he murmured as he bowed. "And I will."

Chapter Two

"You can't leave me with this situation." Lady Meriwether's soft tone didn't dull the steel in her voice. Then she added, "Your Grace," almost as an afterthought.

Christian Vareck, the Duke of Randford, surmised by her stance that she was a no-nonsense individual, but the twisting of her hands revealed her understandable anguish at discovering she was one of Meri's many wives.

The slightest twitch tugged at one of her red lips. They reminded him of a rose his mother had grown in the conservatory of his ancestral seat, Roseport. As a boy, he'd stood by his mother's side as she pruned and grafted Roseport's famed roses into works of art.

This particular Lady Meriwether's mouth definitely resembled one of those crimson masterpieces. Under the spectacular color of a perfect bloom lay the thorns designed to skewer any hand that dare threatened. He'd lay odds on it.

Lady Meriwether tilted her head and peeked down the hallway, seeing if anyone could overhear them. "You just proved why many believe that chivalry is dead."

"I only speak the truth," Christian countered. "My brother and his estate aren't my concern."

She brought her smoldering gaze back to his. The woman's hazel eyes flashed, turning them into a beautiful golden green.

"I meant to say half brother," Christian corrected.

The slight tap of her toe indicated her patience was waning. "Half, step, or whole. He was your family."

"I'm agog you're defending him after what he's done, particularly to you, Lady Meriwether." He shouldn't be astonished that she upheld Meri's memory. Christian's half brother had possessed a certain finesse and appeal that women loved.

"My name is Katherine. Katherine Greer before I married your brother." She released a long-suffering breath. "As the Duke of Randford, surely you can help sort out the details."

"You would assume wrongly. This isn't my problem to fix. It's Meri's estate which Mr. Hanes supervises. He asked if I could stop by. I've done my duty. Now I'll be on my way." He deftly placed his hat on his head, then adjusted it with a tug. "An honor to make your acquaintance, Lady Meriwether."

His insufferable half brother had made a fine pickle of these marriages, but Christian Vareck's duties lay elsewhere. Namely, settling into his position as the Duke of Randford and trying to help his men who came home to nothing after returning from the war.

However, before he left Lady Meriwether standing in the hall, he stole a long gander at her person. She honored Meri's passing by wearing a mourning gown with a short gray silk spencer. Truly, a lighter color would suit her hazel eyes and light brown hair better. Meri's tastes must have changed since Christian had been at war. His half brother normally favored light-haired women with full bodies and voluptuous bosoms.

Katherine Greer possessed none of those features. She had

a lithe form that Christian had always preferred. It had to be her gaze that had first drawn Meri's attention. Her large resolute hazel eyes fit perfectly with her heart-shaped face. The finishing touch of a delicate, refined nose made her pretty. However, her calm, steadfast demeanor at the situation signaled a woman who would not crumble at the first sign of trouble.

Christian had been back in London for a week, and since the war, he could appreciate beauty in the most unusual of places, even the family's solicitor's office and under such a tenuous situation. A man had to find amusement where he could since there was none on the battlefield. Plus, there were no guarantees a man would have enough time on earth to find other pleasures or even happiness.

Meri's demise offered proof of that fact.

Christian moved toward the exit.

"Your Grace, please wait." She took several steps forward, blocking the pathway. "Two women in Mr. Hanes's office need your guidance. If this isn't handled prudently, then we'll all be ruined. You, above all others, know this is an impossible situation."

"My half sibling was a virtuoso of the impossible." He delivered his most sincere smile. "For instance, he was forever finding improbable and impossible situations to land in . . . just like that mud puddle."

"That's a little glib, even for a duke." She clasped her gloved hands in front of her in a stance better suited for a governess with a wayward charge.

"Lady Meriwether," he said patiently. "I asked Hanes to sort things out. Like you, I've just discovered what your husband has done. We can't expect answers immediately." He dipped his head once to indicate he was leaving again.

"You can't leave. We"—she waved a hand between them—"are in this together. If word leaks what Meri has done, we'll face real scandal. Those women in Mr. Hanes's office need help. They'll be ruined." She took a step closer. "I hate to be crass, but you're the duke, the head of the family, which makes it your mess. You need to clean it up."

Without hesitating, he took one step back for safety. He groaned dramatically. "*Lady Meriwether*, lucky for you, I employ people to clean up messes. This office for instance. They're the best legal minds in London."

She laughed softly, but her eyes sparkled with a renewed aggravation. "Your brother retained the same *people* too." She lifted one perfect eyebrow. "The *best legal minds in London* apparently don't have a clue how to proceed."

Her gaze pinned him in place.

He narrowed his eyes. "You wear sarcasm well, Lady Meriwether."

"I take that as a compliment," she purred, then tilted her head in challenge. "What are you afraid of?" she asked softly. "Me? The others?"

"Madame . . ." He lowered his voice. "I've faced Napoleon's finest infantry in conditions that would curl your toes. I've seen fires and horrors on the battlefields that make hell look like a well-groomed park." He allowed his gaze to rake over her form again. "Trust me. I highly doubt you or this dilemma can scare me."

Instead of being offended, she smiled slightly. "We shall see, Your Grace."

"Oh, the rapture. I can hardly wait," he answered sardonically. It was bad form on his part, but Meri's antics always brought out the worst in him. "Now, I must beg your leave."

As he headed down the hallway, she called from behind. "Your Grace? When can I expect my dowry to be returned?"

He turned around sharply. "As you've probably surmised, Meri seems to have either spent it or misplaced it. My money is that he gambled it away."

Katherine let out a tremulous breath, but her eyes never blinked. A subtle tightness formed around her perfect lips. He'd always been susceptible to red lips—not the painted ones of courtesans and actresses, but real ones like hers. Today, such a weakness caused his chest to squeeze. "How much is it?" he asked in the most even voice he could muster.

"Two hundred pounds," she said.

He didn't blink. "Was there anything else?"

She shook her head gently.

"Are you serious?" he asked.

His half brother had married this woman for two hundred pounds? Meri's habit was to spend three times that amount on his horses and racing every month. Christian should know. He'd been the one to pay his bills over the last three years.

She lifted her chin in an act of defiance. "Rest assured, I never joke about money."

Her golden-green eyes suddenly dulled, losing their earlier luster.

Christian inwardly winced. After being in London for only a week, he'd insulted the first woman he'd had a real conversation with outside of his staff.

She straightened her shoulders as if ready to bear any verbal blow he'd bestow. "It may not be a great amount to you, but it means the world to me. It represents everything," she said quietly. This time, she was the one to turn from him.

"Lady Meriwether?"

She stopped but didn't face him.

"I beg you to accept my humble apology. Though it's no excuse, I've not been in polite company for a while. My manners are rusty," he said gently. "Truly, it's not a joke to me either. I'm sincere when I say I'm finished with my half brother's mischief in more ways than one. However, I'll discuss your money with Mr. Hanes. That's all I can promise."

"It's not enough." Without any other acknowledgment, she walked straight toward Mr. Hanes's office.

Bloody hell. Leave it to Meri to part this world with a monumental scandal in his wake. Christian had half a mind to dig up the hoodlum and give him a blistering lecture. Perhaps then he'd find out what Meri had been thinking, marrying three women and spending their dowries.

When Christian walked out the door, an attending footman opened the carriage door. Without breaking his stride, Christian entered the coach, then settled in the forward-facing seat. He stopped his hand midair before knocking on the roof.

Indeed, those women faced real ruin. For a moment, the urge to return and offer assistance grew fierce. He had a true talent for maneuvering people out of dangerous situations.

But not this time.

For his own sanity, he had to cut all ties to his brother.

Half brother.

Without second guessing his decision, Christian rapped twice with his knuckles, sending the carriage lurching into the London traffic. As the coach picked up speed, his gut tightened in revolt. He couldn't leave those women, particularly Lady Meriwether like that.

She'd asked what was he afraid of? Failure perhaps?

He'd failed before with Meri and would probably do so again if he got involved with his half brother's last escapade.

But he'd try, even if it meant he'd have to go through hell again.

By now, the carriage had traveled for several blocks. Christian knocked on the roof, then leaned out the window.

The driver expertly controlled the reins as he peered over his shoulder. "Your Grace?"

"Let's return to Hanes's office."

What a pretentious lout.

Katherine refused to give him another glance after their introduction had finished. To think she'd even entertained putting *that* man in the same category as a beloved family member.

She'd prefer to claim a rat as kin rather than the Duke of Randford. Rat and Randford fit perfectly together. The Duke of Ratface. The Rat of Randford.

As Katherine approached Mr. Hanes's office, debating whom she was insulting worse—the rat or Randford—Willa waited outside the door with a scowl on her face.

"Shall we depart? I'd like to stop by the workshop before we return home." Katherine pulled her gloves tight and extended her hand to take the cloak draped over Willa's arms.

"Kat." Willa shook her head vigorously. "Those poor women."

"The two still here?" Katherine dropped her hand.

Willa nodded, then turned her head from side to side to see if anyone else could hear the conversation. "They have no place to go. We can't leave them here."

"I'm well aware you have a tender heart for those who are vulnerable—"

"As do you," Willa interrupted. "Remember all those kittens you brought home?"

"Those women are not strays," Kat pointed out.

Willa leaned close. "You're right. But they can't fight this on their own. Neither expected this news today. Same as you. They both told me that by coming here, they thought they'd be welcomed into the duke's home. Seeing how the duke acted today? They'd have better luck staying at Carlton House."

Katherine sighed.

"Kat, they're alone," Willa implored.

"Those women married my husband. You truly can't expect me to offer them lodging in my home?" she asked while peeking around the door into the solicitor's office to glance at the other two wives. What had Meriwether seen in them that made him forgot his vows to her? What did they have that she didn't?

Both women had their heads together. One was holding the other's hand in an attempt to give comfort. They were trying to help each other through this crisis.

Her momentary jealousy melted at the sight. She should be bristling with resentment, but instead, her heart pounded a beat in sympathy. But for the grace of the heavens above, she could be either of those two. The husband they shared had turned all their lives upside down. It was his fault. As much as she hated to admit it, the duke was correct. The fault lay with the "trigamist" she and the other two had in common, not one another.

"Do they understand what has happened?" Katherine pulled her cloak around her shoulders.

Willa nodded once decisively. "By the time I entered the room, they were peppering questions at the young clerks who had explained the situation."

She shook her head. "It's madness to try and help. I can't do it."

"Kat," Willa soothed as she placed her hand on Katherine's arm. "The one with child has an aunt she's responsible for. Her name is Mrs. Venetia Hopkins. I met her in the entry while we were waiting." Willa edged Katherine toward the door. "The dark-haired woman who is dressed impeccably has nowhere to go either. She's by herself and seems ready to bolt for the door. We must help them."

"Why?" Katherine answered, acting uninterested in Willa's answer.

"Because they're no different from the others you take under your wing, except they married your husband."

Katherine searched her resolute eyes. Willa had her pegged correctly. Katherine's boutique, a business she'd been building over the years, offered luxury bedding and pillows to the elite of society. After her mother had died, she'd started the business as a way to keep a roof over their heads. Neither she nor Willa had accrued any savings, so they had to fend for themselves. Slowly, Kat's business had blossomed into a successful endeavor that currently employed ten unmarried women who were on their own. It was Kat's way of paying her good fortune forward by hiring single women. Within the next six months, if things continued in the same fashion, Katherine would employ twice that number.

The women sitting in Mr. Hanes's office were the same—on their own without husbands.

"All right," she said reluctantly. "I can give them lodging for a day or two." With Willa beaming in her direction, Katherine entered the office.

The two women glanced up when she and Willa crossed the threshold. "Hello, I'm Katherine, Lady Meriwether Vareck."

The pregnant woman nodded then gracefully stood. "I . . . suppose it's correct to say I'm Miss Constance Lysander. Please call me Constance." She turned to the third woman in the room. "This is Miss Blythe Howell."

Katherine stole a glance at Willa, who shrugged.

Miss Howell, the sister of a viscount, had ordered a fortune of bedding from Katherine months ago. After sending it to Miss Howell in Cumberland, Katherine's invoice had never been paid.

Miss Howell nodded. Keeping her gaze glued to the floor, she stood briefly, then returned to her seat.

"Lady Meriwether, Miss Howell and I were discussing

what we're going to do about our . . . shared situation." A gentle smile fell across Constance's face, indicating the woman was no threat to Katherine.

Miss Howell eventually lifted her gaze to Katherine's. "One of the clerks mentioned you own Greer's Emporium."

"I do," Kat answered.

"Then you and I are acquainted," Miss Howell said.

"We are. Though we've never met in person, I recognize your name." Katherine sat in a chair facing the other two women, and Willa followed suit. "It seems our husband was rather busy this past year."

"I could kill the bounder," Constance muttered.

Miss Howell's eyes grew round.

"What?" Constance challenged. "Look what he did to me. I'm due to deliver in weeks, and today I discovered my marriage is a fraud and the man I thought I married stole my dowry?"

"Perhaps it's a misunderstanding," Miss Howell said.

Constance glared at her.

"How could it be a misunderstanding?" Katherine asked quietly. "We were all called here for the reading of the man's personal will."

"You're right." Miss Howell sighed gently as she rubbed her forehead. "I don't want to admit that Meri did this to me"—she glanced at Constance and Katherine—"or you. I gather from Mr. Hanes's clerks that Meri had a different one assigned to each of us. It wasn't until today that Mr. Hanes realized we were all three married to him." Her gaze locked on Katherine. "I'm in your debt. I owe you money. Meri married me four months ago, then left several weeks after. He didn't give me any allowance. I don't have a farthing to my name, I'm afraid." Her gaze dipped to her hands for a moment. "I'm trying to make sense of what has happened here."

Katherine's heart softened at the woman's words. "Miss

Howell, I feel the same as you, wondering how this could happen. Your brother didn't come with you today?"

"St. John? He couldn't be bothered. He only cares about what horse is favored to win the next race," she scoffed softly. "If horses and gambling aren't involved, St. John isn't interested. He's in Austria as we speak, looking to add to his stables." She shook her head as a tear slipped down her cheek, which she quickly brushed away. "I shouldn't have spoken so freely. Please, I beg of you not to say a word to anyone."

"I won't say anything," Katherine answered.

"Nor I. We'll all be ruined if this gets out," Constance agreed. "My dowry is not accessible either." She leaned back in her chair, rubbed her belly, and stretched as if her back hurt. "I overheard one of the clerks say the money isn't available. Whatever that means. I only hope it means it'll be here soon."

Miss Howell nodded.

"Do you have anywhere to stay?" Katherine asked.

Both women shook their heads.

"I thought perhaps the duke would offer lodging in his home." Constance shifted in her chair once again.

"I'd move us into my brother's townhome, but he didn't open it this season." Miss Howell frowned. "Constance, you look uncomfortable."

She nodded. "I normally rest in the afternoon. But first, we must find somewhere to stay this evening. I can't travel back to Portsmouth today, and neither can you return north."

"The truth is we can't return home until we discover what's happened to our money," Miss Howell said.

Willa cleared her throat and shot a glance Katherine's way.

"Right," Katherine agreed at her companion's gentle nudging. "First things first. You're welcome to stay at my house."

As the women started to protest, she held up her hand. "I insist. It's easier for all of us. Plus, we can compare notes on how Meri hoodwinked us all."

They all nodded in agreement.

Willa smiled at Katherine, then went to help Constance. As the two walked out of the office, Miss Howell sidled next to Katherine.

"My full name is Blythe Elizabeth Howell. My brother calls me Bliss, but my friends call me Beth," she said gently. "I'd be honored if you'd call me Beth."

Kat smiled. "Of course, with one caveat. Call me Kat. Did you bring a lady's maid? She's welcome too."

Beth smiled, but sadness reflected deeply in her ocean-blue eyes. "No. I'm alone." She swallowed, but the unease was written on her face. "I've never been in this situation before."

"I doubt if any of us have ever been in this situation before." Katherine linked her arm through Beth's. "Let's go home. I'll make a pot of tea, and we'll see if we can convince Willa to bake some lovely iced biscuits for us."

Chapter Three

After maneuvering through the London traffic, the carriage finally pulled up to the solicitor's office, and Christian waited for his new footman, John Iverson, to open the door. Iverson had served under him in an elite squad of the Ninety-Fifth Regiment stationed in France and had no home to return to, so Christian had offered him a position.

When Iverson saluted as he stepped down from the carriage, Christian smiled. "There's no need for that."

"I forget, Captain . . . I mean, Your Grace." The young man's cheeks flushed slightly.

"We're all getting used to a new routine." He placed his tall beaver hat on his head. "I'm not certain how long I'll be." Without waiting for an answer, Christian crossed the street, mindful of the traffic.

As Christian was about to enter Mr. Hanes's office, a grubby hand holding a cup appeared out of nowhere.

"Eh, sir?" A beggar rattled the cup with a coin inside under Christian's nose. "Have an extra coin for a hungry man?"

Out of the corner of his eye, Christian glimpsed Iverson coming toward him, ready to intervene.

"It's all right." He turned his attention to the grubby young man and reached into his waistcoat pocket. "Let me see what I have."

"Captain? Is it you?" the beggar asked softly.

The man before him was dressed in rags and smelled as if he hadn't bathed in a month. Yet something was familiar about him as Christian stared into his blue eyes. "Reed?" he asked in astonishment. "Phillip Reed?"

"In the flesh, sir," The beggar's gleeful smile slowly melted. Reed bent his head and stared at his cup. "If I'd known it was you, I'd not have made a nuisance of myself."

"You are not a nuisance." Christian pulled a guinea from his pocket and pressed it into the man's hand. The coin was a paltry offering in comparison to Reed's accomplishments as a scout exploring the countryside and watching the enemies' movements during the war.

"Your Grace," a voice trilled from a few feet away.

Christian glanced at the woman waving a yellow silk handkerchief. Her lady's maid followed. Christian silently sighed as Lady Everton approached. Desperate to have Christian attend a ball she was hosting next week, Lady Everton had sent two invitations to his house since he'd arrived. Christian had politely sent his regrets, but the woman wouldn't take no for an answer.

He bowed slightly. "Good afternoon, my lady."

Lady Everton sailed to his side then curtseyed. "Your Grace, how lucky that I find myself in your delightful company." She glanced toward Reed and did a double take. Her repulsion was evident with her upturned lip. With a backward step, she swept her hand in his direction. "Shoo you," she admonished.

"Lady Everton, this is Mr. Phillip Reed," Christian said curtly. "He served under my command and deserves your utmost respect."

Her mouth opened, and she blinked rapidly in confusion. "I didn't realize. I thought he was a street beggar."

"An apology will suffice," Christian drawled.

"I'm sorry, Your Grace."

"Not me. Him." Christian wanted to roll his eyes. Instead, he nodded in Reed's direction. "And a 'thank you for your service' might be appropriate."

She swallowed and glanced between the two men. "Of course. How rude of me. I apologize and thank you." She stepped closer to Christian and lowered her voice. "About my ball next week, I wonder if you'd reconsider?"

"I'm afraid not." Christian kept his face expressionless. "I'm already engaged." He had no idea how he'd occupy his time that night. But as sure as the sun rises in the east, he wouldn't attend any event at her house in the foreseeable future. "Now, if you'll excuse us?"

"Of course," she said. "Until the next time, Your Grace." She ignored Reed and dropped another curtsey and held out her gloved hand.

Christian examined it for a moment then reluctantly took it. She stood, and before Christian could release her, she stuffed her silk handkerchief in his hand.

"A token of appreciation, Your Grace." She smiled demurely and proceeded on her way.

Reed looked at her retreating figure, then gazed at Christian. "Does that happen often?"

"More than you can imagine." He shook his head at the interruption. "Let's discuss more important matters. Did you find employment?"

"No, sir. The cabinet maker I worked for hired a replacement after I left. He doesn't have any extra work. I've even visited every other cabinet shop around." Reed studied the ground and shuffled one foot. "No one is hiring."

Christian's stomach twisted at the news. Reed was a hard

worker. When he hadn't been roaming the French countryside, he'd generously offered to repair the men's boots at camp in his spare time.

Unfortunately, this is what most of the brave soldiers came home to.

Nothing.

"Where are you staying?"

"Well . . . here and there." Reed let out a ragged breath.

Which meant he was sleeping on the streets.

Christian ground his teeth together. His men sacrificed their lives and livelihoods to protect the country with no repayment or appreciation. "You can work for me. Lodging included."

"Captain, are you sure?" Reed wiped the grime from his face across his sleeve.

The hope in his voice doused Christian's earlier anger at the man's circumstances. "It'd be my pleasure. I could use a good man like you."

"This is all I have to wear," the man said sheepishly. "Nowhere near fancy enough for your home."

"Remember Morgan, my batman?"

"Yes, sir. Fine man."

"He's my valet now. He'll find you something that you'll be comfortable in." He pointed to his coach. "Ask for Iverson and tell him I sent you. I have an errand here, then we'll be off."

"Ycs, sir." Reed stood at attention and saluted, then sprinted off to the carriage.

The tightness in Christian's chest loosened somewhat. He still had to face Meri's wives. If only finding a solution for them was as easy as it had been for Reed. Without delay, he went to the solicitor's door and entered.

The bell above the door chimed his arrival. One of

Mr. Hanes's clerks peeked around a door, then quickly walked toward Christian.

"Your Grace." The young man stopped and bowed. "Did you forget something?"

His mind. Christian shook his head. "Is Mr. Hanes available?" He pulled off his gloves then tucked his hat under his arm.

"I'm afraid not, sir. He left for an appointment." With a pencil stuck behind one ear, the young man stood with his hands clasped in front of him.

Christian lowered his voice. "Is my half brother's wife here?"

"No, sir. And neither are the other wives."

"Do you know where they went?"

The clerk shook his head. "I'm afraid not."

Meri's antics were becoming even more complicated. "Will you have Hanes call on me when he returns? I need to find those ladies."

"Of course, Your Grace. You should know all the wives departed together. That might make it easier to find them."

"As in, they left at the same time?" Christian asked.

"As in, they all left in the same carriage at the same time," the clerk answered.

Christian held himself still, unwilling to express his shock at the news. Finally, he took his leave with a nod.

Once he found where they'd gone, he'd send a note asking to call upon them. As he crossed the street to his carriage, a cold knot of dread blossomed within his chest.

Why did it suddenly feel as if he were about to face a firing squad?

Christian's valet, Jacob Morgan, pulled two silk cravats from the wardrobe. Though two years younger than Christian, the twenty-eight-year-old Morgan possessed the demeanor of a man almost twice his age. He'd been by Christian's side every single day while Christian had served as captain in one of the regiment's companies. After three years, Christian had decided the army could do without him, but he'd also decided he couldn't do without Morgan and brought him home as his valet. Lucky for Christian, Morgan had readily agreed to accept the post.

With care, Morgan adjusted the patch over his left eye. With his tanned features and long blond hair, Morgan resembled a pirate until one saw the exquisite cut of his morning coat. There wasn't a brigand alive who could imitate Morgan's impeccable tastes and elegant style. Thankfully, he relished the opportunity to make Christian appear the part of the perfect duke.

"Is your eye bothering you?" Christian finished buttoning his black brocade waistcoat.

"No, Captain." A painful grin creased his lips. "Maybe. Truthfully, it's an annoyance."

"It's only been a month," Christian said. "Perhaps you should have Dr. Artemis take a look and see how the healing's coming."

"Not that sawbones." Morgan shook his head. "No disrespect, sir, but he always wants to cut something off when he sees me."

"Shall we find someone else to help you?" Christian turned from the mirror and studied his valet.

"No, sir. I'll manage." He held two cravats in his hands, debating which one for Christian to wear. He chose the one without lace.

Knowing Morgan, he would try and hide the pain so as not to be a bother. "I'm going to send a few notes around to some colleagues whom I respect. Maybe they can recommend someone for you." Christian took the neckcloth. With the other hand, he picked up two letters he'd written. "Will you see these posted?"

Morgan glanced at the missives in his hand. "I wonder how Lord Sykeston and Lord Grayson are faring?"

Christian scowled. "Grayson is well. He's coming to town soon. Sykeston hasn't answered my last letter so I thought I'd reach out again."

"Wise thinking, Captain," Morgan agreed. "Good to try and reestablish your friendship with Lord Sykeston. Speaking of men who've returned home, I've got Reed settled in the kitchens. He's helping the cook rearrange the pantry."

"Thank you." Christian tied the cravat into a simple mathematical knot.

"Captain, if I may speak freely?"

"Of course," Christian answered.

"It's kindhearted to help these men." The valet gently smiled. "But, respectfully, you can't hire them all. The next man you hire will have to sleep on a cot in the kitchen. We're out of room."

Christian smoothed his waistcoat to keep from fisting his hands. Every time he thought of one of his men begging for food or shelter, he wanted to punch something. He glanced in Morgan's direction, and the empathy in the man's eyes spoke volumes. He felt the same as Christian, but he made a good point.

If Christian didn't come up with another idea for employment soon, there might be a revolt in his house. The cook was already grumbling that there were too many "cooks" in the kitchen. His housekeeper had been quite direct that the extra servants meant more work for her housekeeping staff.

Before Christian could reply, a knock sounded on the

sitting room door adjacent to Christian's dressing room. Morgan immediately answered, then returned. "Mr. Hanes has arrived."

Christian nodded, then entered his private sitting room, where the visitor currently was setting up his portable desk. As the family solicitor made a motion to stand, Christian held up his hand. "There's no need. Thank you for coming. I wanted to see how today ended."

Mr. Hanes pushed up his wire-framed glasses, then blinked slowly. Such an action made the man look like an owl regarding his surroundings. "They all wanted to know the specifics of their dowries and marriage settlements. Unbelievable sight," Mr. Hanes said in wonderment. "They walked hand in hand out the door together like a merry society of widows. Then they entered Lady Meriwether's carriage and left."

"They went to her house?" Christian asked.

"Yes, Your Grace."

Christian eased his large body against the sofa facing the solicitor. Morgan brought forward a small tray with brandy and glasses and poured two. He handed one to the solicitor, then the other to Christian. After the day Mr. Hanes must have experienced, it wasn't at all surprising he finished his glass in one swallow.

He didn't partake, but Mr. Hanes wiped his lips and gestured for another. Morgan lifted his brows but, without a word, poured the man another.

The image of Katherine's face after Christian had inadvertently hurt her feelings over the amount of her dowry still haunted him. Nor could he conceive how she had married his scandalous half brother. The woman had an assuredness about her that was in direct contrast to Meri's flightiness.

Perhaps it was true that opposites attracted.

Christian placed the glass on the side table, then leaning forward, rested his elbows on his knees as he devoted his full attention to Mr. Hanes. "Have you found out any more information?"

The solicitor ran a hand down his face. "Not yet, Your Grace. Your brother sent information about each wife to three different clerks at my office. I've posted letters to each parish, seeking information about their marriages. The only one I'll have soon is Lady Meriwether's since she married in London. With what the other women have claimed, it appears that Miss Constance Lysander and Miss Beth Howell were married to Lord Meriwether after Miss Katherine Greer."

"What was he thinking?" Christian muttered.

"I don't know, Your Grace." The solicitor exhaled deeply. "I'm trying to discover how long he stayed with Lady Meriwether before he traveled to Portsmouth. That's where he met Constance Lysander. He met Miss Beth Howell at her brother's Cumberland estate. It's all very complicated. It may take weeks to uncover the full extent of the scandal."

Christian leaned back against the black velvet sofa. "Well, I don't want you to delay. Pay Lady Meriwether's dowry amount to her immediately. Did Meri leave her anything else?"

The man shook his head and set down his empty glass. Morgan stepped forward to offer another drink, but the solicitor declined. "According to his will, Lord Meriwether left everything to you."

"To me?" Christian asked incredulously. "We hadn't spoken or corresponded in over three years."

"I'm aware of that, Your Grace," the solicitor said softly.

Christian bristled under the solicitor's steady gaze.

Finally, Mr. Hanes took off his glasses, then hesitated a moment before speaking again. "Seems Lord Meriwether left Miss Howell's Cumberland residence a little more than three months ago, then traveled around the countryside before . . ." He released a sorrowful sigh. "We're still waiting for the rest of his personal effects to arrive from his lodgings in Perth."

"I'll send two of my footmen." Christian had the perfect footmen in mind. "Both served under me as infantrymen and are excellent at reconnaissance. They'll get the job done quickly and efficiently."

"Your help is appreciated." Mr. Hanes slipped his folded eyeglasses in his pocket. "However, sir, I must recommend that you not pay anything to the wives from the ducal coffers, at least not at this time."

"Why?" he asked. "They're legally due their dowries."

"We don't have confirmation who the real wife is."

Morgan blurted, "But you said that Lady Meriwether was the real wife and the other two married Lord Meriwether afterward." He stepped forward, then immediately bit his lip. "I apologize, Captain."

"No harm." Christian nodded at his valet's quick thinking. "I wondered the same thing."

"If you pay Lady Meriwether, then the other two will come forward and demand payment." Mr. Hanes lifted a brow. "I don't have proof of the marriages or the marriage contracts. Your brother didn't write me. Though Lady Meriwether's dowry amount is small, there's a great deal of money involved. Miss Lysander claims her dowry is two thousand pounds, and Miss Howell states her money amounts to twenty thousand pounds. Until we know what's in the marriage settlements, I must advise against it. It would put the dukedom in an untenable position if you paid these women and then discovered all was for naught. What if their claims are false? That no dowry was paid? What if there are other wives?"

Christian stood, and in response, so did the solicitor.

"I plan on calling on the three tomorrow. They've suffered enough at my half brother's hands. I can't in good conscience let that stand. I will pay their dowries. If there are other wives, God forbid, then we'll cross that bridge when we get to it." He clasped his hands behind his back.

"Of course, sir." Mr. Hanes bowed and took his leave.

"I'll get your evening coat, Captain." Morgan exited after the solicitor, leaving Christian alone.

He didn't even want to go to the theatre tonight, but it was expected of him. The Prince Regent had specifically asked if he would attend so he could be acknowledged publicly for his service. Christian walked to the window that overlooked the courtyard with the small garden attached. Instead of finding comfort, he felt nothing but emptiness. How many nights had he looked at this same scene when his father and stepmother had thrown outrageous parties with London's most dissolute? How many times had Christian awoke in the morning only to discover the drunks and laggards, half-naked from their late-night revelries, still asleep on the lawn?

Too many to count.

One thing he learned from the war. Inside, men were still the same breed no matter their social status or where they came from. Tonight's attendees in all their finery would not differ much from the actors and actresses who had converged on Rand House for those monstrous parties. Society would only be there for the latest *on-dits* they could share in tomorrow's drawing rooms.

For some odd reason, Katherine Greer's face wouldn't leave his thoughts. What kind of a wife had she been to his brother? The type of woman Meri would fall in love with would want to be entertained nightly at lavish events with outlandish people.

She didn't appear to be that type of person. Proof was the fact that she took the other wives home with her.

He rested his head against the window and closed his eyes. The amount of two hundred pounds felt like a burr under his skin.

The type of woman Meri was attracted to would've had money. That's why his attraction to the likes of Miss Howell or even Miss Lysander made more sense.

Why did his brother marry Katherine Greer? Who was she?

More importantly, why had she wanted to marry his brother, the biggest wastrel in all of England?

Katherine poured another cup of tea for Beth while Constance's aunt watched Kat's every move. She wouldn't call it rude, but it definitely set her nerves on edge. "Mrs. Hopkins, may I offer you another cup of tea? Perhaps another lemon tart?"

"No, thank you." With neat gray hair and startling dark blue eyes, the older woman daintily pressed a napkin against her lips. "You must call me Aunt Vee." She chuckled slightly. "After all, we are living together now."

Constance patted her aunt's hand. "We're only staying until we resolve this business about the dowries."

"And the marriages," said Beth, who had appeared relieved once they'd arrived at Katherine's house. When they'd entered the carriage for the ride home, Beth had insisted she sit in the middle between Willa and Aunt Vee. It was almost as if she were hiding from someone.

"You're welcome to stay for as long as you like," Katherine added.

"Oh, that's lovely. We're running away from my brother. He wants to have me committed." Aunt Vee turned to her niece. "We can live here forever if need be, Constance. At least until you have the baby."

Constance's eyes widened. "No, Aunt Vee. We can't live here forever, and you shouldn't tell that story." She rested her hands on her swollen belly. "We're not running from anyone."

Willa entered with a tray of iced biscuits in her hands but stopped when she heard the conversation. "Why does he want to have you committed?"

The older woman shrugged. "Seems my brother is bothered when I have tea with my husband."

"Aunt Vee, please," whispered Constance.

Before Katherine could change the subject, Willa asked, "Why does that bother your brother?"

"My husband has been dead for twenty years," Aunt Vee said earnestly. "We have tea once a month. I always serve my apricot tarts from the jelly I make. They were his favorites."

The room fell silent. No one even blinked.

When Willa started to laugh, Aunt Vee joined in.

"Ack, my relatives do that all the time with their dead spouses. That's not madness." Willa set down the tray, then wiped her eyes. "However, the majority of them like to imbibe in a bottle of whisky before they invite them to tea." She walked to Aunt Vee's side, then took her arm, leading her from the room. "I want to hear more about your husband and this brother of yours."

Katherine set her cup and saucer down. Leave it to Willa to find a way to give her time alone with Meri's other wives. She reached over and took Constance's hand. "Is it true what your aunt said?"

Constance nodded, and her reddened cheeks grew even more scarlet in color. She stared at their clasped hands. "If my uncle has her committed, he has control over her house and her modest allowance. The house is what he wants. It has a lovely view of Portsmouth and the sea. There have been stories told in our family that our ancestors hid fortunes found from shipwrecks in underground cellars on the property. Of course, no one can find any of it, but the legends continue."

"Do you have any other relatives?" Beth stood and took Aunt Vee's vacant seat on the sofa next to Constance.

"No. My parents are gone, and I promised my mother before she passed that I'd protect her oldest sister. Aunt Vee can't live by herself or my uncle would throw her into an asylum, so she lives with me." She took a deep breath and lifted her gaze to Katherine. "She's not insane. Just a little above the clouds."

Katherine nodded. "I've three hundred pounds in the bank for operating my business. If you need part of it, I'd be glad to help."

She would have had five hundred pounds available if she could get her dowry back. Though a modest amount, it allowed her to be seen as a lady, one whose loving family had provided for her. Though Katherine's mother was the best mother in the entire world in her estimation, it didn't negate the fact she was still an actress who'd borne a child out of wedlock. She didn't have an extra coin for a dowry.

So Kat had taken it upon herself to provide one. She'd saved every single penny of it, and she'd adopted her great-grandmother's real surname—Greer—not her mother's surname of James or her stage name of Fontaine. No one in good society would have had a thing to do with her if they knew the truth of her birth and upbringing.

Let alone if they heard a peep of what happened to her in York.

"Thank you for your generosity," Constance said with a sad smile.

"How much do you need?" Katherine asked.

"I have some money we can live on. However, I had more, or at least I did, until I met Meri. My father left me his maritime business of refitting ships in a trust, thus keeping it safe. Thank heavens." She leaned back against the sofa. "How did you meet Meri?"

It didn't escape Kat's notice that Beth moved a little closer to Constance. They all wanted to hear one another's stories. "A year ago, he peeked into the window of my linen store at the Beltic Arcade. I went outside to see what he wanted. He was so captivating, I let him in to the shop. That day, he purchased a set of bedding. He was the most gorgeous man I'd ever seen."

Beth nodded in agreement. "He could charm a nun to give up her habit."

"Pftt." Constance let out a breath. "Well, I'm not a nun, but he charmed the clothes off me." She glanced at her protruding middle. "Now look."

"I'll help you too. I'll stay with you through the birth." Beth glanced up at Constance. "If that's all right?"

"I'd welcome your help." Constance smiled grimly. "I need all the friends and assistance I can gather."

Beth turned her gaze to Katherine. "And if it's all right with you?"

She smiled. "Of course."

Beth fiddled with a biscuit on her plate. "When did Meri leave you?"

Katherine had debated how much to share, but in that silent moment, the earnest looks on the two women's faces reassured her. They would not hurt her, since they were in as much pain as she, perhaps even more. Their circumstances were certainly more desperate than hers.

"Well, it was a whirlwind courtship of sorts. In three and a half weeks, we were wed." She took a sip of tea.

Constance's eyes widened. "The banns were called immediately?"

Katherine nodded. "We married at a small church. After the ceremony, we returned to my home, where Willa had prepared a massive wedding breakfast. Meri ate and acted happy. He flirted in his usual manner, then hours later, he told me he had to go to Portsmouth. He left immediately, and I never saw him again."

She stared out the window to keep her tears at bay. She didn't mourn Meri. She grieved for the loss of a true marriage and a chance at happiness. She had wanted marriage to wash away the sin of her illegitimacy and her past. But that had been a fantasy.

"Meri enchanted me the same way he did you," Constance added. "Perhaps if my parents were still alive, they would have seen through his charade." She dipped her head again. "For God's sake, he was the son of a duke. I thought him honorable. . . . Proof that one's rank in society is no reflection of the quality of the person. He stayed with me a month. I thought he was the answer to my problems. Only, he created more." A tear raced down her cheek. "I'm sorry, Katherine."

Katherine swallowed the tightness in her throat as she shook her head. "I'm sorry too. For you. For your baby. For Beth and for me." Now, another would soon face the stigma of being a bastard, and Constance, the poor mother, would suffer every time her child experienced the cruelty from the slights and deliberate insults that would come their way. Kat wanted to shake her fist at the heavens and demand why such a cruel fate had been given to all of them. They were three women who faced real ruin. Constance and Beth were well-bred ladies who didn't deserve such treatment, and Katherine wouldn't allow them to suffer because the duke wanted to wash his hands of Meri.

Beth knelt between them. "Meri captivated my brother. All they talked about were horses and racing." She pursed her lips, then exhaled. "My brother arranged my marriage, gladly conveyed my dowry, then gave Meri most of our family fortune to invest. Meri stayed for a week. My brother should have been the one to exchange vows with our husband."

"Oh, you poor dear," Constance whispered. "Your brother is a viscount?"

Beth stood tall and straightened her dress. "Yes. St. John Howell. For the last three years, he's been trying to marry me off. He thinks he's being a good brother, but his judgment is questionable. He's made bad matches for me before, but thank heavens, they didn't come to fruition. I'm afraid he'll be desperate for me to marry once this gets out. I don't want to go home nor be recognized here. I just want to live in peace. But I'll do whatever I can to help you all."

Katherine offered each woman a smile. "We're friends now. And friends help friends." She reached and took Constance's hand with her right and Beth's hand with her left. "There's only one thing to do."

"What's that?" Beth asked.

"I'm going to the theatre this evening," she announced.

Both women's eyes widened.

"It's a little unorthodox, but at my shop, I heard the Duke of Randford is attending tonight at the behest of the Prince Regent. He should be the one to help us fix this mess. I plan to find him and have a nice long discussion with him. Would either of you like to join me?"

"No," they both said in unison.

Constance giggled slightly. "You're braver than I am."

Beth examined Katherine critically. "You have the keen instinct of a rebel even though you're such a little thing."

"A veritable warrioress," Constance added.

"Some of the best surprises come in small packages," Katherine said. "Please make yourself comfortable. I need to get ready."

With a wave, she left the room, and with each step, the more confident she became. After an enlightening afternoon with her two new friends, Katherine knew the path before her. She'd not allow them to suffer. Nor would she allow the baby to be born in an unmitigated scandal if she could help it. A certain duke would soon discover that Katherine would not stop until he helped Constance and Beth.

As important, she had to protect her business, which meant she had to keep her own secrets safe. The scandal swirling around her and the other two wives was a recipe for disaster. If anyone found out she'd married a trigamist, she might lose the chance to outfit the Prince Regent's bedchambers. The Prince Regent would be loath to entangle his pride and joy, the Royal Pavilion, with her problems, no matter how superior her linens were to the competition's.

She would protect her chance to win that contract. With a royal warrant for appointment, Katherine would turn her business into an indisputable success. She had worked hard, but more importantly, she put her heart and soul into her products. Winning the contract would ensure her future security. The money earned would be her own, and nothing could damage her or her reputation ever again.

Of course, she couldn't allow anyone to discover where she came from or why she had married Meriwether.

All of it led to a logical conclusion. This untenable situation she and the other women found themselves in would not stand. If the brilliant Duke of Randford could outwit and outmaneuver Napoleon's forces, then he could certainly find out what had happened to all their dowries and fix the mess Meri had created.

Unlucky for the duke, but lucky for Katherine, she planned to meet him at the theatre.

The duke might soon fancy that walk in hell's park he had spoken about in Mr. Hanes's office rather than tangle with her.

Chapter Four

Christian could feel his valet's anxiety clear across the carriage. As the seconds ticked by, the poor man's face turned paler. The situation turned dire when he pulled his cravat away from his neck. Under no circumstances would a self-composed Jacob Morgan allow a perfectly tied neckcloth to be ruined.

"Jacob," Christian said slowly. "We're in the theatre line, waiting for our carriage door to be opened."

His valet nodded once, then turned his head. As he pulled the window curtain aside, the streetlamps outside lit the inside of the carriage. Sweat glistened across his brow. He grimaced once, then dropped the curtain.

He cleared his throat and leaned back against the rear-facing velvet squab in Christian's carriage. "At times, this carriage feels like a box. If someone would attack us at this instant . . . we would be defenseless."

"I have a pistol in the storage compartment below me." Since he and Morgan had returned to London, they'd settled into an uncomplicated routine. His valet was a loyal and easy man to spend time with, but sometimes his observations, like the one he'd just uttered, suggested he'd come home from war with more than an eye injury. "But we're not close to the battlefields anymore." Christian smoothed his cadence. "We're safe."

"Indeed, sir." Morgan drew back the curtain once more. He wiped his brow with a handkerchief, then blew out a breath. "There are quite a few women here. I wonder how many handkerchiefs you'll receive tonight."

"Hopefully none." Christian smiled slightly and leaned forward to take in the view. "Today, I only received—" Suddenly, he stopped. "Oh, for the love of God," he said through clenched teeth. "Is that Lady Meriwether coming straight toward our carriage? She appears to be in a high lather and has someone with her." Christian knocked twice on the roof. Immediately, the driver stopped the slow crawl.

Morgan glanced at the window. "She must be upset if she's coming here."

"Indeed. Will you find the Prince Regent and explain that an emergency arose? I'll not be able to attend the theatre tonight."

"Of course, Captain. I'll hire a hackney and meet you back at Rand House."

Before Christian could offer more instruction, the crisp sound of a knock echoed in the carriage. He peeked outside the window to see the women had arrived. Lady Meriwether's stare was glued to the door handle. In seconds, Morgan turned the latch, opened the door, and leapt to the ground.

Christian drew in a deep breath. The only avenue available was to leave the area immediately before she could inflict any real damage. With a determined face, she had the look of a person preparing for all-out battle with certain victory to follow. He exhaled when he glanced at the open door. Thankfully, only one person accompanied her. Lady Meriwether's companion, the one who looked at Christian like he belonged in a pail of pigwash.

Morgan pulled out the carriage steps.

"Company has found us," Christian drawled. "I'm afraid this isn't the best time for receiving."

"I'm not giving, so that's not a problem. At least not for me," Lady Meriwether replied.

"I meant that I'm not entertaining guests," he shot back.

"I meant I'm not giving up." She smiled, and for a moment, he stared. He'd been correct in his earliest assessment of her. She was pretty, and her tenacity was an admirable trait.

But the woman was beyond exasperating.

Their exchange would have been comical if Christian had been in the mood to laugh. Without warning, the audacious woman stepped into the carriage. Christian had no recourse but to move his legs to make her entry easier.

She gracefully stepped around him, then settled herself on the seat opposite him. Her companion followed. Christian nodded at the woman, who sat next to Katherine.

"My lady, it is a *long walk* to the theatre." Christian pulled back the curtain leisurely. "At least half a block. I'm afraid I've decided not to attend tonight's performance. You'll have to find other transportation. I'm on my way home."

"Excellent, Your Grace. I'm not attending the theatre either. Did you know I live within walking distance of Rand House?" Without waiting for his response, she continued, "You can take me with you since we live so close to each other. We can have a nice little chat." She situated herself on the seat facing him directly, then sat ramrod straight. She adjusted her elegant purple velvet pelisse around her. As a direct result of her movement, the fabric shimmered in the light from the streetlamps. Pleased with herself, she nodded, then folded her gloved hands neatly in her lap. "If you'd be so kind? That's what family does for one another."

"It'd be my pleasure," he grumbled. She was practically moving in if her actions were any indication.

"Where are my manners?" she cooed.

Exactly. Where were her manners? Probably back at her house where she undoubtedly misplaced them.

"This is Miss Willa Ferguson."

"Allow me to do the same. My valet, Jacob Morgan."

The confounding woman smiled graciously at the valet, who stood outside the carriage. Not a hint of horror crossed her face when she gazed at Morgan and his eye patch. "Hello, Mr. Morgan. I'm Lady Meriwether."

"Good evening, my lady." Morgan executed a perfect bow.

Lady Meriwether's companion nodded also. "Call me Willa, Morgan. Would you tell me what happened to your eye?"

"I lost it in my last battle," he answered.

Every muscle in Christian's body stiffened. He'd seen the way men and women would gawk at Morgan's injury, then quickly turn their heads and whisper in hushed voices. It caused his loyal friend all sorts of anguish and embarrassment.

"Does it cause you much pain?" Miss Ferguson asked. "Itch? How long has it been?"

"Yes to both. About a month." Always a good soldier, Morgan stood tall and answered her questions politely.

"Miss Ferguson, is this really necessary? Are you trained in medicine?" Christian demanded.

Miss Ferguson completely ignored him. "Come to Lady Meri's house."

"Lady Meri?" Morgan asked.

Willa nodded. "That's what we call her. I've some salve

and a special tea blend that will put the bloom back on your cheeks. My da lost his eye in a farming accident. Said if it hadn't been for me, he didn't know if he would have survived it." Her gruff voice melted into a pleasing Scottish lilt. "Laddie, it'll help you heal, I promise."

"I don't know if I can. I'm always available for the duke." Morgan tipped his head in preparation to leave.

"Mr. Morgan," Lady Meri said softly. "Willa's knowledge of herbs and medicines is legendary. She helped my mother with her pain when she passed with a lung ailment. You're welcome any time at my home."

Morgan suddenly smiled as if the sun rose and set on Lady Meri. "Thank you for your generosity. Both of you. When I have a free moment, I'll stop by."

"You should make time," Christian said. "You complained about it earlier."

"Perhaps tomorrow you could come if your employer would allow it?" Katherine turned her bewitching smile Christian's way, nailing him in place. "Of course, only if the duke can manage to dress himself?" the impudent woman added a little too sweetly.

"Jacob, why don't you visit first thing in the morning?" Christian held Lady Meriwether's gaze. "Madame, I accomplish the majority of things myself. I brush my own teeth and hair. I can saddle my horse"—he tapped his chin as if contemplating a list—"I even can feed myself." He waited for a dramatic pause. "Oh yes, I'm quite adept at running my estates. In my recent past, I've successfully led my regiment into battles without a casualty. Currently, I uphold my duties in the House of Lords." Satisfied that he'd shown her he could rise to the occasion and be accommodating to his valet, he delivered a smile worthy of seducing a siren. "Based upon my experience, I think I can manage my own dress when it's required."

Her breath caught suddenly, and she shifted in her seat.

Christian had hit his mark. When he set his mind to it, he could be as charming as Lucifer.

"My, you are accomplished, sir." Her brow furrowed, and she stared straight through him. "Have you even been to the House of Lords since you've returned to London?" She turned in profile to her companion. "Are they even in session?"

Damnation. He'd made a tactical error in his litany. He should have left that part out.

Willa smirked. "Nae, lass."

"I'm visiting next week," Christian offered.

A slow smile spread across Katherine's face. It reminded him of treacle, a little sweetness to hide the bitter bite of the medicine.

"No time better than now to get your medicine." Willa stepped down from the carriage with Morgan's assistance. "Kat, I'll take the young man home with me, then we can meet you at the duke's house. I can instruct his housekeeper how to apply the medicine and how to brew the tea."

"Splendid idea," Lady Meri answered with a satisfied nod at Miss Ferguson's suggestion.

Both he and Morgan had been completely outmaneuvered by these two women. Christian settled back against the forward-facing squab and stared at the ceiling.

It would be a long carriage ride home.

"Captain?" Morgan asked.

Christian sighed. "Go. I'll see you back at Rand House."

Morgan closed the door, then knocked on the paneling to signal to the driver that Christian was ready to depart. Darkness shrouded the interior of the coach as the driver expertly guided the carriage out of the waiting line. Without direct light, it was difficult to see Katherine across from him.

An awkward silence ensued while a frisson of electrical

current hummed between them. Or at least, that's how it felt to him. Years had passed since Christian had been alone with a woman in such a confined space. At war, he always stayed at camp with his men. Even when they invited him to join in their revelries at the pubs and businesses friendly to the English, Christian politely declined. It wasn't in his nature.

He inhaled deeply. The fragrant scent of violet drew him in her direction, and he rested his elbows on his knees to lean forward. In the twilight, the rest of his senses were heightened.

"Is Miss Ferguson talented with her teas and herbs? Morgan is a good a man. I'd hate to see him hurt or given false hope." Christian let the words trail to silence.

"Very talented. Morgan is in good care," Katherine answered. "Willa was renowned in our old neighborhood."

"Where was that?" he asked.

"Up north." Without offering anything more, she pulled aside the curtain to glance outside.

"Why does she call you Kat? It's a little unorthodox, isn't it?"

"It was my mother's pet name for me, and Willa isn't simply a companion."

The rustle of velvet warned she had moved, then her knee brushed against his. At the sensation, he stilled instantly, his body tensed with a hunger for more. He fought the urge. He was a gentleman, firstly. A respected former member of the British military, secondly. And finally, she was his half brother's wife.

Unaware of the turmoil he battled, she continued, "She's my family. Willa was my mother's companion. Now she's mine."

Her mellifluous voice wrapped around him as the word

mine burrowed into the recesses of his mind. For a wild moment, he wanted nothing more than to make her his.

Ridiculous thought.

He broke the silence between them. "You mentioned you lost your mother. When?"

"About ten years ago. I was fifteen." Her face relaxed, revealing her affection as she spoke. "She was always there for me. She told me never to take anyone for granted, work hard, and always try my best. Good advice from an amazing person and mother."

It was exactly the way he felt about his own mother. "I lost mine when I was six."

"Was she ill?"

He shook his head. "She died from injuries suffered in a carriage accident."

"I miss mine every day." Katherine's voice held a hint of loneliness in it. "It's hard, isn't it?"

"Indeed. I miss mine too." He shifted in his seat. "She was quite the gardener. I helped her tend her roses. We'd spend hours upon hours in the hothouse. I still continue to grow and graft roses. It was her hobby and . . . now it's mine."

The woman across from him was either a menace or a magician. He'd told her things that he'd never spoken aloud to anyone before. Surprisingly, it actually felt quite nice.

"May I call you Katherine?"

"Yes," she said quietly. "Or you can call me Kat."

"Call me Christian." How long it had been since he'd heard his name on the lips of a woman? He rubbed a hand down his face. "I take it you had an uncontrollable need to see me, Katherine?"

She nodded. "After you left Mr. Hanes's office, I found myself with the other women Meriwether had married. Their names are Miss Constance Lysander and Miss Beth Howell.

I discovered they're in dire straits. Neither have anywhere to stay." Her voice trembled slightly.

He wasn't certain if it was from outrage or empathy.

Perhaps both.

"One is with child and the other, the sister of a viscount, is scared of discovery. They realize that if society hears of this, then all of us will suffer. You understand that."

He nodded. Lord, did he understand that. The stench of his brother's madcap scandals never stopped.

She continued, "They're staying with me."

He sat motionless, waiting for more. Her smooth, honeyed voice serenaded him, making the moment feel almost intimate, like friends confiding in one another, sharing their secrets.

"Why did you take them with you?" It was the only question he could think of so she'd speak again.

"But for the grace of fate, I could be one of them. Meriwether could have married me second or last."

"That's noble of you." He struggled for something else to say. Most women, if forced into that situation, would be aghast to offer such help. But the enigma across from him wasn't most women.

"Christian . . ."

The minty scent of her breath kissed his cheek. He'd always had a weakness for mint leaves, but the hesitation in her voice caused his gut to cinch.

"Constance will deliver within weeks. We must do something."

He had promised himself not to become entangled with any of these widows when he'd first walked into Hanes's office. However, the plights of Kat and the other two women were real and couldn't be denied.

The carriage arrived in front of his home, where lanterns

lit the drive. The sight never failed to move him. Sometimes with happy thoughts, but mostly it reminded him of the garish parties that his father and stepmother would host for the demimonde and the theatre actors they had loved to entertain. Thankfully, there would no longer be wild, outlandish screams of merriment or howls of gaiety to rent the air.

"Shall we finish our conversation inside?" he said formally. "We'll wait for your companion and my valet to return, then my carriage will take you home. There are some things I'd like to discuss with you." He leaned against the squab, creating distance between them, and she followed his lead. "Believe it or not, I want the same thing as you."

"Meaning?" she asked warily.

"A way out of this mess."

Christian held out his hand to assist Katherine from the carriage. The instant she touched him, she could have sworn she'd been scorched by fire through their gloves. The overwhelming warmth in his large hand set off an incredible sensation of heat through her limbs. When her feet touched the ground, she released him. She had to regain her equilibrium before she tackled the subject at hand again.

That was what she should be thinking about.

Not his hands or his warmth.

He held her elbow as he helped her up the steps of his London home, a grand mansion in the neoclassical style. The trigamist had never brought her here, probably because he had other wives to attend to.

She should be ashamed to refer to him spitefully as such. But really, she had to keep her distance from the memories of her dead husband. He'd proven he was no saint.

Perhaps his older brother was the same.

Katherine stepped into the entry, immediately blinking

at the brightness. The overhead chandelier hung from the center of the ceiling, its light reflected by hundreds of mirrors on the wall, each encased in a latticework overlay. The decadent pattern matched the blond and white tile of the marble flooring beneath her.

A stoic butler met them at the door. "Your Grace, welcome home."

Christian nodded as he handed his greatcoat to the man, then helped Katherine remove her pelisse. "Lady Meriwether, this is Wheatley. He's served our family for over thirty years."

"How lovely to meet you, madame." The butler stood immobile, much like the Greek statute of Dinlas directly behind him.

"A pleasure," she answered. If she wasn't mistaken, the faintest hint of a grin broke against the older man's mouth.

"When Morgan returns with Lady Meriwether's companion, Miss Ferguson, please send them to my study."

The butler nodded curtly. "Of course, Your Grace." As they turned to leave, the butler stopped her. "My lady, may I offer my condolences on your loss. The young master was always a favorite with the staff here and at Roseport."

The duke stiffened beside her.

"Thank you, Wheatley. I appreciate your kindness."

Before she could say more, Christian latched his arm around hers and escorted her down the hall. She took two steps for each one of his. It was as if he were running away, but from what?

"Pardon me." He slowed his pace once he realized she was having trouble keeping up. "I always walk fast. It's a habit I acquired in the military."

"What else did you acquire in the military?" she asked as they walked down the hallway.

He slowed his step even more. His dimples appeared

briefly when a grin flashed across his mouth. "Habit wise, I don't mind a tepid cup of tea to start the day. I eat fast. Plus, I learned to fall asleep as soon as my head hit the cot."

"Was it hard . . . all those years?"

"The lack of material comforts was insignificant. The war itself was horrific." Before she could inquire more, he opened the door. "Here we are."

As soon as they were in the study, he waved his hand at a set of club chairs in front of the massive burl wood desk centered in the large room. Though the room was well-kept, samples of paperhangings for the walls and vivid brocades and silks were spread haphazardly across a matching library table, giving it a hint of frenzy.

Instead of taking a chair, Katherine headed to the table to better inspect the samples. "Are you redecorating?"

At a side table, he had his back turned to her, pouring a glass of brandy. He grunted in answer.

Her fingers caressed the fine silk. Such beautiful fabric would make an excellent cover for her feathered bedlinens. "Is the silk from Spitalfields?"

"I have no idea. I've given the assignment to Morgan to handle. He knows design well enough, likes fashion, and said he looked forward to the task." Christian took a swallow, then poured another glass.

"If I were the one decorating, I might add some primary colors." She swept her hand across a royal blue wool with exquisite crewel work embroidery. "You don't want it to be dull. You'll be working in here. A little color does wonders for creativity."

"I told him nothing flamboyant, and I don't want that blue you're fondling either. If he chooses everything the color of mud, it would suit me." He shook his head. "Forgive me. I sound like a grumpy old man. Perhaps you should offer your advice to Morgan."

"If that's a challenge, I accept." She glanced around the rich black, green, and white furnishings. In her opinion, it was classic and tastefully done. "It's a beautiful room. Why are you even redecorating?"

"Because this was my stepmother's handiwork."

The brittleness in his tone had returned, much like when they'd first met. Obviously, she'd hit a nerve. She dug a little deeper under the samples and found a lovely brown and cream striped satin that would perfectly match the light color of his desk. The brown shade reminded her of the leather of a new saddle. She'd remember this color and incorporate it into her new collection of linens. She laid it on top so Morgan would discover it.

Somehow, Christian had made his way to her side without her even knowing he was there. An apparition made more noise. "Do they teach you that in the army?" she asked.

His brow furrowed into neat lines. "How to pour a glass of brandy? My commanding officer also instructed me on the fine art of pouring sherry." He held out a glass.

"No, I meant sneaking up on people." She laughed as she took the sherry. They toasted each other as friends would.

"A requisite part of an officer's training, I'm afraid. Never let the enemy see you coming." The smile on his face made him appear years younger than when she'd first met him in the solicitor's office.

My God, he was handsome when he smiled. She stepped back and took a sip, never taking her gaze from his. "Am I the enemy?"

He appraised her, looking for any chinks in her armor. She'd experienced such evaluations all her life when others had discovered that her mother was an actress. Women thought her below them in social status, and men thought her easy prey for bed sport. But Katherine had protected herself by weaving fanciful stories of a doting father who was a cherished husband to her mother. She'd continued the tale by sharing that the poor soul had been lost in a tragic shipwreck, never to be heard from again. Such fairy tales were easy to spin, and people believed her. Meri had. Instinctively, she drew to her full height and tilted her chin barely an inch. She'd not be cowered by a man such as the duke, who had little regard for family. It was the most precious gift one could receive.

"Are you the enemy?" His voice had taken on a dark, silken quality, one that reminded her of his brandy. A sip started off smooth but would soon burn. "You'll have to tell me. But be forewarned, Katherine, I've been trained to crush enemies without a look back."

Her eyes widened. "I'm not your enemy. I'd hoped you would help with Constance and Beth. I don't want their lives ruined. You"—she waved her hand between them—"and I have to figure out a way to protect their reputations. An innocent baby is involved, one who didn't ask for the burden they're about to be born with. Neither did Constance. She thought she was protected under the sanctity of lawful marriage. So did Meriwether's third wife. But you can help these women," she offered.

"Honestly, I'm not certain how I can help. I came back to Mr. Hanes's office to talk to all of you, but you'd left." He swiftly but elegantly turned, then strolled away. "Hanes is trying to determine if your husband left anything that might belong to you or the other wives. He's also attempting to determine the validity of each marriage."

She gasped slightly.

Immediately he turned around. "Are you all right?"

She coughed to hide her unease. "I swallowed wrong."

What if they discovered that Meri had never consummated the marriage? Would it make any difference? What if anyone discovered she wasn't a true lady?

"If it's acceptable, I'll call on you tomorrow. Perhaps together we can find some options for everyone."

The tightness in her shoulders loosened at the offer of help. "Really? I thought you didn't want any part of it?"

"I don't want any part of Meri, but I have no qualms with the three of you." He took another sip.

"What time? The earlier the better for me. I've several appointments tomorrow at my shop in the arcade."

His intense stare found hers. "You work?"

"Yes. I have my own business. I make linens and bedding."

"Interesting." The lines around his eyes relaxed. "How did you get into that?"

"I've always liked to work, and after my mother died, I had to find something to do to help me with my grief." It was stretching the tale a little.

She had been grieving, but mostly it was to put food on the table. Her mother had ensured they had food daily, even if it meant taking parts others would shun. Kat had learned about necessity and sacrifice at a young age.

"I enjoy working also. I like to be productive." He placed his empty glass on his desk and studied her. Silence slowly surrounded them. "Katherine, let me be frank. You said I can help those women. I'll do what I can, but let's make certain we understand each other. I'm not that type of hero."

"What does that mean?" she asked, nervously smoothing the nap of a black velvet upholstery sample.

"I may be decorated for heroic deeds . . ." He rubbed his neck as he studied the Aubusson rug below their feet for a moment, then caught her gaze, his long black hair falling across his face. "But I'm not a hero, romantic or otherwise, particularly when it comes to Meri." He shook his head slowly. "I washed my hands of him years ago. I'll offer whatever assistance I can to you and the other wives but don't expect miracles. Meri's indiscretions are the devil to untangle. They always have been. But this one tops them all."

"Did you hate him?" Katherine asked. Christian had been cold in the solicitor's office, but his response tonight reminded her of a wounded animal, one that would attack to protect itself.

"A person has to care before he can hate." His eyes grew hooded.

If she were a betting person, she'd lay money it was a way to conceal himself before he revealed too much.

When he turned to walk back to his desk, she saw the family portrait propped against the wall. The father embraced his son who leaned over his lap, while the mother, dressed as Pomona, the goddess of fruitful abundance, stood behind them with her hand resting on her husband's shoulder. A lone figure, a boy older than the other, stood stiffly off to the side, obviously uneasy with the sweet bucolic scene in the small garden.

But the painting wasn't what caused Katherine's gaze to widen in shock.

It was the small pieces of foolscap that had been pinned through the portrait. It completely destroyed the work of art. There must have been at least fifty of the small pieces of paper.

"What is that?" She pointed to the portrait.

"It's a map of sorts. How I keep track of important items or things that need my attention."

"It looks like a family portrait." She moved closer to study it. Indeed, the individual pieces of foolscap all had writing on them, each held in place by a straight pin. The only individual without a single piece of paper was the boy who stood far away. "Is that you?"

"Hmm, yes," he hummed. "Ingenious, isn't it?"

"What's ingenious about destroying a portrait?"

"I've found a new purpose for things of no value," he answered. "It makes a perfect place to keep notes. I started the habit while mapping troop movements to various battlegrounds." He turned to her and smiled. "Rest assured, we didn't destroy any art while over in France. We used empty canvases for our work."

He was absurdly calm, without a hint of embarrassment showing on his face, as he walked to her side. He tilted his head and examined his handiwork.

"You've ruined a piece of art. A family heirloom."

"Art is in the eye of the beholder," he countered. "I behold rubbish."

Before she had time to respond, Willa and Morgan entered the study.

Katherine turned to the door, thankful for the interruption.

Apparently, Willa and Christian's valet had become bosom friends. They had their heads tilted next to each other. Willa made some quip, and Morgan held his stomach, laughing.

"My God, it's a miracle," Christian said behind Katherine. "I haven't seen him laugh like that for months. He's been in such pain since he lost that eye. Your Willa must be some kind of a magician."

"Indeed," Katherine said as Willa winked at her to let her know that all was well with Morgan.

"Or a Scottish witch?" Christian teased, his low voice holding no traces of his earlier detachment. "I really don't care if she is one. What she's done for Morgan is beyond incredible. He appears to be back to his normal self."

With his stoic face ready to crumble, Wheatley appeared at the door. "Your Grace?"

"Yes, Wheatley?" Christian didn't turn from the sight of Willa and his valet enjoying each other's company.

"Your assistance is required in the entry. A racehorse by the name of Poison Blossom has been delivered. Apparently, it was Lord Meri's, and he wanted you to have it."

"Bloody hell," Christian muttered under his breath, then completely focused his attention on the butler. "Send it around to the stables."

"I'm afraid that's impossible, sir." Clearly uneasy, the butler continued, "*It* is in the entry and refuses to move."

"My lady, if you'll excuse me?" Christian was already halfway across the study. "Miss Ferguson?" he called out to Willa. "Perchance, do you have any miracle medicines for charming a horse?"

"Nay, but I have an evil eye when needed," Willa offered without a hint of boastfulness.

"Bring it, if you please," the duke called out as he turned the corner into the hall.

Without a doubt, the man made her head spin. He was a master of flipping back and forth from an unsociable beast who claimed not to care about family to a charming, reserved gentleman.

Katherine thought herself quite adept at hiding the truth, but the duke took such skill to an entirely different level.

She and Willa followed Morgan to the entry hall. Taller than most other men, Christian stood with his hands on his hips, surveying the scene before him.

Pure pandemonium had erupted around them. Groomsmen, liveried footmen, and several of the scullery maids were arguing over how best to remove Poison Blossom from the premises. Kat and Willa found a place against a curved wall out of the way.

The horse stood in the middle of the marble entry, refusing to budge as two men from the stables tried to pull her around and lead her outside. By the determined swishing of her black tail and all four feet planted, she was having none of it.

Christian didn't pay any mind to the chaos around him. All his attention was devoted to the horse.

Poison Blossom's ears flickered forward and back in increasing agitation.

"Enough," Christian called out. The command in his voice brought everyone to attention. Immediate quiet infiltrated the room.

An angry Poison Blossom turned her attention to Christian. Her tail swooshed in irritation as the white of her eyes became visible.

"Everyone back away from her." Christian took a step forward. Without objection, every single person moved away from the horse except for the groomsman who held her lead. "John, what do we have here?"

"Your Grace, this man brought Lord Meriwether's racehorse all the way from Cumberland."

A man in work clothing stepped forward, nervously clutching his hat. He dipped his head in a respectable but abbreviated bow. Even he didn't want to lose sight of Poison Blossom when she was in such a nasty mood. "Your Grace, I'm Miff Mitchell from the White River Stables. That's where she's been staying. I was told to bring the horse here."

Christian slowly swung his gaze to Mr. Mitchell. "What can you tell me about Poison Blossom?"

At the sound of her name, the horse whinnied and stared straight at Christian.

Everyone else, including Katherine, had stayed in their positions, quiet as church mice. It was as if they all were spellbound by the sight of the duke facing off against the noticeably pregnant and vexed black beauty.

"Sir, she is the finest and most successful racehorse your brother—"

"Half brother," Christian corrected.

Mr. Mitchell nodded. "That your half brother owned. A bit high-strung, but she has a heart that won't quit when she's in a race. She's foaling, and there's high speculation that her offspring will follow both her and its sire, Black Thunder, in their racing success." The man laughed. "Two of the best racehorses in the country."

Katherine studied the horse. It was apparent she'd been well taken care of. Her black coat glistened in the light, and her legs had been wrapped to avoid injury. She was full of energy. And big.

Very big.

The entry had shrunk in its opulence and size with the horse and Christian measuring each other.

"Thank you, Mr. Mitchell." With his gaze glued to the horse, Christian continued his survey. "I have a question. How is it that she's in my house?"

"Your Grace," the man said sheepishly. "She doesn't like to wait. I reckon she had enough of the outside as I was explaining her situation to your butler. She made herself at home."

Poison Blossom threw her head as if taunting Christian.

"What's happened, Poison?" Christian's voice deepened into a silky smoothness that reminded Katherine of a perfect cup of chocolate, one designed to ease a person into a new morning. "Hmm?" he coaxed as he stepped forward and patted her neck.

The horse threw her head and shifted backward. Several footmen scattered out of her way to avoid being kicked.

"Here now." His deep voice hummed in answer.

She threw her head again.

"Poison, stop. You're all right," he soothed while staring at her.

That voice should be outlawed.

The horse stared right back. Eventually, she shifted and then leaned forward in Christian's direction. All the while, the duke kept stroking her nose and murmuring sweet things into her ear.

"Your Grace, she goes by Blossom," his head groomsman said quietly.

"Of course, she does," Christian said in that same sotto voice. "A beautiful girl like you reminds me of a flower."

The horse pawed the floor in answer.

"Aren't you exquisite," Christian soothed. "A proud beauty who just wants some rest, I would imagine. A bag of oats, fresh hay, and cool water are yours." Christian took a step closer, and immediately, the horse blew out a breath. "Perhaps a carrot after your long journey. Not to mention, a nice, clean stable that will keep you warm."

His voice ignited little sparks of something . . . some sensation that made every inch of Katherine's body come alive. She couldn't identify exactly what it was, but she knew it was dangerous. There was no denying what she was seeing. The Duke of Randford was having a conversation with a horse and making it feel as if it were the most important thing in his world.

As his voice lowered even more in a gentle rumble, Kat leaned in his direction, much like a flower to the warmth of the sun. "Oh, my," she whispered.

"'Oh, my' is the right of it, lass," Willa agreed.

"Did you see what he did?" Katherine whispered.

"Aye. A true cock of the walk in every sphere of society he deems to grace his presence with." Willa sighed. "You'll have to be on your toes with that one." Willa pointed at Christian and Blossom. "Will ye look at that?"

Christian passed by them, leading the horse toward the door without a buck, bite, stomp, or kick in protest. Blossom's clip-clop sounded sure and steady across the marble floors. As soon as the duke had exited with the horse following, murmurs floated through the room as the Randford servants commented on the duke's success with Blossom. Almost immediately, the stable hands and groomsmen followed him outside.

"Another female who succumbed to a Vareck man and his ability to woo," Willa whispered. "He reminds me of your husband."

"No. Meri was nothing like the duke," Katherine answered, keeping her gaze glued to Christian's back until he was out of sight. The Duke of Randford was different. Without any effort, he'd bewitched that horse to do his bidding. He made such a feat look easy.

And much too perilous for any woman who crossed his path.

Like the perfect fit of his evening coat and breeches, he wore his self-assurance with ease. It enhanced his aura of power, and his gentleness with the horse bespoke a man with a heart.

According to the gossip rags, when he'd arrived in London on horseback, women lined the streets and threw their handkerchiefs in his direction. The caricature detailing the event resembled the medieval ladies from days gone by favoring a knight errant.

Who could resist him?

No one. That was the answer.

Heaven above, he was coming to her house tomorrow.

Then and there, Katherine decided it would be best to keep out of his way, or she would be following him around like Blossom.

Chapter Five

Christian reclined in the chair with his neck exposed. Normally, he shaved himself, but after a sleepless night, he had asked Morgan to do the honors for him.

Sleep wasn't the only thing that made him feel uneasy this morning.

Katherine. Just saying her name left him edgy.

When she'd pressed him to help the other two wives, he'd felt that old, familiar dread reach out and pull him under. Would he ever be free of his family's self-centeredness? The idea that his half brother would ruin these women without thought of the consequences made Christian's chest ache, not to mention his head feel as if it were about to implode.

He didn't like to see any woman suffer, but what could he do except pay the wives their dowries and offer assistance when the second wife's baby was born? How else could he shield them from the scandal that threatened to erupt if anyone heard what Meri had done?

That's what a *noble* Duke of Randford should do—protect his family. By keeping those women safe and their reputations intact, he'd be safeguarding Meri's memory and protecting Katherine and the other two wives while sweeping his half brother's disastrous actions under the proverbial carpet.

If Christian's father were alive, he'd have ignored the women. Years ago, too self-consumed to consider others, his father had overlooked Christian for his new wife and Meri. Christian had never said a word, but he had watched his father's actions carefully. Christian had learned that arrogance, self-importance, dissimulation, and obliviousness were the hallmarks of being a duke.

But such behavior wouldn't serve Christian well in his future endeavors since those traits had proven unbeneficial on the battlefield. He fought next to candlemakers, farmers, and cobblers. They all protected one another. Men had to work together if they wanted to survive, no matter their rank or background.

He had promised himself he'd never forget the lessons he'd learned in war. Now that he was back, he would cultivate a way to help his men recapture their lives. For some men, they came home to nothing. Left to fend for themselves, sweethearts, wives, and families simply disappeared, never to be heard from again. Others came home wounded inside and out, with little hope of healing. Some of the men like Reed had to fend for themselves on the street.

Once he took his seat in Parliament, he planned to introduce legislation to provide more assistance to the valiant men who returned home without work and a place to live. He was going to lobby his peers at every social event he attended.

It all brought back what was missing in his own life. Only in the army did Christian find a place where he was part of something. However, when his father died, he had to return to Rand House.

He'd never call it home as he never truly belonged there.

He closed his eyes and tried to summon more pleasant thoughts. Again, it came back to Katherine. He could think about the softness of her skin. When she'd placed her hand in his as he offered assistance out of carriage, he had fought a mammoth battle not to squeeze her fingers. For underneath the kidskin gloves, there was an underlying suppleness and a gentle touch. He would wager on it.

But such tenderness belied a persistence that made her unique. She wasn't afraid to go toe-to-toe with him when there was something she wanted, namely him helping the wives out of this mess. Thankfully, he wanted the same thing.

"Captain, are you ready?" Morgan quickly and efficiently sharpened Christian's razor on the leather belt.

"Yes," Christian answered.

After Morgan applied the softening, creamy soap, he carefully stroked the blade against Christian's skin.

"Tell me about this medicine Miss Ferguson gave you yesterday." Christian closed his eyes as the ritual continued. "The two of you seemed thick as thieves when you walked into the study."

"Willa is quite the medicine woman. She told me her father had lost his eye in a wheat thrashing accident. She said he was in terrible pain." Morgan continued the shave as he spoke. "She created a salve from adder's tongue and a few other herbs." He lifted the blade from Christian's skin and wiped it on clean linen toweling. "As soon as she applied it, the pain and itching stopped. This morning, the redness is down. Willa gave me a bitter tea made from privet to help with inflammation. I'm to drink it morning and night."

"That's astounding," Christian murmured. "Did you see the other wives while you were at Lady Meri's house?"

Morgan shook his head. "They'd retired by the time I arrived. Willa is very protective of those women, especially Lady Meri. Willa has been with her since she was a small child. She speaks of her as a mother would, with great affection and pride."

Christian grunted. With the last swipe of the blade, the shave was finished. He took the toweling and removed the last of the soap from his face. "Did you discover anything else?"

"Willa told me Lady Meri is a self-made woman." Morgan went about the task of cleaning the blade and putting away the shaving utensils. "She's created a very successful business of making and selling linens. Apparently, the *ton* keeps her quite busy. So busy, in fact, she's created a club of sorts."

"What do you mean a club?"

The valet shrugged. "She has a shop in the Beltic Arcade that only allows women inside. It's by appointment only. She's invited other female merchants into the shop to sell their wares."

"I've never heard the like. That's a very exclusive area. Men aren't allowed?"

Morgan shook his head. "A revolutionary idea, if I may say, Captain. It's widely successful, according to Willa. All the ladies in town love to shop there. It's like their own gentleman's club, so to speak. It's designed to discourage the riffraff from intimidating and heckling the ladies, Willa said. There are several men who haunt the area. When they tried to enter once, Willa barred them with a wave of her knife. Apparently, she keeps one on her person at all times. Lady Meri immediately hired an ex-pugilist to guard the doors, so they won't try it again."

"Unique to say the least." Christian admired an industrious streak in any man or woman. It laid the foundation for success in life. It wasn't surprising that Katherine enjoyed working. Quick and creative, she found solutions to problems.

Completely different from her husband, which made their marriage all the more unusual.

A smile tugged at his lips as he finished tying his own cravat. She confronted him at the theatre. Most of the women he'd met since he was back in London were in awe of him. But Katherine challenged him. She was completely refreshing from the other women he'd come across in his week back in town. He had nothing in common with them, but Kat was different. She was building something that very few could ever hope to accomplish, a successful and well-respected business.

Maybe Meri had recognized her as exceptional. Perhaps that's why he married her.

A knock sounded on the dressing room door, and Wheatley entered.

"Your Grace, the carriage is ready." The butler bowed slightly.

"Thank you." He took a final look in the mirror as Morgan helped Christian into the form-fitting morning coat. He adjusted his cravat one last time. The sooner this fiasco was finished, the sooner he could concentrate on his work, helping his men find jobs.

Though, if Christian were honest with himself, he hoped there would be other reasons to see Katherine in the future. He started for the door, then stopped abruptly in his tracks.

With Katherine's business acumen, she could help him create a business or a charity to help the men. She was a successful entrepreneur who had experience creating jobs. Instead of being wary of traveling to her home, he should look at it as an opportunity. After he finished speaking with the wives, he'd ask for her help.

Why hadn't he thought of this before?

Then the truth hit him square in the chest.

Never before had he shared anything in common with his half brother, much less cared for the company Meri kept.

But now there was Katherine.

"Morgan, will you tell the driver that I'll be there in a few minutes? I think I'll stop by the conservatory and cut some roses before I travel to Lady Meriwether's home. Best to be prepared."

Chapter Six

The sound of the firm knock heralded the arrival of a visitor. Katherine stood on the staircase landing and took a deep breath as Willa opened the door. Their meeting today would hopefully set the course for her, Constance's, and Beth's futures. The duke stepped inside with his arms full of the most beautiful rose bouquets Kat had ever seen. The pink, red, and yellow blossoms made the ones available from the street vendors pale in comparison.

"Good morning, Duke," Willa said solemnly as she closed the door.

"Good morning, Miss Ferguson." The deep rumble of his baritone voice filled the entry.

"Call me Willa."

He nodded briefly.

Kat quickly descended the remaining five steps and stood by her companion's side. "Good morning."

"Good morning." His smile was pleasant, if a bit tentative.

Willa looked at the flowers in his hands, then slowly raised her gaze to his. "I don't think flowers are going to fix the mess these women find themselves in."

The duke examined the roses. "I suppose not, but I've always found that"—he glanced in Kat's direction and held her gaze with his—"if you share a bit of yourself with others, it makes the conversation a little more cordial." Keeping three bouquets in his other arm, Christian held out a small posy of red, pink, and yellow roses to Willa. "These are for you. Thank you for helping Morgan."

For the first time Kat could ever recall, a gentle blush colored her companion's cheeks.

"Ack. It was nothing," Willa murmured, taking the small bouquet in her hands.

"It was something to me. Morgan isn't just my valet. I consider him a friend."

"He said the same about you." Willa brought the bouquet to her nose. "I thank you for these. If you'll excuse me, I'll finish making the tea tray," she murmured, then left for the kitchen.

Kat waited until they were alone. "That's lovely of you to think of her." The roses' sweet fragrance filled the air.

"I appreciate what she did for him." Christian glanced about the entry. "You have a beautiful home."

"Thank you." Kat answered. To some, the turquoise walls and black and white floral upholstered pieces might appear garish. Yet it was nice of him to compliment her tastes. "I like color."

"These are for you," he said softly as he handed her a massive bouquet of red roses.

"They're lovely." Kat inhaled the sweet scent, then lifted her gaze to his. "They smell as beautiful as they look. Red is my favorite color."

"It's mine too." He took a deep breath and rocked back on his heels, clearly a little unsettled.

"Perhaps you should share that with Morgan as he decorates your study."

His gaze locked with hers, his eyes narrowing as if considering her statement. Eventually, he nodded. “Excellent idea.”

“Won’t you come in?” She extended her hand in the direction of a small hallway that would lead to the sitting room where Constance and Beth waited.

“Katherine, I’m a little . . .” He studied the two remaining bouquets in his hands and let a somber sigh escaped.

“Apprehensive?” she offered. “We all are.”

“Then, I’m not alone.” A rueful smile spread across his lips. “When I was at Rand House, I was looking forward to this visit, but all I could think about was what Meri has done to all of you.”

“Christian, it’s all right.” She lowered her voice. The dark depths of his eyes churned with emotion. “They don’t blame you. None of us do. But it’s a kind gesture you’re here. They were a part of your brother’s life.”

His gaze swept across the room again. “Because of him, three lives are teetering on the edge of ruination. I’ll try my best, but I hope they have additional thoughts on how I can help.” He swept his hand in front of them. “It’s time I meet these women. Lead the way, my lady.”

How could she have ever considered him too proper and staid beyond reason? The poor man stood there, clutching the other bouquets as if his life depended on it. She stilled for a moment. When she’d first met him, he didn’t want anything to do with the three of them. Yet, he was there ready to meet Constance and Beth because she’d asked him.

Well, perhaps *badgered* was a better word for it.

It didn’t make any difference. He was there to help.

She bent close and murmured, “They won’t snap at you.”

“If they do, I’ll growl back.” He smiled slightly with a nod.

Without hesitating, Katherine walked to the sitting room and stepped inside. “The duke is here.”

The ladies stood in the middle of the room. Beth raised her eyebrows. Constance blinked slowly, then nodded.

Katherine smiled at Christian as he stepped to her side. He would be perfectly fine with her friends.

When she turned to Christian to make the introductions, a genuine smile lit his face, and his deep brown eyes held a warmth she wanted to lose herself in. She sucked in a breath at the sight. He was a man with the natural ability to make any woman, no matter the age, swoon.

Beth dipped a curtsey.

"Your Grace, this is Miss Blythe Howell from Cumberland," Katherine offered, then turned to Beth. "The Duke of Randford."

"Your Grace." Beth dipped a curtsy. "My friends call me Beth. I'd be honored if you would too."

"Beth." Christian nodded, then held out the bouquet of yellow roses. "For you."

Beth's eyes widened as she took the roses. "These are magnificent."

"Thank you. I grew them myself." He turned to Katherine, signaling he was ready to be presented to Constance.

"Your Grace, this is Miss Constance Lysander from Portsmouth," Katherine said and turned to Constance, who looked woefully miserable standing before them. "The Duke of Randford."

"Good morning, Miss Lysander. It's a pleasure to meet you." Christian bowed slightly. "These are for you." He handed the pink bouquet to her.

"The honor is mine, Your Grace. Thank you." She looked at the bouquet, then smiled. "I can't manage a curtsy, I'm afraid. Anything beside a little hand wave is out of the question at this time."

"It's not necessary." He stepped to her side and held out his hand. "Let's get you settled first. Allow me to help?"

Constance hesitated for a moment, then placed her hand in his. Slowly, he bowed over it in a show of respect, then cupped her elbow with his hand. Gently, he helped her as she sat down on the black-and-white striped sofa.

Tears blurred Katherine's eyes for a moment.

Perhaps he was a man a woman could trust.

Yet, she'd trusted Meri, and look where she was now. She blinked carefully, willing herself to reconsider. Christian hadn't lied to her. Nor had he abandoned her and the other wives. At least, not yet.

"It's a little early for tea, but I think we all might need some for fortitude." Katherine took a chair.

By then, Willa had brought in an elegant tea tray. Beth sat next to Katherine. Christian claimed the seat next to Constance.

As plates were prepared and tea poured, he looked around the room, examining the furnishings.

Katherine couldn't help but notice the fraying of the rug, the one she'd bought used at the market or the scratches on the gilded table that she'd refinished herself. It sat between them and held the tea service. The duke might consider her home gaudy as she'd woven an accent of pink into the décor along with the turquoise and black motif from the entry.

His gaze slowly swept through the room until it rested on her.

She waited for what he would say. She was proud of the home she'd created for her and Willa. It wasn't the finest of furnishings, but it was clean and reflected her tastes.

"Your home is warm and welcoming. It's an expression of you," he said. "Would it be acceptable if Morgan stopped by and saw what you've done here? It might give him some ideas for my study."

Katherine let out the breath she hadn't realized she'd been holding. "Morgan is welcome to visit anytime, Your Grace."

He nodded before leaning forward, his clasped hands dangling in front of him. Silence stole between the four of them. The only sound was the gentle clink of the silverware against the plates and cups as Beth served everyone.

He took a sip of tea, then set down his cup and saucer. "If it's any consolation to the three of you, I'm deeply sorry that you're in this position." His deep voice seemed to soothe the nervous energy in the air. "If there's anything I can assist with or anything you need, I hope you won't hesitate to ask."

"Thank you." Beth set her cup down also. "So far, I'm managing."

"We'll need to discuss the future and how to protect your reputations," he offered.

Katherine sat on the edge of her seat and waited for him to offer more.

"Lady Meriwether is the easiest of the three of you. I'm ensuring she receives her dowry," Christian said directly to her.

Katherine's heartbeat had accelerated when he said her name. She forced herself to breathe evenly. Her worry about money had been eliminated, at least for a little while. She smiled slightly in acknowledgment.

Christian's gaze swung to Constance. "Your situation, Miss Lysander, is more delicate."

"In more ways than one, I'm afraid." Constance placed a protective hand over her abdomen.

Christian watched Constance's movement, then caught her gaze. "I'll repay your dowry, hire the best medical care available, and move you to one of my estates, where you can deliver the child. If that would suit you." He cleared his throat and grimaced slightly. "Pardon me for being frank." He released a breath as if coming to a decision. "This is uncomfortable, but if you want me to see about a family who would be willing to take the child, I can do that."

Beth took a sharp breath.

Kat sat on the edge of her seat, ready to comfort Constance if needed. Sometimes that was the only solution for women in Constance's position. They'd be shunned if they had a child out of wedlock, even if they thought they were legally married. Thank heavens her own mother had wanted Kat.

However, people of a lower class like her mother didn't have many options if they faced a pregnancy and were not married.

Christian released a soulful breath. "On the way over here, I thought of something else. Perhaps I could raise the child in my household as my ward."

Constance shook her head vehemently. "Thank you, Your Grace. I know you had to offer about another family, but I must decline. I'm sincerely touched you would offer to raise my child, but I've thought about this carefully. The babe is mine, and I will raise it."

"Of course." Christian's expression stilled, and he grew even more serious. "I will support you both. You'll have the protection of my dukedom. I promise you'll have my help for as long as you need it."

Constance shifted slightly and turned his way. "Thank you, but that won't work. Once word gets out, I'm ruined and so is my child. Everyone in Portsmouth knows me and my family. They believe I'm Lady Meriwether. I own a ship renovation business I inherited from my father. It's a respected institution, and when word gets out I delivered a child out of wedlock, I have little doubt that more people will suffer than just me and my child. Many of the employees have been there for generations. I don't want the business to fail because of this."

Christian blew out a breath, and the pain on his face tugged at Kat's heart. "My half brother's foolishness is like a pebble dropped in a calm pond. The ripples continue to spread."

"I may have a solution for my situation." Constance straightened her shoulders. "Do you by chance know Jonathan Eaton, the Earl of Sykeston?"

Christian's gaze darted to Kat's, and she shrugged slightly. She had no idea what her friend was about to say.

He turned back to Constance. "I do. I consider him a friend."

"Thank heavens," she exclaimed. "I consider him one as well." Her pleasant alto voice deepened slightly. "Will you reach out and ask him to come to London at his earliest convenience? I want to marry him."

They all fell silent.

"Constance?" Kat asked. "This is the first you've mentioned him."

Beth picked up an iced biscuit from the tray. "He is a renowned marksman, a trained killer for the army."

"Was," Constance corrected. "I've followed the stories about him. He's from Portsmouth also, and a hero. He once told me if I ever needed him, he'd be there . . . for me."

Beth put the uneaten biscuit down on her plate. "He's become a recluse since he's come home."

"It doesn't make a difference to me," Constance said with her sweet tone, but her steadfast decision was clear. "He's the one. I want to marry him." She turned her attention back to Christian. "That's my solution. Katherine has generously invited me to stay. I'll wait for his reply here."

Christian's eyes widened. "Of . . . course. I'll write him immediately and ask him to travel to London." He took a sip of tea as if to wash away his astonishment. "I'll talk to him and deliver your proposal."

Constance relaxed against the sofa. "Thank you."

After a moment, everyone's gaze turned to Beth.

"My turn," Beth announced. "Let's talk about my fortune.

I have no concern for my brother's money, but my dowry is something I'd like returned."

"Agreed," Christian said. "Would you like to go home to Cumberland?"

She tilted her chin an inch. "Absolutely not. Like Constance, everyone near my home believes I'm Lady Meriwether. Unlike Constance, I'm not certain what I'll do." She lifted her chin an inch. "It's best if I stay here until . . . until everything is resolved." Her gaze flew to Katherine's. "If it's still acceptable with you."

Katherine leaned in Beth's direction. "You can stay with me and Willa for as long as you like."

Beth smiled, and the relief on her face was palpable.

Christian nodded solemnly. "I'd best be on my way." He stood and waved. "Please don't get up on my account. I'll be in contact soon." His gaze locked with Katherine's. "Will you see me to the door?"

"Of course." Kat stood while the other two women remained sitting. They all said their goodbyes to the duke.

As soon as they were in the hallway, Christian leaned close. "Is there someplace we could talk privately for a moment?"

"Follow me." A chill skated down her spine. She quickly chastised herself as she escorted him into an empty music room save for a piano covered in a Holland cloth. She shouldn't worry. There was no indication that Christian had discovered anything about her true identity.

He softly shut the door behind him. "Well? How do you think it went?" His mouth twisted wryly as if he was pleased with himself. "I think it went as best as it could under the circumstances."

She examined him for a few moments without cracking a smile. "Do you really want to know my opinion?"

"I wouldn't have asked if I didn't." His brow creased into neat little lines.

"I don't give praise easily, you understand," she teased.

His face fell a little.

"But I think it went very well, indeed." She smiled, and a matching one appeared on his face in return.

"I can't tell you how relieved I am." He paused, then looked around the barren room. "I take it you haven't had a chance to decorate this room?"

"No. I didn't want to waste the funds. I need it for my shop." She shrugged. "Besides, Willa and I don't play any instruments."

His gaze swept across the room again until it landed on hers. "I have a proposition for you."

Kat clasped her hands in front of her. "What kind?"

"I want to start a charity of sorts, but I want it to make a profit," he answered. "I'll pay you double your dowry amount if you'll help me."

"Why do you need one?" Now, she was intrigued.

"I want to start a business for the soldiers in my regiment who've come home. Most have lost their jobs, many have lost their families, not to mention their pride. Some are homeless."

"I don't have much experience with soldiers." Yet she'd seen the homeless men roaming the streets during the day. The sight never ceased to pull at her heartstrings. Anytime one had approached her, she'd given them a coin or two. It always reminded her of when she'd been in the same position, standing on a corner, scared but hungry, struggling to raise her hand to ask for a pence.

Never should anyone have to do that to survive.

"I've heard you're excellent in creating a thriving business. That's what I want." Christian's brown eyes swept over her face as if memorizing her features. "And you're the person I want."

Her body stood at attention while little sparks of something exploded inside her at the rumble in his whisky-dark voice. Much like she'd experienced when a fireworks display ignited over Vauxhall. When he lowered his voice like that, it sounded like a man telling secrets to his lover.

She shook her head slightly to lift the sensual fog surrounding her. He wanted her for her commercial acumen, not kisses.

He frowned slightly. "I beg of you, don't say no, yet. They're good men who deserve a new beginning. You can help provide that. You're the person I need," he whispered. "If you'll say yes right now, I'll pay you triple."

Now, he was using his Poison Blossom voice on her. She had to put a stop to this immediately.

"I can't answer now. You have to let me think about the offer." This was madness to even consider such a thing. She was inundated with orders and had to prepare for the Secretary of the First Lady of the Bedchamber's visit. He would be the one to recommend the linen supplier to the Prince Regent's Royal Pavilion. But four hundred pounds would ease the business's financial strain. "I have a lot of work ahead of me in the next several weeks." She paused for a moment. "I don't help just anyone."

"Good thing I'm not just anybody." His smile sent her pulse racing. Then the crafty, dastardly, not to mention charming, man laughed aloud, the rich sound bringing a vibrancy to the room. "Will you at least give it serious thought?"

"When do you need an answer?" Her voice was steady in contrast to the millions of butterflies flittering around in her stomach.

He took her hand and pressed his warm lips against her knuckles, never letting his gaze stray from hers.

She bunched her other hand by her side into a fist to keep some semblance of control.

"When you're ready." He bowed deeply. "Madame, your servant." He turned for the door, then stopped. "I consider it a good sign that you haven't said no. But I beg of you, don't keep me in suspense."

When the coast was clear, Kat let out a sigh. Whether in relief or disappointment, she couldn't determine. If this was the real Duke of Randford, then he had nothing whatsoever in common with a rat.

And that made him all the more treacherous.

Chapter Seven

Katherine never felt so alive as when she was at work. It was what she loved best. Looking around the elegant floor of her shop made her giddy.

Greer's Emporium offered luxury home furnishings from draperies, pillows, and china to her own extensive collection of linens. Everything needed to outfit a bed and an intimate boudoir could be found here. The down was imported from Sweden, the linen from Ireland, and the finest silk available from Lyon. The embroidery on the bedcoverings was a work of art.

Indeed, her store was just as she envisioned it. Decorated in dusky pinks, Wedgewood blues, ivory, with accents of gold leaf, the shop catered to feminine tastes.

Immediately, she wondered what Christian would think of such an endeavor. Would he approve of it as he'd done with her modest home? "Christian," she said aloud. The sound rolled over her tongue like a rich, decadent dessert. He was certainly that and more. A little too much of such richness, a person might become ill.

But it would be heaven to imbibe, she was certain of it.

She twirled a pencil between her fingers. His offer of four hundred pounds was tempting. With that money, she could hire more employees, train them, and purchase enough inventory to outfit the Prince Regent's home along with the increase of business that would surely occur with the royal appointment. It would allow all that without the worry of juggling finances. But with that money came extra responsibilities, namely helping him establish a business for soldiers that would be profitable enough that they could become self-sufficient.

It wasn't an easy feat, nor did she really have any time in her day for anything extra. She sighed softly. The truth was she had to turn the offer down.

But it left a bad taste in her mouth. She'd dearly love to help him.

A dangerous proposition on so many levels. She shook her head slightly at the thought. She was merely feeling gratitude for what he'd done for Constance, Beth, and herself.

After the morning's first rush of customers, she sat down to her daily bookkeeping. A hopeless cause. She pushed it aside as she couldn't concentrate.

The duke wouldn't leave her be—at least her thoughts of him. He'd presented a side to her that was sweet and everything charming. She could easily see him captivating not only the Prince Regent, but the entire country. At their first meeting, she thought him grumpy and cold, but how wrong she'd been. Undoubtedly, his earlier aloofness could be attributed to the shock he encountered coming home to such a mess, but that was life. Fate had dealt Katherine several surprises just as staggering.

Even dukes weren't immune to destiny's power.

"Good morning, darling." A beautiful blond woman exquisitely dressed swept into the emporium like a welcome ray of sunshine. Her favorite customer, Helen, the Countess of

Woodhaven, entered. She wasn't simply a customer, but one of Katherine's dearest friends after she married Meri. She'd met Helen when the countess had walked into the shop without an appointment. Immediately, they'd hit it off and had become fast friends.

A smile escaped when Katherine leaned back against her chair. Whereas Kat had a slight build, Helen was tall, a perfect English beauty with a rosy complexion and bright blue eyes. But it wasn't her height or features that made people take notice and seek her company. It was her welcoming personality and charisma.

"Good morning, Helen," Katherine called in answer and pushed away from her bookkeeping. "What do I owe for the pleasure of your company?"

Helen swatted her hand in the air in a show of genuine affection. "You charmer. You know I'm here to place another order for your sumptuous linens. Remember?"

"For your brother, Lord Abbott." It was *bloody* difficult to keep up with anything right now, when one's life teetered on the brink of disaster. She winced slightly at the foul thought.

Helen glided to Katherine's desk. "I've decided on the linen you showed me the last time I was in." She waggled her eyebrows. "The one in ivory and the most expensive." She turned her head to see if anyone was around, then lowered her voice. "I heard Father telling Miles that he had to start taking his responsibilities as heir more seriously. He wants him to marry." She leaned closer. "The sooner the better. When are you out of mourning?"

"Helen." Katherine sighed. "Please. You and I have discussed this before. I am not interested in marriage. At least not now."

"That gives me hope you'll consider it," Helen pushed.

"You know my circumstances. I'm a bastard masquerading as a member of society. I don't even know who my father is. What if my father was or is a swindler or charlatan?" If her father were such a man, it might explain how Kat had built a superficial persona that had everyone fooled. "I would be a horrible match for your brother."

"It makes no difference to me." At Kat's huff of exasperation, Helen continued, "Come now, my dear. It wouldn't make any difference to Miles either. He's handsome, wealthy, and a happy sort of fellow. If you marry him, then we're family. He'd make a marvelous husband to a woman. Why can't that woman be you?" Helen pushed away from the desk and walked over to a set of samples that Katherine had pulled from storage for another customer. "I don't want you to have to work. I want you to be as happy as me."

"I enjoy my work," Katherine protested. "There are people who have a way to earn their keep because of me. Other vendors, my own staff, and even the farmers in Sweden who send me their feathers. If I play the part of a spoiled widow, what will they do?" She shook her head vigorously. "I wouldn't be happy not working."

"Spoilsport," Helen playfully chided. "I know you thrive here. I can see it in your face. But can I help it if I want you to have more time for yourself? Then we could see each other more."

Katherine walked to her side, then lightly fingered the linens edged in lace. "I'm lucky to have your friendship."

Helen smiled that incandescent smile again and squeezed Kat's hand. "I'm lucky too. I meant to ask how your visit with the Randford solicitor went?"

Kat wanted to tell Helen the truth, but she'd promised the other wives that she'd keep their secrets. "Oh, you know how solicitors are."

"Boring." Like a hummingbird flitting from flower to flower, her friend's attention was drawn to the samples before her. "Are these new?"

"Yesterday, I received that Belgium lace. One of my York suppliers imported it. Do you like it?"

"I adore it. I want a set of linens made with it for my husband and me." Helen turned to face her. "Speaking of Benjamin, we're hosting a small dinner party tomorrow in honor of the Duke of Randford's return. He's accepted the invitation. What do you think of him?"

"I think he's a . . . very special man."

A crease formed between Helen's brows. "What do you mean?"

"He's courageous and fearless, as a war hero should be." If anyone would interest Kat in marriage, it would be him . . . or at least, someone like him. Heat, the kind that told too much, bludgeoned her cheeks.

"Are you smitten?" Helen asked.

"Of course not," Kat answered curtly.

Liar.

"Good." Her friend nodded in approval. "Miles will be there," she said in a singsong voice.

"Helen," Kat protested.

"Give him a chance. Please say you'll come," Helen begged. "I want to show you off to all the eligible bachelors sitting around the table."

"I'm not certain."

"Katherine, it's very informal. Only Benjamin's closest friends will be in attendance."

"Who did you invite?" Kat asked. As Helen rattled off the names, Kat quickly calculated if anyone attending could possibly be from York and might recognize her. It was silly, but she always did that before attending an event.

"If you're worried what others might say for you attending an event during your mourning period, don't be." Helen put down a piece of lace she'd been holding. "Randford is attending, and no one will say a peep against him. Nor will they do so to you. My family's friends are not so high in the instep that they subscribe to the endless rules and dictates that the *ton* tries to force on everyone. Besides, you might meet others interested in what you've built around here. You need to attend more social gatherings and let yourself be known to a wider group of people." She waved her arm around the room. "You might meet potential customers."

Helen had a point. For heaven's sake, she'd been in her husband's company for only six hours when he left her. Why should she have to mourn? Plus, Christian would attend, which meant she'd be able to see him again.

"I don't have anything to wear." She smoothed a hand down her dress. "This is the type of dress I have in my wardrobe. Sensible working clothes. I don't even own an evening gown."

Helen narrowed her eyes as her gaze swept over Katherine's simple muslin dress. "You're about the same size as me. I could loan you a dress." Helen nodded confidently.

"You're at least a foot taller than I am. One of your dresses would never fit me."

"I'll send over my lady's maid. She can shorten the hem," Helen argued, then her voice softened. "I really want you to attend. For me? Will you consider it?"

"No, I'd feel like a poor relation. It's impossible." But suddenly, an idea took root. Kat could put together an ensemble that would be appropriate for such a dinner party hosted by the Earl and Countess of Woodhaven. With her inventory of lace, velvet, and brocades for the custom pillows and bolsters she made, one of her mother's old dresses could easily be transformed into an appropriate evening gown. Her employees were too busy with the shop's orders to help. But if Constance and Beth could sew, it would make the impossible easily conceivable.

Such logic made the decision easy.

"On second thought, I'll come," she said decisively.

"Marvelous, darling." Helen took both of Kat's hands in hers and smiled.

"Besides, it's only fair. If the duke doesn't follow the strictures of mourning, then why should I?" Kat declared with a nod.

"What's good enough for the Duke of Randford is good enough for me," Katherine murmured to herself as she carefully wiped the mud off her shoes after she entered the door to her home. Repeating the phrase one hundred times on her walk home was slowly helping convince her of that fact.

Yet the truth niggled deep down inside. She was still a bastard and he was still a duke. Worse, she was still a fraud, a woman pretending to be a lady, and he was still a duke.

"There you are, Kat." Willa met her at the door with a loving smile. "Your guests are in the sitting room enjoying a little something before dinner."

Katherine took a deep breath. "The house smells wonderful. What are we having?"

At that particular moment, her stomach rumbled with the intensity of a small earthquake.

Willa narrowed her eyes. "You missed luncheon again, didn't you, lass?" She shook her head as she hung up Katherine's pelisse. "I'm serving chicken curry soup, breaded sole with capers, and a lovely raisin rum pudding."

"I'm lucky to have you." Katherine kissed Willa on the cheek quickly. "Not only are you a brilliant medicine woman, but a superb chef. I mustn't let the duke know about your hidden talents or he'll steal you away."

Willa laughed slightly. "His performance with Poison Blossom made me take notice. But never fear losing me to him. His valet is more to my taste. He came over for me to check his healing."

"How is Mr. Morgan today?" Katherine asked as she untied her bonnet, then hung it on the rack.

"I swear that young man has a lightheartedness in his step that was missing two days ago." Willa took Katherine's arm as she escorted her down the hall. "But he has trouble at night. The war haunts him." She shook her head, then smiled gently. "If I were a few years younger, I'd go after the lad myself," she whispered as they arrived at the sitting room.

"What does age have anything to do with soul mates?" Katherine teased.

"Don't tempt me, lass," Willa answered.

Constance and Beth looked up at the same time.

"Katherine, you're home." Constance tried to push herself off the low-seated sofa.

"Don't bother," Katherine answered as she waved her to stay put. "I'll come to you." She took the seat opposite the other wives.

Beth shut the book she'd been reading, then scooted to the edge of her chair. "How was your day?"

"Lovely and busy." Katherine picked up a biscuit that was a leftover from the earlier tea the two women had shared. She finished the delicious treat in two bites then wiped her mouth with a napkin. "Where is your aunt?"

Constance pursed her lips slightly. "Upstairs resting."

Katherine nodded as she brushed the crumbs from her hands.

Beth turned her green-eyed gaze to Katherine's. "If you don't mind me asking, why did the duke want a private conversation with you?"

"Of course, and I don't think he'd object if I shared it with you. He wanted my help with establishing a business for out-of-work soldiers. He offered to pay me a handsome sum that would help me prepare for when the Secretary to the First Lady of the Bedchamber comes to inspect my shop and factory." She blew out a breath, upsetting a loose piece of hair across her face. "I could use the money, but I don't have the time to devote to his project."

"Will you refuse the offer?" Constance asked.

"I'm afraid so."

Beth leaned against the sofa and regarded Kat. "What would you need to say yes to him?"

"What I need is someone who will oversee shipments and ensure my employees have everything they need as they work." She couldn't trust just anyone with that position.

"I was thinking about my circumstances today." Beth folded her hands in her lap and sat sideways like a proper lady, making the move elegant. "I want to stay hidden for a while, but I need something productive to do. What if I helped you, and then you could help the duke?"

"That's a wonderful idea," Constance offered. "Aunt Vee and I are self-sufficient here, and if anything arises, Willa could help us."

Beth nodded enthusiastically. "Kat, before you say yes or no, you should know that I managed my brother's house, including the staff. I even helped him with his horseracing hobby, overseeing the stables and purchasing the proper feed for the animals. I could do this for you." The pleading in her voice was unmistakable. "Please, let me help?"

This was a gift from heaven. It would free up so much of Kat's time. "Are you sure you want to do it? I could only pay you a small sum, say ten shillings a week."

"No money necessary. You're giving me room and board." Beth nodded decisively. "I'd be honored to work for you."

"Really? I couldn't allow you to work for free." Kat's smile grew. She loved to negotiate. "What if I forgave the debt you owe me for the linens?"

"Done!" Beth announced. "Let me start tomorrow."

"Perfect," Kat agreed. "Then I can help the duke. Now,

I have a favor to ask you both. I have a good friend, Lady Woodhaven, who has invited me to a small dinner party tomorrow in honor of the duke. I need a dress for the occasion. I have nothing that would be suitable for such an event."

Constance's brow drew together in subtle lines. "I'd loan you one of mine, but I left my regular gowns back in Portsmouth."

Katherine shook her head. "I can wear one of my mother's dresses. They're old-fashioned, but I think I could make it into something presentable if you'd help me."

While Constance nodded her agreement, Beth slowly stood, then walked to the window. Her expression was perfectly stoic, but her eyes reflected a world of worry. "I've been to several of Lady Woodhaven's dinner parties. They're lovely affairs, and the highest levels of government will have representatives there. Woodhaven has high political aspirations within the House of Lords." Finally, she turned back in their direction. "You won't be able to make a dress grand enough in a day's time for tomorrow's event. You must borrow one of mine, and I'll help you alter it."

"I'll help too," Constance volunteered.

Beth gracefully walked back to them but didn't sit down. "Do you think it's safe to attend such an affair?"

"Meaning?" Katherine tilted her head. "Are you talking about observing the mourning customs?"

Beth shook her head. "We shouldn't have to mourn what's happened to us. I meant, what if it becomes common knowledge that we're staying here with you? Katherine, you might face horrific questions."

She stood and crossed the short distance between them. "Beth"—she took her friend's hands—"it's perfectly safe. Helen wouldn't allow anything like that to happen to me." She lowered her voice. "She's trying to help and believes if

I attend more functions, I'll grow my business and build my name. It's wise advice." She squeezed Beth's hands gently. "Helen would be proud to be a part of our group and would welcome your friendships. She's the type of person who would defend us against anyone who would think less of us because of our circumstances."

"Does she know about us?" Constance asked. Lines of worry creased her forehead.

"No, she doesn't know about any of it because you asked me not to tell her. However, she'd come to me if she'd heard a whiff of any rumor. If anyone has their pulse on the gossip, it's Helen. She's highly respected. And discreet," Katherine added softly.

Beth stared at their clasped hands. "You'll have a lovely time." A melancholy seemed to have shrouded her friend in a pensive mood.

"I'm not really attending for the enjoyment of the event. Things will change for the better. I'm sure of it. Sooner rather than later, you'll be able to go back to your old life," Katherine offered.

Beth squeezed her eyes shut for a moment. "I don't want to go back. I'm done with that life." She waved a hand in dismissal. "Don't mind me. Now, let's get you ready for that party."

Katherine's eyes blurred with tears as her gaze swept from one to the other in gratitude. "This means everything. I want to win that contract."

"I think it's a brilliant idea if you go to the event." Constance stood slowly, then joined them, putting an arm around Kat. "Go forth and find new customers!" she declared, laughing.

"Indeed." Beth nodded. "Plus you'll be on the front lines of society to see what is happening in the war of rumors."

If Katherine was attending the "front lines" tomorrow, she would be in full battle regalia. She vowed to be the most ravishing woman there.

"Come, let's eat," Katherine said when her stomach started to protest the lack of food. "I'm starving."

"Then, shall we see what I might have that would be perfect for you to wear tomorrow?" Beth hooked her arm around Katherine's.

Constance hooked her arm around Katherine's other one just as they had when they left Mr. Hanes's offices.

Three women determined to fight for their own futures.

Tomorrow, Katherine would tell the duke she'd work with him. An image of him on his knees in gratitude popped into her thoughts. Perhaps a kiss or two might be required when she accepted his thanks.

Oh heavens, where had that thought come from?

Chapter Eight

"Woodhaven!" Christian accepted his friend's hand in welcome as he stepped into the brilliantly lit entry of the earl's home. A footman stood by to take his greatcoat and beaver hat.

Christian hadn't seen the Earl of Woodhaven since the day before he bought his commission. He and Woodhaven were close since they had started Eton the same year. But their bond had become unbreakable when they were both bullied by older boys. Christian constantly received harassment for his father's choice of a wife, and Benjamin was tyrannized because he was on the small side. Whereas Christian always fought his way out of a situation, the earl preferred to talk his way out of a confrontation.

By Christian's way of thinking, his method succeeded whereas Benjamin's usually ended with either a bloody nose or a black eye since the earl became tongue-tied when the bullies descended on him. During those harrowing times, they'd become allies, and more importantly, friends.

Now, Benjamin was only a couple of inches shy of

Christian's height of six feet three inches, proving that fate always had the last word.

"Randford, welcome." Benjamin pulled Christian close and pounded him on his back. "It's good to see you in one piece." The earl's gaze swept down the length of Christian's form. "No injuries?"

"None to speak of," he answered with a slight smile.

"Come. I want you to meet my wife, Helen." The earl turned toward the massive staircase that led to the family quarters.

A lovely blonde dressed in a yellow evening gown stood on the last step talking to a woman with her back to the room. The woman beside her was dressed in an ethereal blue silk gown that mimicked a clear summer sky, a vision of all the wonderful things he had to look forward to now that he was back in London.

Christian's gaze slowly swept upward from the back of her dark blue satin slippers. Her legs gracefully flowed upward into perfectly shaped hips and a narrow waist. He'd always been a man who appreciated the unique curves of a woman whether full or slight. She turned in profile. The style of her hair swept forward to hide her face. But he had a clear view of her bodice. Her breasts were pushed together by the engineering marvel of a perfect set of stays. They resembled pillows.

How fortuitous that he'd accepted Woodhaven's invitation.

As his gaze caressed the long line of her neck, Christian held his breath hoping—praying—that her face would be as bewitching as her body. He held his breath as she finally faced him.

Then silently exhaled her name, *Katherine*.

And she was coming his way with Woodhaven's wife.

Christian tried to compose his expression into one that showed he was unaffected by such a display of feminine beauty.

"Randford, my wife, Helen. She's a thief." The earl's smile clearly indicated his devotion.

"Oh, you." Helen playfully batted at her husband's arm. "You really shouldn't say such things. People will start suspecting me if their jewelry is missing."

Benjamin bent down slightly and pressed a kiss against his wife's cheek. "I'm telling the truth. You stole my heart." He took her gloved hand in his and pressed another kiss atop her hand.

"You say the sweetest things," Helen whispered softly, then turned her attention to Christian. "Welcome, Your Grace. We're honored you're here this evening."

"The pleasure is all mine," he answered with a slight smile. Almost immediately, his traitorous attention drifted to Katherine.

She looked away and silently blew out a breath, then adjusted her stance. An enigmatic smile spread across her lips. But the twisting of her fingers betrayed her anxiousness.

Like her, Christian felt every nerve on edge. It wasn't akin to the awareness he always experienced when a battle loomed before him, but something more primitive—more primeval. It was more like a surge of desire.

He shook his head slightly at such a reaction. Perhaps he and Katherine were a little out of practice at attending social events. It was certainly true on his part. He leaned toward her. "Are you nervous?" he whispered.

"A little."

"Me too." He glanced at Benjamin, but the effort offered little help. The man was completely besotted by his own wife and looked as if he were about to throw her over his shoulder and cart her upstairs for a long bout of lovemaking.

Katherine dipped a slight but perfect curtsey before him. "Your Grace, I'm delighted to see you here."

"Lady Meriwether," he answered. "The same for me." He

took her hand and bowed. "You look lovely this evening," he said softly, then cleared his throat.

Completely unaware of Christian's disquiet, Benjamin and Helen were in a discussion over the seating arrangements for dinner. But Katherine tilted her head and regarded him. The woman was too discerning for his tastes, but Christian held her gaze.

"Are you not observing the formal dressing constraints of a widow's mourning?" Immediately, he regretted asking such an asinine question.

Her eyes widened before she laughed softly. The sweet sound did nothing to calm his senses. If anything, it whipped his discomfort into the stratosphere. The woman before him was Meriwether's wife. He shouldn't be attracted to her.

"Your Grace." She leaned forward slightly, the movement giving him an excellent view of her bodice. She arched that infuriating perfect eyebrow in challenge. "How you honor your brother is an inspiration to us all." Then as if she knew his inner turmoil, she smiled.

Christian leaned forward, matching her movement until there was barely six inches between them. "An excellent play, my lady." He delivered a charming smile. Keeping his voice low, he continued, "I'll accept my due, my just desserts, for such a question."

The enchanting minx teased him with no hesitation. It felt wonderful. Perhaps she had an answer for him about his proposal. He prayed that it was a yes. Otherwise, he didn't know where to turn for help.

But they shouldn't talk business tonight. Not with this crowd of distinguished gentlemen. He should spend his time getting to know his fellow peers better, so he could garner their support for his new endeavor.

That meant he should treat Katherine as he'd treat any other lady of quality.

He'd ignore her all night.

Like that was going to happen.

"Do you know many of the guests?" he asked.

"No, but I look forward to meeting them." Then, she did the unthinkable and wrapped her arm around his as Benjamin and Helen led them into the salon to meet the other guests. "Honestly, I'm hoping we'll sit together at dinner. I have so much I want to discuss with you."

As soon as they entered the intimate room, several of his old friends approached. Soon a snifter of brandy was in his hand. Christian held it but didn't imbibe. Tonight, for some reason, the smell reminded him of France, and he couldn't stomach even a sip.

Throughout the various conversations he was engaged in, he found his gaze skating the room, seeking out Katherine. She was a vision in that dress. The bodice was cut in such a way that it accentuated her perfect skin, while the flow of the garment enhanced her lissome form. She and Helen were the only ladies present in a room of five men. The rest of the gentlemen in attendance seemed to swarm about Katherine. None of them were married.

He forced himself to look away and took a deep breath. Such a casual study was to be expected. He'd been trained in the army to take note of situations and scrutinize people. Look at the stance of their bodies and watch their behavior, particularly on the battlefield.

Christian fisted his hands. He'd never been trained to make observations about flirting, however.

Though the men present seemed to be upstanding members of society, in his opinion, they were vultures ready to offer all sorts of comfort to a grieving widow.

What was the matter with him tonight? Katherine had proven she was entirely capable of looking after herself. He couldn't forget that some of the men were powerful members of the House of Lords who could help his business for displaced soldiers. He might convince them that a separate charity needed to be formed for housing the men too. That was the ultimate goal of attending the dinner party.

A gentle peal of laughter rang through the room. Instinctively, his gaze found hers. Her amusement at the quip slowly faded. She blinked, then a smile slowly bloomed across her face.

He smiled, but by then, her interest had been drawn to one of the gentlemen by her side.

Without her attention, Christian felt empty.

He dismissed such an outlandish thought. The reason for such hollowness had to be the simple fact he was hungry. Without thinking, he took a sip from his glass, then coughed.

The stuff tasted foul.

Benjamin rushed to his side and pounded on his back. "Are you all right?"

"I'm fine." Christian sniffed and blinked to clear his eyes. "Do you, by chance, happen to have some whisky?"

Before the earl could answer, his wife slipped next to his side, her attention devoted to Christian. "Your Grace, perhaps now would be the perfect time for you to escort me into dinner."

"Of course," he replied. It was always mandatory for the highest-ranking peer to escort the hostess into the dining room. Momentarily, he forgot that he was that person at tonight's gathering.

"Still want that whisky?" Benjamin asked.

"No, thank you. Not with dinner ready to start."

The earl nodded to him, then smiled at his wife. "I'll see Katherine in."

For some reason, the thought that a very married Benjamin would escort Katherine into the dining room made Christian breathe easier.

Good God, he was spending too much time thinking about her. Thankfully, they arrived at the table, and Christian helped Helen to her chair at the end. Benjamin helped Katherine to her seat at the opposite end of the table.

Their seating positions meant that Christian and Katherine sat diagonally across from each other. Too far to have any conversation, but each could see the other's every move.

Katherine's attention was diverted to the man who sat to her right. A man in his early forties, Bryce Merriman, the Earl of Shelton, cut a striking figure at the table. Head of a committee that allocated extra monies for road improvements, he was someone Christian needed to become better acquainted with.

Christian's privilege was something he hadn't earned, but he was determined he'd use it for others less fortunate. He had his entire future mapped out. In the next critical months, he would become friends with various powerful men, like Shelton. With Christian's fortune, military experience, and the vast wealth of his estate, he was a man of influence. Members would want to woo him for his vote to swing their way.

Christian would be more than delighted to support worthy causes. In return, he'd expect those members to support him with his own agenda, namely finding employment, a sense of belonging, and hopefully happiness for the men who had returned from the war.

He fisted his hands at the unfairness of it all. After what his men had sacrificed, they should be able to depend upon their country for assistance.

At least he had one thing to thank his father for—his title. And being a duke would certainly help.

Perhaps that was why Christian was put upon this earth. It was a question he'd always asked himself. It was like a compass and helped him ensure he was on the right path in life.

And the right path was certainly not toward Katherine's eyes or her delightful laugh.

As he leaned back in his chair, Christian had a clear view of her. She seemed to be enjoying herself this evening with her attention equally divided between Benjamin and Shelton. A skill necessary if one was to be a successful hostess.

Her gaze settled on his, and she smiled that same impish smile again.

"Your Grace." Helen smoothed her serviette in her lap. "I'm hoping that my brother, Lord Miles Abbott, will attend this evening. If only for a little while."

Christian reluctantly dragged his attention from Katherine to his hostess.

She smiled sweetly, then glanced briefly at Katherine. "I hope you don't mind me asking, but were you expecting Katherine to adhere to the strict mourning customs?" She turned her steady gaze to him. The determination in her eyes made them shine like forged steel.

"Why do you ask, my lady?"

"Please, call me Helen." She scooted forward in her chair and turned her head in such a manner that they wouldn't be overheard. "I ask because I'd like to see Katherine make a match with my brother. That's why I invited him here this evening. I'd like for her to meet him. They'd get along famously."

Christian didn't move. He'd been taught as an officer never to give away any hint of what he was thinking. Any unease or anger could be used against him. It wouldn't do when confronting the enemy.

But who exactly was the enemy?

More importantly, who was he fighting for? Katherine?

The whole idea was absurd.

He inhaled as deeply as he could without giving away the disquiet that rolled through him like a cool ocean wave.

Slowly, he released his breath. With the calmest façade he could muster, he said, "I wasn't aware that she is seeking to remarry so soon after my brother's passing."

For the first time in three years, he'd referred to Meri as his brother. Slowly, he placed his serviette beside his plate. What in bloody blazes was happening to him?

It would be easy to blame Meri as he was the reason Christian joined the war. He had proclaimed himself finished with anything in this world related to his father, his stepmother, and Meri. Yet, his half brother's spirit seemed to haunt him at every move and every turn.

But the undeniable truth? It was Katherine who haunted him tonight.

Helen reached out and placed one hand over his. The warmth of her skin did nothing to melt the ice that churned through his veins, fighting to take control.

"I'm sorry if I've taken you by surprise, Your Grace." She withdrew her hand slowly and turned her gaze to Katherine. A warm smile of true friendship graced Helen's face. "Katherine is dear to me. She's a new friend, but one of my closest. I'd give anything to have her be part of my family. My brother is heir to my father's earldom. He could offer her security."

"Of course, the sanctity of marriage offers security for those who respect the institution. But what about the notion of to love, honor, and cherish? You don't want either of them to risk a hasty marriage without anything in common." Christian could have cringed at the irony he spoke. There were no guarantees that the notion of "love, honor, and cherish" was accepted universally. His own family had thrown those words into the pig trough. His father didn't love his mother. Nor did he honor her when he kept a mistress. Meri didn't honor or cherish Katherine or the other women he had married. It only proved that Meri loved himself.

For God's sake, why had he turned down that whisky? He'd trade his dukedom for that drink right now.

"Miles is a good man. I think he and Katherine would make each other happy." Helen's tone turned more direct. "Your brother's early demise demonstrates that none of us should dally when it comes to marriage."

That statement Christian could agree with. He stole a glance in Katherine's direction. She laughed at something Woodhaven said. The look of happiness was becoming on her. He'd never seen her look so pretty.

For the life of him, he couldn't understand why she married his profligate brother. What better opportunity than to be sitting next to her best friend to discover the truth?

He turned his attention to his hostess. "May I ask you a question? Was their marriage a love match?"

Helen silently placed her fork across her plate. "What do you think?" Before he could respond, she answered her own question. "It's not for me to say. They married quickly, then *he* left her," she hissed quietly.

"What's your speculation?"

Helen narrowed her eyes, clearly taking his measure.

"Your brother was a fool." No one else could hear, but the anger in her voice was unmistakable. "*Your* brother left her shortly after the ceremony. That's not a love match in my estimation."

"How shortly did he leave?" he asked, dreading the answer.

"You should ask her." She shrugged slightly. "It's painful for Katherine, as you might imagine. But I ask you, what kind of man would leave a woman like that?" Her voice turned sharper. "She's fashioned one of the most successful shopping emporiums in all of London. She's created jobs for people who have no other opportunities in life. Her linens are works of art. With a little help and support from a man worthy of her, she could yield immeasurable power over the commercial and economic leaders in this country. She'll leave a legacy any family would be proud to claim."

With her cheeks pinkened and her eyes blazing, her attention was devoted solely to Christian. But the rest of the table had turned to look at Lady Woodhaven, who was clearly distressed.

She lowered her voice to a whisper. "Furthermore, she deserves someone who will value her. Not some wandering, roving lout."

"Darling?" Woodhaven's brow creased into neat rows.

With a queenly grace, Helen leaned back in her chair, then smiled at her husband before turning her attention to their guests. "Don't mind us. We were discussing how those wandering American barbarians prefer their tea without milk. Utterly undomesticated. It's not worth a single thought in our opinion. Is it, Your Grace?"

"Indeed," Christian agreed readily.

With a nod to the head footman, Lady Woodhaven signaled she was ready for the next course.

Christian couldn't help but steal a peek every now and then at Katherine. She was remarkably adept at making those around her feel comfortable if the smiles and chuckles from her end of the table were any indication. Each time her gaze would meet his, she would smile as if she didn't mind that he frequently glanced her way.

Over the rest of the dinner, the company continued to be in high spirits. A round of toasts were offered on his safe return. Right before the two ladies were set to depart for tea so the gentlemen could enjoy a glass of port, a man entered the dining room with his arms outstretched.

"Helen, I thought you were going to wait for me," the gentleman crooned, then nodded at Benjamin.

"Miles, you were able to come." Their hostess stood immediately and quickly closed the distance to the newcomer.

"Allow me to make the introductions." Helen looked around the room. "I believe you know everyone except my good friend, Lady Meriwether, and of course, the Duke of Randford." Helen quickly brought the gentleman to Christian's side. "Your Grace, may I introduce my brother, Lord Miles Abbott."

Christian took a quick but thorough assessment. Well-built and fit, the viscount had height, but he stood several inches shorter than Christian. With blond hair and blue eyes, the man resembled Meri.

Undoubtedly, women would say Lord Abbott's visage was handsome. Katherine would appreciate a man like that.

Christian automatically disliked him.

With unbelievable forbearance, Christian stood and extended his hand. Lord Miles Abbott took it in a hearty handshake.

"Your Grace, it's an honor and a privilege to meet you." Abbott smiled. "Your heroics on the battlefield are legendary."

A rush of heat scalded Christian's cheeks from Abbott's praise. "Thank you, but it's His Majesty's army that deserves the accolades."

"I see you're modest too," Abbott quipped, then looked to the other guests and laughed.

"No, I'm not." He'd not let them forget who made the sacrifices. Christian's voice sharpened. "The courageous men who worked under me are my betters. None of us should forget their bravery and willingness to serve."

Abbot's eyes widened in alarm.

The room immediately fell quiet.

"Some sacrificed everything, including their lives." His gaze slowly swept the room as he memorized each shocked face. Some glanced away, embarrassed. Earlier, he'd wanted their help and approval, but in that instant, he didn't give a whit if their delicate sensibilities were bruised by his words. "And the ones who came home to nothing or arrived on our shores with scars, missing limbs, and nightmares as a result of their unselfish service deserve your accolades. Instead, they have received nothing."

"Are you suggesting we pay them, Randford?" the Earl of Shelton asked.

Murmurs rolled through the room at the earl's question. Christian's anger at the unfairness of it all rose with the vengeance of a roaring wildfire.

"Yes. That's the least we could do for them. I think we should provide for their futures after all they've done for us. So we understand one another, it isn't me or any other decorated officer, general, or Whitehall official who deserve your gratitude. It's the bricklayers, the farmers, the cobblers, and the cabinet makers." People like Phillip Reed, who society ignored or tried to sweep from their thoughts. "They served when they could ill afford to do so. But someone had to do it, and they readily stepped forward to protect everyone in this room. Their whole lives upended. They deserve so much more."

By all that was holy, Christian would see they were given their just rewards. His fists ached from holding them so tightly. It was the only way he could keep his ire in check. He forced himself to breathe. He should have never attended the dinner party. His performance was probably the death knoll for any of these guests to support his cause. But they needed to hear the truth.

Damn, but he needed to leave immediately.

Silence weighed heavy all around the room. After his impassioned speech, everyone stared at their plates, hoping someone would say something. But no one dared.

Except Katherine.

With an innate elegance, she stood slowly. "I, for one, am

humbled by that truth. We should never forget their sacrifices. They've earned a place where they are welcomed and appreciated. More importantly, all of us"—she waved her hand slowly around the room—"should honor them every day. Thank you for reminding us, Your Grace."

"Hear, hear," Benjamin called out. His words seemed to have soothed the others as rumblings of praise for all the forgotten soldiers filled the room.

Christian's gaze locked with Katherine's. Her eyes glistened with unshed tears, and in that moment, he *knew* she heard what he'd been saying. She didn't look away from him. He gathered every speck of strength he could from her gaze. In that moment, some tether was created between them. He wanted to be bold and pull it tight until he could hold her for a moment of comfort.

God, his brother was a lucky man to have had her in his life. What must it be like to have a person who truly saw what mattered most and felt the same as you?

Their invisible bond broke when Abbott cleared his throat. Katherine glanced toward the newcomer.

Abbott turned to his sister. "I'm ready to meet the other guest of honor."

Helen escorted him to Katherine's side.

"I'm pleased to meet you, my lord. Your sister has told me so much about you." Katherine extended her hand.

"Likewise," Lord Abbott purred. Immediately, he brought her fingers to his mouth as if they were already intimates. When he lowered Katherine's hand, the viscount continued to hold it. "If I'd known such beauty was to grace my sister's table, I'd have made my father wait until tomorrow for our weekly meeting."

Laughter rang through the room.

Christian changed his mind about the viscount. He didn't dislike him.

He hated him.

"I'm afraid I don't understand," Katherine said. If the pink of her cheeks was any indication, she was uncomfortable with the fact that everyone was in on Miles's joke except her.

"Everyone in society knows that to keep the Earl of Canton-Wells waiting is not something you do if you want to keep your head attached to your body," Christian announced, keeping his gaze glued to Katherine's. "The man has a notorious reputation for being punctual and refuses to see any guest if they are even a minute late."

Helen turned and regarded Christian. "That's a perfect description of our father. Have you met him?"

"No, but the previous Duke of Randford was once invited to a dinner party your father was hosting, and the earl refused to seat him because my father happened to be five minutes late." The earlier heat that had flushed Christian's cheeks marched upward. In fact, it marched so high that Christian could only see red.

The cause?

Lord Abbott had his big paw wrapped around Katherine's hand and refused to let go.

As Christian walked around the table to reach her side, Lord Abbott drew back and stared into her eyes with a nauseating romantic gaze.

"Is something amiss, my lord?" she asked, clearly less animated than before as she tried to pull her hand away.

"Yes," he sighed before lowering his voice. "It's been forever since I've seen such beauty as yours."

But Christian was close enough to hear it. Somehow he managed a straight face as he drew near to Katherine's side.

The man shook his head as if coming out of a trance. "Helen, why didn't you introduce us before?"

"Because I don't socialize often," Katherine answered

instead. With a forceful tug, she successfully broke Abbot's hold of her hand.

By then, Christian had sidled up to Katherine. "Lady Meriwether—"

"Is it that late already?" Katherine interrupted. "How time flies. Yes, I am ready to leave." She delivered a wooden smile to Abbott. "Delightful to make your acquaintance, my lord."

Lady Woodhaven started to protest, but Katherine held up her hand. "Helen, I apologize, but Randford and I have some business to discuss. He has graciously offered to see me home. Thank you and Woodhaven for your generous hospitality."

With a stunned look on his face, Lord Abbott bowed briefly. "Lady Meriwether, I'll count the days until I see you again."

"As will I," Katherine muttered under her breath.

"Would another lifetime be too soon?" Christian said softly for Katherine's ears only.

When her startled gaze shot to his, he lifted his eyebrows innocently, then proceeded with his own farewells. The faster they were out of there the better.

However, for Christian, the night wouldn't end until he found out what Kat's decision was.

He needed her now more than ever.

Chapter Nine

Katherine followed Christian out of the formal dining room without uttering a word. They traveled down the hall that led to the entry, where they gathered their belongings. Soon, he escorted her outside to the carriage. A footman had already pulled down the steps and opened the coach door.

Christian stopped, then turned. "I've heard that Lady Woodhaven has a spectacular garden pond with some unique plants. Would you be interested in a stroll? Unless, of course, you need to return home because of your day tomorrow?"

His voice was smooth but the side-eyed glance he gave her revealed he knew her excuse to leave early had been a ruse.

"That would be wonderful. The pond is one of a kind, rectangular in shape with a small fountain attached." She still felt riled from the appraisal she had received from Helen's brother. The man had stared at her as if she were some sweet treat. When he'd held on to her hand while she tried to pull away, it felt as if she were caught in a net. Thankfully, Christian had reached her side and provided her with an escape.

Christian handed their hats and wraps to the footman. "Iverson, we'll take a little stroll, then we'll be ready to be on our way."

"Yes, Your Grace." The footman nodded.

Christian held out his arm, and she slipped hers around his. Soon, they were out of sight of the carriage and had made their way to the garden. The bubbling of the fountain greeted them, along with the sweet fragrance of flowers. They entered a wooden archway covered in blooms that led them to the pond. Several small lanterns provided light for the paved pathway.

Once through, Katherine took a deep breath and exhaled.

They stopped, and Christian reached into his evening coat and pulled out a small flask. "Take a sip."

Without protest, she did as he directed. She didn't particularly care for whisky, but she needed something to take the chill away. "Thank you."

"You look as if you've seen your husband's ghost." He took the flask and drank after her. "Did you know Lady Woodhaven's brother would be here?"

"Yes," she said softly. "I've never met him before. Helen wanted us to meet. She thinks we'd be a good match, but I told her I didn't want to remarry." She was babbling like the fountain, but it allowed her a moment to tamp down the dread that someone would recognize her as Elise Fontaine's daughter. Lord Abbott hadn't known her true identity, but he'd examined her for so long, she was shaken. Fear wasn't always logical and often appeared when she felt uncomfortable or in new situations. "I didn't care for the way he held my hand. Was it that apparent?"

Christian stared at her with unwavering calm. "I'd be lying if I told you no. However, I don't think anyone noticed except for me. Everyone's attention was on my exchange with

Lord Abbott." He waved his hand toward a bench beside the pond. "Come, let's sit down."

"I don't care to sit." Instead of following, she walked to the fountain at the opposite end of the pond. Another wooden archway led to the small formal garden that Helen had lovingly restored. Several of the flowers Katherine had personally planted herself when she'd come to visit. Never had she felt as welcomed in society, or really by anyone, as she had that day. She'd been accepted by a peeress, and they'd become dear friends. Helen was the only one she'd ever confided the truth of her birth, but she'd never told her friend that she was a convicted thief. Katherine took a shallow breath and carefully released it.

A large warm hand touched her shoulder. Somehow, Christian had come to her side, once again without her hearing him take a step. Instead of being frightened, she found his touch more soothing. For a moment, she wanted to place her hand over his and draw from the strength that resided there. He, of all people, had seen her distress and helped her escape from Lord Abbott's perusal.

"Better?" Christian's voice was as smooth and dark as the whisky they'd shared.

"Yes, thank you." She turned around and faced him.

The look of concern in his eyes made him even more handsome than she had thought previously. Though he didn't move an inch, she could feel the power of his confidence and his composure.

But he hadn't been that way earlier. With his speech this evening, he'd surprised her with his passion for wanting to help his men. He truly cared about them. He reminded her of a river that possessed careening currents and swirling eddies underneath its surface. Simply put, he was a man with untold depth beneath that calm demeanor.

"If you don't want to discuss Abbott, that's fine with me." As if uncertain whether he could touch her again, he raised his hand slowly, then with the lightest of fingers, pushed a wayward curl behind her ear.

There was tenderness in his touch, or was she imagining it?

"Thank you for saying what you did in there. I made everyone on edge, and your words soothed the tension from the room."

"It needed to be said." She closed her eyes and released a breath. The warm, silken feel of his long fingers skating across her cheek made her want to lean into him.

"Those who haven't been to war can't truly understand what I was saying." His voice dropped to a whisper. "But you did."

How long had it been since a man had talked to her with such concern and kindness?

The answer was simple.

Never.

Of course, she and Meri had shared things, but it was all an act. She knew that now. Meri had cultivated the fine art of what to say along with when and where to hold a lady's hand. There hadn't been any true affection in his attentions.

But to think that Christian had any real concern for her was absolutely ridiculous. Kat straightened her shoulders. She always pushed forward and would do so now. Yet, there was no harm in enjoying his touch. Was there?

Of course not.

"The day we met, I found one of my men begging on the street. He had no job or home. I can't tell you . . ." He took a moment to compose himself. "I don't expect you to understand, but I can't let that stand."

She understood well enough. The indignity, not to mention the hopelessness, of being at the mercy of strangers and praying for kindness and a coin. How she wanted to tell him she understood more than he could imagine.

He drew his hand away. "I take it that you didn't come to the party for Abbott but for Helen's sake."

"Among other reasons," she said softly. She wanted to grab his hand and place it on her cheek again.

"What are those?" The deep rumble of his voice warmed her more than the whisky.

"Business, but mostly I'm here because *you're* here. I have an answer for your proposition."

"My proposition?" He leaned forward slightly and clasped his hands behind his back. His brown eyes seemed to shimmer in intensity as his gaze never left hers. "Sounds wicked." His whisper floated around them in the night air before he laughed.

She couldn't help but join in. He'd lost his earlier seriousness and replaced it with a playful attitude.

"My proposition that you help me find a way to employ my men?" His laughter faded, and a slow smile broke across his lips.

For an instant, she was breathless as her heartbeat sped up at the sight.

"Now, I'm intrigued. I assume it's the right answer," he teased.

"It is the right answer if it's mine," she volleyed in return.

Slowly, he lifted an eyebrow in challenge. "My, what confidence you possess."

She shrugged and said offhandedly, "I've always found such a trait attractive."

"As do I . . . especially in you." His voice grew quiet, the hushed stillness interrupted by the gurgles of water.

Goose bumps covered her arms. Like a handsome giant ready to devour her, he stood before her. Instead of being frightened, she wanted to continue to poke and prod him until she found out what his weaknesses and limitations were. She wanted to jab him with questions until she finally uncovered the many layers that made him so unique.

She stared at his full lips and wished for something she shouldn't. The air between them grew heavy, much like a storm ready to unleash its fury. They stood silent, considering each other.

Suddenly, the air sparked with something new, an energy that seemed to vibrate between them.

"You're a spirited woman, Katherine. Sparring and teasing with you makes me feel alive in a way"—his voice turned sinfully dark—"I haven't felt in years. I'm aware of my surroundings so much more, and that includes you."

On the proverbial cliff, Katherine stood ready to leap. Exhilaration of the unknown slammed through her.

"How so?" For a moment, she wanted to withdraw the words. She never flirted, nor did she seek men's attention. Meri had been the exception. Now, she wanted to hone such a skill. For heaven's sake, she felt out of breath. What was it about this man that she had such a strange reaction?

"Hmm, let me consider all the ways I'm aware of you." His eyes grew hooded, and his mouth seemed on the verge of a smile.

Christian was the most relaxed she'd ever seen him. Immediately, she grinned in return. "I'm waiting. How are you aware of me?"

"Well, for one"—he held up his index finger as if making a point—"the first time I saw you, I was struck by how beautiful you are." He then put two fingers in the air. "I'd be remiss if I didn't say I found you charming in the way you weren't afraid to go toe-to-toe with me when we first met."

"You're trying to lower my guard."

He drew nearer, and his breath kissed her cheek. "Am I succeeding?"

They were so close that she could smell his shaving soap. The scent wrapped around her, and for a moment, she breathed it in. "No," she said softly. "You're just a man."

"The things you say are pure poetry." Another low rumble of laughter vibrated in his chest. "I'm just a man who hasn't kissed a woman in years. More than three years, in fact." He bit his plump lower lip.

This was what it was like to have captured a man's full attention. Did he want to kiss her?

Oh, God. What if he did?

She should be shocked. He was her husband's brother. But honestly, she might have participated in a marriage ceremony, but she'd never had a husband.

The deep cadence of his voice could hypnotize her. Her blood heated, warming her from within. Below her belly, her body clenched, then released. It throbbed. His words wove a web of seduction around them that she never wanted to escape.

"Just a man," he repeated as his gaze darted to her lips. "I'm just a man who wants . . ." Christian closed the distance between them, then cupped her cheeks before he gently tilted her chin for a kiss. Their gazes locked. Want and desire flared in his eyes, igniting the same within her.

Immediately, she leaned against him, lifting her mouth to his. She blinked slowly, on the verge of closing her eyes. "Christian." Her whisper floated through the night.

Until a flurry of movement erupted beside them in the rosebushes.

Christian darted in front of Katherine, shielding her. "Who's there?"

A bird burst through one of the rosebushes, flying straight up, the rapid flap of its wings whirring the air around them.

Almost instantly, a white-haired cat darted out of the bushes in pursuit, then stopped. Knowing it had lost the chase, the cat sat in a deigned pose of indifference before commencing to groom itself. Only the swooshing of its fluffy tail betrayed its aggravation at losing dinner.

"Well, this is awkward." Christian's voice simmered with barely checked laughter as he moved to her side. "Did we disrupt him or did he interrupt us? I'm not certain who is owed the apology here."

With her heartbeat back under control, Kat chuckled. "Didn't they teach you the proper etiquette for this situation in duke school?"

"I missed that day." The half smile on his face was endearing. "But I did attend the lecture on how to pose for a ducal portrait with your dog." Chuckling, he took a step back and regarded the cat.

Without a glance their way, the cat turned with its head held high and tail straight in the air and walked back into the rosebushes.

The distance that separated them felt like a mile. Katherine wanted to take a step forward and recreate the intimacy they had shared but thought better of it since he'd changed his stance. He now stood with his feet apart, shoulders wide, and once again, he clasped his hands behind his back. This was the war hero she'd come to know over the last couple of days.

"I apologize," he said while studying a rock on the ground. He toed it gently, then a plunk sounded as it fell into the pond.

"There's no harm done." She cleared her throat and clasped her hands in front of her to keep from twisting her fingers. "I was enjoying myself." She smiled slightly as she locked gazes with him. "With you."

"Katherine . . ." The rest of his response melted into silence. He rocked back on his heels. It had to be her imagination, but a slight flush colored his cheeks. "You were married to my half brother. You're still grieving. I shouldn't have been so forward. I'm no better than Abbott." He took a deep breath and released it. "But I thought . . ." He studied the ground again. "I thought we might . . ."

Where was the man who just delivered a blistering lecture to the guests at Helen's dinner party? *For the love of heaven, say it and put me out of my misery.*

After a few moments when he didn't complete the thought, she did the honors for him. "That we might have found something in common? Perhaps share something together that we'd both enjoy?"

"Yes." A slight grin broke across his lips. "An eloquent way of putting it."

"Would you like to hear my answer now?"

"Now seems the most perfect imperfect time," he said softly.

"How's this for eloquent?" she teased with a jaunty smile. "Yes."

"Really?" The sudden joy on his face was infectious.

"I'll be more than happy to help you. I've come up with a few ideas." In for a penny, in for a pound. "Perhaps you could start a furniture refurnishing business? The men could start out with small pieces."

"For instance?" His brow furrowed.

"Lap desks, writing desks, and smaller pieces that would easily fit as accents within the boudoir or sitting room of a lady." Before he could say no, she continued. "Ladies in my shop are always interested in such things."

An arch of his perfect brow was his response.

It was an excellent idea. She simply had to convince him. "Your charity could sell them at my linen store until demand increases. Once the business is viable, you'll need your own shop."

He remained silent, which wasn't at all how she thought he'd react.

"It's perfect, Your Grace," she declared. "You use repurposed artwork. Most of the pieces I have in storage are gorgeous and unique. They merely need a little care and love from your men who would do the work."

"You have an inventory?" he asked.

"I have a room full of them. I pick up various pieces when I visit the market every week. I know what my customers need to complete their perfect bedrooms." She wasn't being boastful, but she talked with her customers about their ideas and what they enjoyed in life. The highest echelon of the *ton* admired her shop while they ordered her goods. Each woman hoped to recreate in their own home what Katherine had built and designed—an escape from the stark reality of life.

Anything that fulfilled their visions and desires for their private chambers was in Katherine's best interests as well. "Some are antiques from abroad. One of a kind."

"Why haven't you started this business yourself?"

"I haven't had time. If I receive the linen contract, I definitely can't do it. All my effort will be on that."

The lines across his face loosened as his eyes widened. A grin tugged at his lips. "It has potential."

"It's brilliant," she argued. "I have an appointment for us to see a warehouse. I think it would make an excellent workshop for your men. But don't think I'm pushing you. If you don't want it, I do. I'll need the extra space if I receive the royal appointment."

"What type of commission would you be seeking?" His gaze never left hers.

"None. Your payment of four hundred pounds is more than enough. If I'm correct about the demand, your men will be opening a shop close to mine in no time. We can help each other by referring customers to one another. A satisfied customer brings in more customers."

He took a deep breath and released it. He stared at the full moon for a full minute before leveling his gaze her way. "I like the idea. I insist on paying for the inventory."

"It's my contribution to the cause. Willa will be delighted to have the house free of the clutter."

"And you'll make time to help me?" he asked with a hint of wariness in his tone. "While you're trying to win the contract?"

She nodded. "Beth wants to help me prepare for when the Secretary to the First Lady of the Bedchamber comes to evaluate my linens. That allows me to help you."

He held his arm for her to take. "Then let's not dally. I need to get you home so you'll be ready for tomorrow. I can't wait to hear what other brilliant ideas you come up with after a good night's rest."

She took his arm, and together they strolled out of the garden toward the carriage. He thought her ideas sound. She smiled in satisfaction before it slowly drifted away.

Working this closely with him would not be easy. Her lonesome heart might want more.

And she couldn't let it.

Chapter Ten

The next day, Christian waited for his friend to arrive. Julian Raleah, the Marquess of Grayson was more than a friend. He was the perfect audience for Christian when he wrestled with a new idea or concern. They'd met at university and had become fast friends. That friendship had grown over the years. Christian felt closer to Grayson than he ever had with Meriwether.

Last night after Christian had returned home from Lady Woodhaven's dinner party, he'd received a note that Grayson would visit this morning. Now more than ever, he needed his friend's guidance.

Christian had spent practically the entire night pacing his room. He'd been overjoyed with Kat's thoughts for starting a business. But there were other matters seeking his attention, namely a solution for Meri's mess. For all his ability to strategize and plan, Christian was in a fog. He still waited for the Earl of Sykeston's response to Christian's request that he come to London. Only then would Christian broach the subject of marrying Constance. But what could he offer

Miss Howell? She couldn't stay hidden forever working in a factory.

It didn't help matters that Katherine was at the center of the fog. Every time he thought of her, things became murkier. For God's sake, he almost kissed her last night. Her empathy and playful banter had been like a spark to a powder keg. It had set off a want—no, a need—that couldn't be extinguished. He wanted that connection to another person. But not just any person, only Katherine.

He propped his elbows on the burl wood desk and rested his head in his hands. When she'd licked her plump red lips last night, desire had run like liquid fire through every part of him. His body seemed to vibrate in response to her. He recognized Katherine as an attractive woman, but he prided himself on self-control. It had kept him alive for all those years in the military, but last night, his famous willpower had gone on an unexcused holiday.

When Lady Woodhaven had shared that Meri had left her quickly after the marriage, Christian had been shocked. But it wasn't surprising once he considered the source.

"Captain, Lord Grayson is here to see you." Morgan stepped aside, and Grayson entered the room.

"Good God, Randford. There's not a mark on you. That's a sure sign you're the devil's spawn." With dark brown hair and determined brown eyes, his friend was a formidable man. All six foot three inches of his body was toned muscle, the sign of a man who worked hard.

With a grin, Christian stood from the desk and made his way to his friend. Instantly, they embraced. "Thank you for coming."

"I'd have been here sooner, but estate business kept me from calling earlier." Grayson pounded him on his back. "Three years. I can't believe you're finally back. How I've missed you, old man." He finally released Christian and studied him as if under a magnifying glass.

After several moments, Christian had had enough. "What are you looking for?"

"I'm counting the scars that can't be seen." Grayson laughed at his own observation. "There are quite a few, aren't there?"

His friend's observation hit a little too close to the truth. "Come, let's share a drink. I have much to discuss." Christian strode to the side table and poured a fingerful of brandy for his friend and the same amount of whisky for himself. By then, Grayson had settled himself in front of the roaring fire that crackled in welcome.

He returned to the marquess's side and handed him a glass. They both silently toasted each other.

"I prayed for your safe return every day," Grayson said.

His chest tightened at the quiet words. At least one person had cared whether he'd returned or not. "Thank you. There were so many others who didn't have the same luck."

The two men downed the rest of their drinks without speaking, in remembrance for all their friends and acquaintances they'd lost in the war.

Christian sat in the chair next to his friend. "Do you ever regret not joining the Navy?"

Grayson shook his head, then got up from the chair. As he made his way to the brandy, he grabbed Christian's empty glass. He poured both of them another fingerful, then returned to Christian's side. "No. I'm needed at the estate." He exhaled, the sound tinted with frustration. "I work in the fields right alongside my tenants. Honestly, some days I want to leave the place and never return. But that wouldn't be fair to all those families who lived and worked on the land for generations."

The grimace on Grayson's face meant he was running

out of options. Due to his father's bad investments, Grayson worked day and night trying to find enough money to keep his marquessate from falling into insolvency.

"My offer of a loan still stands," Christian offered.

"No, I cannot do it. I don't know if or when I could ever repay you. I wouldn't take advantage of our friendship." Grayson took another sip of brandy.

"I could offer you money as an investor in your experiments."

His friend shook his head. "It's still too risky. Harnessing steam into powering engines is my dream. There's a bigger thrill in making electricity and capturing it in a bottle than running a dusty, dirty estate. But like you, I have other responsibilities."

"If you decide otherwise, the offer will always stand," Christian said.

"Thank you." Grayson grew quiet, then sat of the edge of his seat, devoting his full attention to Christian. "It wasn't until last month I heard of Meri's demise. I'm sorry."

Christian nodded. "Because of his passing, I have no heir. Another responsibility that needs to be addressed. The duchy isn't my only priority. But it's the only one tainted by my father and his second wife."

Grayson lifted an eyebrow in challenge. "Really? That's what you think? You have the ability to craft the duchy into anything you want. It's not tainted—only you think that."

With a dismissive grunt, Christian looked away.

Grayson laughed. "It'll thrive when you turn your attention to the dukedom. You're a natural at managing large endeavors. Look at how you led your troops on the battlefield. You know how to organize people for a common goal. Besides, you were groomed for the task from birth."

A log broke, sending sparks up the flue. A peaceable silence descended between them.

"Welcome home, Christian." He held up his glass in a toast. "To you, my friend."

"Thank you." Christian held up his own glass. He took a sip, then exhaled as he examined the leaded crystal glass in his hand. "I'm glad you're here. Meri left me with a situation that makes his most outrageous escapades look like a Sunday church service."

"Poison Blossom?"

Christian groaned. "You heard?"

"All of London is agog as to what you're going to do with her. Half the racing community is taking up collections to see if they can buy her from you."

"The situation I'm referring to is more than a pregnant racehorse. Today, I received another bequest from my half brother, the deed to a small apartment."

"Might come in handy," Grayson quipped.

"Apparently, he had a paramour," Christian answered. "She sent a letter this morning." He picked up the note that arrived with a scented handkerchief enclosed. "She said it was Meri's wish that she offer her services for the entire month, but only if I would allow her to stay in the apartment."

His friend's eyes grew round. "What? He gave you his mistress?"

Christian leaned back in the chair and glanced sideways at Grayson. "Hmm, yes. He signed a contract for a year's worth of her services. For the first time in his life, he paid in advance. He must have finally won a race. There's still a month left in their arrangement."

Grayson whistled slightly.

"There was only one decision." Christian shrugged, then took the seat opposite the marquess. He wanted to be able to see every reaction that clouded his friend's face when he told the entire tale. "I immediately instructed Hanes to end the contract but allow her to keep the apartment. She's free to find another benefactor. I don't need that type of gift. Can you imagine how society would view me if they knew that Meri had given me his paramour?" He rested his elbows on his knees and caught his friend's gaze. "There's more."

"His wife knows about the mistress?"

"No," Christian said. "None of the wives know about her. Thank God."

Grayson choked on a sip of brandy. Once his coughing fit stopped, he wiped his eyes with a handkerchief he pulled from his pocket. "Pardon me. I didn't hear you correctly."

"You did. I said 'wives,' as in more than one."

Grayson simply stared at him in disbelief. After a moment, he spoke. "Bloody hell, Christian. Tell me."

A half hour later, after telling the sordid tale, Christian was the one who got up and refilled their glasses. "I'm waiting for Sykeston to answer my letters. I'm hoping he comes here soon. But how I can help Miss Blythe Howell, his third wife, keeps me up at night."

"Wait. Beth?" Alert, Grayson lifted his gaze from his glass to Christian's. "Beth is Miss Howell's nickname," the marquess said.

"Do you know her?" Christian stood, then started to pace. It was the only way he could keep his thoughts in order.

"I do. Our families were friends when we were little. I never cared for her self-centered brother, but Beth . . . is a rare individual. She possesses an impeccable character. She's intelligent, hard-working, and cares for others."

Christian stopped in front of the fire. "Sounds like you two have a history."

Grayson shrugged.

It was common knowledge that the marquess had been trying to find an heiress to marry.

"If I've overstepped, forgive me."

"You haven't." Grayson reclined and stared out the window.

"I wanted to offer for her. Even talked to her brother. Shortly thereafter, I discovered the marquessate was practically bankrupt. She's an heiress, but her brother didn't approve of me. Thought I wasn't good enough for her. What a farce that is. He has an uncanny ability to find the worst men as potential grooms." His eyes widened when he realized what he'd said. "I didn't mean that."

Christian stayed any further apology by holding up his hand. "We both know how Meri was."

Grayson exhaled. "I may not have money, but at least I would have cared for her and made damn sure she was happy." His voice rose in frustration.

"I worry about her," Christian confided. "She wants to stay hidden. If Sykeston marries Constance, then she is safe from ruin. But if word leaks about Katherine and Beth, then their reputations are in danger."

He debated whether to tell Grayson all the story or not. But the hell with it. He was his friend and confidant. If anyone could help him sort out this mess with Katherine, it was the marquess.

"There's even more." Christian sat at his desk and ran both hands through his hair. Perhaps such a movement would wipe away the errant thoughts that had populated his mind since last night.

Grayson placed his empty glass on the desk and waited for Christian to continue.

"Last night I almost kissed Katherine."

"That's the first wife?"

"Yes." Christian stood abruptly, then walked to the window. The elm tree in the courtyard captured his attention. It was the one that he and his mother had planted when he was five years of age. She'd died shortly thereafter. His mother had encouraged his love of botany. She had shared her passion for all things green, and now he wanted to do the same with his children one day. Twenty-five years later, his elm had flourished and stood taller than any other tree on the property. For some reason, it reminded him of Katherine. "She's beautiful," he murmured. "And kind."

"Go on," Grayson encouraged. "I can see you're struggling with the attraction."

"Lord Miles Abbott was invited to the dinner hosted by his sister. Seems Lady Woodhaven would love to see a match between Katherine and her brother." He struggled not to put his fist through the nearest wall.

Jealously. That was the only way to explain it. Never had he experienced such an emotion because of a woman.

His heart contracted in his chest with a dull beat. But he'd suffered from jealousy before. His father's fondness and favoritism for Meri. He swallowed the foul taste that marched up his throat.

"It goes against everything I stand for to want Katherine." Christian turned around and looked to his friend. "She's part of Meri, which makes her part of my father. Not to mention that the church doctrine frowns upon it."

"The church wouldn't interfere in this." Grayson leaned back in his chair and narrowed his eyes. "Are you worried what others might think?"

His question went to the heart of the matter.

"It's not as if this would be a unique situation under ecclesiastical law. Look at the marriage of the Earl of Sheridan. He married his brother's widow. If you wed Meri's widow, the marriage would not be void. Without an heir, there is no interested party who would bring suit." Grayson nodded confidently. "Besides, the Prince Regent is so enchanted with you, he would intervene on your behalf, if necessary." The assuredness in the marquess's gaze made his eyes blaze. "I'd even introduce a bill in the House of Lords to ensure it was legal. You have nothing to fear."

Christian rubbed the center of his chest. Throughout the war, he'd felt nothing. He'd felt no need to share his life with another. He hadn't missed the feel of a woman curled around his body. His regiment had kept him busy every hour of the night and day. One didn't have the luxury to think of family betrayals, or life, or even women, outside of the next day. But now that he was back in London and back home, he could think of nothing else—particularly Katherine.

Christian returned to his seat. "I want to do more with my life than be a duke who tends to his estates, produces an heir, then waits to die. I want to help the men in my regiment find work and a meaningful life now that they've returned to England. I've helped some, but there are so many more that need assistance. They put their lives on the line for our country and me. I want to see they're paid back for all they sacrificed. Would I be taken seriously if I lust after Meri's wife?"

"Ramrod and bollocks." Grayson leaned forward. "Of course, you would be."

"There's more." Christian stared at the desk. "I asked her to help me start a business, a charity of sorts. We're going to meet later to see about a warehouse that she thinks would be an ideal location."

"Good. May I make an observation? Not a single soul would care one whit whom you lusted for. Particularly if you're doing good work." His face grew animated. "Indeed, I like the idea. If I had the money, I'd host an event introducing it for you."

"That's kind of you," Christian agreed. "I'm not so certain it's wise to depend upon Katherine. She was Meri's wife."

"Come on," Grayson chided. "That's a little narrow-minded, isn't it?"

"This attraction to her reeks of scandal. I want this charity to succeed." Christian steepled his hands together. "To accomplish that, I need people's good opinion to make it happen."

Grayson laughed, a genuine sound of good humor. "You've been away so long, you don't understand society anymore, my friend. Those fools live for gossip. As soon as one rumor surfaces, another pops up and grabs their attention. They're like pups learning to hunt. They may learn to point, but one squirrel racing by completely captures their attention." He laughed at his own joke. "Take my advice. If you're interested in this woman, then you shouldn't worry about society. You should worry if it's a good match for you." He leaned forward in his chair. "Besides, society will forgive you anything. You're a duke and a bloody war hero, a man who risked his life to save others when certain death faced them." Without allowing Christian to answer, he continued, "Are you concerned if you married her—"

"Marriage? My God, man! I simply wanted to kiss her." Christian shook his head. "I'm talking about an attraction, that is all."

"Is it?" Grayson narrowed his eyes again.

Frankly, Christian felt as if his inner workings were being examined under a microscope. Christian cleared his throat to quell the riot of emotions that swept through him at the direct questions and observations. Deep down, he knew that Grayson was right.

Christian leaned back against his chair. "I can't answer that. She's the only woman I've met since I've been back in London who challenges me one minute, then can turn around and delight me." He exhaled deeply, but his troubles were still lodged in his foremost thoughts. "But for God's sake, she married my brother. Why couldn't she be someone else?"

"Such as?" Grayson drummed his fingers on one thigh.

"Someone who had nothing to do with Meri." He stared straight at Grayson. "She's in commerce. Runs a linen business of some sort."

Grayson smirked. "Is that a problem?"

"It's perfect. In fact, she's thought up amazing ideas for the charity. With her astute business sense, she probably helped Meri with money. The problem is . . . it's as if he conjured her from thin air, married her, and now he's tormenting me with her." He held Grayson's gaze.

The marquess lowered his voice. "Don't live in the past."

"Damnation, I'm not. I'm different. You don't go to war for three years without changing." He shot out of his seat like a cannon, upsetting the chair in the process. Without acknowledging what he'd done, Christian stood the chair upright. "You, of all people, should understand that better than anyone."

"Then help me see the problem?" Grayson countered.

"Why would an intelligent, not to mention savvy, woman like Katherine marry my brother?" Christian growled. After a moment's silence, he walked around and leaned one hip against the desk's edge in front of Grayson. "Well, that took the wind out of your sails."

"I didn't know I was a ship. I thought I was your friend."

"You see my point." Christian wiped a hand down his face. "Everyone has always preferred Meri." He swallowed the bitter taste in his mouth. "I vowed not to become involved with anything or anyone associated with him."

"What about the other wives? You're involved with them."

"They're the exceptions. Meri destroyed their lives. But Katherine? I've broken my own vow over her. The truth is . . . I don't know whether I want to kiss her, take her to bed for a night, or . . ."

"Perhaps marry her?" Grayson pointed out softly.

The thought summoned all sorts of emotions inside him. He enjoyed her wit and banter. Her ability to create an idea for helping the soldiers was sound and, frankly, innovative. She understood what mattered to him. He'd always been an outsider peering inside at his own family. Always wondering why he didn't fit in. But with her, those feelings were forgotten.

"I don't know if marriage is even in the cards."

Grayson stared at him with an incredulous look. "Why not?"

"She said she wasn't interested in marrying again." The words were so low, he wasn't even certain if his friend had heard them.

"Well, I have faith in your abilities. You could convince her otherwise." Grayson leaned back in his chair, resulting in his straight black hair falling gently in front of his eyes. "I need to make time to get the mess cut," he murmured, pushing the offending mane aside.

When he moved, Christian saw the bandage. "What in *bloody* hell happened to you?"

"It's nothing," Grayson said dismissively. "A slight burn with my latest steam experiment." He pulled his coat and shirt down to hide the bandage that covered his wrist.

"Katherine lives with a woman who's gifted with medicines. She helped Morgan with his eye injury. You should see her. I could take you over to Katherine's house and introduce you."

"Really? That's good to know." Grayson thinned his lips to keep from laughing. "How interesting that you seem to have a world of knowledge about the fair Katherine." He leaned forward, capturing Christian's attention with his hawklike gaze. "What a gift to be married to a woman who could love, support, and appreciate you." He picked up his glass and examined the remaining amber liquid. "You should marry her, introduce her into society as your wife. Everyone adores a love match."

"Whoa there, my friend." Christian raised his hand palm out. "You're getting ahead of yourself."

"I don't care to be ordered about as if I'm a plow horse." This time it was the marquess who exhaled loudly. The fire flamed in support of his weariness. "Use that brain of yours and figure this out."

"Easier said than done," he protested.

"What in God's name is that?" Grayson rose from his chair and walked straight to the family portrait that served to hold Christian's memos.

"What does it look like?" Christian picked up a document from his desk and feigned studying it. "It's a handy item to keep my notes organized."

The marquess examined the painting, then turned his steely gaze back to Christian. "Notes? It looks like you're posting debts owed to you." Grayson pointed to one slip of paper tacked to Christian's father's head. "This one says you paid for Meri's stable fees at Tattersalls on the twenty-second of December 1809." He glowered at another. "Good God, man. You paid for Meri's gambling debt in 1812. Two hundred and thirty-three pounds to the Earl of Hendron. You're still keeping these?" He shot a look that went straight through Christian. "This is proof you need a good kick in the arse. You need to come to terms with your feelings for him and put them to rest."

"What are you about?" Christian groused.

"Meri and your family. Put them to rest forever," his friend repeated, ignoring his question. "Do you hear me? This isn't a good sign that you've come back from the war with a sound mind."

Christian threw the document back on the desk. "On second thought, I don't care and don't want to know what you're thinking."

Grayson ignored him and turned his attention back to the notes tacked through the painting. With a huff, he prowled back to Christian's side. "They are gone. Every. Single. One of them. Including Meriwether." He shook his head slightly. "I don't know if you're grieving or losing your mind."

Christian opened his mouth to respond, but the marquess raised a hand to silence him.

"Allow me to finish." He lowered his voice. "I know your family hurt you, particularly your father and his preference for his other family. But it's in the past. You're here now. Let go of the ghosts and come to terms with it. Look forward to your future, one that should include a kind and wonderful woman."

"That's what I'm trying to do," Christian argued. "Look at you. You're in the same situation as me."

"Hardly. Instead of stabbing pieces of paper through your father's and his late duchess's faces, you need to take a look inside that empty hole in your chest where your heart used to reside. See if you can resurrect it and determine what it is you're feeling for Katherine." Grayson sat back down and regarded Christian with a raised eyebrow. "I'd like to meet her."

Christian tamped down the urge to scowl. "I'd be happy to make the introductions. Plus, I insist you meet the other wives. Perhaps you and Beth will find yourselves in a love match?"

The marquess laughed. "You were always a horrible liar." He leaned forward and rested his elbows on his legs, the bandage from his burns clearly visible once again. "Don't be a fool here. You'll lose her if Lady Woodhaven and Abbott have their way."

"I'll lose whom?" Christian asked.

Grayson's gaze never left his. "Prove you're a hero to

Katherine." He lowered his voice, but his exasperation was readily apparent to both of them. "No matter what you feel or what you say, Meri is still your brother."

"Believe you me, I'm aware of that sad fact."

"Christian," Grayson warned.

"Was." Completely ignoring his friend's vexation, he continued, "Meri was my half brother." He nodded in silent acknowledgment of his friend's point. "Katherine *was* his wife. Which means"—Christian enunciated each word precisely—"she no longer is."

Grayson smiled. "Now you're thinking clearly."

Chapter Eleven

Katherine strummed her fingers across the small square pillow her mother had given her the night of her fifth birthday. It was right before she left for her nightly performance. Filled with sweet lavender scent, it normally comforted Kat. But not today.

After her mother's death, Kat had struggled. She couldn't find work. No one would hire her. Months later, Willa had traveled to help a cousin who was deathly ill, but she'd decided not to take Kat because the risk of infection was too dangerous.

Willa thought she'd only been gone for a week, but several had passed, and Kat found herself without food or money. Every time she'd tried to find employment, she'd met rejection. One day, defeated and hungry, she'd stood on street corner, trying to summon the courage to beg for a coin or two.

Her stomach lurched, and she closed her eyes as the horror of that day washed over her.

A group of ragged boys came up to her, and one put an apple in her hand. A random act of kindness that had been a gift from heaven.

Until it had turned into something from hell.

Almost immediately, an angry grocer came upon them, demanding to know who had stolen from his fruit stand again. The boy who gave her the apple pointed at her, then shouted, "She did it."

A constable appeared from nowhere, and the boys scattered into the alleyways.

She'd never been that scared in all her life. It was akin to being stripped naked in front of the whole town as people spat and shouted at her. That day never ventured far from her thoughts. It had marked her. She couldn't walk the streets of York without someone whispering or turning their backs on her. It made her illegitimacy seem like child's play compared to being declared a thief.

"Katherine Elise James," Willa scolded as she strode into Kat's bedchamber. "Why are you moping about this morning?"

Kat cringed at the use of her real name. No one called her that but Willa. "Hush," she scolded. "Someone might hear you."

"It's your name." Willa harrumphed. "I came to collect the dirty laundry this morning. I didn't expect to collect you too."

Kat fiddled with her teacup.

"Lass, what is it?" Willa's tone softened.

She closed her eyes.

"You're still in your dressing gown. Are ye feeling poorly?" Willa clucked as she laid a hand across Kat's brow.

"I'm fine." Kat stared out the window that overlooked the street below. If Willa took a gander at her face, she'd ferret out what was wrong in an instant.

"You're not fine if you're sitting here. You're normally at work by now. A team of horses can't keep you away from the workshop. Now, look at me, Kat."

She propped her chin in one hand, then slowly turned to Willa.

After a quick but worried inspection, Willa's eyelids snapped open. "Are ye grieving?"

She shook her head and tried to smile. "A late start to the day. Help me dress?"

With her usual efficiency, Willa walked to the small cabinet where Kat kept her work clothes. In seconds, she was before Kat and had slipped a chemise over her head. Next came the pretty floral stays Kat had made for herself when she lived in York. After tying them tight, Willa placed a work gown, one that had been died mauve for mourning, over her head.

"Ack, I'll be glad when you're out of those widow's weeds." She took Kat by the shoulders and led her to the modest dressing table. "I'm worried about you, lass."

"As am I." Kat sat so she could face Willa. "At Helen's party, men smiled at me. I felt pretty. Like a princess at a ball."

"Must have been some party." Willa chuckled. "Any one in particular?"

"It doesn't make any difference." Kat turned back around and faced the mirror on the wall, watching her companion's reaction.

Willa raised an eyebrow. It was the look she gave when she collected confessions.

"The duke." She looked down at her lap, hoping to find the courage to explain. She released the pent-up breath she held. "I had on Beth's blue silk dress. He looked at me as if I were the most breathtaking woman he'd ever seen."

"The duke is a smart man." Willa bent down and took Kat's chin in her hand. "You, my love, are stunning."

"You're partial."

A grunt was Willa's answer.

"The duke wanted to kiss me at Helen's." Kat's voice broke, but she forced herself to continue with the story. "But he didn't. A cat chasing a bird interrupted us . . ."

Willa's face softened. "Did you want to kiss him?"

She nodded. "For the first time in my life, a good, decent man wanted me." Hoping for a distraction, she picked up the small pillow again. Lightly, she traced the embroidered heart in the pillow's center and remembered her mother's words. *When we're apart, remember this heart represents mine. All my love for you resides here.*

What Kat wouldn't give for her mother to be with her now.

Willa gently brushed her hair, the simple routine soothing the tempest that had her heart twisted. "You play with that when you're unsettled."

She pushed the pillow away. "Do you know what else I wanted?"

"No." Giving Kat her undivided attention, Willa lowered the brush to her side.

"I wanted to be someone else. Which would be easy for me. I'm an expert at pretending to be a lady when I'm not."

"Katherine"—Willa squeezed her shoulder—"any man would be lucky to have you."

Kat shook her head.

"Look at me," Willa commanded.

Kat raised her gaze until she could see Willa's determined face reflected in the mirror.

"You can accomplish anything. Look what you've done already in your short life." Her eyes blazed with affection. "Fate works in mysterious ways, lass. If you hadn't married your husband, you never would have met the duke."

"Perhaps." She blinked to keep her tears in check. "I just want to love someone and have them love me in return. I've jeopardized that dream with all the fanciful tales I've built my reputation around. If the truth ever spilt free . . ."

"The truth is, you made a mistake," Willa said, patting her shoulder in comfort.

"A mistake? It isn't that simple. No one would have seen past my true circumstances if I hadn't left York and told the story about a pretend father," Kat argued. The taste of bile threatened, but she swallowed. If only she could swallow the bitter memories as well. "Because of that, I have my own business. Who knows where I'd be if I hadn't? Probably still hanging my head in shame, or worse."

"Lass, you're here because of your hard work. A good man who loves you will see the truth."

"Do you think a man will love a thief?" She didn't hide the challenge in her voice as tears stung her eyes. "That's who I am."

"You're not a thief." Willa cupped her cheek, forcing Kat to hold her gaze. "A good man will understand your story. And I reckon you'll find him someday. Sooner, rather than later," Willa soothed.

"Did you ever want someone for yourself?"

"Aye." Willa stared at the window for a moment before turning her gaze back to Kat's. "I discovered I wasn't the marrying type, but I wanted children. The good Lord didn't agree, but he gave me another gift."

"I've never heard this story." Kat's heart clinched to think her loving Willa had suffered. "What gift did you receive?"

"He gave me you." In a rare show of emotion, Willa wiped her eye, then started brushing Kat's hair again. "Let me ask you another question."

Kat sat still and waited.

"Perhaps being true to yourself is what attracted the duke in the first place?" She slid the brush through Kat's hair again. "Mark my words. Trust your instincts. Be yourself and see what happens."

Her instincts told her to hide. How could she be herself

while maintaining the balancing act she'd performed for the last year? She had the title of a lady and acted like one. Because of her status in society, the *ton* had accepted her and her business with open arms.

Now, all of a sudden, she felt like an imposter. She bit the side of her bottom lip. She'd never been one to shirk hard work and the impossible. The success of her linen enterprise was proof. But if the *ton* ever found out the truth of why she rushed into marriage, along with her humble beginnings, they'd banish her.

The day of Grayson's visit, Katherine had sent a note to Christian for him to meet her at the warehouse near the Thames. He was a few minutes early, so he strolled through the busy area toward the designated building at the end of the block. The well-maintained street was bustling with activity. The scent of the river lingered in the air, along with the shouts and the grunts of workers unloading a cart of kegs into one of the buildings.

Christian released a happy sigh. It was a day to enjoy life and the city. The day had never been sunnier or cleaner, meaning the coal-infused air was noticeably absent.

He adjusted his hat to keep the sun from creeping into his eyes, or so he let the passersby think. In reality, it hid the smile that tugged at his lips. Since he'd spoken to Grayson, it was simply remarkable that everything seemed to be flavored with Katherine—her smell, her expressions, the small sounds she made when she was aggravated with him. They permeated the facets of his life.

Even her simple smile caused a chain reaction within him. How lucky his half brother had been to listen to her laugh. The fool should have never left her. If Christian had married her, he was certain he'd never tire of her laugh.

Or her.

Christian rounded the corner at a brisk pace and stopped forthwith before plowing into a woman who had her head bent and was heading in the same direction.

"Hello, Katherine," Christian said as he tipped his hat.

"Your Grace." A vision in a gray velvet pelisse, Katherine greeted him with a warm smile. A matching hat sat at a jaunty angle on her head. "You're right on time. It's right down here." She pointed to the end of the street.

"Shall we?" He presented his best charming smile and raised his arm for her to take.

Her pulse fluttered at the base of her neck, making it hard to control the wild urge to press his lips there.

She adjusted a leather satchel that she carried under her arm, then wrapped her other arm around his before they started down the street.

"I'm thinking about my day. After this, I'm going to my workshop to drop off a few orders." Her eyes widened. "You should come with me. See my workshop and how it's set up. It might give you some ideas for the work areas. The men who'll refinish the furniture will need them."

"Your workshop?" For a moment he forget to breathe. Her eyes practically sparkled as she talked about her work. "I'd like to see it. But I didn't know you owned a workshop."

"I rent the space."

"May I ask a question?" Christian asked.

She nodded.

"What did Meri think about you working?"

She stopped midstep, then turned to face him. Her unique scent rose to greet him. Her lips pursed in a moue of displeasure as she said, "Your Grace, this isn't a hobby. It's a livelihood."

"I meant no offense." He tucked himself closer to her side to give a little more room to a workman who passed by with a keg on his back. Christian purposely kept close after that.

The street was getting busier and busier with men working. "I wondered, because you're very serious-minded about your endeavors. My half brother didn't possess such critical skills."

She relaxed at that explanation.

"Thankfully, I did continue to work. Imagine what my circumstances would be if I hadn't. Perhaps I'd be living at Rand House with *you*." She smiled ruefully. "My finances, I suppose, are . . . an inappropriate topic of conversation. I apologize."

"There's no need," Christian answered, not taking his eyes off her. Her passion made her entire face glow with an invigorating excitement that was contagious.

"Here we are." She unlatched her satchel, then pulled out a ribbon with a key attached. "The owner already gave me the key."

He held out his hand. "May I?"

With a wry smile, she examined him as if he might be poisonous before slowly placing the key in his palm.

As he unlocked the door, he said, "Rest assured, I don't attack innocent bystanders, at least not after breakfast."

She waggled her eyebrows slightly. "I can't vouch for myself."

"You haven't broken your fast?"

"I've had a full breakfast. However, I might still attack."

"You're a vicious one." Christian opened the door with an exaggerated flourish. "My lady"—he leaned close—"I need you too much, so I will take the risk of your bite."

She narrowed her eyes playfully. "I've discovered that all is fair when dealing with someone who underestimates you."

"I would never underestimate you, but I appreciate the warning." A deep laugh rumbled in his chest. She was delightfully sharp-tongued today.

"I'm glad we understand one another," she playfully

mocked, then walked in with an elegant ease that marked her as a lady. "Follow me."

He'd follow her anywhere right now. If he had his druthers, they'd spend the entire day together, meandering the city streets and eating from the street vendors. Perhaps she'd show him the markets where she bought her trims and odd pieces of furniture. It sounded like heaven.

Katherine stopped in the middle of the floor and turned in a slow circle. A gorgeous smile lit her face. "It's perfect, don't you think?"

For an instant, he thought they were looking at two different things. Dreary was the only way to define the space, but the excitement in her voice was irresistible. "Define perfect."

She shook her head. "You're not seeing the potential."

The main room was huge with several offices in the back. Windows on one side of the room were coated with a film of grime, but the sunlight filtered through, highlighting the dust that coated the floor. Several pieces of lumber and a few discarded desks were stacked against the other wall. "With the battalion of servants I've recently hired, I could send over a crew. They'd have the place clean and everything set up within a day."

"Exactly." Without waiting, Kat strode to the back of the building. She pushed the latch on a windowed door, then entered. "This is the main office. I thought your head foreman could use this."

The room was pitch black, but he followed. He took two steps then stopped when something, much like a ghost's hand, brushed across his face.

Katherine wrestled with something. Within a few moments, the room was flooded in light. A lit candle sat on the desk next to a flint box. She turned around, then stared at him as if he had two heads. "You're . . . you're wearing a cobweb."

"That's what I felt. I thought perhaps the place was haunted." He chuckled as he tried to wipe his face.

"Allow me." Kat pulled a handkerchief from her pocket and came to his side. "You look like . . ."

He bent until they were eye to eye, his gaze locked with hers. "A gothic creature? A monster from the marsh?"

A hint of pink tinted her cheeks, and for the first time that he could ever recall, she seemed flustered. "I might suggest a beast from the bog."

"You know me so well." He laughed.

"I need to touch your face," she said softly.

"Please," he murmured.

The fingers of one hand swept across his cheek with the tenderest of touches as she gently brushed the other side of his face with the handkerchief. Without thought, he placed his palm over her hand, stopping her movement. He closed his eyes and concentrated on the warmth and silkiness of her palm.

"What's wrong?" Her voice trembled slightly.

"Nothing." The urge to kiss her grew nigh unbearable. "And everything."

They both grew closer until an inch separated them. Before he could ask if he could kiss her, Kat made the decision for them. With a slow deliberate movement, she swept her lips against his.

His heart pounded so hard, he thought it would break through his ribs. At the touch of her lips against his, Christian cupped her face to deepen the kiss.

"Is anyone here?" a voice rang out.

At the sound, Katherine instantly pulled away. "Of all the rotten luck," she said under her breath.

"Who is it?" His voice had the roughness of sandpaper. Such was the effect of Katherine on him.

"The devil's own spawn," she hissed. "It's Skeats."

Kat smoothed her dress, but it did nothing to slow her pounding pulse, not to mention her slight panting. She was in trouble if such a small kiss could provoke such a strong reaction. She took a deep breath and prayed she didn't appear out of sorts.

Her competitor was horrible. For his timing, his interruption, and his general disposition. "Marlen Skeats is my main competition for the Prince Regent's business," she whispered to Christian.

"We should greet him." He gently pushed a stray lock of her hair behind her ear.

His light touch caused her pulse to pound even harder. But the calmness in his gaze provided some much-needed poise. With a decisive nod, she turned and went to face her nemesis.

Not that she couldn't handle her competitor, but it was nice to have Christian beside her. "Good day, Mr. Skeats," she called out.

"Good morning, Lady Meriwether. A vision as always." Though the words were harmless, they sounded much like a snake's hiss before it attacked. Tall with red hair and a ruddy complexion to match, Marlen Skeats reminded her of a balloon she'd once seen. They were both filled with hot air.

"What a surprise to meet you here." Kat caught herself before she started twisting her fingers together.

"Is it really? I'm certain we're here for the same reason." He smiled, but it held little humor.

She huffed a silent breath, then turned to Christian. "Your Grace, this is Marlen Skeats. He owns a fine bedding shop similar to mine."

Christian didn't extend his hand for the customary shake. Instead, he swept his arms behind his back, making himself look menacing. He nodded once in acknowledgment.

"Mr. Skeats, may I present the Duke of Randford?"

"Your Grace." Skeats bowed deeply with an effusive greeting that made her stomach churn. He didn't fool anyone. "It's an honor to meet an officer of your caliber."

Christian stood motionless, but his eyes narrowed.

Skeats, who was completely oblivious to Christian's unfriendliness, took a quick glance around the room. "This place is perfect." He smiled and addressed his comments to Christian. "Lady Meriwether and I are in competition for the right to outfit the Prince Regent's Royal Pavilion." He turned to Katherine. "The real reason I'm here is to see about letting this space when I receive the contract." He noticeably paused. "I meant *if* I'm the successful winner." He tilted his head and offered a sickly sweet smile.

Katherine resisted the urge to smirk at his insincerity.

"I'm afraid you're too late, sir." Christian's deep voice sharpened. "We've already taken the space."

"We?" Skeats's eyes grew round.

"Lady Meriwether is helping me organize a charity business for my men who've returned from war in need of employment." Christian eased his rigid stance and edged closer to Kat.

For the first time since Skeats's arrival, she relaxed somewhat. As much as one could when in her competitor's presence.

"You'll have to look elsewhere," Christian said.

"Such benevolence on your part, Your Grace. Well, I guess you've proven that the early bird catches the worm." Skeats's gaze narrowed, then extended a hand to Kat. "May I see your handkerchief? Is that your handiwork?"

"Yes." Kat extended the cloth she'd used to clean the cobweb from Christian's face.

"What exquisite needlework." Her competitor examined it for several moments. "Not a stitch out of place." His thumb traced the simple pattern of a flower that Kat had learned from her mother. Eventually, he handed it back to her. "Beautiful."

"Thank you." She placed it in her pocket. "If you'll excuse us? We've another appointment."

"Of course." Skeats walked toward the door. Halfway there, he turned on the ball of his foot and faced them. "Lady Meriwether, I've seen that pattern before, but I can't recall where. It's very unusual." He tapped his finger against his lips. "May I ask where you found such a thing?"

Everything within Kat stilled to a grounding halt. How could she have been so careless? The pattern was a variation of the Yorkshire rose. It was the first pattern her mother had taught her. Only on her personal possessions did she use it.

She debated what to say. Finally, she decided upon the truth. "My mother taught me the pattern. She learned it from her mother. I really can't say where it's from." She smiled but feared it was rather weak.

Skeats nodded. "Thank you for sharing it." He waved a hand and left.

She blew out her breath. She was overreacting. Even if he did recognize the rose, he would only believe her family to be from Yorkshire. The pattern was hers alone.

Besides, he didn't know her real name, Katherine Elise James, the thief who had been caught stealing and convicted within an hour.

Christian locked the door before he gave the key to Katherine. As they started the opposite way from where Marlen Skeats went, Christian caught Kat glancing over her shoulder. Her earlier ease had scattered to parts unknown.

"Let's stop for a second." He took her hand then ducked under an overhang covering a doorway. It allowed a momentary break from the bustle of the busy street behind them where they could chat somewhat privately. Still clasping her hand in his, he studied Kat's face. "What's wrong?"

"Nothing." She bit one perfect lip. "I'm perfectly fine."

And he was the King of England. "Kat, you were wringing your fingers in the shop. You looked over your shoulder to see Skeats's direction." He smiled in reassurance, then lowered his voice. "You're definitely paler than when you kissed me."

"Really, I'm fine." She tilted her gaze to him with a smile. Finally, her cheeks were starting to color again. An excellent sign, except for the twitch below the left corner of her eye. It was exactly how she looked when he'd first met her after they both discovered Meri had three wives.

"Does Skeats worry you? Has he done something to you?" The thought that she was scared of the man brought forth the need to find Skeats and have a very frank conversation with him. If that didn't work, then Christian thought it fair game to beat him to a bloody pulp.

"He's harmless, but his business has been a staple in London for decades. He's probably the odds-on favorite, but I know my goods are superior to his." She stared at the ground as she adjusted her satchel. "That's all."

The desire to erase whatever bothered her and comfort her became overwhelming. He wanted to hold her, but they were next to a busy street. Instead, he squeezed her hand. "Kat, look at me," he coaxed.

She didn't move for a second, then finally, tilted her gaze to his.

"If and when you ever need someone to talk to or if you're scared, all you have to do is ask. I'll be there. Even if it's in the middle of the night. Promise me, you'll ask." He stared into her eyes, the swirls of gold and green mesmerizing. Only when she nodded did Christian exhale.

"Let's go to my workshop." She dropped his hand and

headed toward the street once more. She turned and smiled, this time a real one. "We can walk. It's only a couple of streets over."

As she led him through the streets, Christian's own internal compass shifted. He'd always possessed an innate awareness of the world around him, but now everything seemed a little more in focus. Katherine was the cause of it.

To lure her out of her musings, Christian said, "I understand that men aren't allowed in your shop. Does that include me?"

"Of course." She adjusted her portfolio under her arm again. "I've found that without men, the shopping experience is all the more delightful for my customers. It's by appointment only. Women can express their wants and desires more honestly. Bedrooms are very important."

"For sleep?" He slowed slightly. He'd never given much thought to the importance of linens, or bedrooms in general.

"Among other things," she said.

"Like what?" He waggled his eyebrows. It was wicked to tease her so, but he couldn't resist.

She waved her hand in dismissal. "Reading, resting." With a grin twitching, she stared down the street, then slid her gaze to his. "Use your imagination."

Right then, he wanted her to completely outfit his bedroom. "You don't think men have the same appreciation of such fine things? Or is it that men lack the capability to choose such necessities? What about bachelors like myself who would want to shop at your establishment?" He truly wanted to know her answers. "Don't you want our business?"

"I do, but I would suggest you either get married or find a sister or an aunt who could shop for you." She slowed to a stop. "Otherwise, you're not receiving any of my linens. It's the way I choose to run my business. Unless you're the Secretary to the First Lady of the Bedchamber." Without waiting for his reply, she continued her walk. "This is my workshop." She pointed at a handsome red brick building. "Of course, you're allowed in here." She opened the heavy wooden door, then strolled right through. "By the by, Your Grace, have you heard any news from Mr. Hanes?"

"No," he said slowly.

"I would appreciate it if you'd keep me informed." She stopped inside a small entry hall that led into another room and looked up at him. "Even if you don't have any news, you should have at least sent around a note to that effect."

"You are a difficult person to please, Katherine." He chuckled slightly.

She took a step forward then stopped suddenly. "No, I'm not," she protested.

He took her hand in his and held it for a moment, the touch an incredible sensation that made him smile in earnest. "Then I'll have to try harder."

A beautiful grin graced her lips in answer. He could have sworn that angels started singing from heaven at the sight. "I would like that, Your Grace. Let's start anew, shall we?"

"We shall. Now, how will you make it worth my while?" he asked softly.

Her breath caught, sending his pulse pounding at the sound.

He held up his hands in surrender and laughed. "Katherine, you have the uncanny ability to make me utter the most outlandish things to you."

"A rare talent I wasn't aware I had." Her lips tilted in a saucy smile.

"Oh, you have many rare talents, I wager," he murmured with an answering grin. "As soon as I return home, I'll see what Hanes has discovered."

She swept a hand forward in invitation. "Come inside."

Christian stepped into the room, then stopped. The entire

place was filled with light from windows that were installed in the roof. The brightness gave the appearance of being in another world. Work desks were placed strategically next to one another in several rows. Bolts of linen, silk, and velvet in a myriad of colors lined the back wall. Embroidery threads were arranged by color in specially made cabinets against another wall. There wasn't a single scrap of dirt or salvage of material on the wooden floors.

"Good day, Lady Meriwether." At the last desk at the end of a row, a slight woman with brown hair stood and waved.

Katherine waved in return with a huge smile. Christian's gut tightened at the sight. For an irrational moment, he wanted that smile for himself. What did that say about him, a duke and a war hero, to be jealous of a woman who'd captured her employer's notice and received such a beautiful smile in turn? It said he was ill-equipped to handle his responses to Katherine.

"If you'll excuse me?" Without a hint that she was aware of his dilemma, Katherine strode across the floor.

The sunlight followed her, and dust motes frolicked in her wake as if welcoming her back. He ran a hand down his face, upsetting his beaver hat in the process. Good God, where were his manners? He should have taken off the bloody hat when he entered. This was what happened when he allowed romantic dribble to spew through his brain.

No, that wasn't true. This happened when Katherine took center stage. Everything else fell away.

Katherine brought the woman over to him. "Your Grace, this is Miss Mary Anne Lucas."

"Pleased to meet you," Christian said with a bow.

"Miss Lucas, this is the Duke of Randford."

The woman blushed, then dipped a deep curtsey. "Your Grace."

"Miss Lucas and I won't be but a moment." Katherine

led the woman back to the work area. The woman hung on every word Katherine uttered. While Katherine appeared to be praising the woman's work, the employee smiled. It reminded Christian of the times he'd given his regiment praise over a difficult battle won. As she pointed to several places on the linen, the woman nodded her understanding. Then the woman bowed her head and said something.

Katherine's brow furrowed for a moment as she listened, then she embraced her employee. Christian wasn't surprised at her response. From what he'd seen of her, Katherine was truly unique and had a sense of empathy that most of the members of the House of Lords should emulate. Perhaps then they could finally get some bills passed into law.

She nodded to the woman, then turned and strode to his side.

Christian had the most inconvenient, not to mention irrational, thought. He wanted to damn Meri to hell for finding her first. But of course, that was redundant. Christian had little doubt that his brother was currently sitting beside Lucifer and basking in his eternal flames.

"Would you mind if I run upstairs for a moment? Mary Anne will be working at home today. I'm going to fetch a special project for her."

Christian's eyebrows shot upward. "You allow your employees to work from home? How do you keep track of their hours?"

"I trust them." She held up her hand to stay any argument from him. "I know what you're going to say. They'll steal from me or say they work more hours than in actuality." She lowered her voice as she looked over her shoulder at the woman. "Mary Anne Lucas is one of my most conscientious employees. She's an unmarried mother with two small children. She needs this position. She would never jeopardize it or her family's welfare."

"She lost her husband in the war?"

"No." Katherine turned back to him. "She never had one." The challenge in her gaze caught him off guard. "Some women survive on their own."

A moment of silence drifted between them, upsetting their earlier ease.

"That was thoughtless of me. Forgive me?" he asked softly.

"Of course." Her gaze immediately softened. "I shan't be long."

He nodded briskly.

The slight tilt of her lips looked like an invitation to sin. It would take little effort to bend down and touch his lips to hers while he begged her forgiveness over again until she'd smile. He cleared his throat in a sorry attempt to rid himself of such a vision. But all he could think about was running his tongue over that mouth.

Immediately, that ever-present tightness in his gut—the one he suffered whenever he was around her—hit lower. The falls of his breeches became increasingly tight.

Pure, sweet temptation.

As Katherine ascended the stairs, Christian found himself smiling. He'd never smiled, or for that mattered groaned, as much in the last three years as he had in the last two days.

And it was all Katherine's fault.

She was simply amazing. Honestly, she made him lose all sense of time when he was in her presence. What was astonishing is how she gave him a new sense of what was important in life.

Which was a rare thing ever since he'd returned to London. He didn't think a woman could make him feel like this.

When Katherine turned to go up the stairs to her office, she could feel Christian's gaze following her every step of the way. It had to be her imagination, but he was practically undressing her with his eyes.

She always felt in control when she was here, but with Christian present, she sensed that power more acutely. What would he do if she kissed him here?

He might return her kiss and finally let her experience what real passion felt like. With a lightness in her step, she proceeded up the stairs until she stopped right below the landing at a site that immediately made her heart rattle in her chest.

Outside her office, hunched in a corner, sat a small girl, Mary Anne's daughter, Isabelle, with tears streaming down her face. Mary Anne had reluctantly brought her to work. Isabelle's grandmother normally watched the young girl, but today she'd been ill. Katherine had assured Mary Anne that her daughter was quite welcome to visit today or whenever necessity required.

For Katherine, this was a family, and she was determined to protect them and their loved ones if possible.

"Isabelle?" Katherine walked to her side. When the little girl didn't look up, Katherine knelt beside her. "What's wrong?"

The little girl took a deep gulp as if trying to swallow her sorrow. "My brother, Neddy, got to go to the fishmonger's stall to fetch our supper. I never get to help." One lock of black shiny hair fell across her face when she rested her chin on her chest. "When I asked if I could go, my ma said no. It was no place for a little girl. I'd be in the way." Isabelle lifted her gaze and stole a glance at Katherine. "Then I asked if I could go to the market across the street where they sell pretty ribbons, but she said no to that too." She wiped her nose across her sleeve. "She said little girls didn't belong there by themselves." She sniffed again. "So where can little girls go and where do they belong? I've been trying to figure it out since my ma brought me here."

Her tender sigh cut straight through Katherine. She'd felt the same way too many times to count, particularly when she'd beg her mother to allow her to accompany her when she had a late performance at the theatre. Her mother had said practically the same thing to Katherine. Thankfully, she'd had Willa, who had always found something for her to do that made her feel better.

"That is a tough question for any female." Katherine squeezed her shoulder. "Would you help me put my office back in order while your mother gathers some things to take home? I don't have all the answers, but I'll tell you what I believe the answer to your question should be."

The girl nodded and sniffed gently. Katherine stood. Isabelle scrambled to her feet, then took Katherine's hand. They walked side by side into her office. Soon, Katherine had her folding the samples of linen, satin, and silk into neat stacks.

Katherine dipped her head until she captured Isabelle's gaze once more. "To answer your question, sometimes it's not safe for little girls to be alone. Your mother was protecting you. But there's nothing that a girl can't do. Don't forget that."

Isabelle's eyes widened, and she crossed her heart. "I won't. I promise."

"To do what you want in life, you have to prepare to make the journey worthwhile. For instance, work hard. Be observant. Be true to yourself. Learn your letters." She lowered her voice. "And hold dear the ones you love."

"Like my ma and Neddy?"

"Them especially. Do you like books?"

The little girl nodded.

"Then I predict learning your letters will come easy to you. Once you learn to read, the whole world is yours."

"Though, I'm not a girl, I wholeheartedly agree with Lady

Meriwether." A deep voice sounded behind them. "That's good advice even for boys." Christian's large body filled the doorframe.

"Miss Isabelle." He executed an abbreviated bow to Isabelle. "Pleased to meet you."

Katherine looked down at the little girl. "This is His Grace, the Duke of Randford."

Isabelle nodded and performed a curtsey in answer to Christian's bow, then said softly, "Pleased to meet you too." Her voice was a little uncertain as she looked to Katherine. "Your Grace?"

Katherine nodded her approval. "Nicely done, Isabelle." She bent and pressed a kiss to the top of her head.

"Don't I receive the same praise for my part?" Christian asked.

Her gaze whipped to his face, where an enchanting smile greeted her.

"Seems only fair," he added with an earnest look, then the rogue winked at her.

"Of course." She laughed, but the breathlessness in her voice betrayed the effect he had on her. If she could see him in such a mood every day, it would become an addiction, one she'd never want to be cured of.

"Lady Meriwether, I have everything I need." Mary Anne stood outside the door.

"But I'm not finished," Isabelle protested.

Katherine knelt until she was eye to eye with Isabelle. "I promise the next time you're here, you're welcome to tidy my office. It's always messy."

Isabelle grinned, then nodded. "I look forward to it."

"As do I," Katherine agreed.

"My lady, thank you for allowing me to take the work home so I can stay with Isabelle there." Mary Anne juggled some fabric in her arms.

"Of course. I hope your mother feels better."

"Thank you. I have someone to watch her tomorrow if my mother doesn't." Mary Anne nodded to Katherine and Christian, then held out her hand for Isabelle, and in a trice, they were gone down the steps, leaving Katherine alone with Christian.

"You have a special affection for the little girl?" he asked.

Katherine stared up at him. The attractive candor in his brown eyes made them sparkle.

"I want her to feel important and understand her worth. I experienced the same thing when I was a little girl. Sometimes you need to know you're wanted or have a place in the world."

"How well I understand that sentiment." He stepped closer until a foot separated them. "Believe it or not, I've felt like Isabelle before." He looked away for a moment as his eyes clouded with memories.

Kat studied his profile. He stood frozen as if trying to tame his torments. He'd been hurt. Then he returned to her with a warm, caring gaze that made her want to tell him all of her safely kept secrets. "But I have no experience with the depth of courage and perseverance a woman must possess to make it in the world. I'm in awe of you, Katherine."

Heat cascaded across her cheeks at the affectionate respect in his voice.

"Thank you," she said softly. His deep voice broke through her chest, upsetting her neatly positioned heart.

"You need to know that I want to kiss you."

Immediately, she took a small step forward until her half-boots met his hessians. They were toe-to-toe, and her heart pounded.

"May I?"

She nodded.

Instead of kissing her on the lips, he bent down and pressed a light kiss on the sensitive skin below her ear. She shivered slightly at the touch. Every part of her awoke as if coming out of a year-long sleep.

"Are you cold?" he whispered before trailing his lips against her neck.

She tilted her head, giving him greater access. "No. Just aware . . . of you." The tickle of his breath against her skin felt like another type of kiss, one more intimate, as if they'd done this before. "I want you to kiss me."

"What if I've forgotten how?"

"I think it's like riding a horse," she answered softly. "You never forget how."

"Oh, Kat. Those are"—he slid his finger slowly across her cheek, the touch incredibly erotic, then tenderly took her in his arms—"the wisest words I've ever heard." Gently, he pressed his lips against hers.

For a moment, she didn't move. The next step was up to her, and she'd not waste this chance. She traced the seam of his lips with her tongue. They were exquisite, as full and soft as she imagined. Her chin touched his where the slight bristle was in direct contrast to the softness of his mouth.

She exhaled slowly, and he slipped his tongue past her lips. He tasted of coffee and cinnamon. Tentatively, she brushed her tongue against his. She didn't want this to end. He brought her closer, testing this newness between them. Her heart thudded against her chest, trying to reach him. Without a doubt, he had to feel it. She could practically hear the pounding echo throughout her office.

Christian moaned when he deepened the kiss, and she obliged by rubbing her tongue against his.

Oh, heavens, it was exquisite.

No. He was exquisite, particularly when he was being so attentive to their kiss.

One of Christian's hands settled against the small of her

back. Pressed against the hard plane of his chest proved the definition of exquisite torture, and she melted against him. Her breasts ached for more. The heat of his body enveloped her. They continued exploring each other's wants and needs, for minutes or perhaps hours. It was difficult to tell the passage of time as they were in their own world with their own rules.

Ever so slowly, he released her from his embrace, then simply stared at her as they struggled to breathe.

He glanced at the door for a moment as if debating whether to stay or go. With a nod for her, he made his decision. "Kat, until we meet again."

Breathless and quite happy, Katherine knew she should take heed, but where was the fun in that? She pressed her fingers against her swollen and tender lips.

There was one thing she was certain of.

She'd never been kissed like that before in her entire life.

Chapter Twelve

The warehouse that Kat had introduced to Christian crawled with activity. The men he'd hired to work at Rand House were busy cleaning and outfitting the place with work areas. It was hard to believe it was only yesterday that she'd shown him the empty building. Within twenty-four hours, it was hardly recognizable. It looked as if it might be open for business within days.

His mouth twitched with a grin. Without Kat, this operation might still be a rumination. She'd sent over a list of vendors that might be able to supply the necessary tables and tools for the refinishing work on the lap desks. He'd given the list to Phillip Reed, who he'd assigned to be in charge of operations.

He couldn't wait to see her again and tell what all had been accomplished in such a short time. But what would he say? They'd shared an intimate moment, then he'd walked out of her workshop without a word. Like a tongue-tied adolescent instead of the polished and refined duke he wanted to be. Last night, he'd fallen asleep still thinking of that perfect kiss.

Well, at least one question was answered. A simple kiss wasn't going to satisfy the hunger he had for her.

Who was he fooling?

It was much more than a kiss.

But he had to tread carefully. They were working together, and he didn't want to jeopardize their friendship. Yet, there was a part deep inside him that knew it wasn't merely a friendship, but something rare.

Whatever it was, they would have to define it themselves.

"Reed, what do think?" Christian asked as he surveyed the warehouse operation.

Phillip Reed studied the surroundings and nodded. "It's a grand location, Captain. We'll have supplies brought in through the back, and the empty storage room will be perfect for storing tools, stains, gold-leafing sheets." He pointed to one of the rooms in the back that had sliding doors as a back entrance. "We can bring in wood there. Once we see how the demand is for the refinishing of the writing desks, we can adjust the business accordingly. It'd be nice to make larger custom pieces. That's my specialty." He tucked a pencil he'd used for drawing the building's layout behind one ear. "I can teach the craft to others."

"How many do you think we can employ?" Christian asked. "Twenty perhaps?"

"That's not enough, but it's a start," Reed said confidently. "I'd say fifty within the month."

"Fifty?" Christian said incredulously. That was a huge amount of manpower for a new business. "Are you sure?"

Reed nodded briskly. "I met with Lady Meriwether early this morning. She suggested we assign some men with transporting the finished desks to her workroom as soon as possible. She wants to tailor some of her linens to match the colors and designs. From there, she'll put the stock in her shop and start taking custom orders. She wants them by the end of the week. She's confident they'll sell. Plus she said she'd use a few of the men to help with delivery of her own products." He shook his head. "The woman is a genius."

Christian could readily agree to that. He'd wanted her assistance and expertise, but her efforts to help went way beyond what they had originally discussed. It was completely unselfish of her to devote this much time to his charity when she had her own challenges. Within the week, she'd be meeting the Secretary to the First Lady of the Bedchamber. Christian had little doubt she'd be able to convince the man he should choose her linens for the Royal Pavilion.

An overwhelming sense of rightness rolled through him as he inhaled. He couldn't have asked for a better person to help him.

Or a better person to kiss.

"She also suggested some of the men travel to the counties where specialty woods are available. Thought they could bring back samples for me to look at. If the wood is of high enough quality, we could start making original pieces here." Reed folded his arms across his chest. The look of satisfaction on his face made him appear years younger.

Reed's demeanor had transformed since Christian had approached him with the idea and put him in charge. He seemed happy, confident, and more of his old self.

Calam Walstrom, one of the infantrymen who had worked as a Randford groomsman, drew near. He nodded briefly to Christian before showing a list with tools, paints, and varnishes for Reed's approval. Calam had been one of the first to inquire if he could work here and learn a new trade. He wouldn't be the last.

After the men finished their conversation, Reed turned back to Christian. "Captain, Lady Meriwether gave me the name and address of a place called Hailey's Hope. It's a charity for soldiers who've returned from the war without any place to stay. The Duchess of Langham and the Marchioness of Pembrooke operate it. Lady Meriwether said they have a new dormitory wing set to open. It might be the solution for some of your men who've returned with injuries and can't work right away. When they heal, we can see about finding them jobs."

"She came up with that solution?" he asked. The woman had an answer for everything.

"She'd asked me how I came to find you once I returned. I told her about me begging." Reed glanced at the floor, then turned his gaze to Christian. "She wasn't prying, but concerned. She offered me money, but I refused. I pulled out the last coin I'd received on the streets and said that I was keeping it as a souvenir. I even told her I'd bit it to see if it was lead or gold. She said she'd done the same thing when she was a young girl." He chuckled then turned serious. "Yours was the last coin I'd been given. I'm keeping it as a reminder of where I've been and where I'm going. I can't thank you enough for this chance, sir."

Christian patted his shoulder. "Reed, it's you who I can't thank enough. We're all necessary for the operation to be a success. Just like we were on the battlefront."

Reed could only nod as he wiped his eyes with his fingers. Christian's chest tightened at the sight.

The shop's front door opened, and both of them turned to see his valet strolling determinedly toward them.

Morgan was soon by their side. He nodded to Reed, then turned to Christian. "Captain, your brother's . . . I mean half brother's personal belongings have arrived in London."

The steady beat of his heart stumbled. Poison Blossom and Meri's apartment were relatively easy matters to handle, but his half brother's personal items were another. Meri had possessed them to the last, a glimpse of his life right before his death. It made his passing a reality.

Christian let out an unsteady breath. "Reed, I must go."

"Of course, Your Grace," Reed said. "Duty calls."

It was the first time Reed had addressed him as such. Indeed, he had a responsibility to help the wives, and that required sorting through Meri's possessions. He prayed there was an easy explanation for the lost money. But knowing his half brother's flightiness and penchant for gambling, the chance of retrieving any money was rather slim.

"Sir, shall I come with you?" Morgan asked softly. "I brought a carriage."

"No, thank you. I'd like to walk. I'm heading over to Lady Meriwether's workshop. If she can spare the time, I'd like to have her with me when I open Meri's possessions."

Whether it was wise or not wasn't a question he wanted to examine too closely.

All that was important now was that it felt right to have her by his side.

Katherine sat behind the desk in her workshop warehouse. Amongst her blotter and inkwell, fabrics, trims, and sketches of new pillows vied for her attention. This week, everything had to be in order since the Secretary to the First Lady of the Bedchamber would visit.

She should be thinking about that appointment instead of yesterday's kiss. She inhaled deeply as her pulse accelerated. Katherine traced her fingers over her lips, the sensation causing a riot of responses from her body. As she'd lain in bed last night, imagining Christian kissing her, her whole body throbbed with a deep ache. It still did, with a gentle pounding that made every one of her senses come to life, as if awakening from a deep sleep. No one had ever touched her, but last night Christian did in her bedroom . . . at least, he did in her dreams.

That wasn't the whole truth.

What she'd fantasized about was not Christian kissing her, but her kissing him. She sighed as the sweet memories consumed her. As she'd pressed her lips against his, he'd explored her with his hands, each gentle touch learning what her body liked. She'd been bold in her kiss, savoring every taste and touch, conquering him in a way that no other woman ever had. He did the same to her. He'd filled his hands with her breasts, weighing and kneading them until she'd whimpered. When he'd rubbed his thumbs against her pouting nipples, her cry at the exquisite sensation became lost as he took control of their kiss. When he trailed his hand slowly down the curve of her waist, she wanted more. She wanted his hand to travel to the place where she ached . . . only for him.

"Kat?" Beth Howell stood in the doorway. "Do you have a moment?"

Instantly, her erotic daydream fractured into a thousand pieces at the gentle voice. "Of course. Do come in."

Beth crossed the threshold of the door and stood with her hands clasped in front of her, a patient pose that Katherine was thankful for. It meant that all was well with production. Days ago, Kat had introduced her dear friend to her employees as Miss Beth Howell, who'd come to town to help prepare for the secretary's visit. Everyone had welcomed her with true affection. They were well aware that the contract meant new opportunities for them all.

Beth had settled in without the need for much supervision. She possessed a keen business and organizational sense, and Katherine trusted her with everything. Kind and fair to the employees, Beth ensured that any hiccup in the production was handled efficiently with little fuss. If a seamstress ran low of a certain ribbon for a project, Beth was the one that dug through the supplies and found more. No job was too big or small for her. In the few days that she'd been there, she'd offered a couple of her own embroidery designs. They were bold and striking, and Kat had immediately loved them. She planned to incorporate them into a new line of linens.

But that wasn't all. Beth was aware of Kat's constant concern about finances, so she'd shared a few ideas she'd developed at her brother's estate on how to control inventory. It would save at least ten pounds a month in expenses.

Simply put, Beth was a treasure. And Kat had no idea how she'd managed without her for so long. Without her help, Katherine wouldn't be able to concentrate on the secretary's visit and assist Christian at the same time.

"I posted a letter to my brother's solicitor and asked that he keep me informed of my brother's travels," Beth said as she picked up several samples that had fallen on the floor. "Do you think Randford would mind if I have any response forwarded to Mr. Hanes's office?"

"I can't imagine he would." Katherine walked to Beth's side. "Any clue when your brother might arrive back in London?"

"No." Beth straightened the samples into an orderly pile on Kat's desk. "I hope he stays in Austria for at least several months . . . until things are settled." She swallowed, then smoothed her hand down her throat in obvious unease.

"What do you think will happen when he returns?" Kat took her friend's hand in hers.

"He'll probably try to marry me off as soon as possible." She squeezed Kat's hand. "I won't do it again."

"Was marriage to Meri so horrible?" Kat asked softly.

"No. But he wasn't interested in me. I can see that now." Beth lowered her voice. "I think I'm the type of person who would prefer to live on my own. I need at least part of my fortune to do that."

"I understand. But what about companionship?"

The brief glimpse of pain in her friend's eyes was quickly

replaced with resolution. "I have you and Constance. We'll be friends for life, don't you think?"

Kat nodded with a smile. "You're welcome to stay with me and Willa forever if you'd like."

"Thank you." Beth leaned close to Katherine. "As long as you let me keep working for you."

"It's a promise." Kat laughed.

By then, they'd walked out of Kat's office and were standing on a second-floor balcony that provided an excellent view of the operation below. Ten employees, all women, worked steadily on the latest orders of feather duvets and pillows. Several of them worked by the windows as they embroidered the pillowcases that would be delivered by the end of the week. Some of the designs were family initials, some aristocratic family crests. One thing Katherine had noticed was the lower the title, the more likely the order would be for linens to feature the embroidered design of the crest. It was as if the lady of the house wanted to remind everyone the position they held in society.

How different her friend Helen's decorating tastes were from the others'. She'd only wanted her first initial intertwined with her husband's first initial on the linens. Helen had said it was a sweet sentiment to their love.

A sudden image of a *K* and a *C* intertwined like lovers popped into her thoughts. She wanted to do that for her husband someday.

She'd never once considered doing that for her and Meriwether.

Immediately, such thoughts vanished as her gaze caught on a person who walked as if he were the owner of the factory instead of her. "Why is Marlen Skeats walking our floor?"

Beth discreetly shook her head while she watched his every step. "I saw him outside the other day. This makes the third time this week he's been in the neighborhood. He thinks because he's the biggest supplier of linens in England, he should automatically win the contract. It doesn't take a genius to figure out what he wants. He must have heard the secretary has an appointment to see our goods."

"His product is inferior to ours." Katherine sniffed, then added for good measure, "The way he treats his workers should be outlawed. A rabid dog is given more respect than he gives his employees."

"When we're awarded the contract, we should hire them," Beth said.

"Excellent idea. I'm going downstairs," Kat declared.

"Do you mind if I wait in your office?" Beth turned so her back was to the floor. "In the off chance he would recognize me."

"Of course. Close the door behind you, dearest." Katherine started down the steps to intercept the interloper.

Several of Katherine's workers glanced up with curious looks when Skeats passed their stations.

By then, Kat had arrived on the shop floor. She slowed her step and smiled in reassurance at each one of her employees.

"Mr. Skeats, what a surprise to find you here." Katherine congratulated herself on the ability to keep her voice friendly. "How may I assist you?"

Whatever he wanted, she would deal with it politely and quickly, then send him on his way. She stopped in front of him, effectively blocking his pathway.

"Good morning, Lady Meriwether." He bowed as one would expect of a gentleman, but Kat knew enough of the man to know he wasn't one. He looked around the workroom. "This is quite an operation, my lady. It's such a shame we have to scrape the barrel for competent workers. If you'd like, I can always send those we refuse employment to your way."

Katherine wrinkled her nose. She smelled something rotten, much like the skunk before her. "Somehow I have managed to find the most qualified people for the positions here. Every single employee from the seamstresses to my delivery boy Rodney, who also cleans the work floors, is exemplary. However, I thank you for your kind offer." She didn't hide the hint of sarcasm in her voice.

"Are you out of mourning already? I thought mayhap a wife of your position, especially one married to a duke's son, might abide a little longer"—he scrunched his thumb and forefinger together in a display of feigned concern—"to a respectable mourning period."

"My late husband would have approved of whatever I did," Katherine shot back in answer. She clasped her hands in a show of contriteness. "Forgive me for my outburst, but may I share the truth?"

"I'm all ears, Lady Meriwether." Skeats smiled. "Do tell."

She leaned in as if divulging a secret. "I never need any man's approval."

"We shall see," he grunted in displeasure. "You'll need the secretary's, and he's a man." Skeats turned around slowly and surveyed the work floor. "What does the Duke of Randford think of your little operation here? I sincerely doubt he approves."

"It really doesn't make any difference what the duke thinks." Katherine stood tall and straightened her shoulders. "I'm not married to him."

A long shadow fell over Katherine's shoulder. She didn't have to turn around to deduce who had joined them. She turned and dipped a shallow curtsey. "Your Grace."

"Your Grace." Skeats bowed deeply.

"Mr. Skeats." Christian's voice was so low, it sounded like a growl. "Are you following Lady Meriwether?"

"Oh, no, sir." Skeats shook his head vehemently.

"Are you following me, then?" Christian asked.

"No, sir. I didn't know you were going to be here. I was in the neighborhood."

"What exactly are you doing here?" Christian gaze bored through the man.

Skeats waved a hand toward Katherine. "I simply stopped by to tell Lady Meriwether how marvelous her operation is." He curled his lip slightly, then addressed Kat. "Since we're both under consideration for the Prince Regent's business, if you need any advice or help, I hope you'll ask."

Only when ice was plentiful in hell would she ask him for anything.

Skeats surveyed the floor once again. "As you probably surmise, I'm the odds-on favorite for winning the contract since I'm the biggest supplier of fine bedclothes."

"Modesty is one of your fortes, I see," Christian mocked with a smile.

Skeats completely missed the sarcasm and took a turn around the work floor, calling out from behind, "Indeed, Your Grace. If my orders become too much, I could send the excess Lady Meriwether's way. Though, I must say"—he reached across a worktable and smoothed a hand over a finished duvet—"the quality of your linens is outstanding. You're becoming quite well-known through the *ton*."

"How kind of you to say so." Katherine caught up to him, then took him by the arm and led him back to the front of the workroom. It was obvious to everyone he was evaluating the shop and their products. Truly, she'd grown tired of his antics.

"Is that Belgium lace?" Skeats asked, making a beeline to the table that contained her inventory. "Where did you get it?"

But Christian blocked him by standing before him. "Perhaps another day, Skeats."

If Katherine wasn't mistaken, Christian had sneered slightly at the man. "I need to speak to Lady Meriwether. As one could imagine, I'm a busy man, and I don't like to be kept waiting."

Then, Christian flanked her side, effectively obstructing Skeats's view of the floor.

"Thank you so much for your visit today." Katherine led Skeats to the door. "Perhaps the next time, you might send a note ahead?" From now on, she'd ensure that the door was locked and the windows covered.

"Of course." He took one step outside and stopped. "Your Grace, one more thing . . ."

She held her breath, praying he wouldn't come back.

"A pleasure to see you again," Skeats called out.

Christian stood immobile, not answering back.

"Lady Meriwether, may the best man win." He waved goodbye.

She returned the gesture half-heartedly. "Or the best woman."

He didn't acknowledge her response but kept on his way.

As soon as she returned inside and closed the door, she fisted her hands. "The nerve of that man. He was not here for a social call. He wanted to find something he could use to undermine my chance of winning the contract."

"I'm afraid that's the case." Through the window directly across, Christian glanced at the retreating figure down the street. "Would you like some of my servants here to keep him out? They could watch the doors. Most are from the military."

"That won't be necessary. I make certain everything is in perfect order. When I'm meeting my appointments at the emporium, Beth is here." She exhaled, hoping to relieve her frustration at Skeats's impromptu visit. "Once the secretary arrives to evaluate the business, perhaps we can all get back to work. Thank you for the offer of help."

He smiled in pleasure, one of those grins that could coax the sun to shine at midnight.

"You're welcome anytime, but I didn't really do anything." He took her bare hand in his and squeezed gently as he bowed. Through the fine leather, his heat branded her. "You were the one to steer him away. It appears that Isabelle isn't the only one who can tidy things around here." He gave her the package he'd held in the other hand. "Here are a couple of books from the nursery at Rand House. I thought Isabelle might enjoy them. One is a picture book and the other a primer of the alphabet."

"How thoughtful."

He slid a glance her way. "I have my moments."

At every turn, he surprised her. Her heart beat a little quicker at the sight of his cheeks reddening. "I'll make certain Isabelle receives these. She'll adore them."

He slowly glanced around the room. "You employ all these people?"

She nodded in answer.

Christian clasped his hands behind his back as he regarded the floor. "This is remarkable how successful your business is. When I was here yesterday, I had no idea you employed so many. Now I'm starting to understand why my half brother married you."

"Is that an insult or a compliment?" Katherine laughed and turned to face him. At the sight of his grim face, she quickly sobered. "What's wrong?"

"Meriwether's personal items, including his papers, arrived at Hanes's offices a little over an hour ago. Hanes is sending them over later this afternoon." He paused for a moment. "I'd like for you to come to Rand House and view them with me. If you're amenable and your schedule allows."

"Of course. I'll inform Beth and meet you there."

He nodded. "It's not something I'm looking forward to."

Perhaps it made his death all the more real for Christian. She suspected that he carried deep feelings for his late half brother, locked away and out of sight. Though others might be distracted by the duke's distance and sometimes churlishness, she saw it for what it was—a veneer to keep his heart protected.

"Until then, Lady Meriwether." Christian bowed his head. "I shall wait for you to call upon me at your earliest convenience." With another nod for her, he swept through the door.

A squall that could blow one over would wither in his presence. Which left Katherine wondering if she could withstand such a force of nature. One thing was certain. She was truly thankful such a force was in her life.

Chapter Thirteen

"Your Grace, Lady Meriwether is here," Wheatley announced.

Christian pulled off his gardening gloves and watched Katherine enter the conservatory. She stopped inside the door, and her unmasked enchantment with the room immediately brought a smile to his face. He felt the same pleasure every time he entered his private refuge.

"What a wondrous place," she exclaimed as she pivoted on one foot, taking in the magnificence of the glass walls. Her gaze darted down the neat rows of rosebushes and orange trees.

"Thank you, Wheatley." Christian nodded a dismissal to the butler, then walked to Katherine's side. "I was hoping you'd come sooner rather than later."

She blushed prettily, the color reminding him of wild roses. "This is an amazing place." She tilted her head back and studied the glass dome above them.

Christian mimicked her movement. "It's my favorite room in the house. If I had my druthers, I'd throw out everything but this, then start anew. Come. I want to show you something." He took her hand in his and led her down the row of red roses, then turned right until they stood in front of his worktable.

"Oh my," she said softly. "I've never seen such a rose. What a stunning crimson. It's almost burgundy."

"It's a Portland rose named after the Duchess of Portland. My mother collected roses, and this was one of her favorites." He clipped off a stem with a large bloom, taking care to cut the thorns. Satisfied with his work, he handed it to her.

"It's beautiful." She brought it to her delicate nose and inhaled. A smile spread slowly across her lips. "How lovely."

"Not as lovely as you," he murmured.

Her gaze shot to his.

Christian took a step closer and rubbed the back of his forefinger slowly across one petal of the rose she held. With their heads bent together, it would have taken little effort to close the distance between them and kiss her. "You must forgive my earlier mood at your workshop. Finding out that Meriwether's personal items had arrived made his death irrefutable, if that makes sense."

Understanding shown in her eyes. "It must be hard to lose a sibling. I don't know, but I'm certain it's like a piece of your heart was chipped away."

Her empathy was one of her most attractive strengths. Instead of refuting her, he smiled. Meri was never part of his heart. As he continued to stroke the petal's softness, he imagined it was her skin he caressed. Each touch would teach him what she liked, what she craved from a man.

He wanted to be the man that brought forth the soft, sweet cries of ecstasy that would slip through her lips.

His nostrils flared as his body grew taut. His cock swelled at the image of him making love to her in his conservatory while discovering every secret she possessed. Each thrust slow and deliberate as he learned what she liked. The sweet fragrance of blooms and the smell of damp soil would surround them. Time would cease to exist when he pleasured her, both losing themselves in each other's arms, not caring what day or week it was.

He took a deep breath and released it slowly.

She reached out to touch another rose in bright pink. He imagined her nipples would be the same shade, perhaps a little lighter.

Such thoughts were enough to drive a man mad.

He leaned slightly, and not touching her anywhere else, he brushed his lips against hers. The softness of her mouth would make the goose down in her workshop feel coarse in comparison.

When she gasped gently, he wrapped her in his embrace and swept his mouth against hers again. The blood in his veins pounded. All he could do was pull her closer as he deepened this kiss. She responded by wrapping her arms around his neck, and a small moan escaped.

That soft sound and the supple taste of her lips could bring him to his knees. Her kiss reminded him of the sweetest wine, and he drank freely. He supped on her strength, her fortitude, her kindness, and her regard for others.

It was foolhardy to be kissing her when anyone could walk in, but a small growl of need rose within his chest. This woman made him want all the wonderful things that life had to offer, like the comfort of holding another. He cradled her close with one hand, while the other traced the curve of her waist upward, counting her ribs.

She placed her hand over his and guided it to the soft mound of one perfect breast.

"Katherine," he whispered against her lips, pulling her tighter as his cock hardened. God, it felt like heaven.

She felt like heaven.

A soft sigh escaped her, an invitation to deepen the kiss.

Then she did something that made his heart stumble in its steady beat. She trailed her hand down his chest slowly until she stopped at the hem of his waistcoat.

He groaned in response, hoping she'd take it further and unbutton the falls of his breeches.

"Your Grace?" Wheatley called out from the doorway. "The tea service you ordered is in your study." He cleared his throat. "Whenever you're ready."

It was their good fortune that they stood surrounded by large rosebushes and his worktable blocked the view from the doorway. Slowly, Christian drew away, not wanting their interlude to stop. "Damnable timing. I've half a mind to dock his pay," he teased, a secret between the two of them.

The pulse at the base of her throat fluttered even faster than before. Her chest rose and fell as if she'd run a race. He knew the exact feeling. The sight of her flushed face, pinkened by desire, was so erotic, he wanted to capture such a vision and hold it in his thoughts forever. He took her in a brief kiss again, not wanting to let her go.

"Katherine . . ." He cleared his throat.

She glanced down and smiled at the obvious tenting in his breeches, then took a step back. Immediately, he wanted to follow. He'd follow her anywhere right now.

"We should go," she said.

Reluctantly, he nodded. The interruption had to be a curse or a punishment that Meri had gladly cast upon him from above.

On second thought, it most likely came from below.

Either way, his brother was playing a cruel game with him.

Half brother, that was.

Christ, he should be concentrating on the correspondence in his office rather than Meri's widow's sweet lips.

What was happening to him?

If any soldier had deserted him like his well-bred willpower just had, he would have called for a court martial of the fugitive.

Meri's personal items were spread across the burl wood library table that matched Christian's desk. It stood centered between a set of bay windows that overlooked a private courtyard only accessible through the study. The samples of upholstery and fabric that Katherine had admired before were missing. The tea service sat on a table surrounded by matching sofas facing one another.

Interesting was the only way Katherine could describe Christian at the moment. After Wheatley had interrupted their kiss, Christian had politely escorted her to the study without sharing a word.

Whether it was because Wheatley had interrupted their lovely interlude or because he was in a high spirit from their kiss was anyone's guess.

She was certainly in high spirits and wanted more and everything from him. When they spent time together, she forgot her past.

Finally, Christian broke the silence between them. "Will you pour?"

"Of course." So lost in her thoughts, Katherine had sat like a frog on a log while the hot water for tea cooled. She quickly arranged a tower of cucumber sandwiches, lemon tarts, and fresh raspberries on a plate, then served him. He looked calm as he took a sip of tea while forgoing the delicious treats.

She took a sip of tea from her own cup at the same time. His large Adam's apple danced as the hot tea slid down his throat. Her gaze wandered to his massive hand holding the cup. It wasn't the normal way a person held a teacup. He didn't thread his forefinger through the handle. Instead, his entire hand surrounded the piece of bone china.

She took her time chewing a bit of tart while he continued to stare at her mouth. Then he glanced at the table where Meri's personal items lay. Immediately, he thrummed his fingers against one of his knees. She quietly wiped her serviette against her mouth, then set down her cup. "I noticed the way you hold a teacup. I've never seen anyone do that before."

"My fingers don't fit," he mumbled. "The blasted cups have tiny handles." He stole another glance toward the table, and the color seemed to drain from his face immediately.

"Hmm," she answered noncommittedly.

It was quite possible, even probable, that he'd never grieved over Meriwether's death. Christian kept things bottled up. But every once in a while, the grief spilt, and she could see the pain. He tried to act immune to hurt, but he was as human as the rest of the population who inhabited the planet. Besides, he had a good heart. He had committed to help Constance and Beth. He cared for Morgan and the rest of his men who had served him. Though he groused, he cared for his servants and probably the same for his tenants. Even the way he took his time to protect Poison Blossom showed his intention for good. He had so much to give others—his leadership, his ideas, and his love.

"Shall we?" He stood and waited for her to join him.

Together they crossed the study to the table. He held out a seat for her before going around the table and sitting opposite her.

"I can sense your unease." She placed her folded hands on the table, a sign that she wanted to proceed without any awkwardness.

He reclined in the chair with an insouciance she might have believed if it hadn't been for him kicking her in the shin with his boot as he tried to settle. "Pardon me." He pulled a satchel toward him.

"Don't worry over it," she answered.

"I wish I didn't have to do this," he murmured, then shook his head. "I'm afraid I'll open this satchel and there'll be another Meri-created catastrophe for me to sort through."

"I'll help you," she offered.

"That's very kind, but I couldn't ask that. He's already caused you enough heartache to last a lifetime." Businesslike, he reached inside and retrieved more papers and placed them next to the ones already neatly arranged on the tabletop. "Meri had two satchels. I thought we'd start with this one first as it contained the majority of his possessions."

"Wait." She reached across the table and placed her hand over his. "I'd like to talk about your brother." He immediately stilled, but she didn't remove her hand. "He admired and wanted to emulate you. You're aware of that?"

His attention never left the papers before him. Slowly, he slid his hand from hers.

"What nonsense." The gentle exasperation in his deep voice was in direct contrast to the way he thinned his lips. Pain radiated from his dark brown eyes. It was all the more reason to continue.

"He wanted to win your admiration. He confided in me several times."

"Of course he confided in you. He confided in everyone. Everyone felt close to Meri. He had a way of wooing one over." Christian pulled several loose pieces of foolscap and three packets of papers toward him, then straightened several letters that sat to his right. "All play-acting on his part."

Katherine sat completely quiet, ready to listen to him rant, but she was determined to help him through his unacknowledged grief, a dangerous emotion that appeared to be festering inside him. The anger, then the contrived disinterest, had to be taking a toll on him.

From the looks of it, the papers Christian had in hand were old racing sheets and correspondence. No matter how he tried to organize his brother's belongings, it wouldn't straighten out the chaos that had befallen Constance and Beth, let alone Christian and herself.

"Not that I'm interested or care about Meriwether, but it appears you want to talk about him." Christian feigned a nonchalance that wasn't convincing. With a contrived sigh, he continued, "Go on, then. What did he say?" He never lifted his gaze.

She took a breath for courage, then began, "Well, Meri repeatedly told me that no matter what mischief he found as a lad, you had infinite patience with him. He said that his mother and father wasted little time on him, but you were always there when trouble found him." She softened her voice. "He was proud of you, Christian. He said you would make your mark in this world, just as you'd done on the battlefield. He wanted to host a welcome party for you when you returned." She reached across the table and took his hand in hers, then squeezed it gently, hoping he'd react in kind. With his head bent, he didn't return the gesture. She hadn't a clue how he was reacting to what she was sharing. "I wanted that too."

"Indeed?" His voice was cold when he finally lifted his gaze to hers. The blast of brilliance in his brown eyes could have easily been mistaken for annoyance, but she recognized the longing that glimmered there. It was a grim reminder of all he'd lost.

"I'm so very glad you're home safe and sound," she added softly.

"Thank you. It's . . . I'm weary of all of this." He waved a hand in the direction of the papers, then leaned back in his chair and drummed his fingers ever so slightly on the table. "I have so many other things I want to concentrate my energies on."

A gentle smile fell across his lips, and in that moment, she imagined it was her he was referring to instead of his charity.

"Meri was a magnet for trouble. If there was anyone or anything illicit, illegitimate, or ill-advised, he found and welcomed it with open arms."

Katherine kept her face still as her stomach tightened at the word "illegitimate."

Completely oblivious to her turmoil, Christian continued, "As a result of my good deeds to save my half brother's neck, I've been thrashed within an inch of my life, suffered a broken nose, had my purse stolen, and been chased by a jealous husband who discovered my brother . . ."

"In bed with the man's wife." She finished the sentence for him.

"Yes," he said curtly. What others might see as abruptness, she saw as a man who was desperately trying to keep his emotions on an even keel.

"I shouldn't have said that about him," he said with a hint of contriteness. "However, those are a few of the consequences I suffered when I tried to defend him. There are millions more," he argued.

"He said you were a marvelous brother."

"Before I left for the war, I completely broke with him and his antics." He shook his head in denial as he slashed his hand through the air. "I was finished with him. The final straw was when Meri took my horse and raced him for a fifty-pound purse. For years, I'd trained the animal. He'd been groomed and directed to obey my every command. A battle-ready horse is hard to come by. Mine was exceptional. Instinctively, he knew how to protect me." He exhaled heavily. "I planned to take him with me when I joined the war, but he turned up lame after the race." He shook his head as if he still couldn't believe it. "My stupid half brother took a war horse and tried to turn it into a racehorse. From then on, I brushed my hands of him. He had no respect for that animal or me."

Horrified at the story, Katherine sat there silently for moment. "Did you destroy him?" she asked softly.

"If you mean Meriwether, no. But I wanted to. Neither did I destroy my horse. I felt closer to it than I did my own family." He leaned back in his chair and directed his gaze to her as if challenging her to dispute his statement. "He has a permanent home in the stables at Roseport, my ancestral seat."

Another confession that proved what a kind man he truly was. "I understand why men would follow you into battle. You're not only brave and determined, but you possess a compassion that must have served you and your regiment well."

"That's kind of you to say." Something in his voice hinted that he didn't believe her.

"I am being sincere, Christian." She paused, letting the words sit between them.

He exhaled then nodded once.

"You already knew you'd enter the military years before you joined." She held his stare. "It's rare for a peer, particularly a ducal heir, to buy a commission, isn't it? I'm surprised your father let you."

"Exceedingly rare. By then, my stepmother and father's theatrics and outrageous parties were a constant in my life. I had to escape. Besides, I wasn't a duke then, and my father didn't care. He considered me dull and too regimented. He only cared about pleasure."

Katherine sat quietly while his words flowed freely. It was as if she weren't there. He seemed to be far away in his memories. But then he surprised her. He took her hand and squeezed gently, then leaned toward her.

"Thank you for saying that you're happy I'm home." He exhaled gently. "It means something . . . a great something."

"It's not just me," she answered. "All of England is happy you're home."

He shook his head with a wry smile. "But you see, there's a difference. A huge difference. All of England isn't sitting here with me and holding my hand."

Christian studied her hand. So small compared to his, but hers had the strength to comfort. When she'd said she was happy he was home, he might have fallen a little bit in love with her.

He shook his head slightly to clear the sickly-sweet cobwebs he was experiencing.

It was all nonsense. He'd never fallen in love with anyone before, but somehow, someway, she had invoked all these wants and desires to come rushing to the surface, begging for viability.

For God's sake, her words were simple and pure. Nothing more. She was happy he'd returned home.

Yet they held power over him. Even if his immediate family had been alive, there wasn't much chance they would have been happy to see him return. Not that they'd wish him gone, but they probably wouldn't have even noticed.

He huffed silently. To spend any more time on such notions proved he was a nodcock loon. Christian vowed to put away all those ridiculous thoughts and concentrate on the task at hand, then finish cataloguing Meri's correspondence. That's what he was here for. Not to fall in love.

He chanced a discreet glance Katherine's way. Her skin

glowed, and she held herself at ease. He'd always found he preferred people who were comfortable with their own company. And with her, he was relaxed without the need of formality. They could even sit and enjoy each other's company without conversation.

He cleared his throat and continued to gently rub her hand. He hadn't stopped since he'd taken her hand in his.

To touch her nurtured something deep inside that he'd always wanted but never dared hoped to find. Contentment. Acceptance. Someone who saw him as a human and not just their heir, or their guarantor in Meri's case.

What it all boiled down to was that he wanted someone to put him first in their life. Because with that person, he'd do the same.

"Your friend Lady Woodhaven mentioned a few things about your marriage to my half brother . . . but I'd like to hear it from you."

She shrugged. "There's not much to tell. Your brother came into my shop one day, and we were married three weeks later. It was a whirlwind courtship."

"Did you love him?" The words trailed to nothing, and for a moment, Christian didn't think she'd answer. He stared, waiting for her to say something. Eventually, the silence grew tenuous.

She schooled her features into a pleasant expression. Yet her hazel eyes briefly flashed as if portending storms. Perhaps it was too painful for her to discuss.

"I shouldn't have asked."

"It's all right." She leaned away from the table, creating distance between them. Her gaze grew cloudy, her expression wistful. "Did I fall in love with him?"

His chest tightened waiting for the answer.

"No. I think we both fell in love with the idea of falling in love. At least, I did." She glanced out the window.

Katherine let go of his hand, and immediately he wanted to take it. Instead, he smiled and said, "You're a remarkable person, Katherine. Meri was lucky to have you, however briefly, in his life."

When she turned her attention back to him, she had lifted her brows in shock. "Thank . . . you."

"May I ask another question?"

"Of course," she said, folding her hands together on the desk.

"Did Meri purchase a set of your linens? I seem to recall a bill from your shop."

When she laughed, the bright sound filled the emptiness in his chest. "He did. That's how I met him. I allowed him in the shop."

"Perhaps you'll reconsider and allow me the opportunity to shop in your fine establishment, then?" He waggled his eyebrows. "If we're going to promote each other's businesses, I'd like to have the experience of sleeping on your linens."

She nodded in agreement. "You should."

"Is that an invitation to sleep in your bed?" He tilted one side of his mouth upward.

"Behave," she scolded with a grin.

"With you, I find it impossible," he answered.

She laughed, and her eyes flickered with mirth. He wanted to make her laugh every day and be the man who gave her pleasure in every way. His reward would be her smile and the sparkle in her eyes that lit them from within.

"Now, sir, what are those piles of papers in front of you?" She pointed toward the papers.

Christian picked up the three separate packets. "Meri has assigned a packet of receipts to each wife." He handed one to Kat. "This one is yours. The others are for Constance and Beth." He shrugged slightly and frowned. "I've glanced at them. They're nothing but receipts and records of transactions. Some deal with the sale of horses and livestock. Some are auction receipts. Others are some type of mineral leases. Frankly, I can't make heads or tails of them. Nor does it make any sense why they've been separated for each wife. They're all from the last year."

Kat untied the bundle and rummaged through the pages. "You're right. They appear to be transactions of some sort or the other." Her brow creased as she regarded Christian. "I'm not really certain what it all means. If you'd like, I'll take the ones for Constance and Beth." Kat tied up the pile and retied the leather strap around hers.

"If it wouldn't be much trouble." He slid the remaining two packets toward her, then drew the bag toward him. "I think that's all the papers here." He slipped his hand in the bag again, where he discovered a hidden pocket sewn into the leather. Inside was a folded piece of paper. When he brought it out, he discovered it was a letter.

For Katherine, in the event of my death.

Chapter Fourteen

Christian held out a letter. His large hands made it seem insignificant. "This appears to be for you."

Katherine narrowed her eyes but didn't reach for it. For some odd reason, all she could think about was how neat and proper her husband's handwriting was. The letters could only be described as elegant and bold—just like Meri.

A dark, portending fear wouldn't leave her be. It rippled through her, leaving in its wake a coldness that made it hard to breathe. Whatever Meri had written, she would not allow it to upset her. He was gone forever and had left her in a perilous position.

It defied explanation why the note was even here. He had posted letters to her throughout the last year. Why hadn't he posted this one?

Perhaps he had confessed his sins or tried to rationalize his actions.

With a surprisingly steady hand, she reached for the note, then slipped one finger beneath the wax seal, breaking it in two.

My dearest Katherine,

If you're reading this, then you've been told of my death. More than likely, you've also been informed that I have two other wives. Words cannot express the sorrow I'm suffering now. Of course, that's not true. If I'm dead, then I'm feeling nothing at all.

Never fear, my dear. I am heartsick and deeply ashamed. If it's any consolation, you were the first wife, if you want to refer to yourself as such. But I digress. Please allow me to explain what happened.

Do you recall the kind, young vicar who married us? When he said, "I now pronounce you man" and before he said, "and wife," I was hit by a force—much like a lightning bolt when it slams against a lightning rod.

It reminded me of the day I met you. You were a spectacular vision of loveliness in your shop window. I was riveted. Within days, I had asked you to marry me on a lark. When you said yes, I thought our marriage would be my opportunity to change for the better.

I wanted to make you happy. You seemed eager to be accepted within society. I could provide that entrance for you. It was such a little thing, but I wanted to do that for you.

But alas, we should have never married.

Such a realization couldn't have come at a worse time. We'd just said, "I do." Truly, it was fate playing a cruel and shocking joke on both of us. Not to mention, it was horrible timing. However, I made a gallant attempt as your husband.

Gallant attempt?

He called six hours of marriage in her company *a gallant attempt*?

Absolutely still, Katherine paused in her reading, determined not to divulge the emotions that churned inside her, ripping her heart to pieces. The feat was monumental since the overwhelming urge to scream at the piece of paper in her hands was nigh impossible to ignore.

A horrible nag awoke from a deep sleep and stretched. She'd thought she'd finally rid herself of that vile feeling, but suddenly, its claws were sinking into her once again and drawing deep wounds, the kind that could slice her open. Her shame would be bare to all, and Christian would have a front row seat.

The reproach and degradation she faced as a little girl when others had discovered she didn't have a father roared through her again. They ignored her as if she weren't there. They pitied her, then whispered behind her back. A bastard. A nothing. A whore's spawn. All those names hurt and stripped her of her humanity.

Her stomach tangled into a knot while her cheeks heated in disgrace. The crushing impulse to hide materialized from nowhere.

That was nothing compared to what she had done to herself. She'd ruined her own reputation after her mother's death by being declared a thief.

The inclination to throw the letter in the fire grew, but she refused to act upon it.

Katherine didn't dare glance at Christian, but she felt him studying her, wondering what in the world was going on. How much time had passed? A minute or two? Surely, it hadn't been an hour, though it felt like an eternity in hell. Without looking at the duke, she stood and quietly walked to the window while clutching the letter in her hand so hard that her fingers ached. A heat hotter than Hades rolled through her, causing her cheeks to flame. For a moment, she gently fanned herself with the godforsaken letter.

Christian might have been able to see her turmoil at the table, but if she stood with her back to him, she could hold the shame close and not let it escape.

Katherine faced the private courtyard, where the beautiful view was wasted on her. All she could see was the letter she held in her trembling hands. She blinked once in a desperate attempt to wipe away the dishonor and humiliation that was her due. She didn't ask to be born a bastard. Yet she wore it because it belonged to her.

But the title of thief? She'd earned that all by herself.

The trigamist had left her hours after the ceremony, and he didn't even know the truth about her. But he was correct when he said he saw desire in her eyes. Oh, how she'd wanted to be considered a proper lady who didn't steal or pretend to be someone else.

What would Helen, Constance, and Beth do if her stealing past came to light? Would they protect her like she had protected Meri and his reputation after he'd left? Her heart froze in her chest. What would Christian say? Would he turn his back and not have anything to do with her ever again? If that happened, would it hurt more than the humiliation she had felt when she'd been caught with that apple?

She clutched her fist to her heart, a pitiful attempt to keep the pain from escaping.

Lothario described Meri perfectly. A man who loved many.

But the undeniable fact was that she wasn't any better than her husband. They both lied and pretended to be someone else. He, a supposed honorable lord, had bestowed upon her the title of lady.

And she had proudly used that title to her advantage every day after watching him ride off on his white horse.

His letter was a confession of his sins. After he'd written it, had any of the weight lifted from his shoulders? God, she'd give anything to be free of her burden.

She studied the subtle embroidery on her hem, hoping she could find the strength not to crumble. For God's sake, she didn't want to cry. She willed herself to keep her emotions contained. Eventually, her faithless gaze drifted back to the piece of foolscap in her hand.

Katherine, my darling, when I met the others, I had to marry them. They're beautiful and humorous and women of outstanding character. I hope you meet them one day. I think you all would share a good laugh over our circumstances. Maybe you'd even say something nice about me.

The truth? I just couldn't keep from saying "I do." Who knew that those two words were so addictive?

I did us both a divine favor by leaving. If I'd stayed, I'm afraid I would have wilted like a flower deprived of water. And a wilted flower is so needy and ugly. So, I replanted myself.

Perhaps you can do the same.

I hope you can find it within your heart to forgive me one day. I truly am sorry.

You are a beautiful, successful, and self-assured lady. I have every confidence you'll have a happy life.

Fondly,

M

Without saying a word, she let the letter slip from her fingers. It floated to the ground, much like a feather caught in a gentle breeze.

What a bloody waste of a marriage.

And what a bloody waste of a dream.

She had no one to blame but herself. She was the one who'd damned her own future.

At that moment, she'd give anything to feel a gentle wind across her face because all the air had been sucked out of her. Her chest tightened as if held in a vise, but she managed the incredible feat of bending down and retrieving the letter. Desperate for air, she silently gasped and stuffed the offensive missive in her pocket.

"Kat, what is it? Are you all right?" The alarm in Christian's voice rang across the room.

She couldn't answer, even if she wanted to. She had tamped down her emotions so tightly, she'd lost her voice.

"Kat?" Christian asked gently.

Without taking her leave, she walked out the door, right past the duke, whose eyes had widened.

She had to escape, but one part of the letter kept taunting her with each step she took. If only she could replant herself and bloom as an entirely different person. Never had she wanted that so much as now. She wanted to be someone else, someone who would be worthy of being a friend to the duke.

Tears threatened in earnest this time. Undoubtedly, her cheeks were so red, one would likely have mistaken it as a fever. She didn't even bother collecting her coat from the footman. Instead, she kept right on walking until she disappeared into the nameless London crowds.

She felt as if she'd been stabbed in the heart.

And she had been the one holding the knife.

As soon as Katherine had exited his study, Christian stood. Whether to follow, he hadn't decided yet. Perhaps Katherine left because she was overcome by grief and needed a moment to herself.

He straightened the three packets of receipts for the wives

to give him something to do. Something caught his eye when he looked down. Meri's letter to Katherine lay on the floor, open and inviting. He'd seen her put it in her pocket, but it must have fallen out. He picked it up, then sat at his desk with the paper in hand.

Frankly, he was a bit terrified she might never return after he witnessed her red cheeks and the haunted look in her eyes. He didn't doubt it was another fiasco that Meri had created.

A brisk knock sounded on the door.

Expecting Katherine, Christian called out, "Enter."

"Your Grace?" Wheatley asked in a quivering voice.

Christian dragged his thoughts from Katherine to his butler, who stood sheepishly inside the study. "Where is Lady Meriwether?"

"She left," Wheatley murmured.

"Left the house?"

"Without a word, sir, nor did she take her cloak," offered the butler.

Stunned, Christian blinked. "Did she say where she was going?"

"No, Your Grace," the butler murmured. "When I went to follow, a delivery arrived."

"Have my carriage readied, please," Christian said as he stuffed the letter in her packet. "I'm calling on Lady Meriwether. She forgot some papers." Christian rounded the desk then stopped when he saw the sheer shock on his butler's face. "What is it?"

His butler's Adam's apple bobbed erratically. "You should be aware that another package, a bequest . . . err, some personal property from Lord Meriwether, has arrived from Cumberland for you."

"Put it in the attic—"

A blood-curdling roar echoed through the first floor, followed by another somewhat more subdued growl. The ominous sounds were so disturbing, the birds in the courtyard abandoned their feeders to escape the menace.

"What was that?" Christian asked as he walked toward the door.

"Your Grace, it appears your brother started collecting tigers. There are two in the entry."

Christian stopped.

Without breaking eye contact, the butler straightened his waistcoat and adjusted his cuffs as was his habit when he was nervous. "Apparently, Lord Meriwether favored having an actual tiger ride in the tiger's seat of his yellow curricle instead of a young man."

"For the love of heaven." Christian sighed, then cleared his throat. "Have their cage moved outside into the courtyard. Keep them away from the stables. I'll deal with them when I return."

"They're on . . . a leash." Wheatley's voice grew weaker.

"I'll go out and have a look. Do you think it's safe for a footman to walk them to the courtyard? We can put them somewhere until I finish my call with Lady Meriwether."

"I don't think so. The staff is frightened. They're afraid to move." Little beads of sweat dotted the butler's forehead. "The animals are quite intimidating. Beautiful, but terrorizing. They keep licking their chops." His voice cracked, and he paused for a moment. "I thought if we could have your calming influence, then the footmen and the rest of the staff might be persuaded to move."

"Of course. Come with me." Christian walked out the door toward another snarl coming from the entry. "You were the only one brave enough to leave the entry?"

Wheatley nodded once as he walked beside him. "Yes, sir."

"You're a good man." Christian patted the loyal butler on

his back and offered a smile. “I could have used you over in France.”

Wheatley beamed at the praise until another roar echoed through the entry.

Christian wanted to roar himself. Meri’s mischief was keeping him away from Katherine.

What in the devil was he going to do with tigers?

Chapter Fifteen

Several hours later, after pulling the recalcitrant animals to the courtyard where a suitable cage was hastily erected, Christian stood outside Katherine's town house alone with her cloak folded neatly over one of his arms and the papers in the other. As he waited for someone to answer the door, he prayed Katherine was safe and well.

The door slid open, and a spry woman stood before him. She was dressed elegantly in a spring green gown of the latest fashion.

Christian tipped his hat in acknowledgment. "Is Lady Meriwether available?"

"Which one?" she answered sweetly.

"Katherine."

"Ahh." Her eyes twinkled in merriment. "Come in." She waved him forward.

As soon as Christian stepped through the door, the woman stopped. "I always forget before I let people in. I'm supposed to ask who you are."

"The Duke of Randford at your service." Christian executed a perfect bow.

"You're the charmer." The woman laughed and closed the door.

"The what?" Christian chuckled.

"The one who brought all those beautiful roses." The woman sighed in contentment. "Such glorious color throughout the house. I'm Mrs. Venetia Hopkins, Constance Lysander's aunt." She glanced at the entry clock. Her eyes widened, then she leaned close and lowered her voice. "It's almost two o'clock. Time for our whisky hour," she said sweetly. "Actually, Willa nips the whisky, and I sip sherry. Care to join us?"

"I'm afraid not," Christian answered politely. "I've never been to a whisky hour before, but it sounds appealing."

"You should make time. A tipple is good for your constitution." The woman looked him up and down. "Based upon your size, you must tipple every day."

Christian laughed aloud. Who was this woman? He immediately liked her.

Willa rounded the corner, shaking her head. "Venetia, it's a little early to start imbibing sherry." She leaned close to the older woman and whispered, "Remember what we agreed. When someone's at the door, you can't invite them to join you if you're not acquainted." She chuckled.

Venetia snapped her fingers. "Oh, that's right. Is two o'clock a little early for a tipple?"

"Yes," Willa answered.

Venetia turned her smiling face back to Christian. "Sometimes I say things out of turn."

"We all do, madame," Christian said.

"Now that's settled"—Venetia winked—"would three o'clock work for you?"

"You are incorrigible," Willa scolded with a laugh before she turned to Christian. "Good afternoon, Duke."

"Miss Ferguson," he greeted with a slight bow. "I'm here to see Katherine."

"Her office is on the second floor on the left just past the sitting room." Willa linked her arm with Venetia's and escorted the older woman away.

Christian climbed the stairs to the second floor, where the sitting room's door was ajar. Christian stopped for a quick gander. This was Katherine's domain, and a delightful place it had turned out to be. It was a bright, airy room with colorful chairs and sofas upholstered in red and pink brocades and silk. But what caught his eye were the pillows and bolsters. He couldn't count them all. There had to be at least fifty in various colors decorating the room.

He turned on his heel with a smile. The colors resembled the crisp, deep colors of the gardens at his ancestral seat. He wanted to take her there when everything was in the first bloom of spring. He could imagine her face at the sight of the gardens overflowing with ruby, scarlet, and crimson roses.

In his entire life, it was the first time he'd ever wanted to take a woman to Roseport. It was a special place where he'd spent the happiest times of his childhood. His mother had made certain of that. They'd spent hours in the fields and in the conservatory tending to the roses.

It was the only place he'd ever considered home, and he wanted to share that part of himself with her.

He continued down the hall, then stopped in front of her office door. Through an opening, he could see the bright light of a candle and Katherine bent over her desk, writing. Her cheeks resembled ripe peaches, as if she blushed from the candlelight kissing her face. When she finished, she carefully lifted the quill from the paper and placed it back in its stand.

That was his cue to enter. He gently knocked on the open door.

Katherine lifted her gaze and, immediately, her eyes widened. For a sweet eternity, neither moved nor said a word. Christian drank in the sight of her. A man could easily surrender his soul by staring into the deep pools of golden green that shimmered in the light. If that man were lucky, he'd drown in such a vision. What good was a soul anyway when he could find the promise of heaven in her gaze?

Such was the power of Katherine Greer.

Today, she was no longer Lady Meriwether. She deserved better than his profligate brother.

But the question that still gnawed at Christian's conscience was whether *he* deserved her. There was only one way to find out.

"Hello, Katherine. May I come in?"

Katherine's smile froze when she saw who stood in the doorway. She'd thought it was Willa. Instead, it was Christian who stood before her, looking more handsome and powerful than she'd ever seen him. She shook her head slightly. She had to stop thinking of him that way. Not after today's humiliation. The best course of action was to put distance between them. To even think of him as anything other than an acquaintance was a surefire way of having her heart stomped on once again by another Vareck man and her own past.

The duke's gaze never left hers. As the seconds rolled by, his stare slowly intensified until she could feel layer upon layer of her well-honed defenses being peeled away by his sharp, all-knowing brown eyes. He was too intelligent not to deduce that she'd been dealt a blow that had leveled her confidence.

It was akin to being examined from the inside out. She swallowed slightly but refused to glance away. The exquisite cut of his coat enhanced his aura of power. He was the perfect specimen of a man.

Yet, the dull ache in her chest refused to quiet. Slowly, she rose from her chair, then as casually as possible, she crossed her arms over her chest. "Your Grace, I wasn't expecting you. Is there something you need from me?"

She kept the words polite but without any infliction that would lead him to think she was upset or offended by the letter. It was a skill she'd mastered over the years when others had asked about her father.

"Yes." One side of his mouth tilted upward. "I need to tell you something. Something very important." The effect of his half smile and his eyes flashing with warmth made him appear years younger.

She huffed a breath at the sight.

He closed the door and locked it, then soundlessly crossed the distance between them. "I meant to mention this earlier." He studied the carpet as if gathering his thoughts, then raised his gaze to hers. "I was in awe of what you did for Isabelle."

Her eyes slowly searched his face. "Comforting a little girl who was crying?"

"Yes," he hummed in that deep voice that reached inside and squeezed her heart. "The attention you gave her was lovely. I saw everything." He smiled gently in the afternoon light. "You took time from your day to make a little girl happy." He deepened his voice. "I enjoyed watching you with her. You made her feel wanted."

"Thank you." She glanced at her desk before returning her gaze to his. Heat marched up her cheeks.

He held up the packet of papers. "I thought you might want these." He placed her cloak on a nearby chair, then slid everything across the desk. "I tucked Meriwether's letter into yours."

She closed her eyes at the sight, then forced herself to look at it, though it took a monumental effort. She was a survivor, a fighter, and wouldn't let a piece of foolscap defeat her—not today.

"You found it. I thought I'd lost it on the street." She stared at the folded letter written by her husband—if she could even call the trigamist that. She pulled the missive out and then walked around the desk to the small fireplace where a warm fire blazed. She moved to flick the offending paper into the fire.

"Wait," he said softly. "Before you destroy it, let me speak."

She turned and regarded him. The overpowering desire to crush the letter into a ball was something fierce.

"Your marriage wasn't your fault, but his."

"I take it that you read it?" she asked softly.

He glanced at the letter before returning his attention to her. "No. That's between you and Meri."

Her vision blurred in a haze for a moment. She would not cry. To do so would be her ultimate humiliation and give Meri's words the power to hurt her.

"I didn't think you'd want me to," he said. "However, I can imagine what it said. You see, I take great offense that someone would hurt you. It's doubly infuriating that it was my half brother who wrote those words."

"Why would you care?" She turned her back on him and faced the fire so she could finish her thought without being distracted by his presence. She didn't want to see his response. The truth was, she'd hurt herself by being gullible and not fighting harder in her own defense. "Your opinion is so poor of your brother . . . undoubtedly such disdain must extend to me as his wife."

"Is that what you think?" The astonishment in his voice ricocheted around the room. While she couldn't see him, she could hear the movement of air as he rushed forward. He stopped so close that she could feel the heat radiating from his body. "Look at me," he demanded gently.

She turned and immediately was caught like a moth in a flame at the intensity of his regard. She couldn't move. He hovered over her, one hand on his hip. His expression and everything about him spoke of an iron will and steely determination.

The breadth of his shoulders, his trim waist . . . God, it was unhealthy to think of his body in such terms. Oh, he was a dangerous man, one no woman could keep from admiring, a war hero duke. But to make matters worse, he was a man who oozed masculinity.

A troubled sigh escaped under her breath. How in the world could she resist him?

She couldn't.

"There are two people in this world who I trust enough to call me Christian. Only two, a dear friend and you." He lowered his voice and fisted his hands. "It pains me that because of my half brother's foolish words, distance would come between us. Do you know why it gives me pleasure to hear my name on your lips?"

"No," she said. His gaze locked hers in place. She couldn't have looked away if she wanted to.

He leaned closer. "I value you and your good opinion. I trust you, which puts you in rare company. It makes me furious to think Meriwether could destroy our friendship. He is . . . *was* an imposter."

Which made Meri a perfect husband for her. She blinked twice, fighting against the swell of shame.

"He pretended to be someone honorable, but we both know the extent of his lies."

His deep voice surrounded her in a warmth that reminded her of the finest velvet in her warehouse. The low cadence was comforting and arousing at the same time. To hear such a sound every morning upon waking and at night before drifting off to sleep would be a gift. To feel his heartbeat next to hers every night would be heaven. But that would never happen—not with her own lies. She exhaled, hoping to keep her wits after such thoughts.

"It's beyond infuriating to think that his worthless opinion could hurt you and make you doubt yourself. You have more integrity and decency than any other person I've ever known. I can see those traits in how you care for your employees and their families, not to mention your Willa. I can see it in your action when you took in the other wives." He stilled for a second, but his eyes never blinked. "My half brother was a fool. Any man would be honored to call you his wife."

His words broke a renegade tear free, and she closed her eyes in a sorry attempt to keep it contained. His knuckle wiped it away in the tenderest of touches. Never before had a man touched her with such care and respect. Another rogue tear escaped, and in response, she clasped the fine wool of his lapels in her fists and rested her head against his chest. His arms encircled her, protecting her from the harshness of the world. For the rest of her life she'd remember this moment.

"Have you ever felt shame?" The question broke free before she could think otherwise.

He didn't say anything immediately, then his deep baritone filled the air. "When I was younger. After my mother died, my family became what can only be described as a somewhat unorthodox circus. They were a constant source of shame for me."

Christian's gaze drifted to the London street below, where dusk flirted with the evening. The only reflection in the window was of her holding his lapels as if he were a buoy keeping her afloat.

He turned his attention back to her. "I expect you might feel some shame in my half brother's words. But it's a reflection of his failure, not yours. He didn't do the work necessary for the marriage to succeed." He smiled gently. "There are no guarantees that any of us will experience or even find love in this life. But if we're lucky enough to obtain it, we must protect and nourish it, much like a seedling until it can stand on its own and weather the elements. Love, if allowed to grow, develops deep roots, whether from a father, mother, husband, wife, or even our own children, that will last for a lifetime and beyond."

"Your Grace. If I didn't know you better, I'd believe you're a romantic, much like Lord Byron, or perhaps Shelley."

"Byron only thinks of himself, while Shelley only loves himself," he scoffed. "Neither are romantics in my opinion." He shocked her by bending down and pressing his lips against her skin where a tear stood suspended, refusing to fall down her cheek. Still holding her, he leaned away and grinned like a wicked rogue. "I admit I surprise myself sometimes."

Underneath his gruffness was a man who possessed the ability to feel deeply. Whoever married him would find herself in a love affair that would last a lifetime.

But she couldn't think of that now. She'd not think of another woman in his arms. Not when he held her so close. He was giving her a moment in time, one she'd cherish forever. A brief respite from the ugliness that shadowed her.

This time when their gazes met, something changed. It was as if they were building a path, stone by stone, between them. Kat had no idea where it would lead them, but she wanted to follow it.

Unable to resist, Kat tugged his coat gently, urging him toward her. When he complied, she balanced herself on the balls of her feet to meet him. His eyes never left hers as she tilted her mouth. With the gentlest of touches, she brushed her lips against his in the same manner as he'd done in the conservatory that very afternoon.

A deep groan vibrated in his chest at her touch, but she wouldn't give him any quarter. She wanted to kiss him repeatedly until he understood what he meant to her.

"Thank you," she murmured.

"Say my name," he demanded softly. "Don't let that intimacy be stolen from us."

"Christian." Her voice had softened with desire, and she repeated it. "Christian, let me kiss you."

"Yes." His whisper buried deep within her, unleashing a want she'd never felt for another before.

She pressed her lips against his and allowed the kiss to evolve on its own. He pulled her tighter into his embrace, all the while holding her steady. In turn, she wrapped her hands around his neck. His long hair was softer than she'd ever dreamed. Unable to keep from touching him, she played with his locks as they slid through her fingers like black silk.

Emboldened, she gently nibbled on his full lower lip. It was like the finest velvet. She licked the seam of his mouth. In response, he exhaled, and she swept her tongue inside.

As they explored what each liked, they held each other tighter, both unwilling to let the other go. Unhurried, he mated his tongue with hers. His hands skated down her back much like a waltz. Two slides down, and one slide up. This continued until one hand rested on her lower back.

He leaned back and his gaze drank in her features, slowly and methodically before he closed the inches between them. It was his turn to kiss her. At first it was gentle but grew demanding and possessive. Her thoughts whirled, and she realized that for the first time in her life, she was experiencing real passion with a man who wanted her as much as she wanted him.

It was seduction at its finest. And she didn't care that it was her doing the seducing. Or was it him? It didn't matter. Only this moment mattered.

Christian pulled her close, pressing her lower body against his. Through the layers of clothing, she could feel his hard length where heat pulsed. Pure male power surrounded her. He wanted her. A familiar wetness grew between her legs, and she moaned. It always happened when she thought of them embracing like this.

His kiss turned urgent, as if he were claiming her, marking her as his. Just as she'd imagined doing the same with him. Honestly, she imagined lots of things besides kissing Christian. She fantasized about them in bed making love. It would be glorious to kiss every inch of his body while she explored. His body was like a tapestry, and she'd take her time admiring every inch of him.

His hands continued to roam her body until she put her hand on top of his, then slowly pulled her skirt up. He broke the kiss, and his gaze turned tender. She smiled in answer, all the while pulling her gown up.

"No one will intrude. Willa's warned everyone to stay away when my door is closed."

"I hope you pay that woman enough for her sound judgment. However, I locked the door behind me," he murmured, then stole a kiss.

Katherine laughed gently against his lips. Without warning, he picked her up in his arms and carried her to a slipper chair that sat in front of the fire. With her gown bunched around her hips, she should have felt like a harlot; instead, she had never felt more beautiful.

The look on his face confirmed it. He dropped to his knees between her legs. His hands gently traced the curve of her calves. When he reached the top of her knees, he stopped. "What are your intentions toward me?"

"I'm not certain I understand." She wiggled, wanting him to continue touching her.

"I don't think we should do anything the other is not

comfortable with. I must be honest, I've imagined all sorts of wonderful things between us." He swept his fingers across her cheek, the touch tender and caring. "But I don't think we're ready for that yet, do you?"

She chewed her lip. His gaze darted to her mouth. He was right. She wasn't ready to make love with him, no matter what her fantasies were. "You're right, but I'd like to explore this attraction between us."

"I would also, but I want you to be comfortable with me." With his thumb, he traced her bottom lip. "May I touch you?"

She nodded.

He took her mouth with his in the gentlest of kisses as his hands skated across her thighs. She widened her legs. Katherine gasped at the heavenly sensation. But Christian didn't stop either his kisses or his seduction. His lips trailed down her throat, and Katherine was helpless to do anything but tilt her neck for his ease. He tongued the indentation at the base of her neck, then kissed the top of her cleavage.

Her breathing became even more erratic. She closed her eyes when he slipped his tongue between her breasts. But he made no moves to strip away her gown. She moaned again, thinking of him touching and kissing her bare breasts and nipples.

But he turned his attention elsewhere. With infinite slowness, he pushed her skirts even higher. His rapid inhalation at the sight of her clocked stockings pulled all sorts of feminine strings that made her heart jangle in her chest. His hands against her thighs was a study in contrasts. While her stockings were ivory, his hands were colored by the sun, and the hair on his wrists was jet black. She laid her hands on his, bringing them to her most intimate place, encouraging him to continue his caresses.

Soon, he parted her cleft, then stroked her with two fingers, his touch sure but gentle at the same time. The languid rhythm of his movement kept time with his kisses.

His lips trailed to the tender spot below her ear. One finger circled the nub where all sensation seemed to have settled. "What would you think if I put my mouth here and tasted you?"

Christian didn't move as he waited for her answer.

She tongued the same sensitive spot below his ear, then whispered, "I'd like that."

With a wicked smile, he bent down, then kissed her *there*. A soft growl erupted from his throat and vibrated through her. The sound was so masculine and primeval, she trembled in response. His tongue wove itself back and forth across the sensitive peak, drawing a need within her for more. With another groan, he lapped at her wetness. She shamelessly tilted her hips, demanding more.

His concentration centered on the nub, where her pleasure was the greatest. He changed the pressure of his tongue against her slickness every so often, making her body clench and tighten in preparation for something. He entwined his fingers with hers, the touch incredibly tender. She had a hard time concentrating as the tension increased. He extracted the most delicate tingles, each one building on the other. She didn't know if she was going to fly to the heavens or break apart into a million pieces.

Any of it was fine as long as Christian was there with her.

"Tell me if I'm pleasing you," he whispered, looking at her.

She nodded.

"Are you ready to come?"

"Are you?" In fairness, she pulled him forward and pressed a kiss against his lips. The taste of her was still on his mouth. She'd never done anything this forbidden in her life.

And she wanted more.

"Hmm," he moaned in response. "I think you should find your pleasure first."

Katherine shook her head, then coaxed him to stand before her, putting his falls at her eye level. "I want to play some more." She tilted her head and captured his gaze. "I'd like to touch you now, but only if you're comfortable with me."

He pulled away and stared at her. The look of shock on his face melted away as his eyes blazed with a molten heat that sent more fire flowing through her veins. Without a word, he kissed her again tenderly on the lips, then whispered, "I'd like that."

Katherine slowly unbuttoned the falls of his breeches as he watched her. His eyes smoldered, and he never looked away as he made quick work of untying his cravat.

In that moment, she was thankful she had kept a book of Meriwether's erotic poems instead of burning it. One poem had been quite graphic about how to pleasure a man.

She let out a tremulous breath as she waited. He pulled his shirt from his waistband, and immediately his member sprang forward.

The crown glistened with his leaked seed. With such a resplendent display, she couldn't help but moan softly. She cupped him in her hands and pressed a kiss to the head. He tasted of salt and musk. Without hesitating, she circled her tongue around him, desperate to savor every drop.

He slipped his fingers into her hair, then cupped both sides of her head to hold her in place. "Lick me."

She rubbed a cheek against him and smiled, then ran her tongue along the length of him. He was all male—hard, hot, and wet. Holding him in the palm of her hand, she slowly exhaled and took him in her mouth, circling her tongue around him again and again.

"Katherine," he whispered. His breathing grew labored, and she relished the effect she was having on him.

Over and over, she explored his length with her mouth. When she took him deeper, he gently removed his hands from her head and stepped backward. "I'll come if you continue to do that." A rueful smile broke across his beautiful mouth. "I haven't been with a woman in . . . years."

"Oh." Instead of a witty and sensuous response that a siren would say to her lover, it was the only word Katherine could think to utter until she blurted, "Would you be comfortable if we touched our own bodies as we watched each other?"

"What?" His eyes widened.

"I . . . I read about it in a book of erotic poems once." She straightened slightly but refused to look away.

Time stood still until a wicked smile graced his lips. "You do have a creative mind, Kat."

He knelt on the floor in front of her, then made a fist around his length and moved it up and down. The act so wicked and lewd, she'd never been so excited in her life at such a sight. But the hungry look on his face as he watched her made the room spin.

"Let me see you touch yourself," he whispered.

Closing her eyes, she reached between her legs and slipped her fingers through her wetness. Her body hummed with pleasure as she found her body clenching and tightening in response.

As she kept stroking herself, Katherine watched Christian's face transform into a hundred expressions. Hunger, want, desire, heat, possession. All of it was pure heaven. She imagined him inside her, driving and pounding as they both found their releases.

Christian gripped his cock while he rubbed his thumb against the wet crown. He reached over and kissed her again while he ran his fingers through her wetness. At his touch, she gasped.

"I want a part of you on me when I come," he whispered. He took her essence and rubbed it on his cock. He grasped his member, then moved his fist up and down, gaining speed. His gaze never left hers. The heat between them sparked, and she'd never felt so alive.

In concert, they increased their pace, ready to find their pleasure.

Katherine's body had started its spiral to oblivion. The sensation quickened as she watched Christian pleasure himself. Unable to hold his gaze, she leaned her head against the back of the chair as her body tightened in orgasm. She closed her eyes as a thousand shards of light burst through her vision. She couldn't catch her breath, but she continued to gently rub her center as she slowly fell back to earth like a feather in the air.

"Katherine, look at me," Christian growled softly.

It took a Herculean effort, but she lifted her head. His eyes bore through hers, and his face slowly grew taut. One muscle in the side of his jaw twitched. His fist worked harder and harder, and she could tell he was close. Within seconds, he leaned his head toward the ceiling and opened his mouth in a silent scream.

In a flash, he put his cravat over his cock as he spilled his seed. The raw power of his release seemed to reverberate through the room.

He sat motionless, then lowered his head as he gained control of his body again.

It was humbling and the most beautiful thing she'd ever witnessed in her life. He stood slowly, and Katherine rose when he held out his arms. He pulled her close, then kissed her as if this were their last hour on earth.

Finally, when their heartbeats returned to normal, he swept her into his arms, then seated himself in the slipper chair with her reclining on his lap. They stayed that way as they both caught their breath. In a paradise of their own making, she was nestled by his side with his arm around her.

He exhaled with a deep sigh. "I've never in my life done anything like that before."

The glow from her own release had started to fade. Silence settled around them. Neither spoke, and for a moment, she thought he might regret what they'd done. "I haven't either."

He turned his attention back to her face and brushed his fingers across her cheek, where an unruly lock of hair had escaped the confines of her simple chignon. After he pushed it behind her ear, he continued to caress her. "You never did anything like that with your husband?"

Automatically, she tensed at the reference to Meri. "Never. Nor did I want to." Immediately, she regretted saying such a thing, but he smiled gently.

He bent down and brushed his lips against hers in reassurance. "Come. Let's set ourselves to right. We can't let your Willa find a way to unlock the door and catch us in such shocking dishabille."

She stood, and he followed. With a tender touch, he helped straighten her skirt and bodice, then fiddled with several lost curls. Only then did he tuck his shirt in and button his falls.

It wasn't embarrassment that stole between them, but the awkwardness of what to say next that kept her silent. Christian must have sensed it too. He reached for his soiled cravat, then stuffed it in his pocket before he smoothed his hands over his coat. Only then did he look at her.

"Would you like to come to my house tomorrow and finish going through my brother's papers and other personal items?"

"I'm done with all of that." Then as if to ensure he understood, she rephrased it. "I'm finished with him."

Christian stared at her, not saying a word, but his gaze questioned if she was certain of her decision. With her resolute silence, she convinced him she was serious. His shoulders relaxed, and he nodded.

Without a word, he picked up his hat from the side table, then moved toward the door. He unlocked it and turned to her once again.

"I wasn't going to say this, but I changed my mind. A duke's prerogative, so to speak." He exhaled deeply. "I'm glad you're finished. If he'd lived, he would have never come to appreciate your beauty and your grace." He turned and grasped the handle, then hesitated. He dipped his head and regarded her. His heavy lids didn't hide the brilliance of his eyes. "It would be remiss of me not to say one more thing."

"What's that?" she asked.

"You're breathtaking when you come," he said softly. "I've never seen a more exquisite sight."

Before she could answer or even react, he was gone.

In his wake, the room grew quiet. Her heart swelled with an admission dredged from a place that defied all logic and reason. She had fallen in love with Christian tonight.

Nothing good would come from it except the folly of heartache.

Chapter Sixteen

The following day, Christian sat at his desk reading a letter from Sykeston. Wheatley knocked on the open door and entered.

If another bequest from Meri had arrived, Christian would simply refuse it.

"Pardon me, Your Grace," Wheatley said. Sweat glistened across his brow. "An urgent message has arrived that needs your attention."

Christian cocked an eyebrow. In his entire life of living at Rand House, he could not recall a time when his butler had interrupted him in such a harried tone of voice.

Panting as if he'd run a race, Morgan suddenly appeared beside Wheatley. "Captain, if I might have a word?"

Christian stood immediately and walked around the desk. Today was his valet's normal day to shop on Bond Street. If Morgan had foregone the trip, then it must be something dire.

Christian motioned for the door to be shut. "What is it?" he asked.

Wheatley closed the door, and his valet pursed his lips, then handed a note to Christian. "It's from Willa. She says Lady Meriwether needs you now."

"Is she all right? Do you know what has happened?" Christian asked as he took the note. A burst of nervous energy accompanied by a thrum of unease overtook him. Much like what he experienced when he was about to lead his men into battle.

Morgan shook his head. "Willa's note is very vague. I took the liberty of ordering your carriage."

"That'll take too much time. I can walk there before they even have the horses completely harnessed."

"I'll accompany you," Morgan offered.

Christian nodded. On the way out, he refused the great coat that Wheatley held out to him. Once he reached the street, he turned left and started toward Katherine's town house. After two steps, he cursed, then started to run.

He couldn't have cared less when two of society's most influential matrons dropped their jaws and halted their walk as they saw him running at full speed through the streets of London. Having his one-eyed valet beside him keeping pace probably added to their shock.

They'd have fainted on the spot if they'd seen him in battle. Nothing kept him from protecting his men.

Now, nothing would keep him from protecting Katherine.

He only slowed down once he reached her front walk. The two blocks shouldn't have been too strenuous, but he was breathing heavily as his heart had already been pounding in alarm when he left Rand House. Morgan tried to catch his breath as he knocked on the door. Immediately, Beth opened it and waved them inside.

"What's happened? Is it Katherine?" Christian's heart was ready to burst through his ribs.

"No, it's Constance." She closed the door.

He and Morgan followed her into the sitting room where he'd first met the wives.

"Katherine." As soon as her name escaped Christian's lips, she turned and ran to him. He held out his arms to embrace her, but instead, she took one of his hands in hers and squeezed.

Of course, they were back to formal appearances in front of others.

She dipped a deep curtsey. "Your Grace, thank you for coming."

A week ago, he would have accepted it as a proper greeting, but after yesterday, this formal air between them could not continue. Obviously, something had upset her since the normal brightness in her eyes had dulled.

Morgan nodded at the ladies, then turned to Katherine. "My lady, shall I find Willa?"

"Thank you, Mr. Morgan," she said gently. "Willa has had little sleep and some added chores this morning. I'm afraid she's tiring. Any help you could give her would be a favor to me."

Morgan nodded, then stepped toward the kitchens.

"Is Constance all right? The baby?" he asked in rapid succession. Things had to be dire with Constance if both Katherine and Beth were away from work.

"Constance may be having the baby." Lines of worry marred Katherine's eyes. "I thought you needed to be here."

"You did the right thing," he said.

Katherine turned to the stranger. "Your Grace, may I present Mrs. Love? She's a midwife I've hired to help."

The woman dipped a curtsey.

"Mrs. Love." Christian nodded.

The midwife didn't bat an eye his way as her attention turned to Kat and Beth. "As I was saying, I'm not certain the baby will be born yet, but each birth is different." Her lips turned down in a slight frown. "However, I don't like the way the babe is resting. It's too early for it to have dropped so low in Miss Lysander's belly. That's what makes me think she could possibly deliver within the week."

"Too early," Katherine repeated, as if trying to get the words to sink in. "Is there anything we can do to help her?"

The midwife nodded. "She should stay in bed until the babe decides to make his appearance in the world."

"You think it's a boy?" Christian asked.

"I've never seen a baby girl anxious to escape its mother's womb. It's always the baby boys." She grinned. "We have to keep the mother-to-be comfortable and nourished."

"We'll keep her in bed," Kat promised.

"Willa and Venetia can stay with her during the day and make certain she eats. I can stay with her at night," Beth declared.

"You know where to find me if there's trouble." The midwife put on her hat and coat. "The pains she's having might be real, or they might be an exercise for the body to prepare itself for the birth."

Both Katherine and Beth walked Mrs. Love to the back door, and Christian overheard the midwife promise to check on Constance every day. After goodbyes were exchanged, they came back to his side.

Beth regarded him without any hint of emotion. "Mrs. Love is one of the most talented, not to mention successful, midwives in all of London. Even if she comes through the back entrance, if anyone recognizes her, then the proverbial cat is out of the bag."

"Meaning?" Christian asked.

Katherine huffed out a shallow breath. "Meaning, neighbors will come calling to find out who is having a baby. Then the talk will start, and we won't be able to keep quiet about

Lord Meriwether's marriages." She turned to Beth. "I'll help you with Constance."

Beth took her hands in her own. "Concentrate on your winning the Prince Regent's contract and the duke's charity. You've been so generous already. However, I think we should be better informed of your schedule in case something happens . . ."

She didn't finish her thought, as they all knew what she was saying—if something happened to Constance and her babe.

"I'll also send you mine," Christian offered. "I could take a turn sitting with her."

Katherine smiled slightly. "Thank you. But only if it becomes too much for all of us."

Beth looked toward the stairs. "I should go to her now. I know Aunt Vee is probably worried sick."

"I'll be up shortly," Katherine said.

Beth nodded at Christian, then took the stairs.

"Aunt Vee?" Christian asked after she departed.

Katherine nodded. "That's Constance's aunt who traveled with her from Portsmouth. She's staying with me also."

"Aha. Venetia. She's the one who let me into your house yesterday." He didn't miss the sudden blush that colored her cheeks at the mention of last night. "Katherine—"

"Your Grace, would you accompany me upstairs to my study?" Her voice was all business. "We must talk."

With his hands clasped behind his back, he leaned forward and lowered his voice. "I adore it when you take charge."

She dipped her head, but he still caught the beautiful smile that graced her lips.

"Just like you did yesterday," Christian murmured.

Without saying a word, Katherine led him upstairs to the second floor. With each step, her delightful backside swung with a perfect rhythm. His palm itched to reach out and touch her. Before his thoughts became too outlandish, they arrived at her study.

As soon as they were inside, she closed the door, then sat behind the Louis XV turquoise and gold gilt desk. "Shall I ask Willa to bring us tea?"

"No. But if you have any whisky, I would appreciate one." Christian took the chair opposite her desk and inhaled. Her signature violet perfume filled the room unobtrusively. Immediately, he felt himself harden. Last night, the room had smelled differently. Her violet and musky scent of arousal had combined into a mind-altering fragrance that had brought him to his knees—literally.

For all his days, it would be a scent he would never tire of, and one he'd always remember, along with the elegantly appointed room. It suited Katherine.

How would Rand House suit her? Most likely, it would suit her like her business. She'd manage it with an aplomb and grace that would rival any past Duchess of Randford.

From a bottle on the side table, she poured a fingerful of whisky, then brought it to him. Within seconds, she started to pace.

He stood and placed his untouched drink on the drum table, then reached her side. Gently, he held her upper arms to stop her frantic to and fro movements. "What can I do to help? Hire full-time nurses?"

"No. That could be even more damaging. What if they talked?" She blinked, and the worry clouded her beautiful hazel eyes. "We have to keep this quiet for now."

"I could ask several of the maids over at Rand House to help you and Willa," he offered. "At least a full-time cook?"

She twisted her hands, then dropped them when she realized he was watching. It was a tell that she was unsettled. "No. I want to keep it contained to just us."

Christian studied her face. What he wouldn't do to take this concern from her. "Keeping things quiet is one thing, but eventually the child will be born and people will know what happened," he said gently. "You don't have to do this alone."

"I'm aware of that." She reached for a small square pillow with a heart embroidered on it and hugged it to her chest. "I'm worried about Constance and Beth. I'm also a little worried about the secretary's visit." She shook her head slightly, upsetting two curls.

"What is that? A keepsake?" he asked softly as he pushed the wayward locks back into place.

She handed the pillow to him. "A little something my mother gave to me when I was a little girl. She said it holds all her love for me." Her gaze settled on the pillow. "It's silly, but I find great comfort in it when I'm troubled."

"It's not silly at all." He traced the small red heart on the pillow. "Your mother sounds as if she was wonderful." He returned it to her, and she put it on the desk.

She swallowed and blinked rapidly, trying to keep her emotions in check.

He couldn't help but cup her cheek in his palm. The recalcitrant pounding in his chest urged him to take her in his arms and never let her go. But he forced himself to stay in place. "Kat," he whispered her name like a solemn vow. "Don't keep everything to yourself."

"It's hard to let go when you've been on your own for so long." She stepped away, then started to pace again. After one pass, she stopped. "Have you heard from Lord Sykeston?"

He came to her side and took her hands, encouraging her to look at him. When she tilted her head, he was blinded by the resolve in their depths. "I just received a letter from him. He's coming to town, but he didn't mention anything about Constance. I think our posts crossed on the road. I've sent a reply to his London house, asking him to meet both me and

Lord Grayson at the Marquess and Marchioness of Halverton's soiree tomorrow evening. It'll be safer there. Halverton has a private room for us. No one will suspect anything if the three of us disappear for a while."

"Who is Lord Grayson?"

"He's my closest friend and a friend to Sykeston. He knows what Meri's done and wants to be there to help."

She drew away, then sat on the small sofa before the fireplace, where the flame's shadows kissed her cheeks.

Which was exactly what he wanted to do to her.

"Lord Sykeston has to agree," Katherine said. "Constance needs a husband before her baby is born."

He put the thought of kisses aside—for now. "I'll do my best."

Christian eased himself onto the sofa beside her. He took her hand and threaded their fingers together. Whether it was a sign that he considered her his or that he'd be her champion, it didn't make any difference. It felt right to be touching here in the study. He was fast coming to the conclusion that he would always enjoy touching her, no matter where they were.

"The earl mustn't mind caring for another man's child, and I don't think he will," he mused quietly. He picked up his discarded whisky and swallowed it in one gulp.

"I want to make one thing clear." Ramrod straight, she sat on the edge of her seat. "I don't need a husband."

Christian put his glass down with deliberate care. Katherine could see the wheels turning in his mind. He eased himself against the back of the sofa.

"I didn't plan on offering you to anyone." A half smile formed across his full mouth, and his eyes twinkled in jest. "But I appreciate your candor." He stretched out his legs. The movement so effortlessly smooth, he looked completely at home.

Immediately, her tension evaporated. His familiarity and playfulness brought a succor she sorely needed. "I sound like a . . ." She let out a sigh.

"A woman who's worried about her friend," he added softly.

"I was going to say shrew." She couldn't help but laugh.

He didn't join in but regarded her with a seriousness that made her squirm slightly. He saw too much with that brown-eyed gaze of his.

"Let me give you money for the care of Miss Howell, Miss Lysander, and her aunt. I don't feel right otherwise. The least you can do is give me the benefit of thinking I'm helping. It has to be costing you a pretty penny to keep three additional people under your care."

"Thank you, but no." She clasped her hands. "I don't need help." She hadn't needed help from anyone after she left York, and she wouldn't start now.

Christian examined her as he always did when he didn't like her answer. With a flick of an eyebrow, he thought to press her into accepting his offer. Defiantly, she refused to look away.

"Always the independent woman, aren't you, Katherine? Does this trait come from your years in York, or did you inherit it from your mother?" He smiled gently. "Perhaps your father."

She clenched her hands tighter. Without looking down, she could tell her knuckles were turning white. "How did you know I was from York?"

"I made the assumption from the rose on your handkerchief."

For a moment, her lungs refused to work as she struggled

for a response. If Christian made that assumption, then Marlen Skeats would make that leap of logic too. He knew embroidery patterns and where they came from.

"Well, we were a typical York family." *What a bouncer.* Could a person go to hell for lying? "My father traveled for business quite a bit. He was lost at sea. My mother never remarried."

Better to experience an afterlife fanning the flames for Lucifer than forego the horror and pity that undoubtedly would cross Christian's face if she told him the truth.

"Do you or Willa perchance know how to make Yorkshire pudding? Could you teach my cook?" When he grinned like that, he looked like a young lad, one who no doubt had charmed all the cooks in the kitchen to give him extra treats.

"Both of us do, and we'd be pleased to share our recipe." Waves of relief spread through her at his change of subject.

Christian took her hand and raised it to his mouth. He pressed his lips against the skin before turning it over and pressing a kiss to the inside of her wrist. "I should go." He dropped her hand and stood. "Walk me to the door?"

She placed her hand on his outstretched arm. His forearm muscles twitched under her touch, reminding her that he was not only honorable, but a vibrant, perfect specimen of a man whom she desperately wanted.

Before she could finish the thought, they arrived at the door. Christian swept her into his arms and kissed her until she moaned in pleasure.

"I've wanted to do that since I left you last night," he murmured against her lips. "All I've thought about today is you and me in this very room." He nuzzled the side of her neck with his nose before pressing a reverent kiss on the tender skin below her ear.

"That's all I've thought about too," Katherine answered.

She pulled back and absently played with the buttons on his jacket. "Do you trust Lord Sykeston?"

"With my life. He's a good man."

"I can't help but wonder if he'll marry her willingly. What if he says no?"

"We'll think of something else. Don't worry yet." He pressed his lips against her forehead. "Keep the faith, Kat. Sykeston owes me a favor, so he'll at least listen to Constance's request."

She shouldn't ask, but curiosity got the better of her. "What does he owe you?"

"Everything," he answered. "He owes me his life."

Chapter Seventeen

The next evening, Christian stood overlooking Lord and Lady Halverton's ballroom. For a small soiree, there seemed to be close to two hundred people below. He reached into the pocket of his evening coat and retrieved the piece of paper he'd untacked from the family portrait. Its location had been his father's face.

For some odd reason, his usual loathing of his family and the enjoyment he experienced when he placed a new pin through his father or stepmother had diminished. It was as if those ever-present feelings had faded in importance.

Only to be replaced with Katherine. He wished she were here. Having her near would be a comfort in and of itself. He turned his attention to the paper where he'd penned a single word: *Sykeston.*

After his sister had married, Sykeston felt his patriotic duty required he join the war effort. Able to speak perfect French and German without any accent, the earl had traveled between British army camps with little interference. When he'd decided to return home after learning of his sister's death, he'd been ambushed on his way out of camp.

His leg had been shot and mangled in the process. Unable to walk, Sykeston's death was guaranteed as the snipers were still shooting.

When they ceased fire to reload, Christian had galloped to him and swung Sykeston onto his horse behind him. A bellow, an ungodly sound that could only come from the hell of war, had exploded from his friend when he'd picked him up off the ground. It still rang clear in Christian's memory.

Steps sounded behind him. One was a steady pace, and the other was an uneven gait accompanied by a walking stick. Without investigating, Christian could identify who was approaching.

"Randford," called out Jonathan Eaton, the Earl of Sykeston.

Christian turned around.

The Marquess of Grayson held out his hand first. Christian clasped it tightly, and both men clapped the other on the shoulder.

"Thank you for coming with him," Christian said to Grayson. He turned his gaze to Sykeston and held out his hand. "Sykeston."

The earl transferred his ebony walking stick to the other hand, then reached for Christian's. Though they didn't clap each other on the back, Sykeston nodded with a look of respect. It spoke volumes. They were still friends, though they hadn't communicated with each other after they had come home.

"It's good to see you healthy," Christian offered.

"If you call this healthy," Sykeston quipped as he glanced at his leg.

Christian hesitated a moment. The earl was prickly about his permanently injured leg. "But you're here."

Sykeston nodded. "And lucky to be alive."

Grayson sighed slightly. "Indeed."

The earl looked askance in Christian's direction. "Tell me what's so urgent that we needed to meet tonight." His lips curled downward. "At a soiree?"

"I thought it safer to meet here than at my home." Without waiting for an answer, Christian locked the door. He led the way to a small salon not far from the balcony. Framing the fireplace, two small sofas faced each other. The earl and the marquess sat beside each other on one, while Christian poured three glasses of whisky. He sat on the opposite sofa.

Sykeston appeared at ease, which would hopefully work in Christian's favor when he made his unusual request. Christian raised his glass in the air, and the other men joined him. When they downed their spirits, Grayson leaned against the sofa.

Sykeston wasn't as nonchalant. "Though I was invited here tonight, I wasn't planning on attending. I normally wouldn't set foot in any place where there was music and dancing occurring, but with your summons, I couldn't refuse. What's this about, Randford? You're not recruiting me and Grayson for some spy mission, are you?"

Grayson leaned forward and rested his elbows on his knees with an intense look on his face. "I'm here for moral support."

"For whom?" Sykeston shot him an askance glare. "Randford or me?"

Christian shook his head. "The reason I called you here today is personal. I saved your life once, and now I need your help."

Sykeston nodded once for him to proceed.

"It's dire." How to explain he needed the earl to save Constance and her soon-to-be born child from ruin because of his brother's selfishness? "What I have to say cannot leave this room."

Sykeston nodded again, then frowned slightly at Grayson's audible exhale. "Do you know what this is about?"

Grayson nodded.

The earl returned his curt gaze to Christian. "Don't leave me in suspense."

"My late departed half brother did something unforgiveable." Christian swallowed, hoping to rid himself of the vile taste in his mouth. It always happened when he was embarking on cleaning up one of his half brother's messes. "He married three women. One is carrying his child. All three wives are vulnerable. No one knows, and I'm hoping you will marry one."

Sykeston's face remained expressionless.

After a long bout of silence, Grayson was the first to speak. "Go on. Tell him all of it."

The earl's intelligence was as sharp and accurate as his renowned marksman skills. How fortunate for Christian that he didn't carry any weapons on him tonight because the expression on the earl's face was—to put it kindly—murderous.

"I need your help, Jonathan. Through the tragedies and horrors we've been through together, I've come to know and consider you a friend. I know you're a good man, and I don't want this woman to suffer because of my half brother's deeds." He lowered his voice. "She's a wonderful woman."

Sykeston's face visibly paled. "Constance Lysander married your brother. Who's the one you want me to marry?"

"How did you know about Miss Lysander?" Christian's shock reverberated around the room. If Sykeston knew, could there possibly be others in the outlying areas of England that were aware of his brother's polygamy?

"She's from Portsmouth." Sykeston pursed his lips. "I've known her since she was a young girl. The Lysander family is wealthy and well-known in the area. Constance is . . . special. She would have been a good match for any man."

"She's his second wife, and Miss Beth Howell is his third," Christian said.

Sykeston's face visibly paled. "Who did he marry first?"

"The former Katherine Greer from York," Christian confided.

Grayson leaned against the sofa then pinched the bridge of his nose. "Beth Howell is also a fine woman. *Christ.* I don't even know what to say, and I've heard the story before. If there's anything I can do . . ." His words trailed to nothing.

Christian shrugged slightly. "My half brother received all three dowries, and I speculate he spent the money on racing. I have my solicitor looking for the remnants of it if any exists. Even if I don't find it, I'll make the marriage worth your while."

Lost in his thoughts, Grayson stared at the floor.

The earl stood with the help of his cane, then with some stiffness, walked to stare out a window.

Out of the corner of his eye, Christian noticed the earl gently tapping the foot of his good leg on the thick carpet. The movement reminded Christian of one a predator would make before it attacked.

"I wasn't aware of the situation," Sykeston said without any emotion in his voice. "If I'd found your brother while he was still alive, I would have challenged him, then killed him . . . without regard to you."

Christian's blood ran cold. Rumor had it the earl had challenged his deceased sister's husband over her death. There were no formal enquiries as Sykeston had friends in high places. If he had challenged Meri, his brother would have faced certain death on a dueling field. "What exactly is your relationship with Miss Lysander?"

Sykeston stood silent a moment longer before answering. "She is . . . was a family friend."

No one said a word.

"Would you marry her?" Christian asked quietly. "She's

about to give birth. She's staying at Lady Meriwether's home along with Miss Howell."

"Why don't you marry her?" Sykeston turned and stared at Christian.

The truth was, when Christian thought of a wife, he imagined Katherine.

"She didn't ask me." Christian lowered his voice. "She wants to marry you. She asked if I would approach *you*. If you can't bring yourself to marry her, I understand, but I promised Constance I would speak with you."

"After all these years," Sykeston murmured. For minutes, he stared out the window.

Whatever history Sykeston and Constance shared, it had to have been something rare. The earl never expressed any interest in marriage, women, or society in general.

"What about my heir?" Sykeston asked as he turned toward Christian.

"You could marry Constance by special license after she gives birth. If the babe is a girl, you can claim her as your own and say she was born after the marriage. If it's a boy, then we'll deal with the consequences. I'll pay for the child's expenses."

"But society will think that I cuckolded your brother."

"Perhaps," Christian answered. "They'll know he left her shortly after the marriage." He leaned forward and let the glass dangle from his fingers as he captured Sykeston's gaze. "More than likely, they'll think you came to comfort her, and you and she developed a tendre for each other."

The earl offered a lifted brow. "Me?" He waved his hand down his injured leg. "If they believe that, then they're more ignorant than I give them credit for."

"Constance said you were old friends." Christian stood and locked his gaze with the earl's. "Why wouldn't people believe you both desired this marriage?"

Sykeston turned back to the window. The simple fact the earl hadn't dismissed his suggestion outright gave him hope.

"I'm asking a tremendous favor, so anything I can do to help you personally is worth it to me." Christian refilled his glass and took another sip.

Sykeston still stood by the window, completely ignoring what he'd said.

Christian walked to his side and placed his hand on his friend's shoulder to garner his attention. "I'll replace her lost dowry. Will that help?"

The earl shook his head slightly as if coming out of dream. "I don't need the money. I'll marry her"—the earl dropped his voice—"before the babe is born."

Christian offered his hand, and the earl shook it.

"I must return to Portsmouth for some urgent business," Sykeston said.

"She may give birth any day now." Christian released the earl's hand.

"I'll hurry." Without another word, the earl turned and slowly walked from the room. Once he reached the marbled hallway, the tap of his cane faded slowly out of earshot.

"He's in a mood this evening." Grayson's gaze followed the earl's slow gait. "He was off his game when he arrived. He hates these social events. I'll leave with him." The marquess nodded at Christian, then followed the earl.

Christian released a breath, then relaxed his shoulders for the first time this evening.

It was done.

Chapter Eighteen

"Here we are." Kat opened the door to the boutique and escorted Mr. Edwin Sherman, the Secretary to the First Lady of the Bedchamber, into Greer's Emporium. The shop was spotless after she'd spent the morning tidying and cleaning the place herself. The windows sparkled and the linens were artfully arranged in the main showroom so he could evaluate each design that she offered.

In his mid-thirties, thin, and rather tall, Mr. Sherman glanced around the room. "May I wander on my own for a moment or two?"

"Please do," Kat answered. As soon as he turned from her, she brushed her sweaty palms down her dress. They'd visited the workshop before coming here. Thank heavens for Beth. She'd had the place perfectly arranged, and Kat's employees were working on a wide variety of projects so he could evaluate the work-in-progress. Each station featured a different product. Pillows, coverlets, and various linens were showcased. Kat had even shown him the inventory and had explained in detail how she would increase her staff and products to meet the Prince Regent's needs. Mr. Sherman had simply nodded but offered little else. She had no idea what he'd thought of her production area.

She forced herself to take a deep breath and evaluated the room as if she were seeing it for the first time. The room's interior was tastefully decorated. She hadn't skimped on choosing the finest paints and wallcoverings for the shop. She'd been fortunate when she'd come upon a furniture auction one day that wasn't well-attended. The beautiful but worn Louis XVI bedroom furniture she'd picked up for a song. Luck was with her also when Mr. Reed and his men had the time to refinish the furniture for the secretary's visit. The results were remarkable. Everything looked brand new.

Even the linens themselves were exquisite. Her employees were some of the finest seamstresses in all of England. If she wasn't awarded the contract, it wouldn't be because of the quality of her goods.

Mr. Sherman removed his gloves then ran his hand over a lovely linen. He picked up the edge of the coverlet, then pulled at a seam. "The stitches are tight and orderly."

"Thank you." Kat reached his side and ran her hands over the matching pillows. "This is for Lady Wilder. She's outfitting her country seat in Essex."

"The Marquess and Marchioness of Wilder?" he asked. Before she could answer, he took out his paper and pencil and jotted a few notes.

"Yes." She cleared her throat and clasped her hands behind her back, hoping to hide their shaking. "She was my very first customer, and one of the most loyal."

"How many bedrooms does she have?" He narrowed his green eyes.

This was a test of her ability to satisfy all her orders. "She has nineteen. She orders a set approximately every three months when she redecorates the family quarters." She smiled earnestly. "If you're wondering how I will manage if I receive the contract, there's no need. As I've mentioned, I have plans to hire additional employees for my orders. My current employees will be dedicated to the Prince Regent's orders."

"Good." He nodded. "Do you have a journal for your orders? Perhaps I can see that along with your bookkeeping? I need to see how financially secure you are." He slipped the paper and pencil back into his pocket.

"Of course. Please follow me." Kat led the way into her private sanctum, her office. She pulled the journals from her desk then handed them to him.

Before Mr. Sherman sat in front of her desk, he walked to the new linens Helen had ordered from her. "Who is this for?"

"My dear friend, Lady Woodhaven. That's Belgium lace." She smiled as he examined the linens. They were some of the most extraordinary pieces she'd designed. "I have someone in York who supplies me."

"Exquisite," he murmured with awe. He pulled out his paper and pencil and made a few more notes.

Kat released the breath she'd been holding. It was the first truly positive comment he'd made in her presence.

He sat down and started skimming pages in her order journal. Carefully, he closed it, then turned his attention to her bookkeeping. He perused the entries much as he'd done with the order journal. After a moment, he lifted his head and stared at her. "The Duke of Randford gave you four hundred pounds two days ago. What is it for?"

She smiled in reassurance. "It's a payment for services. I'm helping him create a charity, a business really, for the men that served under him in the army. Many came home without work. The duke is trying to help them establish their lives. It's a marvelous idea, don't you think?"

He grunted noncommittedly as he glanced back at the bookkeeping. "What kind of business?"

"A workshop that will refinish various antiques such as lap desks and small side tables to match my linens." She felt a swell of pride at everything she and Christian had accomplished in the last week. "The duke is passionate about the idea and helping his men. With his commitment, I have no doubt it will be a success. I'm honored to be working with him."

Not only honored, but delighted. Thoughts of Christian and his regard for his men made her feel as if she were a part of something bigger. Something that helped her as much as it helped Christian's men. It was the first time in her life after the "incident" that she could recall helping others without having to worry about her secrets. Honestly, it was the first time Katherine felt she could do anything she wanted without the world falling apart around her.

And she had Christian to thank for getting her involved.

"I'm sure it will be a success, but it's also troublesome." Mr. Sherman glanced down at the paper again. "Will you have enough time to fulfil the Prince Regent's contract if you work for the Duke of Randford also?"

"Yes." She nodded decisively. "The business plans I showed you at the workshop are ready to be implemented. My friend, Miss Howell, is more than qualified to run the workshop while I handle the hiring and training of extra seamstresses and the everyday business in the boutique. My work for the duke will be coming to an end soon. But I'll still help his shop by offering the items for sale in my emporium."

"Lap desks and tables," Mr. Sherman murmured, and he jotted down several notes. "The Prince Regent loves small unique pieces." He stood, and then for the first time in their hours together, Mr. Sherman smiled, one of satisfaction. "I appreciate your time today, Lady Meriwether."

"You are most welcome. Thank you for considering me." The kindness in his voice gave her hope that the interview had gone well. "If you have any further questions, please send them to me and I'll answer immediately."

He put away his pencil and paper for the last time before placing his hat on his head. "I have all the information I need. I'll present my findings to the First Lady of the Bedchamber. A decision should be made by the Prince Regent within the next ten days or so. Good day."

After he exited the shop, Kat strolled to the bay windows that faced the London street, where a startling blue afternoon sky commanded her attention. The visit had gone as well as could be expected. She rested against the window jamb.

The worry she thought she'd experience after Mr. Sherman left was nonexistent. She had done her best and, whatever happened, it was out of her hands. Now, all she could think about was seeing Christian again and telling him everything.

Amazing how the passage of a few short weeks and a particular duke could change her entire world.

Now that Constance was confined to her room for rest, Katherine and Beth spent every evening there before bedtime. Katherine always made it her last stop before retiring. But sometimes work called her back to her study after their evening chat. Beth and Aunt Vee had started taking turns sleeping in a cot in Constance's room so they could be of assistance if needed.

It was remarkable how Constance kept a cheery attitude through all of this. If it had been Katherine, she would have been beside herself. She was certain she'd have suffered from boredom after the first day, but Constance took it all in stride. She kept herself entertained by reading the latest gothic novels, fashion plates, and gossip rags, all of which lay in a haphazard manner across the bedside table.

Katherine made her way to Constance's room. Aunt Vee

sat happily by the fire, knitting away while Beth sat in a chair next to Constance's bedside. Papers were spread all around the counterpane, one of the first projects that Kat had ever completed.

"May I join you?" Katherine called out softly.

"Oh, you're here," Constance exclaimed. "I was about to send Beth to drag you out of your study. All work and no play makes Katherine a dull girl."

Beth laughed at the silly poem. "Makes Jack a dull boy," she corrected.

"But it makes me a happy woman," Katherine added as she sat next to Beth.

"We've only known each other a short time, but I'd say you're happy," Constance agreed. "Certainly more so than when we first met."

"I second that." Beth's eyes flashed with merriment. Since she'd been staying at Katherine's home and working for Kat, the change in Beth had been miraculous. She'd gone from being secretive to outgoing.

Katherine could easily see the women staying on with her after the contract was signed. She would have enough money to take care of them for many years to come. Hopefully, the increase in business from the royal appointment would allow them all to retire in style.

That was if Christian didn't find her friends each a husband. Besides, she might not win the appointment. She shouldn't get her hopes up too high, at least not yet.

Beth tapped her finger against her chin. "Oh, I've seen something that makes Katherine happy besides her work."

Constance's mouth tipped upward in an evil grin. "I'd say it's not something, but someone."

Beth leaned forward, and in a loud playful whisper said, "Do tell."

Constance giggled. "I think it rhymes with Brandford, Sandford, or perhaps—"

Aunt Vee looked up from her knitting. "Randford."

Heat spread from Katherine's neck to her cheeks. "What makes you say that?"

Constance smoothed the down coverlet in front of her. "Every time you see him, you come alive." Her glee turned to seriousness. "I, for one, think it's wonderful. After everything you've been through, you deserve some happiness."

Beth nodded. "I couldn't agree more. You've taken us in and given us a safe place to stay while this muddle is straightened out. We all want you happy."

"Each of you deserve the same," she argued. "Besides, you're reading more into this than there really is. He's trying to do what's best for all of us."

"Of course," Constance agreed a little too quickly with a cheeky grin. "Particularly when he comes out of your study without wearing his cravat and his hair is mussed."

The heat assaulted Katherine's cheeks. "What? Why would you say that?"

"Willa," Beth said. "She mentioned that she'd never seen him with a hair out of place until . . . he left your study the other night. Makes me wonder what kind of work you two were sharing."

"Stop, both of you," Katherine pleaded, holding both of her hands up and laughing. "You know that Willa likes to exaggerate." She pointed to the bed. "What's all that?"

Constance let out an exasperated sigh. "I decided to go through my packet of receipts from Meri." She pointed to the pile. "Basically, it's a hodgepodge of purchases he made with various people. There's no rhyme or reason to any of it, but it appears he used my dowry to finance most of it. Some are horses, mineral rights, jewelry, and even deeds. None of it is a sale between two people. There's always a third person involved in the transaction. Meaning, he trades with person A who trades with person B. But it looks like Meri gets nothing in return. From what I've gathered, it's the same with your individual receipts." She picked up a receipt then blew a lock of hair that had fallen across her eyes. "If I can find what he received, then perhaps I can find out what happened to our dowries."

"You did all of that today?" Beth asked slowly, glancing at the papers before turning her gaze to Constance.

She nodded. "I'm recording it all in this journal."

"Anything Beth or I can do to help?" Kat said.

Constance shook her head. "Thank you, but no. I like to work on puzzles. Besides, you two have had a busy day. Now, tell us how your meeting went with the secretary."

Kat's eyes widened as she recalled the absolutely perfect day it had been. "Mr. Sherman is a lovely man. He spent all afternoon with me." She addressed Beth. "If it hadn't been for you, I don't know if I could have had everything in order. Thank you."

Beth placed one hand over Kat's. "You're very welcome. When Mr. Sherman was at the workshop, I thought him very thorough."

Kat nodded. "At the arcade, he inspected the finished goods. He actually looked at all the incoming orders to ensure we can handle the increase in business if we're awarded the contract. I think it went well. Now, we wait."

"Oh, that's lovely, Katherine." Constance collected the papers into an orderly pile then pushed herself up to a sitting position and rubbed her belly. "What did he say when he left?"

"He told me a decision would be made as soon as possible. I don't know how I'll be able to wait." It was so rare for her to bare her soul to another, but with Christian and her friends, she was finding it easier and easier to share her true self with all her hopes and fears. "I'm hoping for the best. It means I can hire more women to grow my business, which will provide financial security for all of us."

"Whatever the decision, it's absolutely amazing you are being considered for such a contract. We're so proud of you." Constance reached out her hand, and Katherine placed it in hers. "It can't help but increase your business."

Beth nodded decisively. "I wager you'll hear within the week."

"We shall see," Katherine said, not wanting to let her hopes soar.

Constance yawned and settled back into bed.

Beth looked at Katherine. "I think that's our cue."

Aunt Vee yawned in tandem with her niece, then put her knitting in her lap. "It's my turn to stay here tonight."

After they all said good night, she and Beth stepped out into the hallway. Her friend stopped and placed her hand on Katherine's arm. "We're teasing you about the duke."

"I know," Katherine said. "This must be what it's like to have sisters."

Beth shrugged. "None of us knows. I have only one brother, and you and Constance are only children. But I like the way we are with one another." Her face turned serious. "We are sisters," she said unwaveringly.

Katherine dipped her head in acknowledgment. "Indeed." She reached up and pressed a kiss to Beth's cheek. "We will always be sisters."

Beth smiled, and the warmth in her eyes made them brilliant like diamonds. "Then, as one sister to another, let me give you some advice."

Katherine nodded. "Go on."

"Once you hear the decision, I think you should inform

Randford immediately. Not by letter, but by visiting him." She leaned a little closer so they couldn't be overhead. "I'm not certain what is going on between the two of you, but if there is something, then you should nurture it."

"There's nothing going on between us," Katherine protested quietly.

"Of course there isn't." The disbelief in Beth's voice was punctuated by the merriment in her eyes. "*Because there's not a single thing going on between the two of you*, he deserves to hear what the outcome is." She stretched toward the ceiling with her arms, an indication she was tired and ready for bed as well. "He'll share in your joy."

"What if I'm not picked for the contract?"

"Then let him comfort you through your disappointment. But I have an intuition—you may call it a hunch—but I believe you'll be celebrating soon. Are you retiring for the evening?"

"Shortly. I have a few things to finish this evening."

Beth nodded then turned to go to her room, murmuring something about work, Jack, a happy woman, and a certain duke.

Katherine headed down the stairs to the main floor, where she met Willa on the landing with a tray of fresh water and towels for Constance.

"Kat, I forgot to mention that the duke stopped by, and Lady Woodhaven sent over a note, and a royal courier left a letter for ye." Willa's stoic face revealed nothing. "I put both on yer desk."

"Did he say anything?"

"No, indeed. Lady Woodhaven's footman was quite tight-lipped."

"Willa," Kat exclaimed.

She smiled. "Neither was the royal courier very forthcoming."

"Enough teasing," Kat growled.

Willa raised a hand in surrender. "All right, lass. The duke said he'd call on ye tomorrow."

Kat sighed her frustration. "Thank you. Now, I should go up to my study and read it."

"Aye," Willa grunted softly. "If ye need me, I'll be in the kitchen."

"The letter sent by the royal courier? Who is it from?" Kat asked.

"Who do you think it's from?" Willa arched one eyebrow. "It's from the Secretary to the First Lady of the Royal Bedchambers."

Without another word, Kat raced upstairs.

Indeed, two letters lay on top of her desk. The first from her friend and the second from the secretary. She decided to open the one from Helen first. If the secretary's letter said she had not been chosen as the royal linen supplier, she'd be devastated and wouldn't want to read the other one.

Dearest Katherine,

I miss you. I'm aware you've been busy with your project for the Prince Regent, but we used to have tea together once a week. The last time was at my house. If you don't want to host, then allow me. Would you come tomorrow?

All my love,
Helen

Katherine let out a slow breath. She had been negligent in her friendship with Helen. She owed Helen the world, and she truly enjoyed her company. Now that the evaluation had been completed, there was no reason why she couldn't visit her friend. If she did receive the contract, then her time with Helen would be diminished to almost nothing. Katherine would have to travel to the Royal Pavilion for measurements, and when she returned to London, new employees would have to be trained.

She immediately penned a return note to Helen, accepting her tea, then sealed it. She'd have Rodney, the young man she employed at the workshop, deliver it first thing in the morning.

With a deep swallow, she placed her quill back on the stand, then picked up the letter from the secretary. The vellum stationary was heavy and expensive. The wax seal was twice as big as hers.

Her heart plodded through its beats as she turned the note over and over in her hand. It could only mean one thing: she was not the chosen vendor for the contract. The correspondence was too light for there to be a contract inside. Plus, this note had arrived only hours from the time she had departed company with the secretary.

She closed her eyes and forced herself to consider other options. Perhaps he wouldn't send the contract immediately. Maybe there had been a delay in the decision making. Everyone knew the royal court didn't move quickly on anything. Or, more likely, the secretary wanted additional information in order to make the decision.

Yes, that had to be it. The quicker she opened it, the quicker she would know the answer.

With great care, Katherine slid a knife under the seal, gently unlodging it from the paper. She carefully unfolded it, then smoothed it out on her desk.

Looking out the window, she said a small prayer and then forced herself to look down.

Dear Lady Meriwether,

It gives me great joy to inform you that you are the chosen new linen supplier to His Royal Highness's

Royal Pavilion. Not only are your linens superior to all others that we evaluated, but the idea of offering matching furniture accompaniments is intriguing.

His Royal Highness is quite fond of the Duke of Randford, and when he heard about your work with the duke's new charity, his Royal Highness asked that I look favorably on your work.

My dear lady, it should come as no great surprise that if the Prince Regent makes such a request, I simply could not refuse.

I will personally prepare the contracts and have them sent to your shop at the Beltic Arcade. I look forward to working with you in the future.

One final note, you may now address your business as a supplier to the Prince Regent by royal appointment.

Please accept my heartfelt congratulations.

Sincerely yours,
Edwin Sherman,
Secretary to the First Lady of the Bedchamber

Katherine gasped aloud and jumped from her chair.

She was the newest supplier to the royal family. That honor alone would triple her business since everyone in society shopped where the Prince Regent did.

For once, it felt as if her past life was firmly behind her. The business she'd created and its success ensured she was worthy of her position in society. It was what she always wanted.

She held the letter close to her chest, then walked to the window to stare at the London night. Though the street outside her window was quiet, she could hear the hustle and bustle of the city in the near distance. She truly was the master of her own destiny.

Beth and her advice popped into her thoughts. *You should tell the duke and celebrate with him.*

Indeed, she would, first thing tomorrow. Now she had to tell Willa, who by the sly look on her face, probably had already figured it out. She'd been the first one who heard the story about the secretary's visit. Willa had assured her that she would be the winner.

With a lightness she hadn't felt since she'd agreed to marry the trigamist, Katherine descended the stairs and made her way into the kitchen. Willa sat at the kitchen table, holding a cup of tea.

"I have news," Katherine called out with a huge smile and not hiding the glee in her voice.

Just then, Morgan peeked around the corner with his own cup of tea. "What is it, my lady?"

"I was chosen to supply the linens for the Royal Pavilion!"

Willa jumped for joy and took Kat in her embrace. "I'm not at all surprised. Congratulations, lass! This calls for a celebration indeed." With her Scottish lilt blazing at the news, she turned to Morgan and pointed to a cabinet above her head. "Wull ye fetch th' whisky doon?"

"Of course." Gallantly, he retrieved the bottle and handed it to Willa. "Congratulations," Morgan joined in.

"Thank you," Katherine said then tilted her head in his direction. It was odd to find him in their kitchen this time of the evening. "How are you feeling, Mr. Morgan?"

"I've been having trouble sleeping," he answered. "Sometimes, my memories won't let me be. Willa was preparing a tonic for me."

Kat was well-familiar with those type of memories. She smiled empathetically. "Willa's tonics are a godsend for me when my memories won't let me rest. I'm sure you'll find them helpful."

"My lady, I didn't know you had the same type of sleep problems as me. What memories keep you up at night?"

Before Kat could answer, Willa did the honors. "The lass worries too much." She turned to Kat. "I knew you'd git the contract," Willa announced proudly as she poured a third cup of tea. Then she put a fingerful of whiskey into each cup. "My lass, may this be the first of many." When Willa held up her cup, Katherine and Morgan did the same.

All three of them took a drink. Katherine's was a sip. Willa's whisky was known for its potency. She turned to Morgan. "The duke planned to call on me tomorrow, but I think I'll visit Rand House early in the morning before he can leave. I must share my news."

"Why don't you come back with me this evening? I know the captain would love to share in the celebration." Even with his eye patch, Morgan's sheepish smile gave him the appearance of a young man. "Actually, I wanted to ask if you could help me with the linens Lord Meriwether bought from you last year. We found them in some of his possessions with a note that they were for the captain's bed. Neither the housekeeper nor I can figure out how to put your beautiful pillowcases on the pillows."

"Is the duke home?" Katherine asked while hiding her excitement that Christian would soon be sleeping on something she'd made.

Morgan shook his head. "No, my lady. But he soon will be."

"Then let's you and I finish making his bed before he arrives home."

She couldn't wait until tomorrow. She had to see him now.

Chapter Nineteen

After an evening with Grayson, Christian was in a delightful mood. His friend had been excellent company, helping Christian see the advantages of receiving his half brother's strange bequests. They'd laughed over Poison Blossom and the tigers. The horse was currently in Christian's London stables and wouldn't be moved until she foaled. Christian had sent the tigers to a tenant at his ancestral estate who had experience with the creatures. Meriwether's paramour had been thrilled when Christian had cancelled the rest of Meri's contract and had given her the deed to the house where she lived. All in all, everything appeared to be working out well for him and the three wives.

He hummed a little ditty as he climbed out of his carriage, then proceeded up the front steps of his London home. Like clockwork, the door opened as soon as he reached the landing to the front door.

"Good evening, Your Grace," Wheatley called out with a smile.

"Indeed, it is," Christian answered, stepping into the entry of his home. After he handed off his beaver hat to a nearby footman, Christian stopped. A delicate fragrance floated through the air, one that reminded him of violets. "Is Lady Meriwether here?"

The butler chuckled. "How observant, Your Grace."

"Where is she?"

Wheatley pointed toward the second floor. "Your bedchamber, sir."

"Thank you." Christian took the steps two at a time to the second floor. Morgan was coming down the steps at the same time. They met in the middle.

"Captain, Lady Meri—"

"In my bedchambers?" he asked.

"Yes, sir. She has a surprise for you. I would have stayed with her, but there's a problem with the laundry. Two of the laundry maids are arguing over the starch in your shirts. I hope it's all right that I left her."

"Of course," Christian agreed. "Go save my shirts."

"If need be, I'll call in the dragoons." Morgan laughed, then proceeded down the steps.

Without looking back, Christian made his way in the opposite direction, toward his bedchamber. Katherine's violet scent lingered. His lucky stars had to be in alignment at the moment. He could tell her about the marriage proposal, and afterward kiss her until . . .

Then it hit him, the full force of realization. For once in his life, Rand House seemed like a true home.

Because of one unique thing.

Katherine.

The thought of her living here made his chest squeeze with a desperate need as vital as air. She would return from her long hours at the shop and he from his day in Parliament. With welcoming arms and warm kisses, both would be anxious to share an embrace and discuss the hours they'd been apart. It was a heady vision, one he could easily crave.

He entered his apartments, closed the door behind him, then headed straight for the bedroom. Katherine stood over his bed, straightening it as if she were a maid.

"I don't recall hiring a new upstairs maid, but if you're applying, I think you're a little overqualified."

Katherine glanced up and smiled. The brilliance of her eyes shone brighter than a perfectly cut topaz. He was riveted by the sight and couldn't take his eyes off her.

"Good evening, Your Grace." She dipped a slight curtsey, then waved her hand over his bed. "Tonight, you'll sleep on a complete set of my bedding."

For a moment, he thought she was inviting him into bed. He shook his head slightly to rid himself of the image of her lying there, waiting for him to join her to share all the erotic and sensual fantasies they could think up with each other. She wouldn't have a stitch of clothing on.

His body tightened as his cock enthusiastically thickened from such wicked thoughts. He forced himself to concentrate on the bedding as he rubbed a hand across the folded sheets and the duvet. It was almost as soft as Katherine's skin.

"This is a lovely gift." He tried desperately to appear nonchalant and completely comfortable with a beautiful woman in his private apartments. Yet she was more than that. She was part of his life.

"This is the set that Meri bought when we first met. Morgan discovered it this evening in Meri's things with a note that it's for you."

"Finally, my half brother left me something that I'll cherish." He winked at her, then took off his evening coat and threw it on a chair that was close to the bed.

She neatly folded the sheet corners, tucked them under the mattress, then smoothed the lovely duvet across the bed to cover the sheets.

Every inch of his body tightened at the sight.

Katherine walked around the side until she stood next to him. "I received a letter this evening."

Christian frowned. Another missive from his miscreant half brother? No. She wasn't upset. Instead, Katherine practically shimmered with excitement. "What?"

"From the Secretary to the First Lady of the Bedchamber." She took his hands in hers and squeezed.

Christian lifted one side of his mouth. He suspected she won the contract based upon the way she was flushed, her pink cheeks betraying her excitement. But he wanted Katherine to tell him so he could watch the absolute joy that would transform her from a beautiful woman into a spectacular one.

"And?" he prompted.

She tightened her hold on his hands as if trying to keep herself grounded and not float away. The biggest grin spread across her face. "I received the royal appointment." Then without letting go of his hands, she bounced on her toes. "Can you believe it?"

"I had little doubt. Your work is exceptional. They wouldn't have chosen you otherwise. Congratulations."

"Thank you." When Katherine reached up and brushed her lips across one cheek. Instantly, that familiar undercurrent that sizzled between them sparked anew. In a slow, easy movement, she drew away, but their gazes locked, and neither of them looked away.

How long they stood there, he hadn't a clue. But what he did know was that he wanted to kiss her more than he'd ever wanted anything in this life. Such was the power she held over him. "Katherine." His voice turned gruff, much like a growl. "We're playing with fire."

She answered by brushing her lips over his. He didn't move but closed his eyes. Unable to bear it any longer, he kissed her in return. The light violet scent wrapped around him, and in turn, he wrapped his arms around her. She sighed in pleasure, and he slipped his tongue past her lips. Immediately, she met his with hers. It was like coming home from a very long war.

The moan that escaped her hit him like a shot, instantly spreading desire through every part of him. He had wanted her before when they'd shared intimate kisses. Each kiss had built upon the last, bringing them closer and closer to the inevitable. Here and now, Katherine stood in his bedchamber.

He pulled her tighter into his embrace and ground his thickening member against her body, ready to mark her as his. This all-encompassing need to be close to her—claim her—wove around them, locking out their pasts and everyone that had come before them.

She gasped slightly, needing to breathe. He kissed her tender neck, trailed his lips across her shoulders, and she leaned her head back, closing her eyes. He licked the indentation at the bottom of the neck, then gently nipped her skin before kissing it. "You drive me mad. I would devour you if you let me."

"Eat your fill," she whispered.

"I adore it when you talk naughty like that." He chuckled against her mouth before he deepened the kiss.

The sweet taste of mint in her mouth was more powerful than any aphrodisiac known to man. But he didn't need anything to increase his desire for Katherine. He burned for her with a want and need that he'd never experienced before.

However, Kat would have to make the choice with how far they would go. He pulled away, then cupped her cheeks with his hands. The trust and desire in her eyes was a heady sight and one he'd never tire of. He was sure of it. "Kat," he whispered. "My Kat." He swallowed in an attempt to find some semblance of good judgment rolling around in his brain. "We should talk about this. I want you in my bed, but . . . is that what you want?"

Her heavy-lidded gaze almost undid him, but they wouldn't take this any further unless she wanted to. The rest of the world mattered little. It was only them, and whatever she wanted, he'd give her.

"I do," she answered. "I want to make love to you." Her pink cheeks deepened to a crimson color that only enhanced her beauty.

He drew a slow, deep breath, then released it. "This hunger between us, this ache is getting stronger."

She nodded. "It feels right."

This woman could easily possess his heart and soul.

Earnestly, she stared at him, then squeezed his hand. "I don't want to risk a child," she said softly.

He trailed his forefinger down one of her cheeks. "Agreed. I'll withdraw."

Katherine pressed her lips against his as she unbuttoned his waistcoat. With each button she released, he groaned in response. This time, she was the one to deepen the kiss as she slid his waistcoat over his shoulders before it fell to the floor. She smoothed her hands across his shoulders, and against his lips, she whispered, "Did you know that the first thing I noticed about you when we met was how wide your shoulders are and how trim your waist is? I can't believe I'll be able to explore every inch of you."

With the back of his finger, he lightly caressed the exposed skin of her décolletage. With a tremulous breath, she moved his hand to the hidden tie of her bodice. Her heated skin made his cock twitch. His eyes never left hers as they untied it together. He loosened the gown, and with a gentle shimmy of her shoulders, the material floated to the ground like leaves falling in surrender to an autumn wind.

Together they discarded her stays. The thin material of

her chemise did little to hide her hardened nipples pressed against the cloth. This was a delectable torment, much like sweet treats in a candy shop window. With reverence, he palmed each breast, and she moaned, deep and wild. The sound reverberated through him. She would be glorious in bed. He had little doubt. Her passion ignited his own.

She stood before him and smiled, then reached for his cravat. Together, they untied it, then pulled his shirt free of his waist. With a tug, he had it over his head. Her gaze met his then fell slowly down his chest. She licked her lips, and her breath quickened.

He couldn't help but straighten to his full height. He wanted her eyes on him, devouring him with each sultry glance.

"How utterly glorious you are. Where shall I touch first? I want to know what you like, where you're ticklish." She lightly scored her nails over one of his nipples. "Are yours as sensitive as mine?"

He hissed in response. His blood pounded fire through his body. A wildfire couldn't compare to the heat this woman managed to elicit from him.

"I take that as a yes." As her gaze tenderly scouted the planes of his muscles, she gasped softly when she discovered his scar. She reached and tenderly traced the rough edge that ran in a diagonal direction down his left side.

He didn't flinch. "I earned this during my second battle. A French soldier had missed a direct stab to my heart but managed to inflict this reminder of all I could have lost in the war."

"Oh, Christian." Katherine leaned down and traced her lips across the scar. "Thank God you're here."

"Those words coming from you makes them more precious than any earthly possession I own. They center me," he said softly. "Truly."

She bit her lip then looked up. "I meant every word. Are there more?"

He shook his head.

"That's good." She took her hand away, then untied her chemise, never breaking her stare. It slid to the floor in a straight fall. With her hazel eyes greener this evening and her light brown hair glowing from the firelight, she reminded him of a wood nymph set to enchant him. But he was already captivated.

Whatever magic she wanted to weave this evening, he'd gladly submit.

"My God, Katherine." His voice deepened on its own accord as his hungry gaze devoured her body. "You're beautiful."

"Now, your turn. I want to see the rest of you."

Christian was correct—when they were together, everything faded except for the two of them. Not shy, she waited for the proverbial unveiling of his body. The wound she'd discovered on his chest had taken her breath away. Another six inches closer to his heart, and he wouldn't be here today with her.

With a practiced ease, he toed off one formal evening slipper, then the other, before discarding his stockings. When he stood, she forgot how to breathe. She had already admired his broad shoulders where muscles rippled, but her heartbeat pounded in triple-time at his trim waist that melted into lean hips. Her body ached as she studied the outline of his erection straining against his black silk breeches. When she raised her gaze, his eyes smoldered.

"Are you sure?" he asked softly.

"Yes. I want this." Katherine stepped forward and trailed her hands down his chest. She deserved this, finally making love to a man, to Christian. When she leaned close, their naked chests touched. The feel of him was so perfect against her. "Now you'll see what it's like to sleep in my bed."

"Oh, really?" he drawled, then nibbled her lips.

She drew back, then lightly nipped one of his nipples in return.

His eyes flashed and he grabbed her closer to him. "You're claiming my bed as your own?"

"The linens make the bed, and those are mine." Bold and confident, she was certain who she was tonight. She wasn't an unclaimed bastard, a no one from York. She was a woman who would share an incredible moment tonight with this man. She slipped her hand between them and unbuttoned his falls. With greedy, impatient hands, she pushed his breeches past his hips. They caught on his muscled thighs, but her gaze was locked on his cock.

Christian stepped out of his breeches; Katherine reached to touch him. If at all possible, he seemed to be thicker and harder than he was the other night.

He grunted when she wrapped her hand around him. It reminded her of a hot, steel rod wrapped in velvet. His signature sandalwood scent mixed with his own musk became a heady fragrance.

Bolder, she took him in a kiss, then touched the tip of his cock where a pearl of moisture lay like a perfect jewel. "Does it always do that?"

His eyes widened, then a perplexing grin creased his lips. Kissing her in return, Christian swung her into his arms. "Always when I'm with you." Without another word, he carefully laid her on the bed. She scooted over so he could join her.

He surprised her when he straddled her hips, then rested on his elbows, keeping his weight off her.

Unable to resist touching him, she smoothed his hair from his face, then undulated her hips to his. His cock pulsed against her lower belly. The intense sensation made her want more. The top of her thighs were already wet because of him. Katherine knew that her body was preparing for when he'd enter her. She'd never felt so sensual and wanton in her life. She pushed against him again.

"Minx," he teased, then kissed her, stealing every sound in the room and every thought she possessed. The only thing she knew was that this moment was theirs.

Christian slid lower and took one nipple in his mouth while he palmed the other breast. The sensation made her see stars. She raked her hands through his hair and then held him to her, begging him to continue. He chuckled slightly but did it again. She moaned as she cradled his head between her hands. He lifted himself then kissed her on the mouth with a slow sensual ease.

Before she could kiss him in return, he returned his attention to her other breast. She arched her back at the sensation.

Suddenly, he lightly nipped her. In response, she mewled softly. He drove her wild, and she never wanted him to stop.

Thankfully, he didn't. He kissed the undersides of her breasts, then shifted a little lower until he kissed her belly. She gently stroked her fingers through his hair while cataloging every touch and caress. He made her feel as if she were precious and wanted.

He kept going lower, pressing his lips against her hipbone. With languid eyes, he tilted his gaze to her. "How would you feel about me going lower?"

"I'd enjoy that," she purred.

He trailed open mouth kisses across her midsection, then stopped. "What if I kissed you there, and you came against my mouth?"

Her heart quivered, and heat rushed to the spot where he

caressed her. This was more than she ever dared hoped for. "Would you enjoy that?"

When he nodded, the silky strands of his hair caressed her skin. "I know I'd enjoyed it, and I think you'd enjoy it too. I want to give you every conceivable pleasure I can think of this evening," he whispered. "If you aren't comfortable, then we won't. Tonight is for us to enjoy each other."

She held his gaze. "I just thought we'd do"—she waved her hand between them—"it."

"It?" He smiled and, in response, her heart did a flip in her chest. "Oh, darling," he sighed. "The preparation for 'it' is the most important part. Don't you agree? The other day you liked it when I touched you here." He stroked gently through her curls, and she arched her hips.

When she looked down, an incredibly erotic sight greeted her.

He was leisurely stroking himself. "I want you to feel everything with me. But you decide how and when."

Her heart melted a tad. She released a shuddered breath. "I want everything too."

Katherine watched as Christian bent down and rested between her legs. He arranged her in such a way that she was spread out before him. She couldn't imagine sharing herself this with any other man except him. It seemed natural. He ran his tongue along her cleft, then held her open with his fingers to give him better access.

He kissed her once, then his tongue danced against her nub in a slow, measured routine that had her gripping the cover, seeking purchase. He circled the sensitive spot over and over, then he would break his rhythm by sucking on it. She closed her eyes and let the sensation consume her.

With a finger, he entered her. She felt a tightness she'd never experienced, but it didn't diminish the driving need for more. She grew more desperate for his touch and arched her hips toward his mouth. His movements quickened.

She was wet and achy, but she didn't want him to stop. Ever. This was a delicious torment, one she'd gladly experience over and over again as long as it was Christian. When he inserted a second finger and stretched her even more, she whimpered with need.

Every sense she possessed was barreling out of control. She could feel her orgasm almost upon her while he gently moved his fingers in and out and his mouth continued to pleasure her.

When she thought she could bear no more, Katherine closed her eyes. Her body stiffened in release as she gasped his name. Pleasure radiated through every limb until it congregated low within her body, then bloomed into a riot of sensation. She felt weightless as her release was ten times more potent than the one they'd shared the other day.

When she opened her eyes, he'd materialized like a specter above her. He was panting gently, and the intensity of his expression meant he was as affected as she was. "Katherine." The sound of her name in his rough voice pierced every part of her, marking her as his.

She lift her arms to hold him, and he eagerly moved over her. She would have him, claim him in this moment of time, and nothing and no one would come between them.

He kissed her neck as he pushed his hot length against her belly in a move that she suspected mimicked their soon-to-be coupling. She stroked his strong back, learning every muscle, bone, and sinew as he moved. All the while, she wondered if he would be able to tell this was her first time.

Christian reached between them, settling himself at her entrance, and barely entered her. He kissed the tender area below her ear. "So tight," he whispered.

Indeed, so tight that she felt like her body was being invaded and she had nowhere to retreat. She wrapped her legs around him, hoping the position would help relieve the pressure.

With a grunt, he continued, "Do you have any idea how good you feel?"

Before she could answer, he drew back slightly, then in one stroke, he was inside her—completely.

For a moment, everything stopped. She shifted her hips higher, which caused the tightness to ease.

"Did I hurt you?" He didn't move—not a single muscle. She could feel him suspended above her, no doubt wondering. She turned her head to the side and closed her eyes. She couldn't look at him. What would he say?

As importantly, what would she say?

"Katherine, look at me." His voice had turned incredibly tender.

With a Herculean effort, she turned to face him and opened her eyes. Resting his weight on his elbows, he loomed before her like a Greek god who'd swept down from Mount Olympus. The cords of his neck muscles were taut from the exertion of staying still.

"I'm going to pull out slowly."

"No. I'm fine." She placed her arms around his neck. "Please don't. I want this. I want tonight with you," she pleaded. "I want *you*." Her gaze locked with his questioning one. "Please."

He shifted slightly, never looking away, and it brought their bodies closer. "We'll go slowly, then."

Both breathed in and out at the same time.

For several moments, they simply stared at each other while she did her best to keep her face frozen. She swallowed. Not wanting to start the conversation that would be inevitable, she nodded. Why had she not thought this through?

Because it was Christian. He was like a bountiful feast to a starving woman, and she'd been ravenous for him.

With her arms wrapped around him, she kissed him again, and his deep groan encouraged her to continue. He pulled his cock out slowly, then pushed in.

"Relax, sweetheart," he said.

The affection in his voice and the gentle movement of his body made her feel treasured and connected with another human being in a way she couldn't have imagined before. He returned her kiss. His movements became surer and smoother. She hitched her legs tighter around his trim waist. She lifted her hips and met each thrust in rhythm. He held her gaze and gradually increased the pace. He whispered her name, sending waves of pleasure through her. Each stroke made her want more of him. With her hands, she caressed the corded muscles of his back, desperate to learn every inch of him. She kissed him with everything she possessed, her heart and soul.

In response, he devoured her with a kiss that made her want to beg for more. She tried to memorize his every facial expression. In that moment, they belonged to each other in an inseparable bond that could never be broken.

Instinctively, her body clenched every muscle when his face contorted into a grimace as he reached his peak. He took her mouth with his in a wrenching kiss of need. She pulled him tight, creating an oasis that was just for the two of them, locking out everything else. He groaned her name, then pulled out of her carefully. His hot seed shot across her stomach. In that moment, she knew she'd seen something extremely rare.

He'd lost control because of her.

Carefully, he shifted his weight and lay on his side. With his hand, he pushed away the lock of hair that had strayed from her chignon, which had to be a rat's nest by now.

"Katherine, do you know what happened here tonight?" He ran his lips along the slope of her jaw. The thrum of his deep cadence centered her, leaving an indelible mark upon her heart. "I held heaven in my arms."

"Oh, Christian," she murmured, laughing. "Why do you do this to me?"

"Do what?" The puzzled but endearing look on his face made her want to pull him back into her embrace.

"The things you say," she answered softly.

"I've never wanted anyone in the way I want you," he crooned quietly. He glanced where their bodies touched, then raised his gaze to hers. "Why me?"

"Why you?" She didn't hide the bemusement from her voice.

"Why did you choose me to be your first?" A hint of mystery shadowed his eyes.

"Because . . . because it felt right. It was you."

He blinked slowly. That's when she saw the uncertainty there.

Katherine reached and smoothed his brow, not taking her eyes from his, willing him to see the truth. "You make me feel that in a crowded room with a thousand others, I'm the only person there." She cupped both of his cheeks, not allowing him to look away. "I've never had someone see me that way in my entire life. I trust you."

He studied her face for a long time without saying a word. "Thank you for telling me," he said softly. He leaned down and pressed his lips to hers.

Only with him did such a sweet, tender kiss let her hope . . . let her believe that the scars she carried for all those years could be mended. She'd shared a part of herself tonight—how he made her feel—because she trusted him.

And he was the only man she would ever want to build a life with.

Then the truth hit her square in the chest.

Her traitorous heart, the one she'd taught to be careful around unrequited love, hadn't protested a peep when the inevitable had happened.

She hadn't simply fallen in love with Christian.

Oh no.

She'd jumped off the highest cliff.

Chapter Twenty

Drained physically from their coupling, Christian flipped on his back. Katherine curled into him and he wrapped his arm around her. Within seconds, their breathing fell into a natural rhythm with each other. For several long moments, they lay there in silence. It felt perfect to have her here beside him. For the world, he'd like nothing more but to hold her and make love to her again, but they had things to discuss.

He turned on his side to face her. Resting his head on his bent arm, he studied her. With his free hand, he reached for hers resting by her side, then entwined their fingers together. "Are you sorry you married him?"

"Yes." She turned to face him. "But by marrying him, I was accepted by society. And with that, my business grew."

"A mercenary, I see," he teased.

"Is that how you see me?" Her mouth threaded into a frown. "An accurate description, perhaps."

"I see you as a brave and accomplished woman." His gaze traveled over her lithe figure. He could take her again right now. She was every man's dream. Lush breasts that fit perfectly in his hands. Sweet lips. And when she wrapped her arms around him, he felt acceptance. No slights, no judgments, just warmth. She was the light that guided him home.

"You have every right to use the Vareck name to your advantage." He tugged her hand to his lips. "I can't imagine the pain you felt when he left."

"I was delighted we'd married." Her voice had turned incredibly gentle. "I thought we'd have a simple but happy life together. It was what I wanted in my marriage. I thought there was a chance we'd find love for each other. I'd have a husband who wanted to be with me. We'd have a family. That's all I desired."

The wistfulness in her voice held him spellbound. It wasn't his half brother she was mourning but her ideal of marriage.

"After he finished the wedding breakfast, Meriwether told me he had business in Portsmouth that couldn't wait. He had his eye on a racehorse that he thought to purchase." She anchored her gaze on the fireplace. "That's when I knew . . ."

"That's when you knew he was a wastrel?" Christian scooted closer to her.

"No." Her voice was barely above a whisper. "That he was leaving me for good. I couldn't acknowledge it. I didn't even try to stop him. But I used my married name for everything. He'd at least given me that."

"His mother was the same way, and so was our father."

Her gaze drifted back to his. "What do you mean?"

"Disingenuous profligates. The worst of the worst. Meri's mother was my father's mistress." He practically spit the words. "Actually, disingenuous is too kind of a term for them. After they married, the parties they hosted made a bacchanalia look like an afternoon garden party. Their orgies were legendary throughout all of London. When I went to Eton, my fellow students would regale me with tales of my stepmother's sexual conquests of their fathers. When we became older, those same students told of her conquests of them. Age made no difference to my stepmother."

He'd clearly shocked her as she didn't move an inch or say a word.

Finally, she broke the silence. "Did you try to defend her?" Her voice wavered.

Her hesitation slipped between his ribs, and for a moment he didn't know whether to bare all his secrets or keep quiet. He decided on the former. This was Katherine, and she'd never judge him.

"At first I tried. But my classmates knew things about my home. Things that they couldn't know unless they were . . . in the bedrooms." He ran a hand through his hair. "I still didn't believe it, but then one day, it was a night of revelry, another theatre party. Meri came to my room. He was eight, and I was ten and three."

"What happened?" She tightened her fingers around his.

The movement was so inconsequential, but it infused him with strength. He'd never shared this with anyone. "Meri said he'd seen some of my *friends* go into his mother's bedroom." He laughed at the mockery of the word *friends* to hide the pain. It still shamed him to this day.

Katherine scooted up the bed so they could be eye to eye. She never released his fingers.

He closed his eyes for a moment at the painful memory. "Meri was visibly upset so I kept him entertained until he fell asleep in my sitting room. As I made my way to my father's study, it was loud and boisterous. Music and uncontrollable laughter filled the halls. The servants were nowhere to be seen." He shivered slightly at the ugliness of it all. "All of it made my skin crawl. I knew my father wouldn't give a care about me, but I thought he'd be upset with his wife. Besides the fact his favorite son was worried."

"Christian," she soothed.

He brought her fingers to his lips. "It made no difference. I always knew whom my father favored. Though he pretended otherwise, I always knew."

"Go on."

He released a deep sigh. "When I went into his study, my father was sitting at his desk with two well-known actresses draped across his lap, one on each leg. None of them had a stitch of clothing on. He laughed when he saw me and said, 'Join us.'"

"Oh, Christian," she said softly.

Christian pressed her palm to his cheek. The softness of her skin was a balm he would not deny himself. "Said it would mark the day I became a man."

She grimaced slightly. "Oh, God."

"Though I was only ten and three, my father, the Duke of Randford, wanted me to fuck a woman in front of him. Unbelievable." He whispered the last before he pressed a kiss to the middle of her palm. "I'm sorry for the vulgarity."

"It's all right." She stroked his face, offering comfort, something he sorely needed. "What happened?"

Christian looked at her. "Disgusted, I turned and left. I'll never forget the sound of my father's laughter as it followed me out the door. He called me a stiff prick. I packed up Meri and ordered a carriage. We went to our ancestral home where Wheatley met us at the door. We were there a week before Meri's mother wrote to him." He lifted a brow in defiance. "My father never asked about me at all. Not. Once." His gut squeezed at the memory. "I meant nothing to him, so he meant nothing to me. From then on, I discovered where my father and Meri's mother were residing before I came home from school. I ensured that Meri and I never were in the same house with them. We always spent the holidays alone together. No one ever challenged me. Not my father. Not Meri's mother. Not even Meri."

"You protected Meriwether." Katherine squeezed his hand, keeping him from losing himself in loneliness. "No wonder he adored you."

He shook his head slightly. "But it was a wasted effort. As Meri got older, he came under their spell and spent more time with them than me. It's speculation on my part, but perhaps the allures of pleasure and self-gratification were too much for him to resist."

Her brow creased into lines of worry. "Did Meri partake . . ."

"I don't have a clue, but our relationship changed from then on. He turned wild and reckless, as if rebelling against me and the world." He let go of her hand. "I tried to talk to him, but to no avail. I lost him and could do nothing else for him." He reached for Katherine and brought her close. The warmth of her body next to his was a heady solace for all his past heartache. "Maybe I could have tried harder. But after he ruined my horse . . ." Saying the words felt as if his heart was being ripped from his chest again. "He didn't care. He had turned into my father. Whatever brought him pleasure."

"I'm sorry." She brought their clasped hands to her heart. "That had to be hard to live through."

No one had cared about his loss. No one but her. The simple act undid him. He bit his lip to keep the tears in abeyance, then took her into his arms and held her. Burying his head into her neck anchored him from drowning in the memories.

"You're kind to say that. In many ways, it was harder than all the times I faced the enemy." Christian kissed her on the forehead, a thank-you for letting him share this part of himself. "But as far as I am concerned, the duke ruined the duchy. He was a poor excuse for a father. He never grieved for my mother. I'm not even certain he loved anyone but himself. His entire life was a lie." He laughed to hide his pain.

"But I'll rebuild the Randford duchy. Ensure that its reputation is transformed and buffed to a shine." He smiled down at her.

"I have no doubt about it," she said with a grin. "You can do anything."

Her smile brightened everything in the room, including his mood. The effect she had on him grew every day, and he was richer for it. Never had he felt this close to another. Frankly, she was the most unique person he'd ever met. Being with her made him want more in life. The charity was a start, but they could accomplish so much more together.

"The charity will help rebuild the duchy. The second shall be a soiree at Rand House." He kissed the back of her hand. "You'll be my hostess and stand by my side. We'll invite all of London to the event."

Katherine pressed her lips together, and her eyes flashed. "I don't know if that would be appropriate . . . at least, for me . . . not now."

"What are you about?" he murmured, truly surprised at her response. "We'll announce your royal appointment and your efforts with the charity. We'll have your linens and some of the furniture on display. We'll even invite the Prince Regent. I want to show you off to everyone. Your name will be famous throughout the land."

Indeed, it was the idea Grayson had suggested, and it was brilliant. It would be a night to celebrate the charity, but more importantly, Katherine and all of her accomplishments.

Bile threatened to choke Katherine at Christian's words. For a moment, she thought she would become ill, but the sensation left as quickly as it came. His idea of a soiree as a way to launch his arrival in London along with the start of the charity was sound.

But she didn't want any part of it. Having ladies come

into her shop was nothing like a society event where she would be front and center. Her customers weren't focused on her. They wanted to shop and have an experience that was uniquely their own. She was just a vehicle for them.

But to appear as the hostess for the Duke of Randford in all of London, she couldn't risk it. Someone might recognize her. My God, would these fears ever leave her be? What would he think of her if he ever discovered the truth? She had little doubt that her face was paler than the full moon outside. She had to escape before he knew something was wrong.

"I think Willa and Morgan should attend the soiree along with Reed and the other men." Resting on a propped elbow, he peered down at her. "We can work out the details later. Probably the one good thing that came out of the war was my friendship with Morgan. I think of him much like you think of Willa." He took her hand in his. "May I tell you a story?"

"Of course," she murmured, not really listening. Her ears were still ringing with his earlier comments.

"In the military, a so-called career scout entered my regiment after it became common knowledge that we wouldn't see any battles for a week or so. He sang his own praises of finding the perfect defensive positions. My commanding officer believed him, but I had a hunch something wasn't right. I believed he was lying to us."

"Did you say anything?" She scooted back, creating distance between them.

"I tried to convince anyone who would listen that we shouldn't rely on the new scout for the next battle until we saw the battlefield for ourselves. It was to no avail. My commanding officer allowed the man to map our battle position. As soon as the French attacked, the coward ran. The rest of us were cornered with no escape. That's where I earned my scar." The anger in his voice was unmistakable. He closed his eyes briefly and took a breath. "Men died that day, Kat." He shook his head as if awakening from a dream. "Morgan saved my life and has been by my side ever since. I learned immediately that honesty to others is the most honorable asset a man can possess."

"I'm sorry you and Morgan suffered." In a poor attempt to cleanse her own lies, she added softly, "I'm sorry too."

He nodded. "I'm sorry I didn't fight harder to expose the man." He leaned over and brushed his lips against hers.

Without glancing her way, he stood in his full naked glory, then walked to an inlaid dressing table where a basin and ewer of water rested. He poured water, then soaked a linen toweling. After wringing it out, he came to her side. "Let me wash you."

"I can do it." She made a move to sit up, but he quickly bent over and kissed her soundly on the lips.

"I want to take care of you. Allow me to do that?"

She froze when she saw the streaks of blood on her thighs. By then, he was already washing all traces of their coupling from her legs and stomach. Once he was satisfied with his work, he returned to the basin and rinsed out the cloth, then cleaned himself.

For some bizarre reason, she didn't even feel as if she was in the room with him, but watching a dream or performance unfold before her eyes.

When he returned to the bed, he lay next to her and brought her into his arms, still seeming completely oblivious to her torment. "I have news regarding Constance. I saw Sykeston. He's agreed to marry her."

Her fog immediately cleared at the mention of her friend. "Tell me." She was desperate to change the subject.

Christian made quick work of sharing his conversation with the earl.

"What kind of a man is he?" Under no circumstances would she allow Constance to suffer another ill-fated marriage. It really wasn't within her power to control, but she'd do her best to protect her friend.

"Honorable and loyal, the best kind. Let's tell her tomorrow." He gently pulled the sheet and duvet out from underneath her, then carefully draped it over her naked body.

Always before, the sensual sensation of the linens hitting her bare skin never failed to please her. But this time, she couldn't enjoy them, even though she lay next to the man she'd made love to, a man who touched her with care and deep regard.

He kissed her neck, then burrowed close beside her. Katherine let out a tremulous breath. He was everything kind and sweet, particularly when he brought her into his embrace.

But she had to get out of there as soon as was humanly possible.

His arms tightened ever so gently around her before he relaxed. "Stay with me."

Within minutes, he fell asleep, holding her.

She held her breath then slowly released it. Her mind reeled with what he'd shared tonight.

It all led to one conclusion. If he ever discovered who she really was, he'd no doubt despise her.

And her heart would crumble into nothing.

Early the next morning, Katherine arrived home and, thankfully, the house was blessedly quiet.

Willa had to be asleep, which left Kat able to take a long soaking bath in the kitchen without anyone knowing. Really, she shouldn't care. She was a successful woman of commerce and managed her affairs quite adequately, if she did say so herself. It was her business who she kept company with and what she did. Her shoulders slumped a tad. Still, if Willa had discovered what happened last night, she would have worried about her, nevertheless.

And for good reason. Katherine ached not only from Christian taking her, but from her heart being ripped to shreds.

Yet, how she longed to be with him again. The tenderness he'd shown her and the sweet things he said had stolen her heart. He wanted to celebrate her, and she wanted nothing more than to do the same for him. He was kind, generous, and had a heart that kept on giving. If the world was perfect, she'd dress and return to his side immediately.

But the world wasn't perfect. Whatever it took, she had to keep her secrets safe.

How could she have been so foolish as to think and hope they could build a life together? Dukes didn't marry bastards. They certainly didn't marry convicted thieves.

Soon, she finished her bath, then made a pot of tea before retiring to her sanctuary, her office. She took a sip of tepid tea and munched on a piece of toast covered with elderberry jelly. Katherine worked on several new orders, then her travel plans to Brighton as best she could.

A gentle knock sounded on her study door.

Expecting Willa, Katherine called out, "Come in."

Helen peeked around the door. "Good morning, darling," she called out. "May I come in?"

Katherine swallowed at her friend's appearance. She took a quick inventory of where the others were. Constance was in bed. Beth would be with her. Katherine prayed that Aunt Vee, the unpredictable one, was still enjoying her morning tea with Willa. Hopefully, for the next half hour, they could chat without Helen being aware that Katherine had house guests.

"Of course, Helen. I'm delighted to see you." Of all the

days, why couldn't her friend have sent a card over first? Helen's visit this morning would be the first real test of whether Katherine was any worse for wear from last night's visit to Christian's bedroom. Helen was almost as ruthless as Willa when it came to Katherine's well-being. If Helen could tell something was amiss in their conversation, then Willa would sniff it out within two minutes. *Bother. The cost of letting people close to you.* "I thought I was coming to your house for tea."

"I couldn't wait to see you." Helen settled into the chair across from Katherine. "Are you feeling well?" Helen asked as she leaned in Katherine's direction. "Why are your cheeks flushed?"

"I ran up the stairs."

"Hmm," Helen murmured. "When Willa answered the door, she said you'd been in your study all morning." She smoothed her dress, then leaned forward. "I understand congratulations are in order for your latest triumph."

"Pardon?" How in the world could Helen have known she was with Christian last night?

Her friend shook her head. "Darling, I'm talking about the appointment as the supplier to the Prince Regent's Royal Pavilion."

"Thank you," she said woodenly.

Helen peered at her again. "What is the matter with you this morning?"

"Nothing." Katherine released a long sigh. "As you can imagine, I have much on my mind." Including a certain war hero duke with wicked lips and a glorious body designed so a woman would lose all her rational sense. "I'm surprised to see you here."

"Are you?" she asked with a purr, then continued in a singsong voice. "Guess who's set to call on you within the week?" Helen was absolutely beside herself today with joy.

"I won't allow you to guess. I want to say it myself." She laughed. "Miles."

Katherine pasted a smile on her lips. "How wonderful. Does he want to purchase more bedding?"

"No, goose," Helen said affectionately. "Stop teasing me. He's going to start courting you." She leaned back in the slipper chair. "I expect a wedding announcement within the month."

Katherine tried to mask her horror, then blinked slowly. "Did he tell you that?"

"Well, not in so many words. But it doesn't take a genius to figure it out. He told me he was going to call on Randford to discuss your situation with him. That only means one thing. He's going to ask permission to call on you."

"I don't know what to say." Her voice sounded weak to her own ears.

Helen's lips dipped into a moue of displeasure. "I thought you'd be excited."

"I'm surprised, that's all." Katherine looked at the papers on her desk and made a show of straightening them. "Well, that gives me all the more incentive to finish my work." She didn't add the word "here," so she could scramble to the workroom. Best to hide out the next week at her places of work so the earl couldn't find her.

Helen stood. "I must leave. Benjamin wanted my opinion on a few bills he's proposing next week."

"I'll see you out," Katherine murmured.

Thankfully, they chatted about mundane things as they made their way downstairs. By then, Katherine had decided their tea would best be postponed until next week. She used the excuse of more work orders that she'd received. Thankfully, there was no mention of Lord Abbott again. Katherine let out a silent sigh of relief when she escorted her friend to the door without running into another wife or Aunt Vee.

"Darling?" Helen stopped outside the front door on the portico. Her footman already had the carriage door open for her. "Someone said in passing they thought a midwife had visited your residence two days in a row." Helen's gaze bored into Katherine's. "It isn't for you, is it?"

"Of course not," Katherine scoffed. "They must have had the wrong house."

Helen nodded. "That's what I thought." She laughed gently. "What a silly thing to have brought up. I apologize. You have not been with anyone since Meriwether."

With a wave, she continued to her carriage parked out front.

Katherine's blood seemed to rush to her feet. Suddenly dizzy, she closed the door then rested her head against it with her eyes closed.

Someone had to have been watching the house if Helen knew the midwife had visited twice.

If Helen had heard about the midwife, who else might have?

Chapter Twenty-One

Christian stood in front of the mirror tying his cravat. How in the devil had Katherine slipped out of his arms and out of his house without him being aware? His military ways were fast deserting him. Back in the army, he slept so lightly that a mouse scurrying across his tent would have captured his notice. But undoubtedly, she had to return home before the others in her household woke.

In a manner reminiscent of an adolescent love-starved fool, he smiled to himself. Probably because he'd never felt so relaxed after a bout of lovemaking.

A knock sounded on the door.

"Enter."

Morgan came to stand by his side without his usual brightness. Also missing was his huge smile. One thing about Morgan, he was a morning person. That was one of the reasons why Christian enjoyed his company.

"*Your Grace*, you called for me?" Morgan never called him that. His valet perused his appearance and nodded in approval.

"When did she leave?" Christian asked, sounding gruff.

"If you mean Lady Meriwether"—Morgan lifted one brow, making it clear he disapproved—"it was slightly after two o'clock this morning." He pursed his lips for a moment, then continued, "She looked pale, and her clothes and hair were in complete disarray." Morgan looked down his nose at Christian. "I only hope that Willa didn't see her like that."

Christian acknowledged the set down with a nod. "I completely slept through . . ."

"Her leaving your bedroom?"

Christian narrowed his eyes. "Are you judging me?"

"Of course not," Morgan answered. "I'm merely making an observation."

"One well taken." Christian retied the lopsided knot of his cravat. "I'm going to see her."

Christian's valet raised that infuriating eyebrow again. "Indeed?"

He forgot his disapproving valet and thought about Katherine. He had no idea what he was going to say to her. *I enjoyed our time together last night, especially the part where we made love. I'd like to do it again.* He wanted her like none before. He wanted to see the perfect blush that colored her neck and cheeks when she was aroused. The whimpers that escaped her lips when he touched her.

It all sounded like a bowl of balderdash.

What did he really want to say? *I've never felt such ease with a woman before in my life. You are the first woman who I trusted enough to share the truth about my family. I physically ache for you. I want to marry you. I want to be the man who lays a rose on your pillow in the morning, holds your hand in the dark, and kisses you as the sun rises.*

Morgan scowled at Christian as if he could read his thoughts.

In response, Christian schooled his features. "I should have been the one to take her home. Why didn't you wake me?"

His valet's enigmatic visage reminded Christian of a frozen lake. You couldn't see how much ice was below the surface, and you certainly didn't want to find out.

"I tried, but it was like waking the dead." Morgan studied the floor, and the silence echoed around the room like a cannon shot. "Captain," Morgan bit out. "If I may inquire? When did you say you were calling on Lady Meriwether?"

He grunted noncommittedly. When he found the courage to apologize for not taking her home.

And for not meeting her first, before Meri found her.

"When I escorted her home early in the morning, she didn't say a word, nor did she look at me." Morgan lowered his voice. "I know it's presumptuous, but *you* need to see her."

"Of course, I need to see her and make it right. Do you think I'm a philistine?" His valet didn't answer him, which made Christian feel even more like the scum in a pond. Katherine was intelligent, possessed a lovely humor, and had that rare ability to comfort others when they were hurting.

He'd wanted to give her everything he possessed. He wanted to spend every hour of Katherine's day, week, and life with her. He'd be content watching her work all day.

He shut his eyes briefly. The truth was, he loved her.

"Thankfully, Willa didn't meet her at the door," Morgan added. "I don't know what I would have said to her if she saw her mistress come into the house at such an hour."

"Thank you, Morgan, for seeing her home." Christian turned around and faced his valet. "I'll leave right now."

"Shall I accompany you?" Morgan asked.

"That won't be necessary." Christian couldn't tell if his valet's offer was out of duty or friendship. Either way, he appreciated the support, something he clearly needed. But he'd visit her on his own. It wasn't every day a man asked a woman to spend the rest of her life with him.

"Just remember, Willa carries a dirk at all times," Morgan offered unhelpfully.

Christian grunted.

A curt knock sounded on the door. Silent, like a clipper ship cutting through the night, Wheatley appeared in the room.

"Good morning," Christian called out. He returned his attention to the mirror as he fiddled with his neckcloth. He wanted to look his finest for Katherine today. "I'm on way to see—"

"Lady Meriwether?" With his shoulders thrown back like a soldier at attention, the impertinent butler refused to look at him. "That's entirely wise, if I may say so, Your Grace." Wheatley finally regarded him with a stare normally used for unwanted visitors.

"I'm relieved you approve," Christian answered, not bothering to hide his sarcasm.

Wheatley shrugged. "But the real reason I'm here is to inform you that another shipment has arrived of your brother's belongings."

"What is it this time?" Christian asked, clearly not interested.

"Your brother's . . . collection of erotic art," Wheatley said sheepishly. "It's statuary. Fifty pieces." The butler sighed.

"Store it in the attic," Christian answered.

The butler's eyes widened.

"Leave it in the front of the house or destroy it if it pleases you," Christian said in a voice that would brook no dissent. He straightened his coat. "I don't care what you do with it. I have business to attend to. I'm off to see Lady Meriwether."

The butler delivered one of his rare smiles, and Christian nodded in acknowledgment. As he exited his dressing room, Wheatley called out a farewell.

“Excellent, Your Grace. Don’t worry about a thing. I know what to do with your half brother’s art collection.”

Chapter Twenty-Two

Numbers swam before Katherine's eyes. Before the shop opened in a couple of hours, she had to complete the bookkeeping today if she wanted to know how much money she had to order materials for the Prince Regent's linens. Some of the lace would take months to import if she didn't order it now. The gold thread that the linens required would cost a fortune.

She let out a silent sigh. Her heart wasn't interested in work today. It wanted Christian, and so did she. They'd shared the deepest intimacy a couple could ever experience, and she'd run out of his bedchamber faster than a spectral being could permeate a stone wall. What could she possibly say to explain her behavior?

Your Grace, I've pretended to be a lady of quality and I'm nothing of the sort. By and by, I'm a begging bastard who has no idea whom her father is, but I've created a marvelous story about his existence. Did I mention that I've been convicted of thievery?

The clock on the wall struck the hour of nine at the same time a knock sounded on the door.

The only person here was Thaddeus Warren, her ex-pugilist bodyguard. Katherine rose from her chair. "Come in, Mr. Warren."

He peeked his head in. "Oi sorry, milady, but the Duke of Randford is here to see you. Since it's not opening hours yet, I thought it'd be all right."

"Thank you. Please send him in." Her heart tripped in its beat.

Warren opened the door wider, and Christian stepped into her office with his hat in his hand.

"Good morning, Lady Meriwether."

Goose bumps ran amok down her arms at the deep thrum of his voice.

"Thank you, Mr. Warren," Christian said with a smile.

Warren answered with one of his own. "You're welcome, Your Grace." He turned his attention to Katherine. "Do you need anything else?"

"No, thank you," Katherine answered, not taking her eyes off Christian.

After the pugilist walked away, Christian closed her office door with a decisive click.

His eyes blazed, and he was slightly out of breath. He reminded her of a warrior who would defeat any enemy he found in his path.

She'd never seen him so ruggedly handsome. His uncommonly long hair lay against one cheek as if hiding the flush of excitement from her.

She wouldn't allow it. She walked to him and gently pushed the hair away from his cheek. Though he was clean shaven, the slight stubble tickled her fingers, kissing her palms. All she wanted to do was run her lips over his cheekbones. Then she noticed a sliver of dried blood around his mouth.

"What happened?" Katherine brushed the back of her fingers against his lips, seeking to comfort the split in his skin.

"I was in such a rush to see you, I cut myself shaving." Christian placed his hand over hers, effectively stopping her caresses.

"Does it hurt?" She couldn't resist this man. On her tiptoes, she brushed her lips against his.

"Not with you tending it."

"You're the first man outside of Mr. Warren and the Secretary to the First Lady of the Bedchamber to enter my office." The warmth of his hand on hers made every sense come alive with want.

For him. She wanted to bottle such feelings for her own, a memory to carry forever.

"I had to see you." The seriousness in his eyes was breathtaking.

Her heart pounded against its cage, desperate to reach him. She knew exactly how it felt. She'd surrender everything to him too.

"Why are you here?" she asked softly.

"For this," he said, then circled his arms around her waist and brought her close. His lips met hers. A deep groan rumbled through him as she opened her mouth so he could deepen the kiss. Chest to chest, the sensuous feel made her tremble. She felt protected enveloped in his arms and allowed herself to revel in the feel.

This wasn't a simple kiss, but one that possessed every inch of her—completely. She met his boldness with the same. Another moan escaped. Whether it was from him or her, she couldn't tell. All her awareness was centered on this man who held her as if he'd never let her go.

She broke away to steal a breath. Christian murmured a slight protest before he pressed the small of her back until she was flush against him. The other hand skimmed her work dress from her hips to her breast. He teased by caressing his thumb against the tight nipple then captured her breast in his hand, kneading gently. A riot of sensation careened through her, sending a heaviness to rest in her lower abdomen like it always did when he touched her.

He nibbled on her lips. The iron taste from the blood of his sore lip rested on her tongue. She licked the wound again, as if stealing a part of him for herself. He wanted her, and that hunger fed hers for him, and only him. It also fed a want deep inside to belong to another. Not to have him would be akin to the inability to draw a breath. She'd gladly drown in the force of his passion rather than be smothered in a sea of banality.

Which perfectly defined her ordinary life before Christian.

Everything in her life had been nothing before he'd swept in like a rogue wave.

He gently pushed her against the closest wall and canted his hips toward hers. His hard length branded her through their clothes.

"Christian," she pleaded against his lips as she sucked in a breath. She wrapped her arms around his neck, holding on before she fell to her knees.

"I had to see you." He nipped at her lips. He cupped one breast in his hand, then groaned like a starving man. "God, Katherine, with all this linen around, please tell me you have a bed somewhere?" He dipped his head and sucked lightly on the tender skin of her neck. "Not that we need it, mind you." His hands seemed to be everywhere, delivering a flurry of movement. Buttons were undone on the back of her gown, ties on her stays were untied, and then cool air met her back.

Christian was undressing her in her very proper and elegant office.

And he wasn't doing it fast enough.

"Follow me." Never breaking their kiss, she led him down

the private hall. They stopped once as if they needed their kiss to keep going. Eventually, they entered her private sanctuary, a perfect hideaway for them. Without breaking their embrace, she reached behind her and locked the door.

It was the room she'd created for her customers to visit when they were deciding on how to redecorate their bedrooms. A bed stood on a round pedestal dais in the center of the room. Soft candlelight flickered from all sides. It was the very embodiment of romance.

By then, he'd managed to lose his coat, waistcoat, and shirt somewhere between the office and the bedroom. She was no better. Her dress had fallen off her shoulders and rested on her waist. Her stays were nowhere to be seen. With greedy hands, he continued pushing the gown and chemise down her hips.

"What do you think about this bed?" She gasped slightly.

"What bed?" he asked, between the licks and suckles he administered to her hardened nipple, "I'll die if I don't have you. You're all I think about." He kissed the other neglected nipple then took her breasts in both hands as he studied her body. "*You* deserve to have a man's complete attention only on you. And I'm going to be the man that gives it to you."

She whimpered at the words.

He was worse than dangerous.

He was devastating when he said things like that.

She wanted to tell him how romantic he was, but she didn't want to argue. Not now. So she glanced down. Never had she seen such an erotic sight. His large hands held her breasts as he rubbed his thumbs over her taut nipples.

"God, you're so incredibly beautiful," he whispered, then kissed her again. He trailed his tongue down her neck.

The sensation sent her senses careening. She was wet—achingly wet for him. She should be hesitant, but all she could think about was having him again. By now, they both were naked. Without any hint she was a burden, Christian swept her in his arms, then gently laid her on the bed.

Just as in her dreams, he loomed over her with a labored breath that perfectly matched her own. As their chests rose and fell together in a rhythm they'd created together, they stared at each other. They were carefully balanced on a precipice. One false move by either of them could spell disaster. She could die of a broken heart, and he might go through life alone.

His gaze never left hers as he swept her hair behind her ear while his fingers moved across her cheek. He brushed his nose against hers, then pressed a gentle kiss to her lips. "I want to make this pleasurable for you without any pain."

"I'm ready," she whispered.

He lowered his body until his chest was against hers. He rocked gently back and forth, his nipples teasing hers. After a moment, he lifted his body from hers and rested on one elbow. He skated his other hand down her body, learning every curve, every dip, every piece of her, inside and out. That was the only way to describe their lovemaking. Anything he asked of her today, she'd gladly give him as long as he continued to look at her the way he was now—like a starving man.

And she was the only sustenance he required.

She whimpered slightly at the change in tempo of their coupling. He turned his attention back to her nipples. They were so hard and puckered that they ached for his touch. All Katherine could do was tilt her hips toward his in a show of need. She was desperate to have him inside her.

But Christian didn't rush. He murmured her name as his hand crept lower, then even lower.

Her skin tingled in anticipation. "Please," she begged.

Finally, he touched her center, the one that demanded he attend to it.

She hissed when he stroked her most private part.

"Too much?" he asked, withdrawing his hand.

She grabbed his hand and held it to her. With her other hand, she stroked his cock, hard and thick. "Not enough."

He groaned in answer and thrust his cock harder against her palm. In response, she rubbed her thumb over the velvety crown, spreading his leaked essence over it. Then she brought her thumb to her mouth and sucked.

He closed his eyes and exhaled deeply before he opened them. It thrilled her deep to her core, the heart of her, to know that she affected him so. He wasn't always the one in control when he was with her. "Shall I take you in my mouth as you've done for me?"

"Later," he whispered then kissed her soundly, all the while still ministering to her, each stroke making her ache even more.

She bucked into his hand, wanting the release she craved.

"Now." Her words echoed throughout the darkened room.

He entered her with two fingers, keeping his thumb pressed against the sensitive nub. The waves of pleasure came faster and faster until she closed her eyes. A crest of sensation, a kind she'd never experienced before, rolled through her. It reached deep inside, stealing her breath, and she gasped. Everything within her exploded into a million pieces, then as her body calmed, those same pieces drifted slowly and reassembled.

Christian immediately took her in a gentle, soulful kiss. "Good?"

She panted, desperate to catch her breath. "Very."

A grin tugged at one side of his mouth. She answered in kind with one of her own.

He balanced on his knees and took her hips in his hands,

tilting her toward him. When he had her positioned just right, he held her gaze. "Put me in."

It wasn't a demand, but the need in his voice squeezed her heart. In response, it beat double time. She guided his member to her center, and then he pushed in little by little.

He kissed her again. Whether it was to distract her or seduce her, Katherine didn't care as long as he continued to hold her. When he was fully seated inside of her, he buried his head into her neck and started to gently roll his hips. She matched his movements, and he groaned against her neck. "You're my haven."

He adjusted her again, and she wrapped her legs around his hips. As his movements became more frantic, he deepened his penetration. Everything within her unfolded as if giving him access to her deepest desires and wants. "Christian," she murmured, holding on tight.

"I feel it too," he uttered. By now, his member was a piston inside of her. Over and over, he drove into her, claiming her and her body as his. He moved harder and faster until she thought she couldn't take anymore.

He stilled above her. He clenched his eyes closed. The cords in his neck were pulled taut. The raw power of him above her stole her breath. As his climax claimed him, he roared her name as he pulled out of her body.

At the same time, she whispered, "I love you." Instantly, her heart flipped in her chest. She held her breath, waiting, but he didn't respond or even acknowledge her.

Once Christian seemed to realize she was there with him, he slowly gathered her in his arms, then rolled until she rested on top of him. With the gentlest of touches, he brushed the back of his fingers across her cheeks. "You've ruined me."

"How so?" She laughed while leaning into his touch.

"You've ruined me for all others." Christian continued to

stroke her cheeks, but his gaze never left hers. "I love you also."

She concentrated on the dark intensity of his eyes. A thousand reasons to shout for joy rushed through her. He loved her. "Really?"

"Truly." With the most tender care, he cupped her cheeks. "I never thought I'd find this. Never thought I'd find you."

The warmth of his body next to hers was a luxury she didn't think she'd ever get used to. Now, everything had changed. He was an addiction, and she never wanted to be cured. She breathed deep, inhaling the scent of their coupling. She'd remember this moment for the rest of her life. Did all lovers experience such intimacy?

"I have a confession," he murmured.

"What?" Katherine leaned close and kissed the indentation in his square chin.

An endearing yet sheepish grin tugged at his full lips. "I couldn't keep away from you if my life depended on it. But why didn't you let me know you were leaving last night? I would have taken you home."

"You were asleep. I didn't want to wake you, and Morgan was kind enough to see me home."

His gaze held hers captive. The weightiness of it made her stomach clench.

"Katherine, I want to redefine our partnership." The room grew suddenly silent. The exaggerated pulse at the base of his neck matched hers. He took her hand and entwined their fingers then brought their hands to rest next to his heart. "I think we should make it permanent."

"As in work?" she answered.

A lopsided grin appeared. "You're not going to make this easy for me, are you? Have it your way." A mere second later, she found herself beneath him. He brushed his nose against hers. "My darling Kat, will you marry me? Live the rest of your days with me?"

"Don't be silly. There's no need to even consider it. Besides, I don't expect or want a proposal." Her acting abilities were phenomenal if she did say so herself, even if her heart raced as if trying to outrun the lie she'd said aloud.

He cradled her cheeks in his hands. But a coolness, almost reprimanding in nature, flashed in his eyes. "I'm serious." He moved one hand until he cupped her jaw, ensuring she'd not turn from him as he spoke. "I know you said you don't want to marry again. I'm asking you to reconsider that decision."

She blinked, then slightly nodded. "I know."

"You're too precious to me. More than anything, I want you as my wife."

Her heart tumbled in her chest. It was everything she'd ever hoped for but couldn't have.

"Don't ask me," she whispered, then pulled away from him to sit up. She wrapped a sheet around her body, then crawled off him, still clutching the sheet. She began to look for her clothing.

"It's a little late for modesty, don't you think?" he said.

"Perhaps I'm cold." She bent down and picked up her chemise and stays.

"Then come back into my arms and let me warm you," he replied, the seduction in his words unmistakable. "Why don't you want to marry me?"

Her insides melted at the deepness in his voice. "It's not that I don't want to, but I can't." Her voice was so low, she didn't know if he could hear her.

She slipped her chemise over her head. Thankfully, her stays could be worn with the lace in the front.

In a flash of movement, he stood before her, stark naked. Adonis would look like an ordinary man next to Christian.

He towered above her with his perfect body, save the scar, a badge of honor. She looked her fill, hoping to remember every inch of his beauty and his grace.

"Don't look at me like that, or we'll be back in bed in a trice." Christian gently placed his hands on her shoulders and held her still with their gazes locked. "Why can't you?"

Her throat burned as tears flooded her eyes. An ache deep in her chest surged with every heartbeat.

He gently pulled her into his arms. "You can tell me."

Her cheek rested against the strong beat of his heart. She needed to borrow some of that strength. It was exhausting to keep it all inside. This was the time to tell him the truth. If she trusted him with her body, she could trust him with her secrets. "I'm not who you think I am."

"Come. Sit with me." After donning his breeches, he sat on the edge of the bed then pulled her onto his lap.

The breadth and size of his body was something she didn't know if she'd ever get used to. As her tears fell, he brought her closer and slowly rubbed one hand up and down her spine. The tenderness and comfort he offered made the tears fall faster. If she shared everything that had happened, he'd understand why he couldn't marry her.

"I have no idea who my father is." She forced her gaze to his.

He leaned slightly forward and kissed her on the brow. "Is that why you think you can't marry me?"

She didn't trust herself to speak without another rash of tears falling so she nodded.

He tilted her chin until their gazes met. "I don't care. I only care about you."

"I'm a bastard."

Christian tried to contain his shock, but he must have divulged too much by the crushed look on her face. "Sweetheart, help me understand. You told me your father was lost at sea."

"It was a lie." Katherine's voice was so low, it sounded like she was speaking inside a barrel. "Only Willa and Helen know the truth. I didn't even tell Meri." She released a shuddered breath. "My mother . . . was my everything."

"She taught you well, Kat. I'm so happy you had her in your life."

She smiled a sad smile through her tears. "I wonder if you will feel that way after I finish. My mother would be proud of my acting abilities because . . . she was a professional actress. Her stage name was Elise Fontaine. She was a woman who loved me dearly and sacrificed so much for me. She took acting jobs that others cringed at. She took parts where the only payment was the contributions collected at the end of the performance. She didn't care about her pride because she made certain I was clothed and fed. Most importantly, she made certain I knew I was loved."

"You were lucky." It was the only response Christian could think of as his mind reeled with the information she was telling him. He swallowed the sudden thickness in his throat.

She deliberately glanced away. "Yes, I was."

"I still want to marry you," he said gently. "I don't care about your mother's acting career. I care about you. Share my life. Become my duchess."

"You need to hear everything I have to say. I married your brother with the foolish thought that it would remove the taint from me." She shrugged slightly, the act so forlorn that he wanted to hold her forever. "Before I met Meri, I learned all the rules and manners expected of a woman in society. I was surprised how easy it was to fool everyone, including him. When he asked me to marry him, I thought I'd captured the Golden Fleece."

He brushed his lips against hers, then whispered, "I say he had when he married you."

She shook her head and smiled slightly. "You don't play fair."

"I beg to differ. I play honestly." He kissed an errant tear from one soft cheek. "I don't care who your father is. I don't care what your mother did for a living. She taught you how to love, Katherine Greer. And for that, I will always hold her in the highest esteem." He turned her face slightly, then kissed the three remaining tears. "The truth is, my darling Kat, I can't let you go. I've found the most perfect, astonishingly impressive woman in the world to love. You helped me realize my dream of helping others and giving me a purpose. As long as we're together, loving each other every day, that's the only thing that's important."

A fresh onslaught of tears fell when she stared at him. Each one stole a piece of his heart.

She looked up to the ceiling and shook her head as if ready to say no. "There's more. I wasn't going to tell you, but you deserve the truth."

He had no idea what was causing her so much pain, and all he wanted was to take it from her and throw it out the window, never to bother her again. The telltale twisting of her of fingers revealed her turmoil. He placed his hand over hers to stop the frantic movement. "Whatever it is, we'll work through it."

"I don't think we can. Shortly after my mother died, Willa went to take care of a cousin who lived about twenty miles away. She thought she'd be gone a day, but it turned into several weeks. I didn't budget my food or coal carefully, and I couldn't find work. So, I went out one morning, ready to beg on the street."

By now, tears were streaming down her face. He tried to

wipe them all away, but they fell in a river. Each one a reminder of her deep pain.

"Sometimes, we do what we have to in order to survive." Desperate to give her comfort, Christian brushed his thumb across one of her brows.

"My mother"—she shook her head slowly—"would have been so ashamed of me that day if she'd been alive." She turned her head. "I stood at the corner of the market district trying to decide what to do. I'd been to every store up and down the street, asking for work. So, I stood there and struggled with what to say as I held my hand out." She tilted her head, their gazes colliding. "I couldn't do it. I couldn't bring myself to beg."

Her voice dropped so low, he had to bend close to hear her.

"A band of boys came running by. They were about my age, but I didn't recognize them. One of them stopped before me, and said, 'Hello, angel.'"

A sob racked through her body, and he pulled her closer if that were possible. "Did they hurt you?"

"Not physically," she sniffed. "He put an apple in my hand, and said, 'For you.'"

"What happened?" He brushed his fingers across one cheek. For a moment, she leaned against him and he brought her close.

"The grocer came around the corner with a constable. They were out of breath, but you could see the anger in their eyes. The boy who gave me the apple yelled, 'She did it.' I didn't know what they were talking about so I simply stood there. You see, they were shoplifters, and I later discovered that they'd been stealing from the grocer for months."

"Sweet Jesus," he whispered. All alone, she would have been at the mercy of the constable. "Did anyone help you?"

"A man named Mr. FitzWilliam came out of his shop. He and his wife owned a local haberdashery. He had seen everything unfold and told the constable that it was the boys and not me." She shrugged. "It didn't make any difference. Within the hour, I was hauled in front of the magistrate, convicted, and sentenced to the pillory. I had to repay the grocer for all the stolen goods over the last month." She leaned her head against his chest as if seeking sanctuary. "I didn't have a shilling to my name."

"Sweetheart, I'm sorry." He rocked her gently.

"Me too," she answered. "Mr. FitzWilliam appeared and paid my fine, then said if they'd allow it, he'd take me home. Thank God, they let him. From that day forward, I embroidered for him. He helped me design my first linens." Her tears were slowing, but her nose was red. "I've never felt so ashamed and humiliated. People jeered at me as Mr. FitzWilliam took me to his shop. He explained to his wife what had happened, and they fed me and had me stay with them until Willa returned."

His heart hurt for all she suffered. A young girl grieving the loss of her mother, then dealing with the terror of being falsely accused.

She took a deep breath, then turned her face up to his. "That's why I can't marry you." She shook her head. "But please don't say a word to anyone."

"I promise I won't." He ran a finger down her long neck. "If I could find those people, I'd put them all in the pillory."

"I'd like to see that." She chuckled briefly, then turned serious. Her brow furrowed in pain. "Do you know that to this day, I can't eat an apple without retching? I hate the sight of them."

"They'll never be served at our tables. I promise you that."

"But don't you see? It'll never work. The church will never allow us. You'll be mocked and your reputation ruined if you associate with me," she argued.

"Don't worry about the church. I promise we'll be able to marry. What's important is right inside here." He pointed his finger to the middle of her chest. "This is what makes you who you are. I see a woman of the highest integrity who I love with everything I am. And do you know what's amazing?"

She swallowed, then shook her head.

"She loves me in return. I know when something rare and precious is in front of me, Kat. It's you." He dipped his head and pressed another gentle kiss to her sweet mouth. "Marry me," he softly pleaded.

"What if someone finds out about York?" The yearning in her gaze gave him hope.

"We'll deal with it then. But I don't care. Do you believe me?"

She nodded hesitantly. The fringe of her spiked lashes rested against her cheeks. Slowly, she opened her eyes, revealing an unfathomable depth he'd never seen before.

"Please say yes." He had no idea how she was going to answer. With the silence surrounding him, Christian couldn't breathe as he waited for her response.

"Christian . . . I will marry you."

He exhaled all his apprehension and pulled her tightly against him. "You will never regret it. I promise."

"I only hope you won't," she murmured.

"Never." He tilted her chin an inch. With infinite slowness, he lowered his lips to hers. He poured everything that he was and would be in the future into their kiss. Each second that passed was a promise he'd put her first in his life always. The same for any children that came from their marriage. He would give her that dream of a marriage and a happy life. More importantly, if it was within his power, she would never have to worry about the past again.

They didn't tarry at Katherine's shop. After they dressed, they quickly made their way to her home to speak with Constance.

It was such a whirlwind. On the carriage ride over, not a minute seemed to go by without Christian leaning over for a kiss. Of course, Kat returned the gesture with one of her own. She was bursting with happiness. Christian loved her, and they would marry even after she'd told him the truth. Just remembering his tender proposal made her feel as if anything and everything were possible in her life.

They'd agreed the soiree would be in two weeks. Though it wasn't much time to prepare, Christian had assured her that Wheatley and Morgan were up to the task of preparing the house for the party. They'd decided that Kat would ask Helen for help in developing the guest list. As the premier London hostess, Helen knew practically everyone in society. Finally, Christian had convinced Kat that they should announce their betrothal at the end of the event.

Shortly, they arrived at her house and made their way upstairs, where they met Willa on the landing with a basket of laundry. Willa's gaze skimmed Kat's face. "You look like the cat licking the stolen cream from its whiskers." She turned to Christian. "You also, Duke."

Christian bent close to Willa's ear. "You're looking at the future Duchess of Randford."

Willa reared back with a grin. "You don't say?" She dropped the basket, then tugged Kat into her arms. "I'm so happy for ye, lass."

A fresh set of tears, this time happy ones, erupted. "Thank you."

Willa eyed her again and nodded. "You chose well."

"Thank you for saying that," Christian said softly. "I'll take excellent care of her."

"You better," Willa teased. "I don't wanna have to use my evil eye on ye."

"We're here to tell Constance about the Earl of Sykeston," Christian said.

Willa let out a sigh. "I hope there's good news for that sweet lass too."

"There is," Kat said.

Willa grinned, then escorted them to Constance's bedroom door. "The duke is 'ere tae see ye."

Both Constance and Beth looked up from their reading. Each of their faces was expressionless. Constance nodded, then straightened as best she could into a sitting position. She seemed on the verge of giving birth. How could a human body stretch like that? Truly, it showed that women were the stronger of the human race if they could tolerate such an amazing physiological transformation.

"Come in, Your Grace." Beth stood and pulled a chair close to Constance's side.

Christian nodded and bowed over Constance's hand. He then repeated the same for Beth. "I've come today with hopefully happy news."

Beth had moved to the other side of Constance's bed. Her brow wrinkled slightly, but she didn't say anything.

"What is that, Your Grace?" Constance spread her hands over the bedcovering, smoothing out the wrinkles.

Christian's gaze focused on Constance. "The Earl of Sykeston has agreed to marry you."

Constance's dark eyelashes flew open, but she didn't utter a peep. Instead, she simply stared.

"Have you changed your mind?" Kat asked.

"No." She shook her head. "It's been years since we've seen each other. I can't believe he said yes." Her voice trembled slightly. "How is he?"

"As well as can be expected." Christian smiled slightly. "He came home with a severely damaged leg. He has trouble walking at times."

Constance's hand flew to her mouth. "Oh, God. Poor Jonathan. I haven't had a chance to see him. He was never home in Portsmouth when I tried to call on him."

Christian leaned a little closer. "He's willing to marry you before the baby is born. He said he didn't care if it was a boy or a girl."

Constance dipped her head. "Really?"

"Really," Christian said softly. "He had to travel to Portsmouth but will be back in London as quickly as he can."

"I can't tell you how relieved I am at the news." Constancc stared out the window with a winsome smile before turning back to Christian. "Thank you for all your help, Your Grace."

"You're welcome," he answered.

Beth stood and clasped Constance's hand. "Congratulations."

"Thank you, Beth."

Affection swelled in Kat's chest for her friends. She leaned over Constance and kissed her on the cheek. "I'm so happy for you and your baby."

Kat wasn't the only one affected as Constance's eyes grew bright with tears. "Thank you, Kat, for everything."

Christian turned to Beth. "I must leave shortly, but I wanted to ask if you've given any more thought to your future?"

"I'm happy as I am. Don't think for a second that I want to marry," Beth said with a sure nod and radiant smile. "But there is something I think we should address."

Constance nodded. "Beth and I would like to ask about Katherine?"

"Me?" What were her friends up to?

Christian leaned back in his chair with a grin. "I'm all ears."

"Marriage is what we want to discuss, but only if she wants to," Beth said earnestly. "But if and when she does, Constance and I believe he should be a man of the highest caliber with a generous spirit." Beth looked at Constance, then turned back to Christian. "She's been incredibly kind and has welcomed both of us into her home as if we were family."

"We *are* family," Kat corrected.

"I'm thinking of perhaps a man who will love her and care for her as deeply as she cares for all the others in her life," Constance offered, then smiled at Kat. "I want her to have someone who sees how truly special she is. She deserves love and so much more."

"That's perfect," Beth whispered.

Kat wiped her eyes at the kindness and love expressed on her behalf. "I can't believe you've thought about that for me."

Christian's gaze met Kat's. The warmth of his smile echoed in his voice. "I believe it, and I'm in agreement with you. I might have a man in mind, but I don't know how perfect he is. However, I can recommend him as he loves her madly."

In that moment, she fell in love with him all over again.

"Do tell us." Beth laughed.

Christian pressed a kiss on Kat's hand. "Will I do?"

Everything within her tingled. She had little doubt he'd always affect her that way. She turned to her friends. "It's true. We're to marry."

Constance clapped her hands as a shout of joy erupted.

"I knew it!" Beth exclaimed.

Kat's heart swelled at the scene. This was her new family, where hugs and congratulations were freely given. Now she knew what it was like to have sisters.

And a future husband who truly loved her.

Chapter Twenty-Three

Christian's dream of launching his charity to potential benefactors would culminate tonight in a successful rout that the *ton* would be discussing for months on end. Kat was honored to be a part of it. Not only that, but she would celebrate beside him when their betrothal was announced.

She caressed the ensemble that Christian had purchased for her to wear this evening. The white silk gown was covered with a lace overlay decorated with small crystals and seed pearls. The bodice neckline was trimmed in crimson ribbon, reminding her of the Portland rose he loved to grow. The shoes matched the deep red trim with crystals sewn in the pattern of the rose on the front. Even the intimate apparel, the stays, chemise, and stockings, were embroidered with tiny dark red roses.

Ever thoughtful, Christian had sent Willa an exquisite gown in a shade of orange that reminded Kat of autumn leaves. Willa had looked ravishing in it with her red hair. Excited for the event, she'd even mentioned she planned to dance with Morgan tonight.

For the first time in her life, Kat felt like Cinderella finding her true prince.

The previous two weeks, whenever they'd been together setting up the displays for tonight's event at Rand House, Christian had found a way to sneak them away for a few stolen moments. Sometimes it was for kisses, other times more intimate expressions of love.

He'd been so sweet and passionate in his lovemaking yesterday. The memories were like gentle caresses, each touching an intimate part of her. Immediately, she thought of his hands holding her, stroking her skin, and sweeping across her face. Heat crept across her cheeks as she recalled the tender whispers of love he'd shared with her yesterday.

"Kat?" Willa popped her head around the door. "Mr. Hanes is downstairs and asked to see you. He says it's an urgent matter."

She laid the dress carefully across her bed. "Did he say what he wanted?"

"No. He dinnae look happy, lass," Willa answered.

Her earlier happiness evaporated. "Come with me?" Katherine took her hand and squeezed.

In answer, the woman squeezed Kat's. "Lead the way."

Holding hands, they walked down the stairway together. No matter the circumstances, Katherine could always rely on Willa. She'd been Katherine's confidant, friend, and most important of all, her family. In seconds, they arrived in the front sitting room closest to the stairs.

Katherine turned to Willa with a tentative smile. "I can't imagine why he would want to see me today of all days. The soiree is in hours."

"Perhaps it has something to do with your engagement to the duke. You know how those solicitors are. They take delight in making matters complicated."

Kat nodded distractedly. "What if it's bad news?"

"If it is, we'll find a way to deal with it." Willa squeezed her hand again. "That's what we do."

"We persist. That's how we survive." Katherine leaned over and kissed her cheek.

"Don't be thinking negative thoughts, my miss. Tonight is your night to shine next to your duke."

"That's good advice." Kat said a silent prayer then opened the door. "Welcome, Mr. Hanes."

The solicitor turned from the window, and Katherine immediately stopped. The solicitor's face resembled the first snow of a long winter. There was no color in his cheeks, and his eyes were sunken as if he hadn't any sleep over the past several days.

"Thank you for seeing me. Under normal circumstances, I would never dare interrupt such an important evening. But this is dire." The solicitor shook his head slowly.

"Of course. Let's sit down." Katherine sat first on the floral brocade sofa where Willa joined her. Mr. Hanes chose an ornate scrolled-back chair that faced them.

Everything within the room grew quiet. The fire didn't spark, and the wind battering the window died.

An ominous sign.

Katherine tried to swallow her unease, but her heart pounded in her chest. If anything had happened to Christian, she didn't think she could bear it. Finally, she broke the silence. "Is it the duke? Is he well?"

"His Grace is fine." Mr. Hanes released a pained breath, then rubbed his knee repeatedly. It was a rather shocking sight to see him so unnerved. It reminded Katherine of the day when she found out there were two other wives besides herself.

The solicitor stared at the floor as if struggling with what to do.

Katherine motioned to Willa. Immediately, she went to Mr. Hanes's side.

"Do you need anything, sir?" Willa asked in her gentle way, as if tending a patient. "Perhaps tea?"

"No, thank you," the solicitor answered before turning to Katherine. "You may want to have privacy for this conversation," he said softly.

Katherine lengthened her spine and tightened her stomach in defense, as if preparing for a fist in the gut. The normal creaking of the wooden sofa legs and the floorboard underneath were remarkably hushed, as if not wanting to break the solemn silence that filled the room. "Willa is my family."

He nodded once. "I'm afraid I have some very distressing news for you."

"The dowries are gone, I presume?" Katherine waited for him to nod.

"That's not why I'm here." Mr. Hanes's gaze never strayed from hers.

Katherine refused to blink. "Go on."

"I'm afraid there's no easy way to introduce what I have to say. Pardon me for being frank, but your marriage is void. Miss Constance Lysander is the legitimate wife of Lord Meriwether."

Katherine didn't react. She sat frozen with every muscle tight like a spring, ready to unleash all the energy it had stored within it.

"What?" Willa jumped out of her seat. "What kind of nonsense is this?" She closed the distance between her and the solicitor, then leaned across his chair.

Instead of the solicitor being intimated by Willa's stance, he straightened in his seat. No more than three inches separated their faces. "I assure you that I have had all three marriages validated, and Miss Greer's and Miss Howell's are void."

"How can that be? She was the first one married." Willa sniffed. "Void. *Pfft.*"

"Void as in phony, a sham, madame," Mr. Hanes answered, as if Willa need clarification.

Katherine's heart faltered in its beat. Or perhaps it was her lungs struggling for air. Within a span of five seconds, her entire world had shattered. She was no longer titled. With such scandal, she might never be welcomed within the *ton*—even with her marriage to Christian.

She could lose the royal contract with any hint of dishonor swirling around her. As important, Christian's charity could be in peril. She blinked, desperate to keep her bearings and find a way out of this.

"Mr. Hanes." She cleared her throat. "Could you explain it to me?"

"Aye," Willa urged. By now, she'd claimed her seat next to Katherine again. She'd taken ahold of Katherine's hand in her tight, warm grip. "I was a witness. There was another witness. There was a vicar. It was all legal." She spoke louder, as if the increase in volume would make it more real. "They signed the register."

"I'm aware of that," Mr. Hanes said calmly. "The reason the marriage is void is a little more complicated than that. The vicar, a Mr. Lawrence Foulkes, had been defrocked the previous month for stealing from the weekly collection and taking more of the monthly tithe than what he was entitled to."

A sneer creased Willa's lip. "I don't believe any of it. Of all the despicable things—"

Katherine quieted her by holding up her hand. "Please, Willa." She turned her attention to Mr. Hanes. "We were married in a church. Why would he still be in his position if he'd been defrocked?"

As soon as she asked the question, Mr. Hanes's Adam's apple moved up and down like a bobber on a choppy lake. He swallowed before he continued, "Well, you see . . . the man owed a gambling debt to Lord Meriwether. Apparently, Mr. Foulkes and Lord Meriwether had quite a past together. After Mr. Foulkes was relieved of his position, he found a secluded church without much activity. Any weekly tithes, he collected for his own pocket. The elderly vicar assigned to the parish had recently retired. No one had taken his place as the congregation was so small."

"But Katherine and I were there every Sunday when the banns were called," Willa challenged.

"I'm sorry, but it makes no difference," Mr. Hanes said to Katherine. "It wasn't his church. He wasn't a clergyman. When the banns were called, there was no one else in the church, no one else around to notice the . . . um . . . unusual activity."

"Typical English," Willa spat. "Should have had a handfasting. That would've made it legal."

Mr. Hanes ignored the outburst. "Truly, I'm as devastated as you are."

"I doubt that," Willa muttered under her breath.

Katherine ignored the remark. "So, Mr. Hanes, you're telling me that my husband arranged for this sham marriage?"

"Lord Meriwether was not your husband," Mr. Hanes corrected.

"Pardon me. You mean there's evidence to suggest the *loathsome and irresponsible trigamist* arranged such a sham marriage?"

Another awkward silence ensued.

"Mr. Hanes?" Katherine's voice grew sharper as her anger began to boil. "Is that what you're telling me?"

"Miss James . . ."

The sound of her real name felt like a slap across her face. But she held herself straight. "It's Greer."

The solicitor's face froze. For an eternity, he didn't say a word. "Another reason your marriage is invalid. You signed the license and the register as Katherine Elise Greer. But you're Katherine Elise James from York."

Willa moved to stand, but Kat stayed her with her hand. "How did you discover that?"

"The duke told me as we prepared the marriage settlement documents. You must use your legal name." He shrugged. "The duke has secured a special license for your wedding. I really can't say more as he wants to discuss the marriage ceremony in more detail with you."

Somehow, Katherine found the fortitude to stand. "Does Christian know my marriage is invalid?"

"I wanted to see you first. You're owed that much." He picked up his leather pocket satchel where he kept his papers. "I'm off to see him now, then I'll be telling Lady Meriwether the news as soon as I inform the duke. Such a shame that I have to tell him about this complication before the charity soiree." He shook his head, his worry clear in his wrinkled brow. "His Grace has been a new man these last several weeks." He pushed his eyeglasses up the bridge of his nose. "Actually taking an active interest in the duchy and its inner workings more than usual."

Katherine stayed him with her hand. "Wait, Mr. Hanes. Tonight means a great deal to him. It's everything he's been working toward since he returned home. Could . . . you not wait to tell him until tomorrow?"

"I suppose," he said, rubbing his chin. "I could see Lady Meriwether then as long as I'm here."

She cringed at the title of Lady Meriwether. "She's not been well."

"I understand, Miss James." He straightened the brim of his beaver hat. "But she needs to know straightaway. You see, if Lady Meriwether has a son, then under the duchy's charter, the boy would be the duke's heir. I need to tell her what has happened." He headed toward the door. With his hand on the knob, he turned to Katherine. "I'm truly sorry for these upsetting circumstances. But this means your marriage to the duke can't be challenged."

She was afraid to ask the next question, but she had to know. "Will your staff keep their silence about this?"

"Of course. Never fear that, Miss James. Good day." He nodded to Willa, then walked out the door.

Numb, Kat slumped in her chair. She wasn't married to a duke's son. She'd never been married at all. If she had the ability, she'd laugh at this cruel farce, but she was still trying to grapple with it all. Meri had said he shouldn't have married her, and as fate would have it, his wish had come true. A little late for him to enjoy but, nevertheless, he wasn't married to her and never had been.

One hot tear fell down her cheek.

Suddenly, Kat had a handkerchief in her palm. Her loyal Willa stood beside her, trying to comfort her.

"Lord Meriwether is not worth your precious tears, lass," Willa crooned gently.

"No, but Christian is." She wiped her tears and gently blew her nose. It didn't alleviate the hollowness she felt inside her chest. "If word leaks that I was not Meri's true wife, I shudder to think what will happen. Chances are the contract will be rescinded. How long do you suppose before the truth of my past life is exposed? It would hurt Christian and his charity."

"Kat, you've had a spell of bad luck. It doesn't mean everything will fall to shambles," Willa rationalized. "You need to leave the past where it belongs. Behind you."

She nodded. "I don't want him to have to bear another scandal tonight. Truth is, I don't want him hurt tomorrow or next week." Katherine put her hands over her face to compose herself, then took a deep breath to hold in her sobs. "Perhaps I inherited a little of my mother's theatrical talents."

Willa sat beside Katherine with an arm around her shoulders. "Your mother, God rest her soul, would have been thrilled with you, and she'd have been so proud of your accomplishments. She loved you like no other. She always told me you had talent, my lass. But it didn't take talent to be Lady Meriwether. Whether you believe it or not, you've always been quality."

"The truth is, I quite liked being Lady Meriwether. It helped my business succeed so I could hire real employees." She pursed her lips to keep the tears from falling once again. "Helen and I became best friends. I'd never had one before, you know."

"I know, love." Willa patted her hand.

The act was so familiar. Willa had been there throughout Katherine's life, helping her lick the wounds inflicted by careless louts who thought themselves superior to her. Katherine placed her hand over Willa's and squeezed.

"Being Lady Meriwether brought me so many gifts," Katherine murmured. "I have Christian."

"And your mother would have adored him," Willa said. The tick-tock of the clock was the only sound in the room for a minute, then Willa released her breath. "Come, Kat," Willa said softly. "A spot o' whisky will help."

Without any protest, Kat followed her until they stood outside the kitchen, where an animated conversation was taking place.

"Are you the husband for the third Lady Meriwether?"

Aunt Vee asked. "My niece is wife number two. She's marrying an earl. The first wife is marrying the duke. Isn't that romantic?"

Katherine turned to Willa and signaled for quiet by putting her finger to her mouth.

As they reached the door to enter the kitchen, Aunt Vee chuckled. "How many you ask? Only three. Lord Meriwether liked to collect them. The duke knows all about his brother's antics."

Aunt Vee stood directly in front of Katherine, blocking her view of the gentleman. A chill skated down her spine. What kind of gentleman came to the back door of a house if he were calling on a person?

Aunt Vee turned and smiled at Katherine. "You're in luck. Here is wife number one. Katherine, I'd like for you to meet . . ." Aunt Vee stepped out of the way. "Who did you say you . . ."

There was no one there.

"Who were you talking to?" Willa asked while peeking out into the back courtyard.

"A nice young man who was looking for a wife. I told him that Beth was available, but that you and Constance are spoken for." Aunt Vee crowded next to Willa. "He can't have just disappeared."

"He's nowhere in sight," Willa said.

"What did he look like?" Kat asked.

"Handsome in a ruddy way." Aunt Vee turned to Kat. "Tall, but not as tall as your duke."

"Could you have imagined him?" Willa asked gently.

Aunt Vee shook her head vehemently. "He was as real as my husband and I having tea every month." She took another look outside. "Perhaps he was blond? It's hard to tell in this light."

A log fell in the massive kitchen fireplace and crumbled into sparks of fire. Almost instantaneously, the embers burned to nothing.

It was a harbinger of her future. Kat was certain of it.

Chapter Twenty-Four

Christian stood before the fire, sipping the whisky. For once in his life, he was looking forward to an event. What was equally surprising? He was hosting it.

A knock sounded on the door. "Captain?" Morgan called out.

Christian looked up and discovered his valet giving him the once-over. "What do you think?" He waved a hand down the front of his eveningwear. His formal evening coat and britches were black brocade, but the crowning glory was his waistcoat. It matched the trim on Katherine's dress and her shoes.

Morgan lifted an appraising eyebrow, then grinned. "I couldn't have done a better job myself, sir. Tonight will mark the end of the handkerchief-throwing parades."

Christian grinned in return. "It's not every night a man announces his betrothal to the loveliest and kindest woman in all of England."

"She'll be delighted," his valet answered. "And so will you."

Christian waved toward the door. "Shall we wait for Lady Meri and Willa in the ballroom?"

They turned left in the hallway, the shortest route to the stairs that led to the ballroom balcony. Once they arrived, the sound of the orchestra warming up and the low chatter of his men filled the room with a strange cacophony of comforting noise. The men were putting the finishing touches to the linens and lap desks on display. Roses from the conservatory provided a riot of color to the room while his servants stood ready to serve the guests that would soon arrive. Wheatley stood at attention by the main doors.

His charity would be the talk of the *ton* tomorrow, and tonight, he'd finally put the shame of his family behind him with Kat by his side.

Christian couldn't wait to see Kat. Perhaps it would be best if they married tomorrow. Inside his desk was a special license he'd acquired at Doctors' Common. Taking Grayson's advice to heart, he would give the *ton* another *on-dit* to fill their heads with.

"There she is." Morgan's voice deepened in awe. "She's beautiful."

Expecting to see Kat, Christian turned to see that Willa had just entered the ballroom by herself, looking splendid in her finery.

"If it's all right, I'm going to greet her." The endearing regard on Morgan's face for the woman was undeniable. It was heartwarming that those two had grown so close. It boded well for when he and Kat joined their households together.

"Please do," Christian answered as his own anticipation mounted. He scanned the room, looking for Kat. His gaze tracked every door in the ballroom looking for her entrance. By then, Morgan had reached Willa. Clasping her hands in his, his valet was saying something in her ear. A beautiful blush colored her cheeks.

The incessant pounding of his own heart urged Christian forward. Where was Kat? He turned to make his way down the steps when a vision of ethereal radiance stood not more than five yards away.

"Looking for me?" Kat's dulcet voice soothed his restlessness immediately.

He released a breath and took in the vision before him. The gown flowed over her body in a perfect fit. When the pearls and crystals caught the light, she resembled a fairy queen ready to command her subjects. Whatever she decreed, he'd gladly obey as long as she allowed him to be by her side for the rest of eternity.

His gaze locked with hers. "You are beautiful," he said softly.

Her eyes twinkled. "So are you."

Without hesitating, he closed the distance between them and took her hands in his. "I can't find the words to do you justice. But stunning comes to mind."

"Thank you." She ran a hand down his waistcoat. "This is perfect." She leaned close and whispered, "But not anywhere near as exquisite as the man wearing it."

He took her in his arms, careful not to wrinkle her gown. With the gentlest of touches, he pressed his lips against hers in the most reverent of kisses he'd ever given her. He pulled away and memorized her face. Tonight would represent their future, and he'd make certain she knew how much he loved her every day.

He pressed a kiss against her cheek then took her gloved hand with his. "Perhaps we should marry sooner rather than later."

"We have much to discuss," she said. "Perhaps we could find a moment or two this evening to talk in private?"

Before he could answer, Morgan strolled toward them and bowed before Katherine. He turned back to Christian. "Captain and Lady Meri, your guests are arriving."

He smiled regrettably. "After our first dance, you and I will sneak away. You have my promise." He offered Kat his arm, and without hesitation, she wrapped hers around his.

As they walked down the main staircase, hearty laughter erupted. The Earl and Countess of Woodhaven had arrived.

"Katherine," Helen called out.

Kat waved in answer and smiled brightly.

Soon, Benjamin and Helen stood before them. Other guests took their place in line to greet Christian and Katherine. Already, the ballroom was crowded and promised to be a rout. Yet, no matter how long they stood there, Kat welcomed each person with a brilliant smile and thanked them for attending. She shimmered with a joie de vivre that made her irresistible to the crowd.

Every so often he would capture her gaze. She gave him the same smile she delivered to their guests, but the brightness in her eyes reached deep within him, illuminating everything he'd attained since she'd come into his life.

He'd found his calling, his home, and his heart because of her.

Katherine slipped outside onto a side balcony, desperate for air. Minutes before, Willa had danced with Phillip Reed, and Kat had danced with Morgan. All during the set, Morgan kept glancing Willa's way. Her Willa had an admirer. If the looks Willa stole at Morgan were any indication, she returned his regard.

She fanned herself and looked out over the courtyard. Couples had escaped the crowded ballroom for a respite in the cool night air. Lanterns had been hung from every conceivable tree branch, making it look like an enchanted forest. Christian's charity was a full-blown success if the orders for lap desks and her linens were any indication. Mr. Reed had been thrilled, but the look of accomplishment and pride on Christian's face had made her heart melt.

Thankfully, Meri's latest mischief hadn't put a damper on this night. She took a deep breath. The cool air washed away her earlier unease. As Willa had said, there was no use in courting bad luck. Unfortunately, she and Christian had never had a chance to slip away and chat. Every time they came together, another guest had claimed his attention. In high demand tonight, he seemed to enjoy every minute of it. The smile on his face could have lit the entire ballroom. It had been the right decision not to have told him what Mr. Hanes had discovered about Meriwether. Tomorrow would come soon enough.

"Miss Greer?"

At the sound of her name, she froze. Slowly, she turned to find Marlen Skeats directly behind her.

"Or is it Miss James?" He laughed slightly, but the mocking sound echoed around her. "We know it's not Lady Meriwether, don't we?"

"I don't recall you being on the guest list," she answered in her haughtiest voice.

He looked over his shoulder at the crowded ballroom. "With this crowd, anyone could make an appearance, and no one would object. The nobs are mingling with the commoners. Soldiers dancing with 'soon-to-be-duchesses.' You're no longer Lady Meriwether. It's as if the whole world has turned upside down."

"Where did you hear that?" Her voice trembled slightly.

"After Mrs. Hopkins shared the news of the three wives, I discovered that the duke's solicitor employs a few loose lips that get downright chatty if you supply them with an ale or two or three after a long day at the office." He leaned one elbow against the marble railing and regarded her. "But I digress. Remember that day when you allowed me to look at your handkerchief?" He didn't wait for an answer. "I don't normally carry tales, but I saw you in the duke's embrace."

He tapped his chin. "Funny that, as a widow, you were already dallying with your husband's brother. Such scandalous behavior."

"You seemed to be overly preoccupied with my whereabouts, Mr. Skeats." She took a step back but stopped herself from taking any more. Some of her anger evaporated, but she held what remained close inside. She would not be fearful.

"I decided I needed to find more out more about Lady Meriwether, a woman who appeared from nowhere to make her mark on London. The pattern on your handkerchief gave me a hint. The Belgium lace you used on your fine linens? That was the second hint. I know of only one person who imports that specific design. I've been writing to him for years, asking for him to supply to me. He always refused. So, I went to York to see him in person."

"You went to see Mr. FitzWilliam?" Kat bit the inside of her cheek hard enough she could taste blood.

"Yes." Skeats nodded with a smile that reminded her of a hyena. "He told me all about you. How you're a convicted thief."

Kat shook her head. "I'm innocent. He told you that."

Skeats lifted a brow. "Isn't that what all thieves say? 'I'm innocent,'" he mocked, then straightened and clasped his hands behind his back. "Whether FitzWilliam supported your story or not, it makes little difference." His cold gaze nailed her in place. "You were convicted."

"It was an apple." Kat sucked in a silent breath. "I'm going to call a footman and have you escorted off the premises."

"Don't do that," he warned. "If I leave tonight, I'll just send letters tomorrow, and that'll make it worse for the duke and the other wives. Come. I want to show you something."

Kat didn't move, but Skeats walked around her. The balcony extended into the courtyard, giving a wide view of the ballroom below.

"See there?" He pointed to the Secretary to the First Lady of the Bedchamber. "You know Mr. Sherman. But the man he's speaking with? The Prince Regent. Next to him is your duke." He shook his head slightly and smiled. "Randford is the belle of the ball, as one might say. Everyone wants to be near the war hero duke and bask in the glory of his success. He's practically as famous as Wellington and as well-loved as Nelson. The Prince Regent is thrilled with the idea of outfitting the Royal Pavilion bedrooms with lap desks and small tables that would benefit the duke's charity. I expect he'll place a rather large order."

"That's the Prince Regent?" Her own voice sounded weak to her ears.

"Chubby fellow, isn't he?" Skeats turned to face her.

"How did you find out about the orders?" she asked.

"I spoke with Mr. Sherman before I found you. Does the duke know the truth about you, Miss James?"

"That's none of your business," she snapped.

"Imagine his horror to discover that his future wife is a pilferer. Mr. FitzWilliam said you were sentenced to the pillory for a day and night. Imagine being pelted with rotten food and manure. Humiliating, not to mention filthy." He scrunched his nose. "Society will be outraged if they hear the Duke of Randford started a charity with a convicted thief and planned to marry her. Where is the money they've contributed going? Was it actually provided to the brave men who came home from war? Or was it being siphoned off by the thief?" He tsked. "You know how rumors start," he said.

She could barely control her anger at such lies. Heat bludgeoned her cheeks. "He knows and still wants to marry me. You can take your threats—"

"And what?" He had the audacity to laugh. "If the duke knows about your criminal past, that makes it all the juicier, doesn't it? Like father, like son. He doesn't care what you do as long as you're in his bed. It makes no difference if you've slept with his late brother. His father was the same way, I've heard." He tapped the side of his face. "I can imagine the print caricatures that will be posted tomorrow. He'll be ruined, not to mention a laughingstock."

She turned to where Christian stood. Indeed, she had never seen him so happy and carefree. He seemed to have come alive under the attention he was receiving. Soon, several of his men along with Lord Woodhaven had joined him.

"All those men he wanted to help will be left standing in the cold," Skeats whispered beside her. "Such a tragedy."

The love she and Christian had shared over the last several weeks possessed a power that was unique and special. It had its own strength. But even she feared that it couldn't endure a scandal of this nature. Thoughts of Christian laughing with her, sharing a part of himself, roared to life. She couldn't bear to think of him hurt over the lies this man threatened to announce to anyone who would listen.

If she didn't do something, she would destroy Christian and all he'd created here tonight. All because of an apple she'd taken in her hand over ten years ago. It was unfair. But, when had life ever treated her any differently?

"You can stop it from happening," he added.

"What do you want?" Kat whirled to face him and straightened her spine, every nerve firing.

Slowly, he strolled to her other side and viewed the courtyard. "I want you to write a letter to the Secretary to the First Lady of the Bedchamber saying you can't fulfill the contract. It's too much of a burden for you. Then, I want you to leave London for good." His eyes narrowed. "Tonight would not be soon enough."

Kat locked her knees to keep them from knocking together. "Why would I do that?"

"Mr. Sherman told me I was next in line for the contract. I'll be out of business if I don't receive it. I can't compete with your goods. However, my grandfather started this business fifty years ago. It won't fail under my watch." His face reddened as if in distress. "All you have to do to save your duke's charity and his reputation is to leave."

A slight sneer tugged at her lips that Skeats was threating her livelihood and her employees. A vision of Beth in the workshop skated through her thoughts. Kat had never seen her so happy. But what made the blood race through her veins was the insidious threat to ruin her beloved.

Kat stole a glance at Christian once more. He stood tall while speaking with the Prince Regent. His tall stature gave her hope and comfort, a steady mast in this tempest created by Skeats. God, she loved Christian more than life itself. If he was hurt because of her past actions, then her future meant nothing.

She'd faced challenges before and failed. It was part of life. There was only one decision to make. "I'll agree to it under one condition."

"What's that?" he asked.

"You never threaten the duke or his family again."

"Done," he said with a smile.

"I'll be leaving immediately and will send the letter to you this evening." Without waiting for his answer, Kat returned to the ballroom.

It was no wonder Skeats was losing his business. The man had little negotiation skills.

She nodded and smiled at the soiree attendees as she went to find Willa. One thought kept her on a clear path. Nothing would stop her from protecting Christian.

Within the hour, Katherine stood outside of Constance's bedroom with Willa by her side. "What did you tell the duke?"

Willa shrugged. "I told him you'd taken ill. Lass, I hated to lie to him."

"You didn't lie. I'm sick of having this burden hang over my head. Are you ready?"

Willa nodded. "You should be prepared to tell them when you'll return."

"How can I? If my plan doesn't work, I may never return." Katherine squeezed Willa's hand. "If that's the case, I have no idea where you and I will settle. It certainly won't be London."

Willa let out a sigh. "Perhaps you should ask the duke if he has a residence we can go to until the scandal dies down."

Katherine swallowed. "I won't be a burden to him. I have to manage this on my own. Otherwise, the scandal will never die, and both Christian and I are ruined. If you want to stay with Constance and Beth, I would encourage you to do so. I'm certain Morgan would love—"

"Not another word," Willa scolded. "Where you go, I go."

Her breath halted in her chest. How lucky she was to have this woman in her life. "Thank you." Katherine kissed her on the cheek. "Shall we?"

Willa nodded.

Katherine knocked on the door, then entered.

Beth sat next to Constance in her bed.

"You're home early." Beth stood at her entrance.

"I'm so glad you're here," Constance said. "Mr. Hanes came to see me."

Desperate to keep her ire at Skeats in check, Katherine tried to sound calm. "Are you all right, darling?"

Constance nodded but kept her gaze glued to her clasped hands.

Willa arranged chairs on the other side of the bed so Katherine could face the other wives. Her loyal Willa sat in one, then patted the seat beside her for Katherine.

Katherine made her way to the chair. She arranged her skirts, then looked to her friends. Besides her time with Christian, one good thing had come from this fiasco. She had family whom she could trust. After a weighted silence, she smiled. "Constance, I'm truly happy that you're Meriwether's . . . wife."

Her friend let out a shallow breath. "I have no idea what to say." A tear trailed down her cheek and, immediately, Beth took her hand. "I'm so sorry."

"There's nothing to be apologetic about. Your baby will be born legitimate," Katherine soothed. "It's no one's fault except—"

"Except the sorry excuse for a vicar who performed the service and the rakehell that married you," Willa announced.

Beth nodded in agreement. "*Hear. Hear.*"

"Whatever you need from me, consider it done," Constance whispered as she wiped the tear away.

Katherine leaned over Constance to kiss her on the cheek. "Don't cry. I'll not have you upset by my change in circumstances."

"I'm sorry too," Beth said. Her eyes welled with tears. "But you still have the duke."

If there was a God in heaven, she would still have him in her life. "Thank you, dearest. You're both so kind to me. But there's more that I need to tell you."

"What else could there possibly be?" Constance asked.

Damnable tears. It they'd only leave her be until she got through this. "I'm leaving for York immediately. I've written a letter of instruction that all my funds be transferred to both of you." She turned her attention to Beth. "I've addressed a letter to the Secretary of the First Lady of the Bedchamber. In it, I've said that I want to rescind the contract because it's too much of a financial burden on me." Beth was about to argue, but Kat held up her hand.

Constance struggled to sit. Beth immediately leaned over and helped her up and arranged the mountain of pillows behind her. Katherine closed her eyes as numbers swam like a school of fish attempting to evade the wrath of a shark. Financially, she had enough to take care of Constance, Beth, and her employees for at least six months if her plans didn't work. The remaining amount, a paltry sum by any measure, would have to be stretched for her and Willa until she could think of another way to make a living.

"I've paid the rent on the town house for the next six months. You're both welcome to stay here."

"I don't understand," Beth said softly.

Constance's forehead rippled into concern. "What's this about?"

"Skeats demanded that I write the letter or he would drag both me and Christian through the mud and destroy Christian's charity."

"How can he do that?" Beth's cheeks bloomed with heat. "The bloody bastard."

"Basically, he discovered I was a convicted thief." Amazing that ever since she'd told Christian what had happened, it was becoming easier to talk about it.

Both Constance's and Beth's eyes widened.

Immediately, Willa came to her defense. "She was innocent."

Kat patted her arm gently. "It's all right. I'm going to tell them the whole story."

Willa's eyes grew as round as Constance's and Beth's. "You are?"

Kat nodded. "I'm tired of living my life in fear." She glanced at her hands and smiled. She wasn't twisting her fingers. If she wanted to have a life with Christian, then she had to take the steps necessary to ensure that she was free from the fears and threats that had haunted her for the last ten years. Their love for each other deserved that, and if she didn't try to rectify the damage, then she didn't see how she could marry him. It wouldn't be fair to him, her, or their marriage.

She turned to her two friends and told them everything. When she finished, Kat took a deep, steadying breath. "I've been living with the conviction for the last ten years. I'm going to York to see if Mr. FitzWilliam might help me."

"I can't imagine the burden you carried, living with that accusation." Beth leaned over Constance and squeezed Kat's hand. "But why did you write the letter that you'll give up the contract if you're going to York?"

"To give me time to see if I can fix this mess and keep the contract. I signed the letter to the secretary as Lady Meriwether," Kat said triumphantly.

"But I'm Lady Meriwether," Constance said.

"Exactly," Kat answered. "It was a stroke of luck that I signed the contract under my company's name instead of my title."

Beth grinned. "That's brilliant, Kat."

"I don't understand." Constance looked between Kat and Beth.

"Kat signed the contract as Greer's Emporium. Not Lady Meriwether." Beth nodded with a sly grin.

"But whether you call yourself Katherine Greer, Greer's Emporium, or Lady Meriwether, won't they know it's you?" Constance asked.

Kat nodded. "But you see, I'm planning on selling Greer's Emporium to Beth for one guinea right now. It doesn't make any difference how it was signed." She winked at Beth. "I won't own it anymore if Beth buys it right now before I send the letter to Skeats. Only Beth will be able to rescind the contract."

"Oh, that's wickedly sneaky." Constance nodded in approval.

"Of course, I'll buy it from you for a guinea," Beth announced, then furrowed her brow. "I actually know the magistrate in York. He's name is Mr. George Dane-Fox. His sister is a dear friend of mine from finishing school. I could write you a letter of introduction."

"That would be perfect." The longer she sat with her friends, the more confident she became that her plan would work.

A faint sound, much like a knock on the front door, drifted into the room. Beth stood and looked out the window, then let out a gasp.

"Who is it?" Willa asked.

Beth's hand flew to her heart. "It's the Marquess of Grayson." She bit her lip as if unsure what to do. "I wonder why he's here."

"I'll go down and see what he wants." Willa stood.

"Let me." Beth smoothed her dress. It was the first time she'd been out of sorts since they'd met at Mr. Hanes's office. "He's an old friend of my family. I'd like to see him."

"Don't mention me," Kat instructed. "I don't want Christian to find me."

"But he could help you." Constance said.

"I have no doubt he'd move heaven and earth to help me. But I must do this myself. Otherwise, people will believe that he sought favors of my behalf." He couldn't help. The best way to put a stop to Skeats was to tell the truth about her birth and her time in York before it was all over the gossip rags.

Today, she learned a valuable lesson. Even the proud and proper Duke of Randford was powerless to change her situation. Only she could.

She vowed then and there that Skeats would not win. Which led her to another valuable lesson. All's fair in love and war.

Especially when one loved a duke.

Chapter Twenty-Five

Christian propped his elbows on his desk and rested his face in his hands. "Katherine is gone." He rose from his desk and tended to the fire. Though it didn't need another log, he threw another one in the blazing hearth for something to do. "Things became so hectic last night, we never had a chance to chat. I went by her home this morning and discovered she's vanished."

Grayson poured himself another cup of tea, then refilled Christian's cup. "Beth wouldn't tell me much. What about her workshop or the Beltic Arcade store? Someone must know where she's gone."

Christian turned and started to pace. It was the only thing he could control in his life right now. "Hanes was here before the crack of dawn. The staff hadn't even finished cleaning the ballroom yet. Katherine's marriage to Meriwether was a sham. The vicar who married them was thrown out of the church for some indiscretion." Would his half brother ever quit making such a shamble of everyone's lives? With this latest news, Meriwether had punched Katherine in the gut—from the grave.

"Do you think that's why she left?" Grayson asked.

"I don't know," he mused. "Katherine is worried my reputation will be ruined if her past comes to light."

"Well, she has a point."

Christian stopped midstep and glared at his friend.

Grayson raised both hands in surrender. "Hear me out. What Katherine says is typically true of society. However, in your case, we both know that you don't care."

"Maybe it was the final straw, and she wants to be done with the Vareck family. Who could blame her?"

"Nonsense." Grayson took a sip of coffee. The wisps of steam rising above the cup disappeared into thin air.

Much like Katherine.

"One thing I've discovered from this last Meriwether mess, I'm just like my father. He didn't care what people thought of his wife and favorite son. I don't care what people say about Katherine and me."

Never in his life did he ever imagine claiming anything so foul as his father. Truth was, Christian was as selfish as his father ever had been.

For Christian wanted it all. He wanted Kat in his bed every night, serenading him with her sweet moans and quick intakes of breath as she reached her climax. When he kissed her, he wanted them to lose themselves in each other's arms as their passion turned playful and slow and tender.

He ground his teeth as the truth pounded into him. He was exactly like his father—not in the lewd, perverse proclivities the previous duke had embraced. It was something more fundamental.

Katherine had taught him the importance of family and how to craft one from the friends who truly cared. She taught him where to find a place to belong. "She is more important than the duchy, my charity work, or even my reputation. She's everything."

If he hadn't fallen in love with her, he'd still be trying to outrun his family and their past. He was free now to start his own future. He'd accomplish so much with Katherine by his side, and he couldn't wait to see what lay ahead of them as they started their lives together. Today it was a distant dream. Why did she leave him without a word?

"Even the Prince Regent didn't care after I shared that Meriwether had married three women." Christian pointed to his desk, where a pile of papers littered the surface. "It's all over London that he increased his linen order last night with Katherine's emporium. When I went to introduce her, that's when I discovered she was 'ill.'" He rested one arm against the mantle and stared into the fire, hoping for additional inspiration. He had to find her. "I want to respect Katherine's wishes, but . . ."

"Your heart won't let you?" Grayson answered.

Christian's heart ached. Hell, everything inside ached for her. "Indeed. I wish I were with her. I want to know that she's safe. Why couldn't she tell me?"

Grayson stood and came to Christian's side. "You could send your reconnaissance-trained footmen to find her. Perhaps hire an investigator."

"I'm not certain that would be a wise decision."

"Probably." Grayson nodded in agreement. "I don't know much about love, but I do know something rare when I see it. I've never seen you so alive as when she was in your life. You became another person, one who found delight in ordinary things. If you feel this way, chances are she does also. I don't think her leaving London means she's leaving you." He took his time piece from his pocket. "I must go. I'm meeting with several colleagues to discuss a new idea that's being proposed by some French scientists. They think there might be a way to harness the sun's energy. I'll be back this evening to see if you've made any progress."

"Until then," Christian said.

The marquess headed toward the door, then turned around. "Where's the portrait? The one you use for keeping track of things?"

"I found someone to restore it." Christian walked to his friend's side. "Or I should say, Katherine did."

"Remarkable," the marquess exclaimed softly. "So, I take it you're going to hang it again in the library?"

"No. It has a permanent place in the attic. As Shakespeare once said, 'An ill-favored thing, sir, but mine own.'" Christian shrugged.

"Good decision." Grayson squeezed Christian's shoulder in affection then left.

Afterward, Christian strolled to the window overlooking the courtyard. Whatever Katherine was doing must be something she felt she had to see to. He ran his hands through his hair. The feeling of helplessness was foreign to him. For God's sake, he didn't even know if she was in London or not. The only thing he knew was that she'd taken Willa with her.

All of it left a hole in his gut. His heart seemed to trip in its beat as if its rhythm was off. For a million times that morning, he wished he would have told her he loved her just one more time.

Wheatley stood at the door. "Your Grace, a young lad by the name of Rodney is here to see you. Miss Greer sent him."

"Send him in." Christian rushed forward, ready to greet the young lad, who worked in Katherine's workshop.

Wheatley waved a boy of about ten years into his study. "Your Grace, this is Mr. Rodney . . ."

The boy fidgeted slightly as if shy. "Smith. My name is Rodney Smith."

"Come in, Rodney," Christian offered.

"I've taken the liberty of ordering a tray of sweets that you might share with the young man," Wheatley said.

"I can't stay for that. I need to get back to my work." The longing on the boy's face at the mention of sweets reminded Christian of himself as a lad.

"Wheatley, would you ask the cook to wrap them up so Rodney can take them with him?"

"Of course." Wheatley softly closed the door behind him.

Christian studied Rodney as Rodney studied him. Tall for his age, the boy looked to be mostly arms and legs.

"Come in." Christian escorted the boy to a chair in front of his desk, then took his own seat. "How long have you worked for Miss Greer?"

"Ever since she found me begging on the street," he murmured.

Christian closed his eyes briefly. That was Katherine. Always concerned for others.

"She's paying me extra to come here." Rodney reached into his cloth bag and pulled out a package wrapped with one of Kat's linen samples and tied with a ribbon. "I'm supposed to give you this."

Christian took the bundle from the boy. Kat's violet scent drifted around him as if embracing him.

"Miss Greer told me to wait until daybreak." Rodney nodded. "I must get back to work."

"Wait, please." Christian would do anything to keep him here a little longer. He wanted to know everything the boy could impart about Katherine. "Did you see her this morning?"

A sad smile lit his face. "Bright and early, like the sun rising. Brought me some iced biscuits. She said she was going on a trip."

"Did she say where?" Christian tightened his grip on the package. "Or for what purpose?"

"No." The boy tilted his head in contemplation. "But she did say she had sold the business and I had a new employer." He let out a sigh. "She told me she didn't know when she was coming back."

The hot stab in Christian's chest made him gasp for air. She sold the business? A sudden vision of his future without Katherine flashed before him. He should have followed his instincts and gone to see her as soon as he'd discovered she'd left the soiree. But last night, Willa had made him believe that Kat's sudden illness was inconsequential. She'd said it was Kat's wishes that he stay with his guests and not worry on her behalf. It had to have been the news about her marriage to Meri. Before Christian could inquire more, Wheatley stepped into his study with a box of treats for the lad, and immediately, Rodney stood.

"It was nice meeting you." The boy nodded politely.

Christian rounded the desk. "If you remember or hear anything else, I'd appreciate it if you stopped by again."

The boy nodded, then turned. When he took the box from Wheatley, he thanked him politely.

"I'll see Mr. Smith to the door, Your Grace," Wheatley said, then closed the door behind them.

For privacy sake, Christian took the package to a window seat at the far end of the room. He sat, then swung his legs onto the thick cushion. The recess was large enough that he could lean back against the wall without having to bend his legs. He studied the package in his hands. Gently, he squeezed the linen covering. The contents gave way to his fingertips.

The embroidery on the linen piece matched the set in his bedroom. As he untied the ribbon, his gaze fixated on the edge of the piece. The figure of a *C* and *K* were entwined in a bold red script. Gently, he traced the stitches that Kat had made before he unfolded the cloth. Inside was a letter and a small pillow.

A small red heart embroidered in the same color thread lay in the middle of a pillow slightly larger than a pin cushion. He closed his eyes and leaned his head against the wall. It was similar to the one that Kat's mother had made for her.

Christian placed the pillow on his lap, then opened the letter.

My dearest love,

I have important business that took me from London. Time is of the essence, so I departed early this morning after the sun rose.

I made this for you last night. It holds my love for you. All of it. If you ever doubt my true affection, just gaze at this pillow.

You have my heart forever.
K

Christian stared out the window. There wasn't a word about her selling her business or whether she would return to him. He didn't even know if he'd hear from her again.

He glanced down at the pillow, then pressed his lips against the heart. Kat had been wrong. This pillow didn't hold her love. He did.

Because of that, he'd live through hell and gladly sit beside Lucifer as long as he found her. He slipped the pillow into a pocket sewn on the inside of his morning coat.

He had no doubt now, Katherine James was more than a thief. The evidence was the empty hole in the middle of his chest. He would find her, then bring her home.

Christian slowly strolled through the London streets on his way to the warehouse, where Reed and his men were busy working. After the soiree, they'd been inundated with orders. Three days had passed since Katherine had left, but it felt as if Christian had endured a decade of torment. He still had little, if any, information about her disappearance.

He'd visited Kat's workshop and her place of business. Both places were empty as if closed for good. Afterward, he'd called on Constance and Beth, hoping they could tell him more about her disappearance. Venetia had greeted him and politely informed him that Constance wasn't feeling well and Beth was attending her. When he'd asked Venetia if she knew anything about Kat, she'd shaken her head and said she was sorry.

After that, he'd called on Helen, who hadn't heard from Kat. She seemed genuinely surprised that Kat had left London. Even Morgan hadn't heard from Willa.

The woman had left without a trace, except the pieces of Christian's crumbling heart littering London.

"Your Grace?"

Christian slowed to a stop then turned. He should have kept on walking. It was his typical luck to run into Marlen Skeats.

A disingenuous smile crossed the man's lips. "How fortuitous to find you this morning. I was going to call upon you."

"For what purpose?" he practically growled.

"A business proposal. I thought we could come to an agreement to help one another." The hopefulness in Skeats's face soured Christian's already dampened mood.

He stared, not hiding his contempt. "I'm not interested."

"Come now, Your Grace, I'm aware of the situation your brother left for you and Miss James to deal with."

"Why are you calling her Miss James?"

"We discussed her situation." A feigned look of pity crossed his face. "She's pulled out of the contract and left London for good."

He didn't answer. It was inconceivable. The contract was Kat's pride and joy.

Skeats nodded with a smug expression.

All sound seemed to have disappeared from the street as Christian hung on every word.

"It was apparent that she didn't have the financial backing to do the work." Skeats rocked back on his heels and puffed out his chest much like a Dorking rooster. "Happens all the time to businesses that don't have the resources to make a go of it." He leaned close as if they were confidants. "Plus, with her conviction as a thief, imagine the disgrace your charity would have experienced being associated with one such as her. It took a little convincing on my part, but she fled with her tail between her legs."

"You convinced her?" he asked while tamping down the urge to roar.

"Yes," Skeats answered, turning serious. "I told her that I'd tell the secretary about her past if she didn't rescind the contract and leave London. A military man such as you can appreciate the rules. They're meant to be followed."

"And what rule did she break?" Christian asked, not keeping the menace out of his voice.

"Once a thief, always a thief. Pretending to be a lady doesn't hide the truth. If you didn't know, she's a bastard. Her mother was a mediocre actress." Skeats lifted a brow. "I have an appointment with the Secretary to the First Lady of the Bedchamber to discuss how I can take over the contract. I'll be more than happy to work with you and your charity to supply the additional items that the Prince Regent wants."

Christian's earlier ire ignited into a full-blown fury. "You sanctimonious arse," he seethed, then raked his gaze over Skeats as if he were offal. "When did you have this discussion with her?"

"There's no need to be uncivil," Skeats added with a sniff. "To answer your question, at your soiree."

"You weren't even invited. Which means you trespassed in my house." He could have the man arrested for such a charge, and no one would even ask for evidence. A duke's word carried that much influence. It took every ounce of strength Christian possessed not to bloody the man's nose. "Do you know where she went?"

Taken aback, Skeats shook his head, then stepped out of Christian's path. "She didn't say, but I'm not surprised she didn't tell you. It's her nature."

Christian methodically forced his hands into fists. Katherine's secrets had been unearthed by the scum in front of him. Skeats had forced her away. She'd sold her business, cutting her ties to London and him. It took every ounce of restraint not to challenge him right there to settle their differences on a dueling field.

Christian stepped closer, then lowered his voice. "It's *my nature* to tell you to go to hell. I will never do business with you, nor will I ever acknowledge your presence." He took another step. "When you see me, you turn the opposite direction. Understand?"

Skeats didn't answer. Instead, he turned and walked briskly until he was out of sight.

The more Christian found out about the night of the soiree, the more convinced he became that he'd never see Katherine again.

He patted his coat pocket where he kept the pillow she had given him. Before bed, he'd placed it next to his side. When he woke from the unrelenting dreams of trying to find her, his heart had pounded in the stillness of the empty night. Automatically, he'd reached for the pillow and breathed deeply. Last night, the scent had diminished in strength.

Another piece of her slipping away.

He wouldn't let it stand. Without a second thought, Christian purposely strode through the streets. Several times he heard his name called. To his acquaintances, he raised a hand but didn't pause to chat. He was a man who wouldn't stop until he found her.

Finally, he stood on Kat's front doorstep. His blood pounded thick through his veins, like it always did when the call to battle sounded. But this time it was different. His ire at Skeats and his broken heart over Kat's disappearance combined into a maelstrom that would not be defeated.

He pounded on the knocker. If there was a God in heaven, Venetia would answer.

He lifted his hand to knock again when the door opened.

Venetia greeted him with a smile. "I was wondering when I might see you again." She leaned close and whispered, "I can't invite you inside and talk to you alone."

His eyes narrowed.

Before he could ask why, Venetia stepped over the threshold, then closed the door behind her. "But no one said anything about the outside." She winked.

"Where is she?" The yearning in his voice was unmistakable, but he didn't care at this point.

"I can't say." Her brow furrowed. "But Willa told me specifically not to mention York to you."

For the first time since the soiree, Christian could breathe again. "I thank you, madame."

She nodded, then opened the door. Instead of walking back into the house, she turned. "Please hurry. I miss them both."

He nodded, then turned for home. As soon as he made his way inside, he called for his sleekest carriage and fastest team of four.

By nightfall, he should be well on his way to York.

Which meant he'd soon find Katherine.

Each creak of the carriage wheels brought Katherine closer and closer to the magistrate's office. It also took her away from Christian. She closed her eyes and rested her head against the leather squab. She couldn't think like that. Whatever happened in the next two hours would be key to allowing her to return to him whole.

Yet, the emptiness inside her threatened to swallow her. If she wasn't successful in getting her name cleared, then she'd have to face letting Christian go. Now she understood how people who suffered from a broken heart could wither away.

She wouldn't think like that. It would work. For once in her life, she'd face her demons and fight until the end. When she'd first arrived, she had little trouble finding Mr. FitzWilliam, who had agreed to meet with her and the magistrate.

Katherine glanced out the carriage window as the beauty of the Yorkshire countryside passed. "Do you ever miss this place?" Without waiting for Willa to reply, Katherine continued, "I used to, but not anymore. You once said we needed to find our way in the world after my mother died. It's not here. Our way is in London."

Willa patted Katherine's knee like she'd done a thousand times before whenever worry had a stranglehold over Kat. "Indeed, lass. We'll find our way back there just as we always do." A spry smile tugged at her lips as she waggled her eyebrows. "Perhaps someday we could take a holiday along the shore. I've always fancied dipping my toes in the ocean. Maybe I could learn to shuck oysters. You could create a soap to chase away the fish smell."

For the first time in five days, Kat laughed. "Oysters are not fish."

Willa dismissed her comment with a wave of her hand. "But they come from the same smelly place."

Katherine stared straight as a new idea percolated. "Soap-making, you say. We could make some, then sell it along with the linens."

"That's my girl!" Willa clapped her hands together. "A fine idea for a new endeavor." She grew quiet for a moment. "Wish I'd taught that Skeats fellow a lesson when I had the chance."

"You mean a lesson with your dirk?" Kat shook her head. "I'm glad you didn't."

Willa started to argue, but Kat held up her hand. "This is for the best. There will be others like Skeats in my life, and I can't have you always ready to defend me with a knife."

Willa's interest had turned to the countryside. After a moment or two, she broke the silence. "Why didn't you tell the duke where you're off to?"

A pesky tear fell, and Kat wiped it away. "He would have insisted upon coming and helping me. It would become fodder for the rumormongers that he paid to cover up my conviction. That would have hurt his reputation even more than it already is."

"You have to tell him, lass."

"Of course, I will. But I have to do this on my own," Kat said softly. She was tired of feeling sorry for herself. It was exhausting. "All my life, I've known that I had been wronged. I've let people use my misfortune against me. With their looks, taunts, and scowls, I've allowed myself to feel as if I wasn't worthy or somehow less of a person. Whenever I would meet someone, my first worry was whether they'd know about my past. That's no way to live. With Christian, I want a life where I can give all of myself."

Willa raised an eyebrow.

Katherine narrowed her eyes. "You didn't tell Morgan, did you?"

"I may like the young man's company, but it doesn't mean I tell him tales he has no business knowing." She huffed a breath. "As if I'd share such a secret with one of the duke's employees. It's your business, lass. Do you ever blame your mother for you being a bastard?"

"I could never blame her. She loved me."

"Do you blame me for not being there and protecting ye when you were arrested?" Willa asked so softly that Katherine wasn't certain she heard correctly.

"No." Then in a firmer voice, Kat said, "I blame myself for being in the wrong place at the wrong time and for not fighting harder." She leaned forward in her seat and took Willa's hand in hers. "I would never hold you accountable for my mistakes." She squeezed her hand. "My mother was the first person who loved me for who I was. You were the second."

Willa wiped a tear from her eye. "Thank you, lass. I love you like my own."

Katherine leaned forward a little more and kissed Willa on the cheek. "And I love you like my own."

Willa straightened and tidied Katherine's cloak like a mother would. "If I were your mother, it would be remiss of me not to tell you there is a third person who loves you. Your duke."

"Do you think he'll be angry?" Kat asked softly.

Willa shrugged. "I don't know, lass. But if he is, I wouldn't blame him."

Before Kat could answer, the carriage slowed to a halt in front of a lovely estate on the outskirts of York. It was the home of Mr. George Dane-Fox, the local magistrate. A footman stood ready and opened the door.

In moments, they were escorted to the study, where Mr. FitzWilliam and the magistrate waited for their arrival.

She stood tall, didn't twist her fingers, and smiled. "Good

afternoon, Mr. Dane-Fox. My name is Miss Katherine James from London, and this is my companion, Miss Willa Ferguson." She turned to Mr. FitzWilliam. "Hello, sir. I can't tell you how much I appreciate you being here."

After greetings were exchanged, Mr. Dane-Fox had them all take a seat. "I read the letter Miss Howell sent. She speaks highly of you. Now, what can I help you with today?"

Katherine took a deep breath for fortitude. She could not fail. Her future with Christian depended on it. "I'd like to tell you what really happened ten years ago when I was convicted of stealing an apple."

Chapter Twenty-Six

"Thank you for listening to both me and Mr. FitzWilliam." Katherine shook Mr. Dane-Fox's hand.

"Of course, Miss James. I was glad to be of assistance." The magistrate bowed slightly and turned toward his study.

The footman opened the door. With Willa by her side, Katherine stepped out into the fresh air. The bright sun blinded her for a moment.

"Look, Kat," Willa whispered. "He's here."

She blinked twice, not believing what she was seeing.

Christian leaned against the side of his massive travel carriage, staring at the ground. The instant he sensed the change in the air, he raised his gaze and found her. She stopped to drink in the sight of him. His face was drawn as if he'd lost weight, and shadows lingered beneath his eyes. It appeared he hadn't slept any better than she had since they'd parted.

He didn't move as she hurried down the steps to meet him. Marble had to be more pliant than his expression. After what seemed like an eternity, she reached his side. "Hello, Christian."

"Katherine," he answered.

No *Kat*. No *sweetheart*. Just *Katherine*, which perfectly matched the formal tone in his voice. She clasped her hands in front of her. "It's good to see you. Actually, it's better than good. It's everything. But . . . how did you find me?"

"I called on Venetia. She stepped outside your house and told me. No one mentioned that she couldn't talk to me outside." A hint of displeasure sounded in his deep voice. "I believe Willa wanted her to mention York to me."

Kat's gaze flew to Willa, who had her back turned and was in a conversation with Morgan. As if she sensed Kat's staring at her, she turned and shrugged in apology.

Christian called out to Morgan, "Why don't you take Willa in Miss James's carriage?" His gaze slid to hers. "I'll take Miss James with me."

A coolness, almost an icy veneer, seemed to encase him. It reminded her of the first time they'd met. He was *that* man again, the one she'd first been introduced to at the solicitor's office.

He helped her into the carriage, then let go of her hand immediately. She sat in the forward-facing seat, and he across from her. Without a word exchanged, he knocked on the roof. The jerk of the carriage caught her off guard, and she placed her hand on the bench beside her to balance.

"Where are we going?" she finally asked after several minutes.

"Wherever you'd like," he answered. The reserve in his voice became unbearable.

"I'd like for you to stop the carriage."

He complied instantly by knocking on the roof. Katherine swung the door opened, then turned his way. "I think we should walk. It might make the conversation easier."

"For you?" he asked.

"No, for you," she answered. "It might loosen you up a bit." Without waiting for Christian to exit first and help her down,

Kat took Iverson's hand and carefully stepped to the ground, then strolled to a copse of trees. If memory served her correctly, an orchard of some type was on the other side. When they were far enough away from the carriage, she turned to face him.

Christian leaned against a tree. His gaze dropped to his hands. Almost in slow motion, he removed the leather gloves finger by finger. When his hands were free, he looked her way. "I take it that your business is completed?"

"It is, and I was successful." She took another step closer. The air hung heavy. That had to be the reason they weren't rushing into each other's arms. She would not allow herself to think anything otherwise. "May I tell you about it?"

"If you'd like." His brown eyes flashed with an emotion she couldn't identify.

Close by, several wrought iron benches looked over a small stream that bordered one side of the orchard. The sound of the flowing water offered comfort. "Would you sit with me? You were my first stop when I returned to London."

He held up his hand, inviting her to precede him. She sat on one bench and waited for him to join her. To her utter disappointment, instead of sitting next to her, he chose another bench directly across from her.

"I suppose I should be honored that I was to be your first," he said.

Those words reminded her of when they'd first made love. He'd been so tender and loving toward her then. But the man before her and his attitude were a mystery right now. She had no idea what he was thinking. If she lost him . . . She wouldn't allow herself to finish the thought.

"I had hoped . . . you'd be as delighted to see me as I am to see you." Though his eyes were hungry and seemed ready to devour her, she wouldn't look away.

"You have no idea," he murmured. "You're all I thought about since the night of the soiree. It's been torture. Pure hell." He glanced over his shoulder at the horizon. "Skeats came to see me. He told me that you had an exchange that night."

"We did. That's why I left."

"Why didn't you tell me?" He stood abruptly, then started to pace. "We're to be married, and you didn't deem me worthy of sharing your travel schedule?"

"You were deep in conversation with the Prince Regent. I had to move quickly."

"For what purpose?" he asked.

"To protect everyone I care about," she answered, then lowered her voice. "Especially you."

"Me?" He stopped as if surprised at the response. "What could that sniveling coward have done to me?"

Katherine let out a tremulous breath. "Skeats told me if I didn't give up the contract and leave London that night, he'd ruin you. He threatened to run to the gossip rags with the information that I was a convicted thief who was embezzling or worse, stealing from your charity."

His eyes softened. "That's why you left? To save my reputation?"

She nodded briskly. "All I could think about was who would be the next to hurt you by threatening me." She looked into his eyes, and those damnable tears clouded her own. "I couldn't let anyone, especially Skeats, hurt you because of me. I love you, and I'll do whatever I have to do to keep you from harm." A tear fell, and she angrily wiped it away. "Furthermore, I'll do anything and everything to defend you and our love."

"Even leaving me?" he asked.

"Yes." The intense hurt in his eyes mirrored hers, but now

was not the time to crumble. Not when she was fighting for them. "Will you listen to what I have to say?"

He nodded once.

"If I told you what I had planned, then you would have wanted to go with me. I had to do this on my own. Otherwise, I don't think I could have married you."

He stumbled a step in his pacing. "What are you saying?"

"I came to York to clear my name." She glanced down at her hands. She still wasn't playing with them, a good sign that gave her strength to continue. "I realized I could never be the wife and partner I wanted to be for you if I still had a foothold in the past. You deserved better, and so did I. I finally understood that simple fact."

"What did you do?" he asked softly. He took a step in her direction and stopped again.

"I went to see Mr. FitzWilliam and asked him to come with me to meet the new magistrate. When we arrived, I asked the magistrate if he'd review my case and listen to what I had to say."

Christian tilted his head. "Did you ask for a pardon?"

"No. A pardon would mean that I was even now a thief." She bit her lip. "Everyone would still think me guilty. I needed to clear my name and claim my future for myself. I hope you understand." Her throat tightened, but she forced herself to continue. "I asked the magistrate to reconsider the case, and he agreed. After he heard Mr. FitzWilliam's statement as well as my own, he reached a new decision."

Christian stood before her without a hint of what he was thinking. Perhaps Willa was correct. He was angry with her.

"He declared me innocent." She wouldn't turn from his gaze. "I can't tell you how freeing this is." For a moment, she didn't know if she could continue without crying. "No one can ever accuse me or threaten me with my past again. Which means they can't hurt you. I know how much your reputation means to you as you rebuild the duchy. That's why I left. I love you more than anything in this world. If I had to give you up to protect you, I would." Tears were freely streaming down her face now, and she didn't care. All she cared about was the man who stood in front of her. "Now, I can stand by your side and give myself to you and our marriage without any reservations or fear." She forced herself to stop so she could take a deep breath. "That is, if you'll still have me."

The trickling water of the stream and the occasional call of a magpie were the only sounds between them. He continued to stare at her. Her entire future felt as if it hung by a thread. A stitch was nothing when dealing with a duke in a moment of time.

Lucky for her, she was an expert at taking threads and turning them into masterpieces.

"But I warn you now, if you don't want to marry me, you're going to have to be the one to walk away." She stood and took a step nearer. "I'm not leaving until you tell me that you love me and you forgive me."

Suddenly, he was before her with his mouth slamming into hers.

It was completely uncivilized, but Christian couldn't keep away her from any longer. He pulled her into his arms and kissed her. Nothing chaste or polite, this kiss contained a savage passion. The fact she was leaning into him and returning the kiss with the same hunger made his heart swell.

When they finally took a breath, her hand went to her lush lips. In wonder, her mouth formed a perfect *O*.

"I've discovered quite a bit about myself since I've met you. There's one need I can't live without. It's you. I need you in my life, Katherine Elise James, more than anything. I don't give a damn about the duchy or my reputation. I've said it before, but it bears repeating. All I care about is you." He squeezed her tightly to him. "Promise me one thing?"

"What?" she asked in that breathless voice that turned his insides into jelly.

"Don't you ever dare leave me again," he growled softly, taking her hand and pressing a kiss to her soft skin. "I want to be beside you, a part of you. Understand?"

She nodded.

Still holding her hand to his lips, he cupped her cheek with his other hand. "I always wondered why I was put on this earth. Now I know. It's to love you." He pressed a kiss to the tip of her nose. "Completely." He pressed another to her forehead, then trailed his lips lightly to her temple.

He filled his lungs with her scent, knowing he'd never tire of it. He'd never tire of her.

"Every day that I can show you how much I care, I will call it a success," he said softly against her skin. He cupped her head with his hands. "I'm happy your past is behind you. I understand your feeling of relief. I feel it too. I've shed the horrid memories of my family because of you. I'm giving you my heart, my love, and everything I possess."

Katherine came out of the sensual fog she was lost in. "I have nothing to give you. I sold my company to Beth and gave my money to Beth and Constance. It was the only way I could think of to keep Skeats from ruining the contract." Her eyes searched his. "I'm worth nothing. No wealth, no home, and no dowry. I spent it all." She sighed softly.

"I beg to differ," he said. "If you give me nothing, then I'll consider myself the richest man in the kingdom." He wanted to rejoice when she combed her fingers through his hair, the touch tender and loving. "Nothing is very important. I myself am very fond of the word *nothing*."

She had tears in her eyes. "You silly man. Why?"

Her love for him made her face glow and, immediately,

he was caught in her warmth. "It's a powerful word. For instance, nothing will ever keep me from you. Nothing will keep us apart. Nothing will keep me from giving you my heart. Nothing will keep me from showing you my deepest abiding love every day. Nothing will keep me from making love to you. Nothing will keep me from begging you to marry me every hour until we say, 'I do.'"

"Enough." At the same time, she was laughing and crying. "Enough," she repeated, then eventually turned serious. "My turn."

"Anything, my love."

"I'm sure you're angry. Do you understand why I had to do this?"

The hurt and uncertainty in her eyes told him how he answered would define their lives from this day forward. With a deliberate ease, he took both her hands in his. "I'll be honest. I was worried, Kat. I haven't slept or eaten in days. Though I didn't like it, you were trying to shield me from scandal by leaving. How could I be angry for you loving me and trying to protect me?"

"Did you get the pillow?" She nodded slowly, but her eyes didn't mask her vulnerability.

He pulled it out of his pocket. "It kept me from drowning in despair and has never left my side since you left. It reminds me of all the wonderful things you are. A woman"—he brushed a thumb across her cheek—"who loves fiercely. She possesses a deep affection for her family, her friends"—he dipped his head until he caught her gaze—"and me." He wiped a stray tear from her face.

"I fought for myself and cleared my name." She bit her lip. "But underneath it all, I'm still a bastard."

"I don't care. I love you." He cupped her cheeks, not allowing her to look away. "Like me, you couldn't help the circumstances of your birth. But unlike me, you were loved,

Kat. I know how valuable that is. It's everything. It makes life worthwhile. You make life worthwhile. Share your life and all your days with me. I promise I'll fill them with love."

She let out a tremulous sigh, then nodded slightly. "So you'll still marry me?"

"Never doubt that." For the first time since she left, all was right with the world. "You'll come home with me?"

She nodded.

He pressed his lips against hers. Everything around them disappeared except this kiss and embrace. When she moaned against his mouth, he kissed her deeper as their hunger for each other threatened to consume them. Such was the beauty of them together. When she whimpered slightly, he gave her no quarter. Under no circumstances would this woman ever doubt her worth in his eyes.

She drew a deep breath and her eyes widened. "Look around us."

He didn't take his gaze from hers. "What do you see?"

"We're in an apple orchard." The wonderment on her face was a sight he'd never forget. "I don't think I hate apples anymore." Her brilliant eyes glistened with emotion.

"Say it again," he pleaded. "Say you love me and you'll marry me."

"I love you, and yes, I'll marry you," she said against his lips before giving him another kiss that threatened to drag him under.

He didn't care as long as she was with him.

"But you don't play fair. Did you lead me into this orchard?"

He laughed. "That was all your handiwork, my love. Besides, I thought all was fair in love and war." He pressed his lips against hers. Then and there, he vowed to kiss her at least five times a day for no other reason than to remind her how much he loved her. "Thankfully, we need only concern ourselves with the love part."

"I think you have the saying wrong. It should be . . . all's fair in loving the duke." She pressed a kiss against his ear and whispered, "And you're the duke."

"No. You have it wrong." Christian laughed as Katherine tilted her head adorably. "I'm your duke."

Epilogue

Rand House
Six months later

Katherine strolled through the halls of Rand House. Each day brought a new treasure to discover. On the inside, it contained a charm and grace that transformed it from something formidable into something beautiful.

Much like Christian.

For the past several months, she'd established a routine where she would meet her clients for appointments at Greer, James & Howell Emporium in the mornings while Beth supervised the workshop. In the afternoons, Beth would handle the emporium appointments.

When Kat had returned to London, she and Beth had decided to change the name of their business as they were now partners. Kat smiled. Now her friend wasn't a bit afraid to reveal herself.

In the afternoons, Kat would work with Christian on his charity or on her new soap venture. Her first batches, though small, had been wildly successful. The violet-and-rose-scented bars were her favorites. Her next foray in fragrance would be to mimic Christian's favorite scent of sandalwood.

Beth had stopped by yesterday evening. Marlen Skeats

had come to her begging for work, and she'd had the utmost pleasure turning him away from the emporium. He was insolvent, and frankly, it was for the best. She and Beth had hired all of his employees.

Katherine stood outside the conservatory, her favorite room in Rand House. She quietly turned the handle and stepped inside. Immediately, the warmth and humidity surrounded her, making that first breath inside the room difficult. The sweet perfume of roses filled her second breath. The orange trees had been moved to the south side of the room. Endless rows of roses filled the remaining area.

As if she conjured him from some dream, Christian came toward her, his long legs devouring the distance between them. The very same legs that had been entwined with hers last night. She couldn't turn from the sight. Determined and resolute, each step seemed synchronized with the pounding of her heart.

When he came within five feet of her, he slowed to a stop. His eyes sparkled and his nostrils flared. He stood before her in all his ducal glory.

Katherine blurted the first words to come to her. "Where is it?"

He lifted a single eyebrow.

"Hand it over." She laughed, then held out her hand while eliminating the distance between them.

"Wife, I have no idea what you're asking."

"Quit teasing," she protested, then proceeded to run through his pockets. Not finding what she wanted, she ran her hand over his waistcoat. "You can't hide it. I want *it* now."

"I married such a saucy wench," he sighed with exasperation. "Fine." He wrestled off his morning coat and threw it to the ground. Then, he unbuttoned his waistcoat. "I wanted to wait until this evening to ensure that you were properly fed, rested, and wooed before we made love." His lips spread into a smile that stole her breath. "But if you want to do it here under the glass dome, I am your servant, Duchess." His deep voice vibrated with laughter around them.

"Stop teasing." She blew a stray piece of hair from her eyes and smiled.

Christian came to her finally and wrapped one arm around her. The heat of his body surrounded her, and she closed her eyes. Who needed a fire when a woman could have a lovely embrace from her husband?

With his other hand, he ran it gently over her rounded middle. "And how is she?"

"*He* is fine," Kat answered with a smile.

"You'll make a glorious mother." His face softened in the glow of the morning light, making him even more handsome than the day before.

"And you a wonderful father," Kat replied.

Christian placed a sweet kiss against her lips as he reached into his waistcoat pocket. "Is this what you're looking for? I hope it meets with your approval," he whispered, running his lips across her cheek until he found her earlobe and gently nipped.

She tilted her head to give him greater access. That's when she saw it, the most glorious orange rose she'd ever seen. "It's beautiful," she said in awe. "It looks like a harvest moon."

"It's the Katherine," he said proudly.

"Oh, Christian," she said as tears threatened. "You've been working on that for years. It's perfection."

He smiled broadly. "Only a flawless rose should be named after my wife."

"I can't wait to show it to Constance, Beth, and Helen. They're coming over tomorrow for tea. Constance is bringing the baby." Her fingers trailed the perfect petals. "This is the best present ever."

His eyes immediately brightened. "Would you come to the

workshop with me today? Reed thinks your design for the new beds and bedframes will be popular. He wants to build a prototype."

"Of course. Let me change."

A jaunty lopsided grin tugged at his lips. It always made her heart skip a beat. He inspected her dress, then slowly leaned close. He trailed his lips across the skin of her neck until he kissed that tender spot beneath her ear. "You look ravishing in that lavender brocade and silk gown. Don't change."

"Thank you." She'd never have enough of this man.

"Speaking of ravishing, I could ravish you now." Christian nipped her skin gently, then soothed it with another kiss.

"Hush," she playfully chided. "We'll shock the staff with such actions if they see us out here. I think they heard us the last time we were in your study. Wheatley hasn't looked me in the face for two days."

"Indeed." Christian waggled his eyebrows. "Yesterday, he actually blushed in front of me."

Kat pressed a kiss against his lips, then murmured, "I want to show you a room I discovered this morning. It'll be perfect for my work area."

Christian shook his head decisively. "What about the connecting room next to my study?"

"It's too small." She straightened his cravat. "I've decided that we'll need a larger room if we're going to be looking at wood and fabric samples for the furniture. Plus, I want a display area for my soaps."

Christian pulled her closer to him and exhaled. "I suppose you're right, darling. I find it amazing how busy we'll be in the next couple of months. Men from the Ninety-Fifth Regiment have already been applying for positions in the new factory. We have orders from Helen and Abbott for new beds."

"Ahem, Your Graces," Wheatley called out as he walked toward them.

"I swear I'm going to dock his pay one of these days," Christian growled.

"No, you can't," she whispered. "When Wheatley auctioned off Meriwether's erotic statuary, he raised five thousand pounds for the charity."

"Good point. My wife, always the diplomat." Without letting her go, Christian answered their butler. "What is it, Wheatley?"

"Another bequest from Lord Meriwether. A prized Hampshire boar," Wheatley said matter-of-factly.

"Put it in the stables. We'll send it to Roseport." Christian smiled, then turned to Kat. "At least, it's something useful."

"I'm sorry, sir, but the bequest is for Her Grace," Wheatley said with a smile.

"For me?" Then as if the baby thought it funny, it started to kick nonstop. Kat placed a hand over her belly. "What am I going to do with a pig?"

"Bacon is always a sound choice," Christian said.

"Sir, based upon its pedigree, this hog is worth a fortune," Wheatley informed him.

"Will you put it in the stable for me?" Katherine asked with a smile.

"Of course, Your Grace," Wheatley said with a bow.

Christian watched their butler leave. "I wonder what that's about?"

Katherine tucked herself closer to her husband. "I don't know. I didn't think your brother left me anything."

"We'll figure it out." Christian rubbed his nose against hers in a show of affection, then pressed a tender kiss against her lips. "I love you, wife. Always and forever."

"And I you." Tears welled in her eyes at the sincerity and love on his face. Never did she think she'd be this lucky to find the man of her dreams, someone as wonderful as Christian. "I don't regret my supposed marriage to your half brother anymore. Because of him, I found you."

Christian cupped her face with his hands. "And I, you, because of him. It almost . . . but not quite, makes me want to claim him as my brother."

She nodded and squeezed him tight.

"I'm the richer for it," he said.

He bent down to kiss her, and Kat closed her eyes, loving the feel of his arms around her. She'd never grow tired of his kisses or the wondrous man himself. When their lips touched, a spontaneous combustion of need and want swirled around them. It always happened when they became lost in each other's arms because they loved each other.

Forever.

Author's Note

I'm sure you're wondering how Meri escaped from being charged with bigamy . . . or trigamy as Katherine called it. It wasn't as difficult as you might think.

Between 1750 and 1815, there were one hundred and seventy-nine cases filed for bigamy proceedings in the Old Bailey, London's Central Criminal Court. Wives and husbands alike were brought up on charges for these crimes. When convicted, the wayward spouse faced a variety of punishments including branding on the thumb, incarceration, transportation, and fines.

Even though marriages were recorded in the parish record books and witnesses were required to validate the ceremony, there simply wasn't a central marriage license registry. A spouse like Meriwether could disappear and then find another to join him in wedded bliss.

In 1823, a stopgap measure was mandated to keep some type of permanent records of who was legally shacking up with whom. Every marriage had to be entered into the parish register, and a copy of every page had to be sent to the bishop assigned to the parish. Thus, we have the makings of a central department for the recording of valid, certified marriages across the country. In 1837, a civil registry of marriages was established in England and Wales called the General Register Office.

I like to think that Katherine and Christian were quite happy that Meri found a way to skirt around such a bothersome legal requirement of sticking with only one spouse at a time.

Read on for an excerpt from

RULES OF ENGAGEMENT

BY JANNA MACGREGOR

Coming soon from St. Martin's Paperbacks

Shall I call a doctor? Where are you hurt?" Constance knelt on her knees and lightly placed her hand over his. The sounds of his fall and the accompanying groans of pain still seemed to resonate around her.

Jonathan's eyes jerked open at her touch.

"Come now. I lied to your valet for you. I said a trunk of my shoes fell. Please don't tell me you're uncomfortable with me by your side touching you."

For an eternity, he didn't say a word, but stared at her. Without taking her hand away from his, he continued to rub his leg. "It's not that."

"What is it, then?"

His voice lowered, and she had to lean toward him to hear. "Very few have seen the gnarled flesh of my right leg. If you faint at the sight, I can't pick you up."

"I won't faint," she assured him.

"It's happened before with others," he argued.

"I'm not that type of person, nor do I faint at the sign of blood." She smiled slightly and was rewarded for her efforts when a grin tugged at his lips. "Katherine's companion is renowned for her knowledge of herbs as well as gifted with medicines. She sent a recipe, and I made a salve for you to help with the pain."

"You made it for me?" he asked.

She nodded. "Mrs. Walmer was quite accommodating."

"My cook allowed you into her kitchen." He ran a hand down his face as if trying to reconcile the fact. "I shouldn't be surprised. You could charm a badger to share his burrow." He shifted an inch in the chair, his abrupt exhale ragged.

The poor man was obviously in a great deal of discomfort. "Let me get it. It can't hurt."

For a moment, she thought he was going to refuse. Finally, he nodded.

After quickly checking that her daughter Aurelia was fast asleep in room next door, she picked up the salve, then returned to Jonathan's side.

She knelt again at his feet. She scooted closer until she was practically between his legs. He widened his stance slightly. The subtle movement released the scent of cedar soap. The rich fragrance melded with his own, a potent and virile male who happened to be in front of her.

Constance bent her head, pretending all her concentration was centered on opening the jar of salve. In actuality, it was to keep from revealing the effect he was having on her. At the last twist of the lid, the scent of peppermint floated between them.

"Ah." She brought the container to her nose and inhaled. "It's very pleasant. I added peppermint oil. It's still your favorite, isn't it?"

He didn't answer.

She silently exhaled. He should know by now that silence had never stopped her before. "I tried the salve on myself. It isn't harsh nor will it leave a stain." She held the jar out to him.

Without wasting a glance at the salve or her, he said, "You do it."

She swallowed slightly. She'd never dreamed he'd ask her to help him, but she wouldn't look a gift horse in the mouth. This might be the only opportunity to break down some of the barriers between them.

"All right."

He grabbed her by the wrist before she could lifted his banyan out of the way. "Don't."

To an outsider, it might have appeared abrupt, as if he wanted to hurt her. Instead, his touch was incredibly gentle as if holding a piece of crystal. She studied his hand holding her wrist. With the long length of his fingers, he could easily encircle both of her wrists with one hand.

"Don't what?" she asked.

"Don't look at my leg when you rub it in." His gaze never left hers as he continued to hold her arm. "Promise me."

The rough and hardened voice infiltrated her chest. Every organ, cell, and other parts of her body vibrated in awareness. It was the first time they had truly been alone without another living creature disturbing them. Even his dog Regina had retired for the evening, content that her master was in good hands.

"I'll only look at your face and the jar."

"Thank you." He released her.

She scooped some of the salve, then rubbed her palms together, releasing more of the fragrance. "The peppermint oil is designed to mask any odors."

"I wouldn't care if it smelled like a horse's . . ."

She couldn't help but laugh. "Who would have guessed that the Earl of Sykeston possesses such a vile vocabulary? I'll have to watch that Aurelia doesn't hear such language." The words trailed to nothing as she peeked at him under her eyelashes.

Finally, a small smile creased his lips. "Well, if that's all she has to be afraid of, she'll be fine."

"I think I'll start at your ankles, then move toward your knee. How far does the injury extend?"

"The worst is above the knee," he answered. "Flesh is missing on my thigh where a ball had to be dug out."

It took every ounce of strength she possessed not to cry out at the horror he must have endured. Not of pity, but of outrage at how much he'd had to brave. Not only had he been shot, but then to come under the surgeon's knife afterward. "Are you ready?" she asked softly.

"Yes."

Constance kept her eyes on his as she deftly placed her hands on his ankle. His skin cool to the touch, and the bones so different from hers. She massaged his ankle down to his heel. His ankle was so large, she couldn't wrap both hands around it. As she trailed her hands up his calf, she prepared herself for what she might feel. A puckered wound, missing flesh, none of it would surprise her.

"How does that feel?" She continued to stroke upward, kneading the tight muscles of his calf. The hair on his legs was smooth but coarser than what she had expected. "Too hard . . ."

The words trailed to nothing when she found the first scar. It felt as if a cup of flesh had been carved out of the back of his calf.

He didn't flinch when she grew quiet. "A little harder, please. That was the second bullet I took. The first knocked me off my horse."

"Then what happened?" She pressed her fingers into his skin, again and again. With the palm of her hand she pushed straight down. She repeated the movement for several more minutes.

He wasn't going to answer, so she reached for more salve.

Then she remembered their stupid rules. "I suppose I wasn't supposed to ask about that."

"What?" He tilted his head as if truly not understanding what she was talking about.

"Asking about your past. What happened on the battlefield that day certainly qualifies." By then, she'd reached his knee.

He winced slightly at the movement. "I think I might have landed on my knee. I'll have a bruise there tomorrow. Right above where you're rubbing is where the first shot hit. It's the reason for my instability. My thigh bone was shattered."

Her eyes widened of their own accord. She waited for him to call her out for it. Instead, he turned his attention to the window.

Her perfidious gaze dipped to his shoulders, then rose to study his profile. He had grown into an extraordinarily handsome man. His eyes had almost closed as if about to succumb to sleep.

Yet his stubborn pride wouldn't let anyone in. He was hurting in so many ways, more than in a physical sense.

"The surgeon insisted that he had to cut off my leg." He faced her. "I declined."

"Oh, Jonathan, I can't imagine the pain and the horror." She skated her hands over his kneecap, then swooped back down for another rub lower.

He narrowed his eyes. "No pity."

"No pity." She swallowed the lump inside her throat and sniffed. To change the topic, she scooped another handful of salve. "I must come closer to work on the rest of your leg."

His stare never left hers as he nodded once.

Scooting nearer, she rested on her knees much like if she was in church kneeling to pray. She reached under his banyan, then trailed her fingers across his skin until she found the last injury.

Forcing her attention to his thigh, she traced the wound to see how large it was. Though this leg was smaller than his other, it was still massive in size and strength, so different from her own. With the tips of her fingers, she could tell where he'd been shot. Angry striations of raised skin accompanied by a depression of about an inch deep and several inches wide along with a myriad of stitches marked his thigh about his knee. She massaged it over and over.

With every exhale that escaped from his parted lips, she could tell if she was too rough or too soft. If they were sharp, then she pressed too hard. If they were shallow, then her ministrations were perfect.

His breath fanned across her cheek as if kissing her. Memories of their first kiss rushed forward, sweeping her closer to him. This was the worst timing in the world to think about kissing her husband. Constance was supposed to be helping him, not seducing him. She made the mistake of looking down.

God help her. Her husband was aroused. Though his banyan was closed still, the outline of his hard cock resting against his midriff was plainly visible.

She closed her eyes yet the image stayed front and center. She took a deep breath, desperate for control. Inside, an incredible heat was building. His scent was tempting her to take what she wanted.

"Constance."

She couldn't ignore the low thrum of her name on his lips. Unable to fight it, she leaned closer and forced her eyes to his. The startling whisky color of his eyes held a fire hotter than the sun. She leaned in an inch, a simple experiment to see how he'd react. If he leaned opposite, he'd have made it perfectly clear he wanted no part of her. He stood his ground.

She wanted to shout to the heavens. But there was still work to be done.

She moved closer.

He still didn't budge an inch.

Closer and closer she leaned, not giving him any quarter. She moved with a stealth that hunters would have envied. And she didn't stop until her cheek rested against his. She couldn't breathe. How long she had waited to feel this close to him—skin-to-skin. His evening bristles teased her to press closer. All she wanted was to cup his other cheek in her hand, then press her lips against his.

A ragged breath escaped as she tried to tamp down the chaos that had erupted in her own body. Feeling and sensations melded together in a combination primed to explode.

She whispered his name in answer. "Jonathan, do you want . . . ?" She couldn't be certain, but it was entirely possible his lips brushed against her ear.

"It's entirely possible that I want what you want, but you tell me first."

She stayed perfectly still. Any movement was too dangerous for either of them. Though their cheeks touched, several inches separated their bodies from one another. His heat radiated toward her, surrounding her, holding her close.

She never wanted to escape.

"Tell me what you want," he demanded softly.

In answer, she moved her hand up his thigh. The muscles underneath her fingers flexed. His hand tightened around hers. Slowly, he pulled it toward his body.

"I want . . ." She slid her cheek across his, the touch incredibly slow and sure and erotic, yet innocent.

A scant inch separated her lips from his. Their breaths

mingled in a prelude that they both knew would lead to another wall between them cautiously dismantled stone by proverbial stone.

If she had her way, she'd much rather obliterate it into bits. However, the moment called for patience.

Slowly, she raised her eyes to his. "Let me kiss you."